Oliver Stark has been writing f[...] a
teenager, he was an avid fan [...] l
made his first attempt at crime fi[...] [...]ess
to say, this never reached public[...]

After trying a wide variety of jobs, from working in a bookies to managing a pub, he finally gave in to his passion for reading and went on to study and then teach literature. Oliver now lives in London with his wife and children.

American Devil is Oliver's first novel, and the first in a proposed crime thriller series featuring Tom Harper and Denise Levene.

Praise for *American Devil*:

'An impressive debut . . . written with pace and a delicate feel for the darker shadows of the American psyche. Stark is an exceptional new British talent. Let's look forward to what he does next' *Daily Mail*

'One of the best thrillers I have read in ages, tightly plotted, intricately planned, not a loose end or an unexplained action or clue anywhere, great characters, great pace, twists and turns aplenty which will lead the reader completely off the track (well, it did this one), and an exciting and thrilling climax which had me on the end of my seat' Elaine Simpson-Long, Random Jottings

'*American Devil* is well written, paced steadily with a climactic finish and chock full of thoughtfully crafted characters . . . Stark delivers an aptly stark portrayal of the modern-day psychopath; drawing on those good old fundamental ideals as religion, love and betrayal. If this is how Stark starts out – we're positively salivating for second helpings' The Truth About Books

'An assured debut, suggesting that Oliver Stark is a name we will hear a great deal more from' Material Witness

Oliver Stark

AMERICAN DEVIL

headline

First published in 2010 by
HEADLINE PUBLISHING GROUP

First published in Great Britain in 2010 by
HEADLINE PUBLISHING GROUP

4

Cataloguing in Publication Data is available from the British Library

ISBN 978 0 7553 7113 6 (B-format)
ISBN 978 0 7553 7010 8 (A-format)

Typeset in Palatino by Avon DataSet Ltd,
Bidford-on-Avon, Warwickshire

Printed and bound in Great Britain by
Clays Ltd, St Ives plc

Headline's policy is to use papers that are natural, renewable and
recyclable products and made from wood grown in sustainable forests.
The logging and manufacturing processes are expected to conform
to the environmental regulations of the country of origin.

HEADLINE PUBLISHING GROUP
An Hachette UK Company
338 Euston Road
London NW1 3BH

www.headline.co.uk
www.hachette.co.uk

To my wife

Prologue

West Virginia, February 14, 1982

He stood behind the white picket fence, hidden in the shadows of a beech tree. It was ten forty in the evening – enough time still to ask her the question. In his right hand, he held twelve red roses with velvet-soft petals. He wanted to give her something real special; after all, she was the girl of his dreams.

Above the large timber-framed house, the moon was so bright that he could see the jumble of kids' toys abandoned on the veranda. His nervous grey eyes rose to the first floor and scanned each window in turn. He stopped at hers and sweat formed instantly down his back. Her bedroom glowed with a soft pink light. The beautiful and untouchable Chloe Mestella, just fifteen years old and already way beyond the reach of him or any of the local boys.

He figured that she'd be fast asleep by now, so he'd have to steal up to her room without her parents seeing. He knew what he was going to say to her when she woke up. 'Chloe, will you be my Valentine? I love you so much sometimes I want to die.' He looked again to the pink-lit window. His head was throbbing as if a train was driving through it.

The boy stepped out on to the crisp cut lawn. The house itself looked like it was sleeping. He thought he could see the roof rising and falling like a breathing chest. What a place to grow up! What a fairy tale! But why couldn't she just be a little bit nice to him?

The problem with these rich girls was that deep down they weren't nice at all. They dressed in pretty clothes and smiled sweetly when they had to, but he'd been at the old log yard after dark and seen what they did in the back seats of borrowed cars, their innocent faces twisting and trembling in the shadows like they were in some kind of pain.

Even the untouchable Chloe had been ruined. Someone had taken advantage of her, rubbed her up in the dell, pulled her clothes about and rutted with her like a farm animal. Grunt, grunt, grunt, went the football star, with Chloe crying out for him to stop. But he carried right on to the finish line, just like he'd been taught.

Holding the roses close to his chest, he crept along the side of the house and lifted his head to the living-room window. Mary and Don Mestella were eating seafood linguine with a couple of friends. Upstairs their little girl was tucked up in bed – a snug warm curl of a body in soft pink pyjamas. It was the perfect family scene and he wanted to be part of it.

The boy pulled at each window in turn. The toilet window opened to his rough fingertips. He pulled himself in through the narrow gap and tumbled head first into the small room. He froze in fear and listened out.

He peered around the half-open door of the toilet as he checked the hallway. Glasses clinked in the living room, but his eyes were fixed on the stairs. It was a short dash across the open hallway. He eased the door further open and placed his left foot on the bright polished floor. From the other end of the hallway something clattered. The boy felt his body seize up. Then a voice called out. 'Hope you're all ready for dessert in there!'

Mrs Mestella. *She was in the fucking kitchen.* He couldn't move. His breath shortened. She was already walking out of the kitchen with a big pavlova held triumphantly in front of her. He couldn't risk shutting the toilet door and catching her eye.

He held his breath, leaned back into the shadow of the dark room and hoped she wouldn't look over. If she did, she'd scream, the pavlova would drop and he'd have a hell of a lot of explaining to do.

His whole body shivered as he watched Mrs Mestella pass by in profile, all her attention on the big white meringue covered in thin slices of bright red strawberry. The boy caught a gust of sickly perfume in his throat and nearly coughed. He held it until she was in the living room, then he darted across the polished wooden floor spluttering into his sleeve. His eyes rose to the top of the stairs. Little steps to his own private heaven.

At the top of the stairs he took off his shoes and padded down the corridor, edging open each door in turn. In the second room, he saw Chloe's younger twin sisters radiating life. Next came the master bedroom with its double doors slightly ajar. He felt like some crazy Goldilocks but inside the fear and anticipation were leaping in his chest.

Along the corridor he came to her door and touched it with his fingertips. It was covered with pictures of fairies. There was a wooden nameplate saying *Chloe's Room – Be Nice*. This was the room she had grown up in. It contained all her innocent dreams.

The boy looked down at his roses. He slowly repeated what he had planned to say. He wanted it all to be perfect but he was shaking like a leaf and the spit had dried in his mouth.

He pushed the door open. The walls were pale rose and there was a small night-light that gave the room that warm soft glow he'd seen from the garden. He took three small steps into the room and there she was – his own sleeping, perfect princess.

He felt as if his whole world had suddenly come to him fully formed from his dreams. His yearnings were so strong he felt fit to burst. He reached out towards the tanned flawless skin of her arm. As his fingers brushed her an electric charge shot right through him. Every nerve tingled.

Her pyjama top had risen up and her hip was visible like the curve of a stone statue. The skin was so delicate and pale. From downstairs, the chatter of voices and sudden bursts of laughter rose up through the house, but they sounded as though they were coming from the bottom of a deep well. He was way up above, in heaven.

The boy placed the twelve red roses on the nightstand, moved to her bed and took the flowered quilt in his hands. He pulled it slowly from her body and let it drop to the floor. He had only wanted a glance, that was all.

But he couldn't help himself now. He moved his mouth to hers and kissed her. His lips were cold and hers so very warm. His hand reached down and slipped inside her top.

Chloe Mestella woke. Her eyelids flickered open. For a moment she was confused, her head still full of dreams. Was this real? The dark shadow above her? In a half second, she realized that this was very real. Someone was in her room. Some stranger was on her bed with his hands all over her. Fear caught fire and rushed wild through her limbs. She breathed in, about to cry out, but a hand caught her. A rough hand covered her mouth and pressed her jaw down firmly.

'Shh,' a low voice said in the pink light. 'Your parents will hear us.' Chloe's eyes flicked left and right. His whole body moved quickly on top of hers and jammed hard against her – so hard against her chest that she couldn't breathe. Her heart pounded; she was sweaty and icy cold in the same moment but her muscles felt tired and weak. It was terror clawing at her. Blind terror.

'Chloe. I love you so much sometimes I want to die. Will you be my Valentine?' She shook her head violently and tried to speak. There were tears in her eyes. She wasn't thinking of the right thing to say, she was just giving him her answer, shaking her head. *Please let me go, please don't hurt me!* The boy held her down harder, like some struggling animal.

He forced his whole weight on to Chloe's mouth. Disappointment mingled with shame. Shame for having hope, for loving her – shame for being refused by the one person he'd hoped would save him. The devil had said it all along. *Give her a chance, if you don't believe me. See if I'm wrong about her. Give her a chance to prove me wrong. If I'm wrong, I'll leave you alone.* With shaking arms he pushed down on her body more firmly, feeling self-hatred squirm in his mind, mocking him. He shuddered with tears as he forced his bony limbs harder and harder against the girl he loved. Chloe couldn't breathe any more. Her legs and arms and torso thrashed about under his weight. She was making too much noise. Way too much noise.

The boy was getting real frightened now. She needed to shut the fuck up and stop moving. If he got caught, that was the end of everything. He pushed harder and harder against her throat, pushing with every muscle on to her chest. Chloe thrashed and kicked more. Then she was still.

He looked down at her, his forehead creased in concentration. Chloe's eyes took on a look he'd only seen in animals before, like when a cow was about to be slaughtered and its eyes grew big and white. They called it 'crazy eye' on the farm. The boy stared. Chloe had gone crazy eye and her arms and legs had stopped moving.

It was hardest to kill the ones you loved. But that's what the devil wanted – he didn't want you killing cheap. This was much more than murder – this was a rite of passage. The devil had been at the boy's ear for years, whispering and telling him things he couldn't have imagined.

The boy was alone in the silent pink bedroom. The devil had delivered as he promised he would. He was finally alone with the girl he loved. And there was so much that he still wanted to do with her. This had been in his head a long, long time.

PART ONE
November 15–21

'Better to reign in hell than serve in heaven'
John Milton, *Paradise Lost*

Chapter One

Police Headquarters, New York City
November 15, 1.52 p.m.

The deputy commissioner's office at One Police Plaza was just across from City Hall in downtown New York. Eight minutes before the meeting was scheduled to begin, Lenny Elwood crossed his office and stopped at the view over Brooklyn Bridge.

His eyes followed the taut steel ropes across the East River. People died all the time, he thought. It was the nature of life. Forty or more people died building the very bridge in front of his eyes. But death these days was unacceptable: unpolitical even. People had the right to live. Especially young people.

At the best of times, Lenny Elwood was a man in a hurry for things to happen, but this wasn't the best of times and he could feel his blood vessels constricting. He breathed deeply and reached to his inside pocket for his statins. On his dark mahogany desk, the week's newspapers were laid out. Each headline jumped up at him as if it wanted to scream the words in his ear. But even they seemed muted next to the picture.

Christ, thought Lenny, there was no need for a headline at all. The photograph did all the talking. His hand moved across the thick black letters and rested on the grainy shot of a bright, childish face. The girl had a ribbon in her long blond hair, large

9

blue eyes and the shine of gloss on her smiling lips. A face that said everything was all right. Except it wasn't.

Mary-Jane Samuelson was a girl with so much life ahead of her. Her expression was full of optimism and innocence. And now that she was dead, hers was the kind of face that sold papers and made America stand up and take notice.

A week earlier, the beautiful debutante had been brutally strangled inside her family's Upper East Side apartment. Mary-Jane Samuelson was just fifteen years old. The attacker had raped and tortured her before killing her with her own pantyhose.

But Elwood knew that things were about to get a whole lot worse. An hour earlier, the dispatcher had called through a second female body with ligature marks round the neck. They now had a potential serial killer on their hands, and Lenny wasn't going to stand for it.

At 1.58 p.m., he opened the door to his office, glared at the two police chiefs in their smart black uniforms and waved them in with a rapid flutter of his right hand.

He watched each of them pull out a chair, sit down, shuffle a little and place his forearms on the table in silence. He sensed their fear and liked how it felt. They knew they had to move things along rapidly or someone would be cut off at the knees.

The men waited in silence around the large polished table. It sat between them like a still pond, all their reflections upside down. The weekly crime meeting early that week had not gone well. High-profile murder cases were bad for the city and girls like Mary-Jane were about as high profile as you got. Lenny had told them that he wanted this sorted immediately and now there was another body. The two chiefs knew this meeting was coming. It was how the NYPD worked these days. Accountability, they called it. But it was nothing more than an old-fashioned back-alley shakedown.

They waited a moment as the tight-lipped PA shuffled her

satin blouse around the deputy commissioner's shoulder and laid a beige file in front of him. She licked her thumb, leaned forward and opened it for him.

Elwood looked at the report. 'Okay, gentlemen, let's get down to business.' His lip twitched with eagerness. 'Why the hell are you letting this maniac kill these girls? We're two down and I've got a handful of shit from you. A handful of shit.' Elwood looked down at his open palms and eyed each man in turn. 'He's cut up two girls in the most populated piece of rock on the planet and you've got jackshit. This is unacceptable, gentlemen. Give me some answers, right now.'

He looked round the table, giving both men a chance to speak up. 'You've got nothing? Nothing at all? The police commissioner told me this morning that he wants this sealed, solved and off the books. You must have something for me, gentlemen.'

The chief of detectives, Bureau Chief Ged Rainer, swivelled on his seat and threw a sarcastic smile to the head of the table. 'Well, if it's coming straight from the police commissioner, why don't we start doing something rather than sitting on our butts all day long? Who'd think he'd never served as a police officer?'

'You think this is worthy of a comedy routine, Rainer? Listen to me and listen good – if Commissioner Garry's reputation is on the line, then so is yours, get it? And he's asked me to come in here and shoot one of the horses. Now I've got two horses sitting here and I've got one bullet. Is it going to be you, Rainer, you fucking comedian?' Ged Rainer looked down at the table, his ears burning. 'Now who's going to tell me the whole story?'

The chief of the homicide bureau, Jim Stanton, finally spoke. 'I got Captain Lafayette outside,' he offered. 'He heads up North Manhattan Homicide. I thought you might want to hear it from the guy leading the team on the street.'

'Sure, bring him in if neither of you have a fucking word to say for yourselves.'

Outside the deputy commissioner's office, Frank Lafayette sat in a brown leather chair. He'd been made to wait too long already. He had better things to do with his time than shine his ass. He had a killer on the loose who liked to cut his bodies open and pose them. He wanted his best man on the job, a specialist – but that wasn't going to be easy. He'd already asked, but Ged Rainer had slammed the door in his face each time. The PA appeared silently at his side like some slinking cobra and showed him into the room.

'Welcome, Lafayette. Take a seat,' said Elwood with a smile that looked more like a sneer.

'Prefer to stand, if I may.'

'Stand, sit, I don't give a damn,' said the deputy commissioner. 'What is it with the detective bureau? You know everyone here, Captain?'

Lafayette nodded respectfully.

'So, Captain, how does it look?' Elwood leaned in, staring fiercely.

'We got nothing at the present time, sir. That's the plain truth. No bullshit. We're nowhere. Detective Nate Williamson is leading the team. He's a veteran and he's got nothing to follow. This killer is clean.'

Leonard Elwood scratched the shaved hair at the back of his head. 'I want more, Captain. Honest to fucking God, it's not enough. How many detectives you got on the case?'

'Near to eighty, sir.' Lafayette stared down at his shining shoes. He knew what was coming.

'And you've got zilch? It's bullshit!' shouted Elwood. 'Rainer, I'm right, aren't I? It's bullshit.'

Ged Rainer leaned forward. 'We don't want a killer on the streets of New York, do you understand, Captain? This isn't the nineties, we can do without the drama.'

'I don't want one either, sir,' said Lafayette. 'But it's not easy catching a pattern killer, if that's what we have. There's no motive, no witnesses, no informants and no leads. They strike where and when they want to.'

'What do you need?' said the deputy commissioner. 'What is it you want from us? I presume there's something or you wouldn't have showed up here, taking shit for these assholes.'

Lafayette paused. Chief Rainer was the guy who'd refused his request and now he was going right over Rainer's head in public. The captain swallowed hard. 'Sir, with all due respect, if we want to move forward on this, we need our best man on the case.' Rainer turned and shot a look of contempt down the table.

'Who's your best man, Captain?' said Elwood.

'Someone who knows how to track pattern killers, sir. One of the very best. You may know the name. Detective Tom Harper. Five years ago, he brought in the Mott Haven strangler, Gerry North. He traced a used dollar bill found in the victim's throat back to a payroll of Gerry North's employer. It gave us a list of thirty-five men. North was the fifteenth guy we saw. Great police work, sir. Last year, he brought in the serial killer Eric Romario. You'll remember that case, sir. Eric liked to break into apartments and wire people up to the line power and switch it on. He killed eight people. Harper worked on the killer's background. He thought the killer would've begun life as a firestarter, so he picked out the records of petty arsonists from ViCAP and traced them through employment records of the power companies. He got a hit list. Eric Romario was on his way to wire up a children's swimming pool when Harper came calling. No one else would've taken that line, sir.' Lafayette looked up. 'He came in late, took over the lead and pulled these guys down. He got somewhere with next to nothing. He's our best guy.'

'Then get him in. What are you all waiting for?'

Rainer shouted across. 'Lafayette, pipe the fuck down. I told you no already.'

'Shut it, Rainer,' spat Elwood. 'If this is the guy who can do the job, then get him in.'

'Harper can do it, sir.'

Rainer was up on his feet. 'He's on suspension for assaulting a superior officer, sir. He's facing termination.' He leaned into Lenny Elwood and whispered something.

Elwood nodded and looked up. 'This is the same guy that knocked Lieutenant Jarvis off his fucking feet?'

'Yes, that's him,' said Rainer. 'A real throwback to the bad old days.'

'He was provoked, sir,' said Lafayette.

Rainer was shaking. 'Detective Harper is not coming back on my team, sir. Lafayette, you're overstepping the mark here. I've already told you that's not gonna happen. Harper's a volatile bastard and we're just about ready to go with the termination.'

'Is he our best detective or not?' said Elwood, firing looks all round the room.

'He's the best, sir,' said Lafayette. 'Unconventional. Aggressive. But most important, he's a specialist in these kinds of kills. He's worked three previous pattern homicides, two in NYC as you just heard and one upstate. These aren't the usual kinds of homicides we deal with, sir: we think this is a pattern killer.'

'He assaulted a superior officer,' Rainer snapped. 'Are we losing our minds here?'

'He lost his head one time and took a swipe at a lieutenant, but he had good cause.'

'Took a swipe?' said Rainer. 'He busted his jaw so bad it's been wired up for a month. He was on the boxing team. He's dangerous. We can't let this guy go around beating people up.'

'And this is our best detective?' said Elwood. 'A pair of fists with a chip on his shoulder?'

'If I could have one man on the team, it'd be Harper. No

question. These girls have the right to expect us to do our best.'

The deputy commissioner's eyes narrowed. 'Will he do it?'

'He doesn't feel so charitable towards NYPD at the moment, but he might.'

'Well, offer him a clean break. Tell him we'll scrub the charge if he succeeds – that's an offer he can't refuse. Get some department shrink to sign him up for some anger management therapy to cover our backs. Bring him in, Captain.'

Rainer was shaking his head vehemently. 'If it comes out that we've put a madman on the case, if the papers get hold of it, we're going to be blown out of the water. I don't think he's our man.'

'With all due respect, Chief Rainer, he's exactly our man. Now go get him, Captain.' Elwood stared hard at Rainer. Their eyes locked for a few seconds.

'With all due respect to you, sir,' said Rainer, 'I'm the senior ranking operational officer here, and for the record, I'm not reinstating an officer who beats up other officers. I've got morale to think about. I'm not doing it. I categorically refuse.'

Larry Elwood rose from his leather seat and pointed a bony finger at Rainer. 'Looks like I've just found my horse, Chief Rainer.'

Chapter Two

Central Park
November 15, 3.35 p.m.

The solitary walkers in Central Park were all wrapped up warm. The wide skies overhead were bright blue into the distance and the air was cold and dry. At the northeastern corner of the park, the suspended homicide detective Thomas Elias Harper crouched on his haunches on the edge of the sandbank overlooking the glittering water of Harlem Meer. He was dressed down in a pair of old combats, a well-worn overcoat and an orange cap. He was alone, with a pair of binoculars tight to his eyes, watching the movement in the trees on the far shore, keeping deadly still.

Then he spotted it again and his heart rose a beat. He focused slowly with his forefinger and caught the image crisp in his sights. There it was, almost flat against the oak bark, a white-breasted nuthatch edging down the tree trunk, its sleek head and white throat darting out for insects. Harper followed the bird across the leafy ground as it hopped on to a forsythia twig and pecked beneath the fallen maple leaves for grubs. He smiled with satisfaction.

The detective moved down through the park, a small knapsack on his back. He reached the brow of a hill in the North Woods and moved across the ravine. He climbed up a low bank to get a good position and stood looking into the dense vegetation, the stream babbling through the trees, the leaves crisp and whispering in the light wind. Reports had mentioned a glossy ibis in the area; he'd been back to the same site for three days, but hadn't had any luck.

Out of the trees behind him, Harper caught a scuffling sound. He listened intently as the sound grew. It sure as hell wasn't a glossy ibis. It wasn't some walker strolling through, either: the movements were quick and determined. Every now and then, the noise stopped. A moment later, Harper could make out the heavy breathing of a man out of condition a few yards behind him. It could be only one thing – a homicide cop.

'Harper!' called a deep voice.

Captain Frank Lafayette had waited an hour outside Harper's apartment in East Harlem before he got a lead from the guys in the fish market and went hunting in the park. The captain, his face a delicate lacework of tiny red veins, put his hands flat on his knees and looked at Harper's back. 'You couldn't take up bowling or some fucking thing?'

There was no reply, not even a flicker. Tom Harper was standing still beneath a small group of bare trees. He was six two, athletic, his close-cropped hair brown, flecked with grey. He had been the NYPD cruiserweight boxing champion for three seasons and the muscle in his back and shoulders still showed.

'Detective Harper, it's Captain Lafayette. I need to speak to you. It's urgent.'

'Keep quiet, Captain.'

'What?'

'I said – keep your voice down.'

Tom had caught sight of a warbler edging forward from behind a rock, a flash of yellow and black, and then it appeared, its quick head turning from side to side.

'Tom, I just need a few minutes of your time.'

'Quiet!'

'For fuck's sake, Harper, stop shitting me here!' shouted

Lafayette. The voice rattled through the woods and the nervous little warbler darted a look towards them, lifted off and flew away downstream.

Harper let his binoculars drop to his side and turned to Lafayette. He glared across. 'Leave me the hell alone.' He strode off through the undergrowth, following the flight of the bird.

'Harper, wait up. I just want a word. We need your help.'

'Well, I'm suspended right now. You not noticed that, Captain?'

'Detective, I know you better than that. I want to make you an offer.'

'I don't need anything from you.'

'You heard about the case?'

'I've seen the girl's picture just like everyone else. You've got a serious killer on the loose and Williamson hasn't got a clue. You're getting pistol-whipped at One PP, so you came to see me.'

'Give me one minute of your time, Harper. Come on.'

'I can't help you, Captain. It's time for me to move on.'

Lafayette paused. He had to get the timing just right. He caught Harper's eyes. 'They found a second body this morning. Same killer, we think.'

'I'm sorry to hear it,' said Harper.

'She was walking home last night and disappeared. Probably abducted.'

'I don't need to know the details, Captain. It's not my case.'

'Look, Harper, these girls were raped and strangled. Same ligature.'

Harper looked into the trees, the details playing on his mind. 'As you know, I'm not available for duty.'

Lafayette moved in close. He took a photograph from his inside pocket and tossed it on to a white rock. 'Take a look. The unknown subject is a mean bastard. After he killed Mary-Jane, he scattered flower petals all over her body like in some ritual.'

Harper looked down at the crime scene shot of a bloody corpse. 'He cut her?'

'Tortured her with shallow cuts, yeah. Likes to watch them bleed.'

'The papers didn't say.'

'We keep the real grim stuff to ourselves, you know that.'

'I'm sorry for these girls, Captain, but I can't go back now. I broke Jarvis's jaw. You know what that means as well as I do. There's a big door and it's shut in my face. My own stupid fault, I know that. I'm not looking for sympathy. I deserve whatever I get.'

'You were provoked, Tom. Everyone knows how you feel about Lisa. Jarvis was a fool, but he's just one stupid cop who tried to get himself a name by getting a rise out of the big guy.'

'Well, you tell him it worked. I'm riled. Lisa wanted out, that's one nightmare, but I don't need some failed detective telling me she's screwing around.'

Captain Lafayette looked at Harper. He was thinner than before, leaner, with a thin line of red around his eyes. Three months earlier, Harper's wife, Lisa Vincenti, had decided that enough was enough. There'd been one lonely night too many and she'd moved out while Tom was working all hours closing the Romario case. Jarvis was a smart-ass lieutenant and a local precinct bully who thought it was worth making a joke out of, and he'd gone in hard. It was a mistake. Harper had been in no mood for jokes.

'Will you listen to my offer?' said Lafayette.

'I need to start over,' said Harper. 'I need new ground under my feet. I need to get a job somewhere else. That's my feeling.'

'What as? A birdwatcher? You know no police department in the country will touch you. You've got a charge over your head. You assaulted a senior officer. Listen, Ged Rainer will have you out by the end of the week. What you going to do then?'

'I'll find work.'

'But I can make the Charges and Specs go away, Tom.'

'How?'

'We've got a killer out there and the department needs you. Hell, I need you. They'll wipe the slate if you come on board.'

Harper paused and stared at Lafayette. 'I can't go back. End of story. Sorry.' He started to walk down the valley, fast.

Lafayette struggled behind him and pulled to a standstill. He couldn't keep up any more. He stared at Harper's back and shook his head. 'What you going to do? Pity yourself the rest of your life? Everyone loses someone, Tom. Get off the fucking canvas.'

Fifty yards ahead, Tom Harper stopped in his tracks. The words got him cold. He counted to ten real slow, keeping his anger from getting out of control, and then he walked on without turning his head.

'He's taking trophies, Tom,' shouted Lafayette. 'He took the kid's eyes out of her head. Try to imagine that while you're out here watching the birds.'

Chapter Three

East Harlem
November 15, 6.14 p.m.

Harper felt the air cool around his neck. Dusk had fallen quickly and any hope of continuing his hunt for the last of the winter migrants had seeped away in the sudden thump of Captain Lafayette's parting words. Tom walked back through the park feeling like someone had hit him hard in the gut. Lisa Vincenti wasn't a weak spot so much as a great big hole in his life. Walk too close and he'd fall right back in and start the whole process of slow-motion drowning all over again.

Lafayette's words continued to rattle around in Tom's head as he walked back to the rented one-bedroom apartment he still called home. The apartment was on the second floor of a decaying four-storey block, in what the realtors liked to call a *transitional area*. That meant that the poverty was still real enough, but the condos and multi-million-dollar developments were only a stride or two away. Transitional – just another fancy word for unfair.

He'd lived along East Harlem's southern edge ever since he and Lisa decided they were a long-term proposition. They'd honeymooned in the two small rooms above the fish market on 110th and Third, eating romantic hot dogs looking out across the Harlem River with their legs dangling through the steel walkway crossing FDR Drive.

Tom Harper and Lisa Vincenti went back twelve years. They'd met as optimistic twenty-two year olds. They connected in the deeps and in the shallows. But after Tom was made a homicide detective, things got difficult. The pattern killer cases absorbed him and Lisa must've got sick of waiting for her husband to come home. She wanted the man she married, not this obsessive guy with monsters in his head.

She had packed up and left. Harper now wanted to leave, just like she had. The apartment and the whole of Manhattan felt like the setting for a story that was no longer his. She'd taken the heart out of it all.

Tom wandered across to the window. His hand rose to his face and felt the stubble. If Lisa walked into the room right now and saw his hangdog look and the shit all over the apartment, she'd blow a fuse. He loved her still and missed her even more, it was that simple. He missed the smell of her skin, the look in her eye, the way she could talk until everything seemed right again. She believed in things, too. She had faith. Not many people did any more; he missed that. He missed the rhythm of being two. Beating a drum with one stick had no rhythm at all.

Tom walked back to the armchair that sat staring at a blank TV screen. Another long night lay ahead of him. Another night of slowly letting the whisky close off the different switches in his brain until he was numb to the whole wide world.

He closed his eyes, but for the first time in months it wasn't Lisa's image that formed in his mind as he lay back in his decrepit old armchair. It was the photograph of a pale and bloody body lying dead in some rich folks' apartment.

Harper opened his eyes quickly and saw the glaring reflections on his window from the street below. The city was a mosaic of shadow and light. Once upon a time, city lights excited him, but he didn't like the promises any more. He reached for his backpack and pulled out his notebook. Each dog-eared page was beautifully illustrated with quick sketches of various birds. Dates, times, locations and notes surrounded each sketch.

He picked up his pen and sucked the end until he tasted ink on his tongue. He drew the faint outline of the warbler from memory. He wrote the date, stared at it and then looked again to the window. His mind wouldn't settle.

Across the room, his cell phone chimed a cheap tune. Harper jumped up and grabbed it. He'd not once given up on Lisa. He was endlessly optimistic that one day she'd want to come back. And he would forgive her – no question. He put the cell close to his ear. 'Yes?'

'Didn't disturb you, did I?' Harper's heart sank. Not her voice. A man's voice. Captain Lafayette.

'You don't give up, do you?'

'Blue Team have just left the crime scene. Don't know much about the victim yet. But she looks the same type and the injuries are similar. Like we feared, we think it's the same unsub.'

'Sorry to hear that.'

'They found her on Ward's Island. She was left out on the rocks in the water. Probably died late last night. The body'll be there another hour or so.'

Harper sat down. 'What's the MO?'

'She's been strangled. Same ritual – torture cuts, left naked. She was also posed.'

'Posed how?' said Harper, pen in hand, tracing the outline of a rock on his notebook.

'Like she's praying.'

'Hands tied together?'

'Yeah, with copper wire.' Lafayette paused. 'I want you to take a look before they take the body. No commitment. Just give us something, Tom. Anything. For God's sake.'

'I'm not ready to go back, Captain.'

'How about you just take a look at this girl, tell me what you can? Maybe what you see will help us nail this bastard. Call it a leaving gift.'

Harper was silent. The figure of a girl with her hands in prayer appeared in black ink on the page in front of him.

'I'm in a black Impala outside your apartment. I'll wait ten minutes. If it's a no, then whatever you go on to do, Harper, good luck and all that. You were a first-rate cop, the best. Don't ever forget that while you're down there in Vegas hunting slot-machine fixers.'

Chapter Four

Darkness was holding fast over Ward's Island. Only the distant lights of Kirby Psychiatric Hospital and the near glow of the crime scene were visible from across Hell Gate Bridge. The whole area was still being scoured by Crime Scene Unit detectives.

The east wind had blustered all day and now raced across the island, whipping up the surface of the water and making it dance against the black rocks. Across the river, Manhattan's teeming grid of coloured lights reflected in the dark water like a street-level rainbow promising wealth and fulfilment. But there on Ward's Island, on the rough grass against the rocks, lay a naked body lapped by the shallow surf. Her guts were torn open and a couple of seagulls had stayed around after dark to take what they could.

The icy wind was also freezing the four officers standing in a half-circle above the corpse, their bomber jackets zipped chin high, their eyes streaming and their faces pale as pig skin. In silence, they stared down at the mutilated body. Officer James Cob was stamping his feet and playing around with his flashlight.

'Hey, Hernandez, did you eat already?' he said.

'No,' said Hernandez. 'How the fuck could I eat out here?'

25

'Here, you like fresh meat?' Cob shone his torch on to the corpse.

'Serious, Cob, knock it off, buddy. You're making me sick here.'

'It's your fucking diet that's churning your guts,' Officer Lees put in. 'He had three hot dogs and a doughnut in the wagon.'

'Why the fuck is she marrying you, Hernandez?' said Cob. 'Can anyone explain how this big fuck is getting hitched to a ninety-five-pound looker? These fat guys are taking all our women.'

'Fuck you and your mother, Cob, I've got the magic touch. They'll be crying out for more when they feel these.' Hernandez held up his chubby fingers and wiggled them in the air. 'They call me the feather, my touch is so light. I'm like a butterfly wing. They just keep howling for more.'

The guys laughed aloud in the darkness. For a moment they forgot that they were on a city shore next to a murder victim. Then silence seemed to capture the small huddle again. Their conversations kept dying out like a match in the wind.

Harper watched from a distance, a shadow in a black coat. It wasn't his case, he was still on charges that would no doubt end in a termination, but he already felt responsible. And being out in the cold sure beat sitting in his apartment and letting the emptiness swirl over and over in his head. He'd done enough of that. Maybe he had even let the self-pity take him over.

He couldn't help but feel the crackle of his nerves at the sight of the crime scene. This was his territory. He felt the tingling at the tip of his fingers like he used to. He breathed deep and walked towards the officer guarding the yellow tape. Harper had a vague outline of the first kill in his mind, mainly from the secondary sources – no real facts yet, just the fragments of other people's horror and a bit extra that the newspapers liked to sprinkle across the story by way of speculation and sensation.

The uniform read the name on the log when he signed in.

'Nice to see you out here, Detective Harper. You taking the case?'

Harper looked at the young officer. 'No.'

'Wish you were. This guy's bad news. I saw what he'd done.'

Harper nodded and moved towards the lights of the crime scene. He could hear the officers laughing as he approached and saw their little game of dead woman peek-a-boo with their flashlights. He wasn't impressed. Whose investigation was this? It looked wide open – no structure, no urgency, just a forensic team and a bunch of patrolmen. The detectives from Blue Team had all left. Since when did Blue Team let things slip this far? The whole of the NYPD should be on top of this case. He walked directly towards the officers and stamped on the edge of a sheet of corrugated iron. It clattered violently.

The four men turned with a start and pointed their flashlights towards the noise. Harper stared right back at them, his granite face contorted by the torch beams. 'Get your fucking lights out of my face, gentlemen.'

He moved slowly across to them, shining his own torch into the officers' faces one by one, taking it all in. 'This is a crime scene. Get away from the body. And have some damn respect for the dead.' His light remained on Cob's face.

'Nice of you to turn up, Detective,' said Cob. 'All the big boys have come and gone already.'

Harper scowled and looked down at the corpse. He felt the anger rise in his knotted muscles and flap like a black flag inside his mind, wiping away all other thoughts. An intense concentration formed in his head.

He turned to the officers. 'All right. Move back. Get out of my way. One of you get across the top on the right and shine a light from that side. Get a move on! Move! Now! You, down on to those rocks.' He took Hernandez by the shoulder and marched him to the water. 'Get down on that rock and shine a light for me from there.'

'I'll get my shoes and pants wet,' said Hernandez.

'Do I look like I care? Go.'

Hernandez looked down at his shiny shoes and pressed pants. His foot stepped down on to the black rock Harper had indicated and he watched his ankle submerge slowly beneath dark freezing water. The other two cops stared at Harper.

Harper started to pick his way towards the body. He reached the rock as Hernandez's light flashed across her face. The light from the officer on the right spread out across her side. It was a horrific sight. She was a young woman in her early twenties. Her skin was white as alabaster. Her naked body lay flat on its back, her hands wired together on her chest as if in prayer, her legs raised and spread wide apart. Her feet and ankles had been jammed into two rock crevices. All over, wet petals stuck to her skin and the rock. Harper picked one up from the rock and turned it in his hand.

He looked closely at the body, careful not to touch or move anything that might be evidence. He was working out the sequence, trying to spot the small things that didn't quite fit. The woman's hair was short and scruffy, her face thin, with well-defined cheekbones. Harper leaned in and looked more closely. His flashlight moved slowly over the corpse. Ten minutes was all he gave himself. He knew he didn't have long before the coroner arrived to take the body off the rocks, so he pulled himself back up to the bank. He stood and faced the two officers who hadn't moved. 'Why are you still hanging around here? Haven't you got something to do?'

'Before we take orders, let's see your shield, Detective,' said Cob with a sneer. 'You ain't got no ID showing. Maybe you ain't a detective at all.'

Harper turned to the poor woman who'd been executed on the cold rock, probably screaming her lungs out where no one could hear. The killer didn't have any human feelings at all and now Officer James Cob wanted to bust his balls.

Harper walked across to Cob and stood face to face. 'You want to know who I am?'

'Yeah, and what you're doing here.'

'And what I'm doing here, is that right?'

'Yeah. You're so quick, you should be a detective.'

'I'm nobody but I'm here to find out why this woman was attacked.' Harper felt his back teeth lock together.

'Personally,' said Cob, 'I'd say she was asking for it, going out dressed like that. She ought to wear a little more, wouldn't you say?'

'You think, do you?'

'She ain't got much on,' said Cob.

'You want to know what it feels like to be down on those rocks, Officer?' Harper reached, quick as a rattlesnake, and snapped his big hand round Cob's wrist. His eyes stared hard.

'Get the fuck off me!' Cob shouted.

'You think it's funny that a woman's been raped and executed?'

'No. I was . . . Come on . . .'

Harper pulled Cob's arm hard and shoved him down towards the corpse, flicking his leg across the officer's weight. Cob fell hard on to the muddy bank, a look of stark panic on his face. He was badly winded and Harper still had his wrist in a vice-like grip.

'Doesn't feel like you're sorry, Cob.' Harper dragged Cob towards the edge of the bank.

'What the fuck are you doing, you madman?'

'Have a look at her face, Cob. Do you think it's funny? Do you think it's funny what he did? Look at her, you animal.'

Cob, with his face in the cold dirt, stared down at the result of hatred and violence jammed on the rock.

'You think your girlfriend or mother would think this is so fucking amusing?'

'Please, man.'

'How fucking sorry are you, Cob?'

'Very sorry. Very, very sorry.'

Harper released Cob. 'Don't ever talk like that about a victim, you asshole.' He twitched and strode off over the grassy bank, taking huge strides, his black coat flapping behind him.

Cob rose from the mud, his back sodden, his wrist aching. He looked at the three officers, Hernandez ankle deep in water, Lees pale at the edge, Poulter back down from his vantage point.

'You fucking nutcase, Cob,' said Poulter.

'What? Who the fuck was that guy?'

'You don't know? That was Tom Harper.'

'What's his problem?'

'Oh, there ain't just one. Everything's his fucking problem,' said Poulter.

Harper's silhouette disappeared over the brow of the incline, leaving the rest to North Manhattan Homicide to clear up and assess. He had what he needed. There was a dead woman on his ground. A young woman raped and murdered for no reason. This was not a random strike – the killer had chosen a defenceless victim simply because she was weak. It wasn't fear that was knocking against Harper's heart now, it was cold determination.

As he walked, the trickle of images was already forming. Harper's mind worked like a hundred cogs, assessing information and throwing out conclusions. He figured that the attacker had come at her from behind. A sign of his weakness. He'd taken her out with a blackjack; it'd left a three-inch gash on the side of her head. He didn't even have to struggle with any resistance. Then he'd somehow got her to his car and driven her out to Ward's. From the road, he'd dragged her to the rocks, raped her while she was still out, then cut her open and watched her begin to die. Finally, he strangled her.

Harper reached the top of the hill. He turned and looked down. The body had been dragged across the ground. Harper followed the line in the grass. The girl was maybe 110 pounds, but the line wasn't true or consistent. Maybe the killer was physically weak. He couldn't even hump a 110-pound body across the ground without stopping every ten yards. Or he was carrying something and using only one arm to drag her. Harper looked again at the drag marks with his flashlight. Yeah, the killer was carrying something with one arm and dragging her with the other. Scrub weak, this killer was physically strong. Very.

Manhattan Psychiatric Center was only a hundred yards away. A possible link, he thought. Ward's Island was home to two psychiatric hospitals. Most of New York's criminally insane were within a mile of this spot.

Harper looked across to the grounds of MPC. Plenty of places to hide. He looked back at the officers on the shore. He let the thought about what he'd do if he found the guy flood his mind. The guy who'd attacked and forced himself on this woman – called her names, shouted at her, made her weep and wet herself and shudder with fear, and then, when she was most terrified, slashed at her with his knife. Slow and painful beyond description. Then there was an act that was strangely redemptive – he scattered petals on her body and put her hands together in prayer. Harper knew why Lafayette had wanted him personally on the case. Killers like this played by different rules.

Harper pulled open the door and got into the Impala. He was thinking, still working out the movements that had been this woman's last.

'What you got for me?' said Lafayette.

'Victim's not from the hospital, she's too high class – she's got an expensive dye job, perfect nails and enough dental work to set you back twenty thousand. She's in her early twenties and she's been well looked after. Her hair's been hacked off. My guess is that he's taken her hair as his trophy. Looks like her right shoulder's been dislocated. So he's abducted her somewhere in the city and then driven her here. He's dragged

31

her across the ground by one arm. I'd say that the killer has probably been scoping this area for some time and possibly the victim too. She's a type. Similar to Mary-Jane. Blonde, refined, wealthy. The killer might even have a reason to be here. I'd say that he's probably been to and from this hospital many times. He might be a patient or even a nurse. That's a good spot he's picked. I think he worked the sightlines. The waterline on the rocks is invisible from beyond this hill. So he's taken the trouble to get her out of sight so he can spend time with her. That's some careful working out he's done. Also, he probably drinks. I'd say he needs to drink before he does this. It's just a hunch. Check traffic, see if they pulled over any drunk drivers in the last couple of months. He's tried to make it look like a random attack, but I think this guy's clever. I think he knew exactly who she was and where he was taking her.

'If it's the same killer, he clearly isn't able to take the women home. That suggests he's got someone at home that he needs to hide this from. Your unsub is probably in a long-term relationship, Captain. Not a good sign if he's used to hiding his activities from a family and a job, because he's going to be good at this. He's in it for the long haul and wants to keep clean. He might have brought her here because of the water. The press reports mentioned fibres found on Mary-Jane's body, so maybe he's just making sure he doesn't make the same mistake twice. Maybe he knows about police procedure.'

'You think he's cleaned her?'

'I think it's possible, yeah. Possibly more than that. I don't know yet. He's also carrying something. Not sure what, but my guess is that it's a camera and tripod. He's playing games, deep inside his head, and he's working up to something. The posing is getting more explicit. I think the killer is getting to like this.'

'You got more in fifteen minutes than Williamson had in a week.'

'You're trying all the tricks, aren't you?' said Harper. 'I said I'd take a look, I took a look. Am I free to go now?'

'Is that what you want? A dismissal, criminal charges and a job with a security firm?' Harper stared out of the car in silence. 'I can make the charges go away, Harper, but . . .'

'But what?'

'But, Harper, you're also considered unstable. You agree to come back on the team, I'll make it happen, but you gotta see someone to help you through the stuff in your head. Don't be a tough guy: you need help. I can smell the drink on your breath and read the signs and it's not a path you want to take. See someone – see a shrink, someone to talk to.'

Harper's hand clenched involuntarily. He held his breath for a moment, looking down into the footwell of the car. 'I don't think I can, sorry. I'll take my chances.'

Lafayette reached across and put his hand on Harper's shoulder. 'Don't let her kill you, Tom. It's her life, she made her choices – don't be a fucking reaction the rest of your days.'

Harper got out of the car. He leaned down and looked in at the captain. 'One more thing.' He held up a small pink petal. 'This is cherry blossom. Ask the question – where the hell did he get cherry blossom in November?'

Chapter Five

Barnard College
November 16, 2.59 p.m.

Dr Denise Levene walked up the steps to the small podium in Held Lecture Hall at Barnard College, right across the street from Columbia University. She didn't often do public lectures since taking up a position with the NYPD, where she offered CBT to disturbed cops.

The audience of 150 was a mix of students and anyone who cared to drop in. They applauded the arrival of the research scientist with dutiful enthusiasm. Dr Levene looked out at the expectant faces. The glare of the stage lights blanked out their features. She never really enjoyed public speaking. She was happiest in the security of her lab working with her taciturn research students. Still, that didn't mean she didn't know how to put on a good show.

Denise smiled at her host, then raised her hand, and the audience hushed. 'Thank you. Thanks for coming.' Her hand moved to the control on her podium. She set her DVD in motion.

In the audience, a striking-looking man in a black suit and a beige mac, his neck low in his collar, was staring intently at Dr Levene. He was bored of waiting. He was often bored. He cursed under his breath and then, under the bench, he took a two-inch pocket knife and pushed it through his pocket lining and about a quarter of an inch into his thigh. Denise Levene was supposed to be an expert on the causes of violence. What would she make of him? He was eager to know.

All the man in the black suit wanted answered was why – he wasn't after a cure, for Christ's sake, just a little bit of an indication of what he was. An idea. A notion. He twisted the knife in his thigh, opening the wound. He watched his own body's reaction to the pain. It was just a phenomenon in his head. No need to react, no need to give way to the urgency of biology. He had always felt more than that – more than merely human. He was sanctioned by his own pain to hurt anything and anyone.

What was pain, anyway? Just a neurological electro-chemical pulse, not a real thing at all. A chimera, like love, like happiness, like life. Like goodness. He looked across at the audience. Scientists were so slow. He yawned and tapped his fingers in agitation.

'What you are about to see, ladies and gentlemen,' said Dr Levene, 'is a journey to the cause of human intraspecies violence.'

'About time,' murmured the man in the black suit.

The audience looked up at a large brain scan. The two great hemispheres of a single brain were projected on to a forty-foot-high screen.

'The following sequence is a brain scan of a child who is in the process of learning.'

On the screen, the brain danced with colour in different areas – reds, blues, golds. Connections sparking and fading at incredible speed. It was like a New Year light show.

'The brain is a learning tool,' she continued. 'It is the one thing in which we excel over other species – the capacity to learn: we are the pre-eminent learning animal. For a long time, scientists presumed that the brain came pre-packaged at birth, like a computer preloaded with software that you just had to switch on. We now know that the brain comes pre-packed but very empty. No software installed, just the bare components. Life is our software, ladies and gentlemen; we write the code as we walk, eat and breathe. And each of us writes a different code.'

She clicked her mouse button and the next video streamed in. 'What you can see here is the growth of a single brain neuron. At birth, we have all of our billions of neural cells. But the brain is not the function of these cells alone. The brain – what we know as our consciousness – is formed out of life's experience, out of the experiences that make up every second of our life. Watch this single neuron get to work.'

The image of the small elongated cell began to shake slightly and small branches started to reach out from its sides and from both ends. Soon these branches were branching in their turn and suddenly, out of the darkness of the screen, they were connecting with branches from other nearby cells that became illuminated.

'You are watching human thought in action, ladies and gentlemen. The single neuron has the capacity to make a million connections. You have a billion neurons. That's a lot of connections. And these connections are made through experience and thought. But today I want to tell you about my research into "non-thought" – the experience of the "unlit" zone.'

She clicked again and the single neuron returned to its pre-thinking state, a single isolated cell in the middle of a field of darkness.

'See this cell: it knows nothing of what's around it. Its relationship to the world is non-existent. It does not know what's out there. How do we, as human beings, experience this darkness in our own minds? Why do these dark areas matter?'

Denise thought it was going reasonably well. Some faces seemed genuinely interested. She clicked again. 'This is the brain scan of a child who has suffered serious neglect between the ages of zero and three. I think that you'll find it quite interesting.'

The slide came up. A gasp of fascination rippled through the assembled crowd. The scan showed a neural network with a dark hole in the centre.

'In circumstances of serious abuse and neglect, the brain does not form correctly, and vast areas remain unconnected – like unexplored regions. What this means is that for some abused or neglected individuals, there is simply no connection between the parts of the brain that create normal behaviour. Some people do not have the mental capacity for empathy, control of impulse or fear of consequence – the roads simply don't go there.'

She leaned closer to the microphone. 'Of course, behaviour can be learned. An individual can observe what empathy looks like and appear to display it. But it is not necessarily genuine. It is merely mimicry of external signs. It is shadow play, like a painting. There are people out there who have set up a whole ghost personality to allow them to cope and act within society. Many of our violent criminals have these black holes and my conjecture is that it is these unconnected parts of the mind that make their behaviour so abhorrent, so alien, and make treating them so difficult. In very real terms, ladies and gentlemen, they know not what they do.'

The final slide came up. It showed five brain scans, each with at least one very noticeable area of darkness. 'Here are five brains. You know who they belong to? These five brains belong to five different serial killers.'

The faces of the killers themselves came up on the screen one after the other.

'Killers or brain damage victims? These are the pattern killers – ghosts with darkness at their centre who try to gain meaning by repeated sensation. Sensation as an attempt to fulfil a hole left by a lack of capacity to feel emotion, empathy or concern.' Denise took a drink of water. The man in the black suit sat impassively, his eyes picking out the single diamond hanging in the dip of Denise's neck.

'We have often tried to imagine the mind of a killer,' continued Dr Levene, 'and I can think of no better image than a brain that seeks but can't feel emotion – it is like a hand without nerve endings reaching into a fire. It does not feel the heat but it is burned none the less. But there are many of these brain types amongst us. Our contention is that they are like sleeper cells, indicating potential violence. And our next steps will be to look at how to reactivate these black holes. With science, to pour light into the heart of darkness. My apologies to Conrad.'

There was a murmur of laughter. Dr Levene looked out at the crowd. She was pleased. She summed up with a flourish of her right arm.

'For want of better language, what we have found here is a place of neural silence, of isolation – of darkness. What we have found, ladies and gentlemen, is that there really is a dark heart at the centre of violent men and women. Violence is not caused by an experience of pain, but by the lack of an experience of human empathy. An absence, my friends, of love. Violence is neurologically the negative image of love, ladies and gentlemen. An unloved brain is only ever half formed.'

The man in the black suit smiled and stood up. He was love's shadow, that was it. *Love's fucking shadow*. That felt just about right. He would have liked to stay to talk to Dr Levene about his own theories, but instead he rose and started to make his way along the row of seats.

In the restroom of the lecture block, the man turned the handle of the glistening chrome faucet and washed his hands. He was pleased that he could feel the sting of the hot water. No problem there, he thought. He leaned forward and carefully splashed water over his face and then looked at himself in the mirror. Denise Levene was not half as clever as she thought she was.

She had no idea about the true causes of violence. Only he did. Him and others like him. The causes of violence were very simple. So simple that killers never told anyone about them. Reasons were private, outcomes were public. He wanted to give Dr Levene an opportunity to see the truth. One day, he would.

He looked in the mirror and smiled broadly.

He picked up his black briefcase and put it on the vanity unit. He had another thirty minutes before the lecture would end and the inspired academics would stream into the lavatory with their vomit-inducing praise for what was, in his mind, a rudimentary and facile account. He opened his case and looked down with a smile.

He had liked the part about the ghost personality. Of course, most actors had the capacity to feign emotion. It was not a feature of some kind of sociological brain damage. He looked down at the make-up, wigs, prosthetics, hair colourings and various other items in the case. He had been in touch with a good theatrical warehouse in Boston. They had supplied everything he needed.

He looked at himself. Not a big change required, he thought. A bit of ageing, that was all.

He took out a bottle of latex, pulled the skin around his left eye taut, spread it over the stretched skin. He repeated the operation for the other eye and then around the corners of his mouth, and his forehead.

As the latex dried, his skin wrinkled up. He took out a brown-grey wig and placed it on his head. He looked up; the effect was immediate. Ten years older, at least.

He put in brown contact lenses and with a small tube of tooth colour he tinted his teeth a deeper shade of ivory.

All in all, his transformation took less than twenty minutes. It was not a perfect job, but he didn't need perfection at the moment. The key to success, he knew, was in costume. People read your clothes quicker than anything. He took out a folded green jacket and a pair of trousers, both with gold braiding. He put them on and closed his case. He looked in the mirror at his assumed identity, smiled broadly and looked at his watch. Time was short.

He had things to do, deadlines to meet, people to kill.

Chapter Six

Barnard College
November 16, 5.10 p.m.

After her lecture, Denise Levene spent the rest of the day doing the rounds of the department, catching up with her former colleagues, and then drinking a good Sancerre with them well into the evening. The general consensus was that Denise had been a great colleague and she was sorely missed. She was a profoundly good communicator, but at thirty-two she was still young enough for the science community to patronize her. A woman had to produce twice as many papers and work twice as hard to get the recognition of a man with half her talent, but that was the way of the world.

It wasn't right, but it was true, like many things in life.

It was partly the endless pats on the head while the glass ceiling was closing over it that had motivated her to move out of research and try to get direct law enforcement experience with the police or the Feds. She'd found a position as psychotherapist for the NYPD almost at once. Those jobs didn't usually attract people as well qualified as Denise and they bit her hand off at the first interview. They offered her a nice office and enough bad cops to keep her interested, and they'd even let her continue her research and maybe find a way to fund it. She'd taken the job on the spot. The head of department at Columbia called her a 'reactionary masochist'. She'd known then that she'd made the right decision. She wanted to be close to the real thing, not hiding away in the safety of academia her whole life.

Her dad would've approved too, to a degree. He was a practical man, a man who liked to get right in. She didn't know how he'd feel about her working for the police, though. That would've been an interesting conversation if he'd still been alive.

The truth was that the NYPD offered her access to men and women who had seen these violent criminals first hand. They offered her access to the behavioural science unit at Quantico. She was excited, no doubt about it. It wasn't the same, interviewing the convicted criminals in prison. Everyone thought it was, but she knew that these killers changed when they got caught. A murderer sitting in a cell, devoid of any targets, was not the same guy as the man still free in the world and open to the temptation of his desires.

Denise was interested in the time before they were caught. It was behaviour prediction that really excited her. She wanted to know if it could be modelled. That was the most interesting thing of all. How these people managed their own minds when they were out there in the world. Was there something predictable in these unpredictable killers? It was understanding how they operated out there that would lead to real developments in profiling. And that would mean more guys like them getting caught.

Denise smiled across the room at someone she didn't recognize. She was tired now and wanted to get off home. As the party was slowing down, Denise managed to find an office off the reception room in which to call her partner, who was out somewhere on the campaign trail. Daniel was a fitness-obsessed, carrot-juice-loving liberal but he was hers. They'd been together five years. He worked long hours as an adviser on environmental issues to a Democrat senator. He was one of the good guys looking after the planet. Denise listened to the ringing. She could see him sitting on a lazy chair in his vest and shorts, a running magazine on his knees, the news on in the background. He picked up.

'How did it go, darling?' Daniel asked in his slow West Coast tones. He'd been unable to attend her lecture and had sent her flowers by way of an apology. The senator always came first, but Daniel made sure it never felt that way to Denise and she appreciated those little touches.

'That's my last one for a while,' she said. 'It felt hard seeing everyone again. But it went well. How was Fahrenheit when you left?'

'He was missing you, but he's got your sister with him now, so he'll be in doggy heaven with chocolate biscuits at every meal.'

Denise loved her dog and her partner in that order. Daniel was wonderful when he had the time but her spaniel offered her the unconditional, uncomplicated affection that she remembered from her childhood.

'I might not stay long,' Denise said. 'I want to go home, get out of this suit and eat a tub of Ben and Jerry's watching *Angels with Dirty Faces*.'

'I'd love to join you.'

'Let's say a prayer to a boy who couldn't run as fast as I could,' said Denise in a terrible James Cagney impression.

'It's a good thing you're not taking up acting.'

'Yeah, it's also a good thing you're out of reach right now.'

'Not like you to be violent,' he said. 'Maybe it's working with the NYPD.'

Denise paused. 'Heh, it's the same cops who put their lives on the line trying to keep the city safe so that liberal assholes can make like they own the place.'

'Apologies,' said Daniel. 'I'm sure they're doing all those liberal assholes a great service.'

'Apology accepted, you liberal asshole.'

Daniel laughed. 'God, I love it when you talk dirty. If I was with you right now—'

'You're big with the mouth, Daniel, but you're never at home to follow these promises through.'

'Saving the planet's an important job. Can't just switch it off.'

'It's not the job I want switched off, it's you. You need to lie back once in a while.'

'Hey, are you watching the news?' Daniel leaned forward and watched the ticker tape crossing the bottom of Fox News.

'No, I'm in an office. What's going on?'

'They're reporting a homicide in New York.'

'What happened? When was this?'

'It's just breaking now. A woman was found dead out on Ward's Island.'

Denise focused. 'Is it linked to Mary-Jane's murder?'

'They're speculating. Fox News are right on the scene with live feeds. You should take a look.'

'I can't here. Tell me what happened.'

'Like I said, a woman killed and dumped on the rocks. It looks as though you might have your work cut out, Denise.'

'Yeah, well, I want to help.'

She remained on the phone to Daniel for another minute, until she signed off with her usual ending: 'Love you till tomorrow.'

She opened the door and looked into the crowded reception room, full of bright and smiling faces, all there to wish her well. Denise's eyes were not focused on any of them. She had to leave quickly. She wanted to see the homicide report.

Chapter Seven

East Harlem
November 16, 6.00 p.m.

Harper's suitcase was sitting packed on a chair, but he hadn't gone anywhere. Not yet, at least. In the background the radio crackled updates on the pattern killer they were calling all kinds of names. Harper had been listening and watching closely since he'd seen the victim's face the day before.

The murder had kept him awake all night. After four hours of restless turning, he just couldn't shake the image of the girl on the rocks from floating around his head. She wouldn't go away. Harper wanted to get out there. He wanted to know how a killer got cherry blossom in the fall. Unlike his endless thoughts about Lisa, he knew what to do with homicide cases. He knew the right questions to ask.

His head buzzed with ideas and possible leads already, but he had resisted a call to Lafayette. He had lost his cool once already with Officer Cob. He'd let the anger get the better of him – he still didn't trust himself to be returned to the unsentimental wisecrackers of North Manhattan Homicide. Every weakness was fair game on the homicide squad.

But there was a violent sociopath out there and one thing Tom Harper knew for certain was that he was only just creeping out of the shadows. It was clear that the killer seemed to have spent an extended time with each corpse. The killer had found his voice: a demented voice that wanted to be heard.

Tom kept thinking as he walked down to the subway, took the south train to 51st Street and walked towards Fifth Avenue.

The main entrance to St Patrick's Cathedral was special to Tom. Lisa was a Catholic and loved the place more than any other. When she walked out on him, it was the first place he looked for her. If Lisa was in trouble, this was where she'd come. And on the odd occasion when they'd argued, this was where he knew to find her. This was the place where she lit candles for her grandmother and grandfather, where she attended Mass and went to confession. The cathedral had been her place of refuge and Harper had often wandered in by her side and watched her walk down the centre aisle towards the altar. What she thought about, Tom didn't know.

Outside, the Gothic spires and pointed arches thrust upwards between the big blue glass windows of the office blocks. Harper looked up at the rose window that formed a perfect point of focus like some magical point of connection, then walked through the great doors. Inside, you could disappear from New York into a vast space for reflection and thought. Harper wasn't sure if he was religious or not, but the place moved him.

The cathedral was just about emptying out. The stone still resonated with the voices of the crowds. Harper found a pew near the back, slipped across and felt the reassuring smooth wood against his hand. He stared up into the great open height and the stained glass. He needed to think about his life and this was the only place he could think of to come for some kind of direction. He put his elbows on the pew in front of him and lowered his head.

He tried to push negative thoughts away and let his mind drift. He let recent images flit through his mind: Lafayette, the photographs, the girl on the rocks, Lisa, the nuthatch, a family of four all hand in hand by the lake . . .

Half an hour later, a tall figure appeared at the back of the cathedral. He looked around, his eyes widening in surprise, and then he spotted Harper in the back pew. He slid in behind him and put a hand on his shoulder.

Harper's eyes opened as a familiar voice whispered in his ear. 'I heard on the grapevine that the department asked you back in. What you waiting for? You can't refuse that. It's not right. Fuck that. It's serious. Come with me, my friend. I'll save you from this cult.'

Harper turned and smiled. His partner of three years, Eddie Kasper, was sitting there, his bright street clothes incongruous in the vast stone space, his voice even more so. No one in the department dared to rattle Harper, but this young black man had no fear at all, and, what's more, he even seemed to like the big guy.

'God, it is quiet in here! Is it like first one to talk has to stay in at play break?'

'People are praying.'

Eddie nodded in approbation. 'I get you, man. You're going through some kind of religious conversion, ain't that right?'

'Eddie. You can't talk so loud in here.'

'And that's just how it is with you these days, isn't it, Mr Silent? No hard feelings on my part, buddy, but you cut me off, don't speak to me and don't answer my calls. I'm not thin-skinned. I can take it, but even I got limits. See the tracks of my tears?'

'I've been busy.'

'Screw busy, you ain't been deep sea diving, you got a phone. I'm your best buddy.' Other people from the pews in front of them were starting to look round.

'What's with the praying and shit?'

'I'm looking for something.'

'Well it ain't in here, man, it's out there, hiding behind every pretty face on the street.'

'Lisa was a Catholic. *Is* a Catholic.'

'My girlfriend wears false nails, but you don't see me in the nail bar.'

'I could imagine it.'

'Come on. These Catholics, man, they believe in God and celibacy and all that. No sex before marriage. These are the ones I fear most of all. Do you think you can catch celibacy?'

'I hope you do. I would love to see the look of disappointment on your face, Eddie.'

'Hey, this is your thing, that's cool. I ain't judgemental. I like a man with quirks. I can do quirks. I myself like to pee with my eyes closed just to see if I can keep to the bowl. It's a challenge thing. And come the power cut, I'm the ladies' best friend. Precision is my thing. So you know, I get this whole quirk thing.'

'It's not a quirk.'

'It is a quirk, Tom. You're sitting in someone else's living room with a bunch of other folk saying nothing and speaking to Mr Invisible. That's a mighty big quirk. Might be the biggest of them all.'

Tom smiled at his buddy. 'It's good to see you, Eddie.'

'That's better, man. Now give me some chest hair.' Eddie wrapped his arms round Harper and pressed his body in tight. 'God, I've missed you, man.'

Harper pushed him away. 'Enough.'

'I'm an emotional man, Harps, I don't have to hide it. I love you, brother. Look at you. Can I say something?'

'What?'

'You look like shit. Don't you eat? Sleep? Wash? Fuck, man, you can't short cut the basics.'

'How did you know I was here?'

'You been here a few times since, you know, since she walked out. I look out for you, watch your back. I was worried.'

'Following me?'

'Not so much following. I see it as guarding and protecting. You need a guardian angel, Harps.'

48

'If you're my angel, then I'm in real trouble, so how about you shut up and let me sort this out with the man upstairs.'

'Don't be asking for a replacement, Harps. I'll sit nice and tight here, quiet as you like.'

They paused. Eddie looked all around him. The silence lasted four seconds. 'Harps, there ain't no hot chicks in here. You should go gospel. I'm telling you, I nearly went evangelical myself when I saw what they got stashed in them Harlem churches. Harlem Gold. I'm telling you!'

Harper laughed. 'Enough, Eddie. They can hear you.'

'Come and talk to me outside or else I will not shut my mouth and I make that pledge in the eyes of Mr Invisible.'

Harper was getting several looks from other people in the cathedral. He stood up and took Eddie outside. Out on the sidewalk, Eddie breathed a huge sigh. 'Good God, Tom, that was hard for me, being so quiet.'

'You weren't.'

'Yeah, but even the notion that I might be expected to be silent freaked me out. That's why I could never get school either. I've got to talk to know what's what.'

The two men looked at each other a moment, taking in the separation of the past few months. Eddie's tone lowered. 'You know my feelings, Tom. I'm sorry about Lisa.'

'Thanks. I mean it.'

'No problem. I tried to talk to her. She wouldn't see me.'

'It helped to know you tried.'

'Her loss.'

'I'm moving on, you know. Lafayette tell you?'

'Yeah, but he also tells me you looked over the scene at Ward's Island. And I know Tom Harper . . . that's not going to leave you alone. I bet it's sitting in your fat head just driving you mad.'

'That's just about right. These are bad kills. Did Lafayette put you on Blue Team?'

'Sure.'

'Is it as loose as it looks?'

'Yeah, it is, and you were right about the Ward's Island girl. Another rich girl who won't get a chance to spend her inheritance. Her name's Grace Frazer. She was knocked to the floor next to her car in the city, then somehow dragged off the street and taken to Ward's. You were right about the camera too. They found tripod marks in the grass above the rocks.'

Harper suddenly clocked a look in Kasper's eye. 'Aw shit, Eddie. Lafayette sent you, didn't he?'

'No, Tom, it's worse than that.' Eddie's face was stone cold. 'What?'

'I just got called in. They found another body down in a parking lot right in the heart of the city.'

'Another body already?'

'I wanted to see if you'd ride with me. We need you, Harps. We really need you.'

'Two corpses in two days,' said Harper. He glanced back to the cathedral. Life, death and the afterlife all in a moment. 'Lafayette wants me to see a shrink.'

'Sounds like you need to, speaking to invisible people and forgetting to wash. You're just like those Ward's Island psychos I've been interviewing all day.' He paused and looked at Harper. 'Come on, Tom, let's do what you do best.'

'What's that?'

'End horror stories.'

50

Chapter Eight

Tom Harper and Eddie Kasper drove in silence from the cathedral into the wealth and privilege of the Upper East Side. Harper looked up at the darkening sky between the towering buildings. His greatest memory was lying beside Lisa on the side of a razor-edged ridge with a view of the stars, watching the flocks of migrating raptors in the dark. Some things were still magical in the world; it was just getting harder and harder to find them.

The rain clouds had gathered by the time they turned on to East 82nd Street. The two detectives felt the strain of the news as the car lurched through the pull and push of rush hour traffic. Finding a third dead girl so soon was highly unusual, even with the worst of killers. Harper wasn't sure what they were dealing with. He felt his own ignorance and chastised himself for not taking up Lafayette's offer the day before. Up ahead, they saw the familiar parade of police cars beating out a frenzy of red and blue lights.

As Eddie pulled up to the kerb, Harper took a quick look at his cell phone. No messages – there never were any more. He closed his eyes momentarily. Life must go on.

They jumped out on to the street. It was a buzz of activity at the scene and the first officers had managed to close off both ends of East 82nd. The Crime Scene Unit had secured the area with blue screens and put up six strong floodlights that filled the air with an unreal glow and caused steam to rise from the damp sidewalk.

Harper and Kasper found the entrance to the car park and hurried down to the underground lot. Their footsteps echoed against the bare concrete walls and they could hear the low murmurings of the cops from two levels below.

Just beyond the entrance, Harper's eyes scanned left and right, up and down. He noticed that the parking lot had limited exit points, maximum exposure, valet parking and cameras at every corner, making it a very visible and difficult spot to escape from. This killer wasn't afraid to choose a high-risk location. Except with crimes of passion and anger, which could happen wherever those emotions exploded, such openness was highly unusual.

'If this is the same killer he's changing quickly,' he said to Kasper as they moved down through the dark underground lot. 'This is a far cry from the lonely waters of Ward's Island.'

'Well, we're about to find out.' Eddie pointed towards the rest of Blue Team gathered around a metal railing at the far end of Level 2.

Nate Williamson and Detective Mark Garcia were standing apart from the others, talking closely. Williamson was big and strong, but his hair had mostly left him; Mark Garcia was handsome and well dressed, and smelt of cologne. Together they looked like a veteran cop with a pimp informer. Harper walked across. He and Williamson had some history. Harper was given the lead on the Romario case after Williamson had got nowhere with it.

'How's it going?' Harper asked. 'What's the situation down here?'

'Fuck me, what's brought you back from the dead?' said Williamson. 'Jarvis dropped his charge or what?'

Harper shrugged. 'Don't know about that. I've just been asked to take a look. See if I can help out.'

'Well, we need all the help we can get,' said Williamson, and put out his hand.

Harper took it and shook. 'You're not pissed with me?'

'I'm three weeks off retirement. Let sleeping dogs lie is what I say. How about it?'

'That's good to hear, Nate, but you know they won't let you retire in the middle of a case.'

'That's the only reason I'm happy to see your ugly face, Harper. I'm hoping you can get me a quick arrest and a ticket for the Bahamas.'

Kasper had a look of surprise on his face. 'Hey, this isn't a love-in. What's the story here, Garcia?'

Mark Garcia leaned over a steel railing and pointed. 'There's a body in the arch at the far end. White girl, early twenties. Similar to the girl on Ward's Island, but this one's worse. A whole lot worse.'

'What kind of injuries?' Harper asked.

Williamson jumped in. 'It's like this. Victim's unidentified at present. She's been stripped, probably raped and cut like the others. It's our very own Jack the Ripper.'

Their faces lit by the overhead fluorescent tubes, Tom Harper and Eddie Kasper stepped across to the large brick arch. The body was at the base of three steep steps that led to an old metal service door. Harper ran his hand over the worn curved tread on the top step and then looked down at the body.

It didn't matter how often you'd stared at the aftermath of violence, it always took your breath away. The victim's pale corpse was lying flat on the wet concrete, half under the arch, the skin of her abdomen and chest peeled back on either side of her torso as if she was on display in some sidewalk anatomy class that had been suddenly abandoned.

Harper took his time looking at the corpse. It was hard to see a human being turned into this mess, but he tried to see through it, to notice what was logical about the death scene and what stood out. At this scene, a lot stood out.

Eddie moved across to Tom, who crouched by the body and stared at the woman's bloodied face. Her eyes were intact this time but it was the same killer. Harper saw that right away.

'What's your take, boss?' said Eddie.

'No idea yet. Poor girl. She went through a helluva lot of fear and pain. That's all I got. Give me a moment, Eddie.'

They looked down at the naked body again. It remained horribly still. The harsh fluorescent lights of the underground garage lent the corpse a greenish glow. The only movement was a couple of insects buzzing around her chest. Harper thought it looked like the killer had opened up her torso for a reason. Another trophy. Not only that, but he wanted everyone to see what he'd taken. Harper looked up at his partner. 'The girl's heart is missing,' he said.

Eddie walked away. It was too much to think about. Alone, Harper sat on the bottom step and looked at the corpse. *So what happened to you?* Her hands were so caked in blood that he couldn't tell if she'd put up a fight or not. *Did you come down here of your own free will? What did he do? Threaten you with his knife to keep quiet and go along with his plans? Did he make you undress – promise to let you go? Or did he sap you and drag you here while you were out cold? Did you know this bastard?*

Harper looked carefully at the marks on the floor. The ground in the arch was wet from a leak that seemed to come from a crack in the concrete above. There was a layer of black carbon from traffic fumes which scuffed up easily and left light marks. Harper looked at the pattern of marks at the bottom of the steps. Two long straight lines extended about forty centimetres from the bottom of the step. Heel marks as the killer had dragged his victim across the ground holding her upper body. That meant he'd probably sapped her. Harper saw another set of marks. Three oblong shapes scratched around as if looking for the right spot. The tripod, no doubt. Whoever it was, he had filmed or photographed these gruesome final scenes.

Harper continued to think it through. *He hit you and dragged you to the arch. Then he turned you. The heel marks twist and then stop. He laid you flat out here, half in view. Why? Why leave your body visible? Wasn't that dangerous? Why not pull you all under the arch? Was that because he wanted to see what he was doing? Needs the buzz of seeing your face as he hurt you?*

Harper looked carefully for any other scuff marks. There were none. He looked at the shallow puddles of blood that had pooled across the concrete. He peered into the darkness of the arch with a flashlight. More blood was thick across the back wall and a few drips hung above him. Harper was no blood-pattern expert, but the arterial spray was unmistakable. The killer would've left the scene covered in her blood. There were flecks of blood-covered paint under her fingernails and scratch marks at the base of the wall. *He raped you and mutilated you out here in the light while you were semi-conscious, then pulled you inside.*

Harper leaned across to the wall. The scratch marks were all in the same place. *How did he keep your arms from moving?* He'd held her down, somehow. Harper imagined the scene, letting the images pass through his mind as a mass of sudden, bloody fragments. *He had his knees on your arms as he cut you, didn't he? He sat there, muffling your screams and watching you real close.*

It was nearly an hour before Harper finally emerged to allow the Crime Scene Unit to get the body bagged and out to the lab. He was just leaving when he spotted something else. It was easy to miss, written faintly in yellow chalk with part of the lettering removed by the dripping from the ledge above. He couldn't read it as it was, so he called the photographer down to get some good shots. Then he went back to the team.

'So what does the clairvoyant say?' said Williamson with a sneer that showed off his gums.

'She was tortured to death down there while shoppers were returning to their cars.' Harper looked at Williamson hard. 'It's unbelievable.'

Nate Williamson felt it too. 'No ligature this time. She didn't survive the surgery, is my guess.'

Harper nodded his head. 'Yeah, I agree. He hit an artery and it will have killed her more quickly, thank God. But listen, the arch down there is large enough to conceal the body, if he'd wanted to. But he hasn't, so there's something important to him in how he's left her, half in and half out. Visible.'

'He might've been interrupted,' said Williamson.

'Yeah. Or he wanted the body found. I think maybe he wanted it found just like it was – posed.'

'What do you mean?'

'I mean it looks like he's been particular in how he's left her and how he's opened her up.'

'Particular, as in flat on her back? How else is he going to leave her?'

'Particular, as in . . .' Harper took another look over the edge of the railings. He could see her head in a circle of blood and the flaps of skin stretched out beside her. 'He's showing us something. The missing heart. I don't know yet. Give me time. What's the Medical Examiner say?'

'He thinks he's used something like a filleting knife and some kind of bone shears – not the kind of thing you carry around in your pocket. Definitely premeditated.'

'Any witnesses? Anyone hear anything?'

'We've got near thirty officers from Nineteenth and Twenty-fifth going round the blocks, but nothing yet.'

'How do you read it, Harps?' Eddie said. 'Who is he?'

'It's not spontaneous. It was planned. He humiliates and likes hurting. He's posed the body. It looks to me that he's got the whole thing figured out – where he kills, how he kills, how he escapes. He's been dreaming this a long time. My take on the victim is that she's just like the others. She's rich.'

'And how can you tell that?' Williamson asked.

'She's got a half-carat diamond in each ear, she's had a nose job, her hands and feet are unused to work, and she looks like she spent most of her life in a gym.'

An hour later the scene was a buzz of police activity. NYPD's Crime Scene Unit was fast, thorough and precise. Staffed, unlike some CSUs, with police detectives – they knew the importance of speed.

The next twelve hours were crucial. If they got a quick lead, they might be able to run this killer down before he got to dispose of his bloody clothes and put his trophies away. Williamson reckoned that he had a car and would put her clothes in the trunk and then maybe leave them until the heat calmed down – but that was a long shot.

Harper stayed at the scene and sat on the low wall at the edge of the lot. He pulled out his sketch pad. A sleek dark grackle stared across the page from a couple of days earlier at the Ramble. He turned over and drew the crime scene with a few quick lines. The dead woman appeared on the page in front of him. Thoughts of Lisa flittered into his mind but he stopped himself. The imagination could be a cruel thing. He focused on the sketch. Without the shock-red blood and bruising, she looked serene – she was positioned with her arms across her pudenda like a Renaissance nude, the butterfly wings either side of her, strange and otherworldly.

What was he doing, this maniac killer? The posing was important. Harper knew that much. It was an act of communication. He was saying something. As yet, Harper didn't speak the killer's language. But something was happening. This was the second kill in two days. His rate was escalating dramatically. Why? Was it some kind of kill frenzy? Time would tell.

'Hey, Harper!' a voice at the far end of the parking lot called out. Harper looked up and saw the tall, thin figure of Eddie Kasper, dressed in his low-slung pants and bubble jacket, his hair braided tight to his scalp.

'Yeah, what?'

'It's just like old times, ain't it?'

Chapter Nine

The Station House
November 16, 9.14 p.m.

Harper had a quick decision to make if he was going to make a difference to the case. He drove straight from the parking lot back to the precinct, the mass of information from the crime scene turning in his mind. He needed to know the deal.

Captain Lafayette was not in his office. He was down in the gym, sweating out his frustrations. He'd been working round the clock on the case, trying to get the breakthrough from Blue Team while keeping the executives from breathing down everyone's necks, but nothing was biting.

He'd left a message for Harper to go down to the gym if he turned up. Tom Harper was the one hope he had of turning down the heat, and talking to Kasper had been his last-ditch effort to pull him into the case.

When Harper arrived in the gym Lafayette was alone. Everyone else was out hunting down witnesses and following up vague possibilities. Lafayette was on the weights. He saw Tom and huffed through another five repetitions. Always one to make people wait.

'Heard you showed up at the crime scene. I was first down there. Worst I've come up against. How about you?'

'Yeah, it's brutal.'

'Serial homicides usually escalate like this, Harper?'

'No. Not quite so quickly, but there are no fixed patterns. They usually take a longer cooling off period between kills. For some reason, the killer got hungry real quick this time.'

'Same guy, right?'

'Almost certainly. As long as you keep the specific injuries and the cherry blossom detail out of the press, we should avoid copycats.'

'What's wrong with plain old-fashioned murder? You want to kill someone, take a gun. One shot. Be tidy, you know.' The chief towelled his shoulders dry. His thick moustache was also dripping. He licked the sweat off the bristles and then towelled his face. 'Offer still stands, Harper. Where are you now?'

'You'll have to be more specific.'

'Look, I can be specific. Do you want to try to save any part of your career by taking the clean slate and helping us nail this case? You'd have to apologize and sign up to some therapy for the aggression, just to keep ourselves in the clear. Rainer is gunning for you, Harper. You need to know that I had to go over his head for this one.'

'Thanks, Captain. I appreciate your faith in me.'

'Fuck faith, Harper. I looked up the stats. You're a closer. The best we got.'

Harper looked around him. 'I'm not sorry for what I did to Lieutenant Jarvis. He called Lisa a slut, and everyone knows I've got a short fuse. He knew what he was doing.'

'I know, I know. Divorce is a pig of a business. He said the wrong thing. Listen, one day he'll realize what an ass he is, but until then you've still got a life to lead. Look, I can probably apologize on your behalf, but will you help us stop this scum from terrifying half of New York?'

'What do they want from me? They're not going to rip up the charges, are they? And Jarvis won't like it, either. He'll take it as far as he can.'

'Jarvis will hate it, but let me worry about him,' the captain said. 'He's got his own troubles. A lot came to light during the internal investigation – he's been intimidating the new recruits and anyone else not able to stand up to him. He'll be lucky to keep his own fucking job. And as for the charges, we can maybe get away with a Letter of Instruction. With psychological assessment and therapy for that temper of yours, I think we can get that signed off by the deputy commissioner.'

Harper rose. 'I can do without the psychological assessment.'

'Just go through the motions for me, will you? It's part of the deal.'

'I got my own way of handling it.'

'I know, and look how successful it is. Come on, give yourself a break. Jump on board. You could do with the focus.'

Harper stood silently, then nodded once and the two men shook. 'Good to have you back on the team, Detective Harper. You get signed up to the department shrink and you're back on Blue Team. Dr Levene works at headquarters. She knows you're coming. Just don't take a pop if things get tough. Keep your fucking hands in your pockets, Sugar Ray.'

'Sure,' said Harper. 'If people lay off me, I'll lay off them. Simple laws of physics, Chief.'

Chapter Ten

Blue Team Major Investigation Room
November 16, 11.15 p.m.

For the first twenty-four hours of each homicide, the focus was on three main points of investigation – victim identification, witness search and forensic leads. Back at Blue Team, Tom Harper went straight from the gym to his old desk and started working on victim ID. He'd not been happy with the speed of ID on the previous victims. It took them eight hours to ID the Ward's Island corpse as Grace Frazer and those eight hours were lost hours.

Harper insisted on going through the CCTV images himself. He knew two things for certain from his visit to the crime scene: one, the woman in the parking lot drove there in a car, and, two, that car had disappeared. Simple conclusion was that the killer didn't use his own car. He'd gone to the lot on foot and after the murder he'd driven the victim's car out of there. It was the only way he could've left in such a bloody state without being seen.

It only took an hour of searching the tape before he spotted the victim's car arriving in the lot. He paused on a single frame and wrote down the licence plate on a brand new silver Mercedes SUV. He called it through and within a few minutes he was looking at the victim's ID. She was called Amy Lloyd-Gardner, and she was twenty-four years old. A quick check on the various databases showed she was a PR executive married to a wealthy young banker.

Tom pulled up a photograph of Amy Lloyd-Gardner from a social networking website and leaned back into his seat. He stared at her face. She was another beauty with long blond hair, similar in looks to Mary-Jane and Grace. The killer was fixated on a certain kind of look and this was his trigger: a bright-eyed, blond-haired innocence.

Harper turned round to look at the room full of officers working methodically through the case details. Somewhere out in the city, Amy's husband was waiting up for her, as yet unaware that his young wife was a murder victim.

She had been on a lazy afternoon shopping trip. She would've had no idea as she wandered around the shops that there was a killer tracking her and waiting for an opportunity. No idea at all. Her car, her clothes, her shopping had all disappeared. That meant that the killer had taken everything away in the silver Merc. But the killer didn't take the body and he didn't need to take the clothes. *He wants to keep the clothes*, Harper thought, and added it to a growing list of the killer's predilections. He called across to one of the detectives and asked him to get the car details sent out to the team and called through to patrol. Within minutes, the car's plate and description was radioed all across Manhattan and New York State. Finding the big shiny car was just a matter of time.

Harper walked through to Williamson to give him the heads-up on the ID. Williamson took the printout. 'Thanks, Harper. Listen, I'll take Garcia and go and see Mr Lloyd-Gardner myself. Shit, what a night call this is going to be.'

Harper was pleased that Williamson would take this one. He needed more time to go through the information from the crime scene. When he returned to his desk, his email blinked with a new arrival, from the guys at the crime scene lab. Harper had requested the photographs as soon as they'd been downloaded and categorized. He clicked through the images one by one. The story retold itself on his computer screen. A sad end to life in a grey concrete garage. The violence of the poor woman's end was there before him in cold close-up. He felt the anger rising and took a moment to detach himself.

He clicked backwards and forwards through the pictures of the corpse. From a certain angle, the naked body with the skin stretched out either side of her torso looked like some kind of butterfly. Was that accident or design? He stared at the screen. Amy's toenails were painted red, and there was a little black ace of spades on her left hip. Her eyebrows had been plucked thin and then drawn in pale eyebrow pencil, and her lips still retained a translucent pink lip gloss. Even on a mutilated corpse, the little marks of recognition and individuality demanded to be known. Harper noticed a mark just below her lips. Smudged lipstick. Maybe the killer had left a print. He zoomed close to her lips, until they covered the entire screen. It wasn't a fingerprint. A faint outline of a kiss lay half across her lips in her own lipstick. The killer must have kissed her, coated his lips in her lipstick and then kissed her again. There was a half-print of the killer's lips sitting right there.

He gave Latent Prints a call and suggested they get a print. Everything needed to be processed, every tiny detail. He never knew, down the line, what would help him nail this bastard and get him locked up. Sometimes it was a single hair, sometimes a significant coincidence, sometimes a cell phone call that put the killer at the scene, sometimes something as simple as a kiss.

What were they dealing with? A sociopath? A thrill seeker or a sexually sadistic serial killer who wouldn't stop until someone stopped him? The team didn't talk much as they wandered in and out of the precinct late into the night. Not even the jokes were flowing yet, just the grim sense of a difficult journey and the knowledge of how much pain and suffering these victims had been through.

Harper picked up the congealed dinner of chicken noodles that had been half eaten a few hours earlier. He was halfway through the first mouthful when he caught the image again in his mind's eye.

Harper moved back to his desktop and clicked on her photographs again. *The hands in prayer*, he was thinking. That little detail from Grace Frazer's murder was sitting right there in Harper's mind and the link to the parking lot killing flashed into his mind. He found the image he wanted. The woman's corpse was shining bright. Her skin was so pale it was almost iridescent, the wings were blood-dark, and the fluorescent lights glistened gold on the bloody circle around her head.

Harper stopped mid-chew. *A halo?*

Yes, he knew that there was something in that image, something that connected it to Grace Frazer. The killer had started to express himself, let himself be known a little. First a woman with her hands in prayer and now he'd made wings and a halo. Amy looked like an angel with her heart torn out.

Harper was fired by the thought and quickly printed three photographs, one of Mary-Jane Samuelson, one of Grace Frazer and one of the Angel. He went up to one of the big boards that had been set up in the investigation room and pinned the pictures side by side. Garcia looked across from the computer he was working at. 'What you looking at, Harper?'

'He's signing his corpses.'

Harper picked up his coat and walked down the stairs. He needed some fresh air and a chance to think. A killer's MO was one thing – it was what he needed to do to kill – but an MO could change, as it had in this case. He had cut them to different degrees, but the signature was what he needed to do to fulfil himself, what he couldn't kill without doing. The angelic wings and the hands in prayer were part of a ritual, just like the cherry blossom, which struck Harper as almost bridal. The killer needed to pose his corpses like dead angels. Harper felt that he knew something about the killer now. He hated goodness and religion. Like a devil, he needed to degrade it all.

Harper stepped across the street towards a coffee shop. It was close to midnight. Outside, the air was good and cool. The winter migrants who had stayed in New York would appreciate the break from the harsh cold wind. Harper's footsteps echoed in the quiet night air. Then he spotted a guy up ahead staring at him.

Harper turned and behind him saw two more big guys walking towards him. All three were over six foot and burly. They looked like security guards, or maybe even police.

'I guess this isn't social, so what do you want?' Harper said, cold-eyed.

'Into the alley,' said one of the guys. His face looked like the side of a mountain.

'Read the shield, gentlemen,' said Harper, flashing his ID. 'I'm a cop, so you might want to avoid trouble and get yourselves home to bed.'

They didn't move, but looked down into the dark alley. Harper thought they were motioning for him to make a move, but from the alley he heard footsteps. His eyes twisted towards the sound and he saw the problem. Its name was Lieutenant Jarvis, and everything suddenly clicked into place.

Jarvis's jaw was no longer wired up but his face was still misshapen down one side. 'Detective Harper,' he said in a slow slur. 'I thought your police time was over. Now someone tells me I've got to eat humble pie while you get the glory spot. After you leaping on me with those fists of yours, doesn't sound fair, does it?'

'No, Lieutenant, it doesn't sound fair.'

'So, what was it you objected to, Harper? You didn't like my insinuations?'

'I didn't like any part of it at all,' said Harper, 'or your tone of voice.'

'Really. My tone of voice. Hey, guys, he doesn't like my beautiful voice.'

They laughed like eager sycophants. Harper looked around

quickly. This wasn't good news. These four guys were all strong, and people fighting together tended to get all excited like a pack of hounds and do real damage. They could bust him up pretty bad. He couldn't see a way out. There were too many of them. He let his arms hang down by his sides.

'These your men, Lieutenant?'

'These guys are just visiting the city. They stopped by and offered me a helping hand.'

'Let it go, Jarvis. I hit you because you called my wife a whore.'

'I still say she's a whore. She's shacked up with a lawyer over in New Jersey. She made that move real quick. Makes you think, doesn't it, Harper? I heard the reason she left is because you used those fists of yours once too often. Well, me and my boys are going to make it hard for you to ever use those fists again. In the name of public safety and women's liberation.'

Harper bristled. But it was just what Jarvis wanted. The bad cop throwing a punch.

'Didn't you hear me, Harper? Lisa Vincenti was fucking every guy in the department while you were out all night chasing Eric Romario. She got real lonely. Liked it every which way, I heard. Now she's done with the department and has moved on to the courts.'

Harper's two hands were fists now, and the anger was rising. He took a step forward. Then stopped. 'I ain't gonna rise to it.'

'You don't need to,' Jarvis spat.

One of the three gorillas stepped forward, then another. They grabbed Harper at each elbow and shoulder and marched him down the alleyway. The third gorilla opened a long canvas bag that was sitting by the dumpster and took out a serious-looking sledgehammer. Harper was held fast as Jarvis moved in.

'You know what this is, Harper?'

'I know what it is and I know what you are – a fucking coward. You do this, Jarvis, and I'll hunt you down.'

'With what? You going to slap me with your big flat hands?'

'I'll hunt you down, Jarvis, and every one of these monkeys.'

'You do that. I just want you to remember the last person you hit with those fists and what a stupid thing that was.'

'Jarvis, this is way beyond necessary. I'm working the case because they need me. There's a killer out there.'

'Put his arm on the dumpster,' called Jarvis.

Harper resisted and strained with all his strength as the three men held him and prised his arm from his side, but they were too strong. Against three of them he couldn't do anything, not with his hands held firm.

They held his wrist down on the lid of the dumpster, so that his fist was lying ready to be mashed to pieces. Jarvis picked up the big carbon-steel sledgehammer. 'Let this be a lesson you don't forget.'

He pulled the long handle up over his head and then held it for a moment. 'Ready?' The hammer flew down at speed. Harper's skill, learned from hours in the ring, wasn't just in the extra pound per inch he could force down those four knuckles, it was in the ability to keep his eyes open when facing danger and to make split-second decisions.

As the hammer fell, the three gorillas closed their eyes and leaned away from the point of impact. It was the natural thing to do. The gorilla holding his wrist even moved his hand up Harper's forearm.

It was a tiny miscalculation on their part, but enough. Harper watched the sledgehammer fall and twisted his wrist and hand about three inches to the right. It was enough to move out of the line of the hammerhead, which thudded with a massive shock into the steel dumpster, the loud bellow of sheet metal against carbon steel echoing both ways down the alley. The four assailants flinched in the aftermath and gave Harper enough of an opening. Harper pulled his left arm free. He already had his targets mapped out. Four blows. He could get four shots off in under two seconds. Trained to do it.

At his best, Harper could throw a punch at around ten metres per second. None of the four guys was more than a metre from him, which gave the first about a tenth of a second to see the straight left coming at him and parry or duck. He had barely clocked it when the full force of Harper's 300 kilograms of pressure burst on to his jaw in the form of a clenched fist. His head flew back, his neck jolted and he was flat on his back, out cold.

The second guy had a little longer, but Harper turned with a right hand uppercut which hit the point of his jaw and lifted him to the tip of his toes.

The third guy was now backing off, which was a damn good thing because Harper hadn't held back with the power and was pretty sure he'd broken bones in both his hands. He turned to Jarvis.

'This time I'll forgive you out of respect for your stupidity, but play a trick like that again and I'll hurt you. Do you understand?'

'Fuck you,' said Jarvis, picking up the sledgehammer. It was about as stupid a move as he could've made. With both hands wielding the hammer, he was a sitting duck. Harper moved his torso out of the way, bounced back on to his front foot and gave Jarvis a repeat performance, this time with the full force of his elbow. Jarvis's jaw shattered like glass for the second time and the sledgehammer clattered to the ground.

Chapter Eleven

Precinct House
November 17, 6.20 a.m.

After a four-hour sleep in the bunkhouse and a trip to the department doctor, Harper took his bruised but unbroken knuckles back up to the precinct house. His role in the investigation was to find a way into the case, which meant getting to know the killer, and he had some catching up to do. He wanted to see the crime scene for Mary-Jane's murder and called Eddie Kasper at home. 'You need to take me through the reports of victim number one. I know the basics – I've got the autopsy protocol right here. I know what he did to her, I just want to see how it happened. This first kill triggered off the next two, that's my thinking.'

'It's six a.m., Harper. Don't you sleep?'

'We got a case to crack. Eddie, I expected a little more commitment from you of all people.'

'Fuck that, I'm kinda busy on a different kind of commitment here. Can't it wait?'

'I'm back on the case, Eddie, and that means you're mine. Now get over here.'

On the other end of the phone, a woman's voice came on the line. 'There's only one woman in Eddie's life and she's lying next to him, so who the fuck are you?'

Eddie and Harper agreed to meet in the Upper East Side

residential street where the first victim was found. Eddie drove up with a look of disapproval on his face. He jumped out of his car and threw the door shut.

'It's no good you smiling, Harper, you don't have to face her. She's not a woman you want to displease. Especially not when it comes to her conjugal rights.'

'It was six a.m. You two were fast asleep.'

'It don't matter to her. I need to be right there on tap, should she have any such need.'

'Well, she's a lucky lady.'

'That's what I tell her. Shit, man, what the hell did you do to your hands?'

Harper started walking. 'I got them caught in a door.'

'Both of them? That's a hell of a door.'

Harper kept Kasper walking towards the first crime scene – a four-bed apartment in a luxury building. Mary-Jane had been found dead in the hallway of her own home.

Harper opened the door to the apartment. The family had since moved out. They'd never move back, either. Their lives had been destroyed. Mrs Samuelson had come home, opened the door and seen her daughter, exposed and bloody on the floor. Harper held up a photograph of the scene.

'She was right there, legs facing the door, head propped up on two pillows,' Eddie said, pointing at the stained carpet.

'He posed her for maximum shock and humiliation.'

'Her mother's not recovered,' said Eddie. 'I interviewed her twice. She's bad, Harps.'

'I imagine,' said Harper, moving through the apartment. 'How did he get in?'

'He had a key or she let him in. No sign of forced entry.'

'You mean you don't know yet?'

'He gets in and out without being seen. The only witness we got on this one is dead. I don't think anyone's come up with anything more yet.'

Harper walked through the beautifully furnished rooms.

The trail of blood ran from the hall into the living room. The windows looked out across Fifth Avenue. 'What do you think happened?'

Eddie shrugged. 'He took her in here. We think he raped her on the couch. They found seminal fluid on the cushions. He wasn't careful with this one. Left us his DNA, but so far no hits on CODIS and if he's not on any DNA database then he might not have killed before.'

'What next?'

'He strangled her, went to the kitchen to find a knife, came back and took his trophy. After that, we think he sat staring at her for some time before he moved the body. Medical Examiner thinks she was lying in that spot in the living room for a good half an hour.'

Harper wandered around the room. 'Two things are different here. I saw the report. The knife he used was from the rack in the kitchen, right?' Eddie nodded. 'He didn't have a knife with him. The second thing that's different is that he left his DNA and fibres all over this one. Amy and Grace were cleaned. I think he took their clothes to be sure, but he left Mary-Jane's on the floor.' Harper looked closely at the carpet. 'Any tripod marks?'

'No. But Mr Samuelson's camcorder was missing.'

'She didn't struggle at all, did she? There's not a thing out of place. My guess is that he controls them with fear and promises. He promises that he'll let her go so she does what he wants. He either has them out cold or he controls them. I guess he felt safe with Mary-Jane because she was younger.'

'Yeah, that's too true.'

'What I don't get is why he goes for such high risk targets. It's strange for a killer to start so confidently. He seems fearless. He takes big risks to kill the most difficult victims. Why? What's so important about their wealth and privilege?'

'Jealousy?' said Kasper.

Harper shook his head. 'It's more than that.' He had read the department reports and autopsy protocols on the first two murders and was convinced that the killer was an organized type of sociopath. He not only had a personal vendetta, he had a thing against society in general. He most likely chose these girls because their deaths caused maximum fear and maximum national heartbreak. Killers usually chose their victims from within their own social strata, but Harper couldn't see it in this case. There was punishment going on here. And then the strange confessional poses and blossom. The poses that suggested the killer didn't feel like he had the right to do what he'd done. He seemed to show remorse.

Harper spent an hour walking through each room, piecing together the last few minutes of Mary-Jane's life. 'All three kills show confidence and hatred,' he told Eddie as they left. 'There's an increasing degree of overkill. In all cases, the killer posed the corpses and took a trophy, and he sprinkled cherry blossom like confetti over the first two. Why is that?'

'He's a fucking mental case. That's the only explanation you ever gonna get from me.'

'Yeah, he's crazy, but he took time to shift each body to expose them. He wants to degrade them – to hide their faces and expose them as if he was suggesting that that was all they were worth. I know they were all wealthy, but if you want my opinion, I think this is personal. He sees something in these girls that no one else sees.'

Chapter Twelve

One PP
November 17, 10.00 a.m.

A couple of hours after walking the crime scene, Tom Harper left Eddie Kasper to talk to the profilers at the FBI's New York field office. Later he arrived right on time for his appointment at One PP. He knocked on the fake mahogany door of the suite on the fifth floor. The little brass sign read *Dr Denise Levene, Ph.D.*

On the wall hung a little certificate: *Dr Denise Levene, a fellow of the American Psychological Association, was honored as Distinguished Psychologist of the Year in 2003–4 for her pioneering contributions in cognitive behavioral psychotherapy.*

A warm voice from inside the office shouted, 'Come in.' Harper did as he was told. He had to these days. He pushed the heavy door across the thick carpet and stepped inside.

There she was, Dr Denise Levene, sitting in a high-backed black leather chair in a white blouse, writing in her desk diary.

Harper stood in the entrance and waited for her to look up. She didn't. It gave him a second or two to run his eyes over her. Blond hair. He hadn't expected that. Young, too. She had a petite frame. Then she looked up and a pair of bright blue eyes held his gaze directly. She was pretty, for a shrink.

'Welcome. Take a seat,' she said.

Harper remained standing.

'Take a seat, *please*,' she said and smiled, all nice and accommodating.

'Look, if you're going to get all hooked on me, why don't you just say something now and we can end this.'

She didn't blink. Good on her.

'Take a seat, Harper.' She was forceful now.

He stood his ground, unsure how to play this one. Levene leaned back in her leather chair and chewed the end of her pen. 'I get it. I'm blonde. I'm a woman. I've got letters after my name. You don't know what to do with me, do you, Mr Harper?'

'It's Detective Harper,' said Tom, flexing the muscles in his shoulders.

'Not according to your file, cowboy. Not unless I agree you're fit for duty. Officially, you're still on suspension.'

Harper sighed. She was a smart-ass. Just what he needed. A curt little city girl with an answer for everything. 'All right, let's get this over with,' he said, moving into the room and sitting reluctantly on a wide brown couch. He was feeling distinctly uncomfortable. After he'd hit Jarvis the first time, they had made him sit through sessions with some tight-faced therapist who responded to every remark with 'Well, that's good. So gooood.' He'd ended up blaming the therapist for destroying his career. Too much thought can kill you as surely as too little.

Levene tipped further back in her chair. She studied Tom for a moment, unafraid of his negativity or of the silence. She was trying to get some angle. Tom felt her eyes on him and he lifted his head and stared back. She was confident. Dealt with his type before, maybe. Knew the road.

'Let's get some shit out of the way first,' she said. 'You don't want to be here. Fine. I can read you like a book. You need to display your cynicism and negativity because you feel threatened in here. I understand that. But you don't need to feel threatened. I'm here to help.'

'I don't feel threatened. You're way off the mark.'

'Not physically threatened, Detective. I mean emotionally threatened.'

'Well, what do you expect? They didn't teach us the moves to deal with an emotional attack at the academy.'

'I like your sense of humour, Detective, but it's just another way of deflecting the blows.'

'I'm not afraid, Doctor. I'm just pissed off that you're wasting my time.'

'You don't think this will help? Fine with me. You just want your shield and minimum fuss. Fine also. I'm not that interested in you, to tell the truth. I've worked with enough guys like you to know that I'd be wasting my time too.'

'Well then, that's all nice and easy for the two of us. Let's just do the minimum and sign this off.'

'Okay. Let's do that. You need a clean psych assessment, right?'

'Right.'

'And you're sure you've got that anger thing under control.'

'Sure.'

'So those bloody knuckles are just for effect, right?'

'Right.'

'Okay. Let's do the minimum. You sign up for ten sessions and I'll sign this psych form right now.'

'Ten sessions? Fuck that. I want the minimum.'

'That is the minimum, Detective. I had planned a couple of sessions, but after meeting you I realize we're going to have to go in deep and that's going to take time.'

'No way. I'm fine. You know that and I know that, so sign the form and let me get back out on the streets.'

'You don't sign up for ten, I'm not letting you out on the street at all. You're not fit.'

'How do you know? You haven't even assessed me!'

'I can see everything I need to – you're spoiling for a fight, you're resentful and negative, and you have no idea what to do with those little things called emotions. So, in my view, you're not ready to be issued a gun. But if you sign up for ten sessions, then that's going to convince me that you do want to help yourself and help resolve the anger. You sign up, I'll give you the benefit of the doubt.'

'So it's Catch-22?'

'No, it's CBT. Cognitive behavioural therapy. We focus on practical strategies to manage your behaviour and we focus on the now. I don't need to go back to your childhood and I don't go looking for your subconscious. I don't try to interpret your world. I couldn't give a damn about why you do things or what you think. All I know is that I can change those things.'

'You sure about that?'

'We agree behaviour we want, call it Behaviour A, and we agree behaviour we don't, call it Behaviour B. In stage one, we set about noticing how much we are drawn to Behaviour A and Behaviour B. Stage two, we put in some rewards for Behaviour A and some sanctions for Behaviour B. So you see, we just retrain your mind a little and maybe your emotions, but they are secondary. We focus on getting the actions we want; the emotions will follow. But first, we got to agree what the problem is.' Denise laid her arms on the desk. She was tanned and her silver charm bracelet rattled against the wood. She looked towards Tom for a reaction. 'If there is a problem,' she said.

'Not my problem.'

'Still a problem, though.'

'Not worth your time. Nice as you are.'

'Let's dispose of the attitude,' said Dr Levene. 'I get it. I get it you don't like me or trust me. I get it you don't really think psychologists can help, period. I get it you like being angry. You're a man. I get it. Why don't you try to be a little more interesting? I could tell right from the moment you walked in that you're a very emotional guy. I can see it in your curled lip and your twitching hands. So be emotional. Make my day.'

Tom half smiled. She was good. He could see why the guys liked her. And she was good to look at too, if you didn't mind the stuck-up, college-educated aura.

'Looks like you're the one with the attitude,' he told her.

'But I didn't screw up my job. That was all you, and looking at you I'd say you did it all by yourself. Hope she was worth it.'

Harper stood. He walked over to her desk.

'That simple, is it?' he growled. 'This is some problem you're about to turn around? Solve my anger? I don't care what you do. I'm here because this is my only option to save some lives.'

'You've got this saving-lives fantasy to a T,' she said. 'Hero cop with bad attitude cos he cares too damn much. Lover walks out, again, because he loves too damn much. Why the hell is the world mistreating Mr Perfect? You need to get your head out of your ass. If she left you, she left you for reasons belonging to both of you.'

Harper was riled. He stared hard at Dr Levene. 'Don't believe what you hear, Levene. I read people too. You talk tough and act tough, but you're scared of me. I can smell it.'

Levene smiled, but his aim was good.

'You want more?' Tom said. 'I come in the door. You're writing but you've got nothing to write. Look on your pad. It's empty. You're play-acting. You've done your second blouse button up too, but I can see by the crease that it's been open all morning. You've turned your personal photos away from me and you've turned your certificates out . . . Jesus, you're the one hiding, not me. Main motivation with you – to get what you want.'

'Right on all but the last point. Main motivation is wildly off the mark.'

'You know what? I think you're flirting with me, Dr Levene.' Tom leaned right over the desk.

'You're in my space, cowboy. Back right off.'

'Get you excited when I'm that close?'

'Yeah, the smell of whisky at ten in the morning really turns me on.'

'Quit your games.'

'You first.'

'You sit here in Suite No. 32B. All the signs that you are a made-it lady. You even solve people's problems. I bet you feel great. But out there, Dr Levene, out there is a maniac who tortures his victims and takes body parts. Watching them die and convulse as he . . . Shit, lady. He tore open a woman's chest, cut out her heart and then went home. Went off to his day job.'

Levene nodded. 'That's the emotion I was talking about. Nice to see it as it really is.' The smile had left her face.

'My problems don't amount to anything worth State dollars, so yes I resent the waste of everyone's time.'

A lesser doctor would have ended the session right there and then. Pressed the small red security button and had this psycho cop from the dark ages towed away. But that wasn't Levene's way and that wasn't how Levene succeeded when others failed. She smiled. Unbuttoned the second button on her blouse, turned the photos out and the certificates in.

'Just seeing how good you are, cowboy. Now let's get to work.'

Tom went for the door. 'I've signed to ten sessions, right? Well, let's keep them short. Session one over. Nine more to go.'

'Then you agree to come back?'

'If it's the only way I can get out there to work this killer, then I'll endure you.'

'Fine. But I want you back here tomorrow. I need to get started right away if you're going to stay out of trouble, Detective.'

Chapter Thirteen

Blue Team Major Investigation Room
November 17, 2.34 p.m.

Harper spent the rest of the morning trying to get Denise Levene's voice out of his head, so he went back to the other two crime scenes at Ward's Island and the underground parking lot. He didn't get much further with his thinking and drove back to the precinct. He wanted desperately to call Lisa, but resisted it. She'd told him not to. She'd said they both needed to work out how to live apart. He parked up, bought fresh coffee and a bagel from a street vendor and walked up into the open-plan sixth-floor office of Manhattan North Homicide.

The detectives who made up the elite Blue Team were all sitting around in the far corner facing Nate Williamson. He'd just received the feedback from the Fed's violent criminal apprehension programme, ViCAP – a database of sickening crimes.

Williamson was a hard-nosed veteran of nearly twenty years. His age alone demanded respect, but he still worked out and he could floor a perp half his age. The Romario case had been his lead at the start. After four months they'd put Harper in charge. It wasn't easy for Williamson, but he knew the younger guys were just that little bit smarter and faster. And Harper had done a good job. Williamson knew that he wouldn't have made the links Harper had made. Not in a million years.

Harper walked into the centre of the room for the first time in a long while. 'Nice time last night, Harper?' asked Williamson, looking at Harper's fists. 'We wondered where you got to.'

Harper tried to shrug it off. 'Got them caught in a door.'

'Yeah,' said Williamson, 'we've just seen the door wearing a face mask.'

'Eddie and me walked the crime scene again. I need to speak to the team, Nate.'

'When I say so, Harper,' said Williamson. 'Now listen up, all of you. The street teams are still scratching around and nothing's giving – a few witnesses with contradictory stories. There's nothing on ViCAP. Forensics have nothing yet, but they reckon he's been careful with his prints again. They'll be able to confirm whether they've got any DNA samples in a couple of days. They found some microfibres in Amy Lloyd-Gardner's hair and mouth and a half-print of the killer's lips on her mouth, but nothing much to go on. He took her clothes. The autopsy will get under way soon, but the ME confirmed that Amy's heart had been removed. Any luck on finding the silver Merc, Garcia?'

Garcia shook his head. 'Nothing. No sighting at all. He maybe has it locked up.'

'Unlikely,' said Harper. 'It's full of evidence. Most likely scenario is he took it to a scrap yard and torched it. You should check all the yards.'

'Will do,' said Garcia.

Kasper nodded from the side. 'I've been speaking to the FBI profile coordinator and we'll put the package together for him if we want his help. Our own profiler is out of action.'

'What's wrong with him?'

'Long term sick. He's probably the killer.'

'Yeah, and I bet he wouldn't even be able to work that one out,' said Garcia. The guys laughed.

'Nothing else?' asked Williamson. There was nothing from the floor. Harper filled the silence.

'I called the Medical Examiner this morning. She found a bite mark on Amy Lloyd-Gardner's breast. Fairly deep, too. They'll get a pretty good imprint from it. He's growing already. Getting more aggressive. Getting to like the thrill, but he needs to do more each time to get the same buzz. I'll work up the details to send off to the Feds, but my hunch is that this is a serial killer and he's just beginning to express himself.'

'Express himself? What do you mean?' asked Garcia.

'I mean, some take time to dare to do all the things they dream about, but this guy is getting there real quick. It's not a good sign. And he's professional – ambush, cosh, drag out of sight and then strip and cut. It looks like he's recording his crimes, too. They like to replay the memories.'

Williamson turned to Lol Edwards, a balding red-haired cop from Maine. 'How about anything from the stores? Anyone following Amy?'

Lol shook his heavy jowls. 'Nothing to report. Can't get anything from the stores in Madison and Park Avenue. We got a better photograph from Amy's husband and it's doing the rounds with the store owners, see if we can get someone to remember something. We should know where she went and what she bought by the end of the day. Her credit card records just came through, so we'll have pieced it all together soon.'

Williamson nodded. 'Garcia, the rest of your report. What you got?'

Mark Garcia stood up. 'Got some good stuff from the eye-witnesses. Seems like there was a guy in a silver SUV next to a woman. We've got three separate sightings of a Caucasian male in a green uniform with grey hair. One saw him when he was in the car, two saw him sweeping the garage. He was wearing these orange shades that some of the gangbangers wear, so they can't do much with his face. But we got this drawing finished. It's only his lips, jaw and nose, but it's pretty good as a likeness – it's a mix of the three separate sightings. They all saw this guy in the underground lot.'

Garcia moved over to the board and tacked the drawing up. The team looked at it. The face was regular and symmetrical, but the eyes were hidden. 'What doesn't he want us or them to see?' said Harper. 'I think he's hiding something that might identify him.'

'What like?' said Williamson.

'Different coloured eyes, something like that. Something he wants hidden because if it went out on a profile, he'd be recognized.'

'That's not a bad piece of deduction, Harper, but he might just be trying to hide his identity like any criminal would. So let's not go chasing guys with eye problems until we got some evidence.'

'Oh, and they said he smiled,' said Garcia.

'When?' asked Harper.

'In the car. He gave this woman a smile and a wave.' Garcia looked to his notes. 'A big smile, she said. She also said the lady in the car was naked. Maybe they were having sex.'

'How were they having sex?' asked Harper.

'It's easy to do, Tom. We've got books and everything if you need them,' said Eddie.

Garcia half smiled. 'Maybe they weren't, but what do you think they're doing if she's naked?'

Rick Swanson, all five foot and 180 pounds of him, sniffed. 'So, there's this couple in a silver SUV and they're naked.'

Garcia interrupted. 'She was, he wasn't. He had a green uniform on.'

'Okay, good,' said Swanson. 'So she's naked. They make out and have a row. He pushes her out of the car, she runs for it. He is in a rage about something, gets out and pulls out her heart.'

'You're a real nice storyteller, Swanson,' said Eddie.

'Fuck my style, is that what we're saying happened?'

Harper tapped the desk. 'No. They weren't making out. He was forcing her and threatening her life. This isn't a trick or affair gone wrong, this is a whole life gone wrong.' He thought for a moment. 'Look, the statement says that he was in the passenger seat. It was her car. He's got in beside her, threatened her and then hit her and dragged her across to the arch.'

Williamson stood. 'No use all this speculating like we're all still in the academy. We need more street work. Okay, guys, let's keep up the hunt. This is a nasty piece of work. Let's get out there.'

Harper stood. 'One more thing – I think the killer is stalking the victims. I think he knows them inside out and exactly where they go.' Harper took a foam cup and poured strong coffee from the pot.

'How so?'

'I took a look at Mary-Jane's diary. She mentions someone following her on two occasions.'

'Could be anyone,' said Williamson.

'Get this, too. On October 4 a guy stopped her in the street and told her she's got lovely eyes. I called her parents: she didn't say anything to them.'

'I didn't know that.'

'That's over a month ago. Could be this killer knows his victims very well. That's why he's so confident. He knows them and their movements intimately. You went to see Amy's husband. I bet he wasn't missing her at all, was he?'

Williamson looked up. 'No. He was out with his buddies.'

'The killer knew she wouldn't be missed. I bet the same is true of Grace.'

'Damn right,' said Swanson. 'She was on her way home and lived alone.'

'It's a maybe at the moment, but Mary-Jane was alone for about eight minutes each day as she walked to her apartment. If that was a random opportune strike, it was sure as hell unlucky for Mary-Jane. I think he knew exactly when she'd be vulnerable. I also looked up the police records. Grace Frazer had reported a man outside her apartment on six occasions. Patrol took a look but never found anyone. With Amy, my guess is he's followed her many a time before and knows where she shops. He also knows her car and where she likes to park – right close to the entrance nearest to Madison Avenue. He found a place where the CCTV wouldn't spot him, too. I might be wrong, but if he had a uniform it would be too dangerous to wear that disguise over and over again in a place with CCTV just waiting for the type of victim he wants. All three suggest he's a careful, planned stalker who waits until the time is right. That's what didn't make sense. They look like risky kills, but he's planned these so well they're actually not.'

The team took it all on board. Harper had got to the heart of the case after a day's work.

'Press interest?' asked Lol Edwards. His skin was pale but he had a red birthmark on his neck that was getting redder by the minute with the excitement or the heat in the room. He looked like his face was going to explode.

'They don't know what's happened exactly and there's only so many tears they can extract from the paying public, so they're holding out for now, but when they get the full horror they'll splash this all over.'

Harper went up to the whiteboard. 'I got one more thing. It's not something that's going to lead anywhere, but if you look at Amy's body from above . . .' Tom drew the outline of a body with wings and a halo. 'See? The two flaps of skin are positioned like wings and she's got a halo of blood round her head. She looks like an angel.'

'Oh, that's sweet, that is, Harper,' said Williamson. 'That's so fucking poetic. You think she fell from heaven?' Some of the other guys laughed. 'You think she got sliced up by the overhead power lines? That's good. You think someone pushed her out of heaven, or did she jump?'

Harper stood centre stage while the team shook with laughter. Finally he smiled and took out a note from the crime lab. 'You remember that chalk writing on the wall by Amy's corpse? We just got it deciphered by the lab.' He handed it to Nate Williamson. Williamson turned it over and read it out.

'*Every angel is terrifying.*' Williamson looked up. 'What the fuck does that mean?'

Harper raised an eyebrow ever so slightly. No need to gloat. Ah, hell, how often do you get to gloat? 'Seems like someone wanted us to think about wings and angels, wouldn't you say, Nate?'

'Fuck you. That's what I would say. We're a team here, Harper, not a bunch of showoffs.'

'The line is by a German poet called Rilke. I think he wanted us to see the wings and halo. He's playing with symbols. He's trying to say something. I think he's trying to say he's a clever bastard. My guess is, he's not educated beyond high school and he hates that.'

'So what does the quote mean?'

'I haven't got a clue.'

'Well, find out,' said Williamson. The team felt the tension and wanted to get back to work. They looked at the photograph of the woman from above and suddenly saw something more than mindless mutilation. Garcia spoke first. 'You saying, Harps, that he posed her and ripped off her skin so she looked like an angel who'd been destroyed?'

'Yeah, that's just what I'm saying.'

'It's pretty stuff, Harper, and it'd make a nice little story, but how the hell does this help us find the sick bastard who cut her?'

'It doesn't – yet.'

'Ex-fucking-actly!' Nate Williamson slapped his hand on the desk as if to call the meeting to a close. 'We got to try to get something more from the witnesses and this composite drawing. And if that fails, Harper, how about we'll call up the Catholic Church and see if any angels are missing from heaven?'

Harper didn't say anything. There was no need. He wasn't playing Nate's game – he saw straight through the old man's bluff and anger. Williamson was afraid of losing his potency again, afraid of being found out for not being quite as good as people imagined he was. Well, thought Harper, who wasn't?

As the team dispersed, Harper walked up to the photographs of the corpses. Each time, they blossomed to life afresh on the static image that was already in his mind. It was a strange sensation, as if the image was layering in his consciousness and becoming more and more detailed.

On the board were ten close-up shots of each of Amy's toes. The nails were red, but underneath the polish on each there was a faint outline of some other design. The forensics boys had X-rayed the images. He looked closer. A spider and web on an orange background, a Playboy bunny on purple with a crystal eye, two yellow-eyed daisies, a tropical sunset, a set of hotrod flames.

He looked again at the nail art. 'Williamson,' he called. Williamson turned and gave him a long cold stare. 'Maybe I got something here.'

Nate lumbered across and pinched his nose in a gesture of nonchalance. 'More spirit guidance?'

Tom tapped the photographs of the girl's toes. 'Amy's toes were painted with different designs. You need to find out which nail bar does these. It might be a point of contact for the killer. Maybe one of the places he scopes his victims.'

Nate Williamson was staring hard at Harper. He flicked a glance at the nail designs. Harper tried again. 'Your investigation needs a lead. I'm throwing you a bone, Nate. Pick it up, for chrissake.'

Chapter Fourteen

The Lair
November 17, 4.34 p.m.

There was no doubting any longer that he was an artist. He could feel it more than anything else. It had become as real as the sky and the moon. He was the artist, the creator, the great artisan. The creative flow had just kept coming, bursting out of him like a fountain from a snapped hydrant. His masterpiece was finally coming together. Twenty-five years in the making. Twenty-five years of slow-burning these images and ideas inside his mind. He had waited and waited and now he was emerging from the close sweaty chrysalis of patience with great wings and enormous power.

He rested his arms either side of the table to steady himself and looked down at the evidence. Amy Lloyd-Gardner's small dark heart rested in a shallow aluminium tray. It had all happened, every moment. It really had happened. The girl's heart had been steeping in the formaldehyde solution for nearly sixteen hours. The killer wanted to preserve it just as it was, full of beauty and mystery, but it wasn't easy. He'd already filled each of its chambers with wax to keep the full rounded shape of the muscle; then he'd injected the tissue itself with a concentrated formaldehyde solution. He was desperate for it to work, but he was still experimenting and couldn't tell whether the heart would disintegrate or hold its shape.

He'd used small animals to test various ways of preserving specimens and thought he had his technique just about right: injecting the tissue with the right solution of formaldehyde, then steeping the organs in the chemical solution so that it entered every cell and stopped the process of decomposition. It sometimes worked well, but other times it didn't. He didn't know why. After all, he wasn't a scientist, he was an artist.

Still, it was the overall effect of his sculpture that would make his name, not the small, less-than-perfect parts. He looked across to the small glass vitrine that contained Mary-Jane's two eyeballs. They were less than perfect too. The dazzling blue that had drawn him to her in the first place had turned cloudy. That was what was so interesting about sculpting with real human remains: you couldn't always get it the way it was in your head. You had to work harder and harder to bring off the things you had seen in your daydreams.

Still, when he looked into Mary-Jane's dull eyes through the carefully made solution, he recalled the moment of her death with perfect clarity. Her look of fear, the slow, tormented cry and guttural pleas. He wanted to relive it all. He wanted every acknowledgement of his sick transgression locked into his little glass cages and preserved in formaldehyde. It was his museum of experiences: the artistic impression of his own dead heart.

After Amy, the killer had cleaned himself up, dumped the car, then gone home and crashed for twelve hours solid in a deep, dreamless sleep. The kills really took it out of him. He felt like a victim in the warm aftermath of a car crash when you sit there flooded with every chemical the body can throw at you, your pants warm from your own urine, your vision crystal clear and images racing at different speeds through your shocked mind. God, it felt good. And then, what's even more thrilling is that you realize you're still alive and the crash wasn't an ending, but a beginning, and you can do it all again. It was like being reborn with more power than ever before.

After Mary-Jane, fear was something he knew about only

from memory. He no longer felt it. The killer moved along his gallery to Grace's long golden tresses. He passed his hand over the silky fine hairs, stroking them slowly and tenderly. He felt the moment of her capture with a shiver of excitement.

Early that day, he had scoped another of his targets. He'd watched her for a while in Central Park, staring through his binoculars. She was sitting with her friends, chatting and laughing. A good student. A real grade-A brain. She was rich and well connected but slumming it with the real students out in Yorkville. He only ever wanted the best. She was a smart cookie, but even she didn't know that he'd been watching her for eight months, ever since she'd caught his attention at one of the art history lectures he'd attended.

He'd been searching out and following his girls for years. He had seven of them now. Seven girls all with the same look, the same smell of money about them, the same wide blue eyes with their look of endless innocence.

He'd been scoping them for a long time. His little lair was plastered with their pictures. He liked to watch them grow up, he liked to see the way their hair changed over the years, their clothes too. He liked to know just about everything about them, even how they responded to threat. He tested them out with all kinds of little things. A dead rat on a car seat, a nasty grope on the subway, threatening graffiti, and sometimes just plain old-fashioned love letters. He liked to watch them as he interfered with their lives. They were his puppets. All along, he knew he was watching dead people. It was just a matter of time, and now the time had come. It was time to reap.

Three of the specimens were now dead. He had the evidence right there: eyes, hair, heart. Four more girls and he could construct the image that had been with him for so long.

He'd soon have every last one in his gallery. Seven body parts to shape his sculpture. The world would see his talent, his brilliance. They'd hate him, he knew that, but they'd have to admit his brilliance. The daring nature of his scheme.

He was going to complete his masterwork and then open his gallery to the world. He called it *The Progression of Love*. Each time he killed, he felt invigorated, and his sculpture was growing.

The killer looked over at the newspapers he'd bought. He needed the headlines and stories for his gallery. It showed how the world was already responding to his work. His reviews. He sat down and started clipping out the pictures and articles and pasting them on the cold stone walls of his lair. He was a little disappointed in the press coverage. They'd not really grasped the significance of what was happening to the city. They didn't seem to get it. They even dared to suggest that Mary-Jane's murder was a break-in gone wrong. How many thieves would take a girl's eyeballs and pose her like that? It took inspiration to work a body like he did, inspiration and hours of mental preparation. It wasn't a random strike, it wasn't anger: it was a culmination of everything he'd ever felt.

Chapter Fifteen

East Harlem
November 17, 6.06 p.m.

Eddie Kasper wasn't smiling when he entered the big open-plan room of the station house just before the evening briefing. He laid an armful of papers down on Harper's desk.

Harper was staring out of the window. He'd spent the last few hours piecing together his theory that this killer had been scoping each of his victims and interacting with them. Mary-Jane's diary was a good place to start and gave him the idea, but the thought that this killer had watched the girl for months before striking was terrifying. Grace Frazer had called the cops about someone hanging around her apartment, but, as yet, Tom had nothing on Amy Lloyd-Gardner. If this guy was stalking them all over an extended period, then there ought to be something. He'd spoken to her husband and family earlier that day and they could think of nothing. The kill was so personal, though, Harper's thinking was that he had interacted with her somehow. He just needed to find out how.

'You heard yet?' asked Eddie, tossing a paper across to him.

Tom looked up. 'I'm just trying to imagine how I'd follow a rich shopaholic. Maybe Amy didn't notice things around her. Or the killer got too close with Mary-Jane and Grace and he watched Amy from a distance. What do you think?'

'You really haven't heard, have you?'

91

Tom turned the paper towards him. 'What?' He looked at the story in the *Post*. The NYPD had done a good job of keeping the press from linking the killings. There was enough heat after Mary-Jane's murder, and they were already getting over fifty confessions a day. They didn't want this to escalate. They'd be swamped. Tom read the small story about Amy Lloyd-Gardner in the paper. Another murder. The reporter had none of the gruesome details. He'd presumed a robbery and the interest level dipped to monotone prose.

'I've seen this,' said Harper. 'If we can keep it like this, it's good news.'

'Yeah, that's right, but it's not going to stay that way,' said Eddie.

'What's going on?'

'Lafayette's just gone in. We need to get to the briefing. Harps. You're not going to like this.'

Tom and Eddie got to the briefing room and found a spot amongst the other detectives working the heart of the case. Lafayette was sweating. His red face looked agitated. Williamson wasn't looking the audience in the eye. What the hell had happened? Not another body?

Lafayette craned his neck and the room slowly went quiet. 'Okay, people. We've got a problem. This has been running since early this morning and we're getting nowhere with it. I just want you all to know, we've been down at One PP all day using any leverage we can get and they won't budge. Not an inch.'

'Not an inch,' said Williamson. 'I've got a copy made, so pass these around.' He handed a thick ream of paper to the end of the row. The pile made its slow route around the room.

'What is it, Eddie?'

'I ain't gonna tell you, Tom. I don't want to be in the firing line.'

Tom watched the pile moving up the rows.

'Just to paint the picture,' said Lafayette. 'The *New York Daily*

Echo did us the courtesy of sending across the copy this morning. They informed us that they intend to go to print tomorrow morning. They asked if any of the details in the story are inaccurate. We've been at them all day. Our lawyers have been trying to get this stopped, but it looks like we've got nothing.'

'What are you talking about?' said Harper.

'Read the paper, big guy. If you can't do the long words call me over. We can sound them out together and wiki them online. Then again, it's the *Daily Echo*, four syllables bad, two syllables good – one syllable even fucking better – so you should be all right. You know why they call it the *Daily Echo*? Once they start blabbering about something, you can never get them to shut up.'

'What am I looking for?'

'Read the report by Erin Nash. She's an investigative reporter who has just blown our case wide open. She seems to have some hotline to the heart of the case.'

Harper had been through the papers that morning. Most of them gave the basic story about Amy Lloyd-Gardner, reflecting what the NYPD had decided to tell them. A homicide in a parking lot in suspicious circumstances. Another woman found dead. Police yet to comment. No one, so far, was linking Mary-Jane, Grace and Amy, and the cops hadn't released any of the details. The pile of tomorrow's paper then arrived in Harper's hand. He took one and passed the pile to Eddie. He stared down at the *Daily Echo*. The headline kind of spat at you in large red and black print.

SERIAL KILLER STRIKES NEW YORK
AN AMERICAN DEVIL'S CAMPAIGN OF SLAUGHTER
by Erin Nash

New York detectives are investigating the gruesome murder of a young woman whose naked and mutilated corpse was discovered yesterday afternoon lying in an upmarket underground parking lot on East 82nd Street, a police source said.

A female shopper returning from a Park Avenue shopping spree discovered the unidentified corpse at 3.15 p.m. lying flat on its back on the dirty asphalt in a pool of blood, said the source.

The victim, described only as a wealthy white woman in her early twenties, had such severe injuries that police detectives were stunned by the extent of the overkill. The medical examiner is yet to determine the cause of her death.

A source close to the NYPD's elite Blue Team said that the victim had been brutally raped before her chest was cut open and her heart removed. It is said that the killer pushed cherry blossom down the victim's throat.

The corpse is the third young female victim to be found in Manhattan in the last two weeks. Detectives are speculating that the murders, all occurring in the east of the city, are the work of a single man, a serial killer dubbed the American Devil because of the way he poses his victims in religious postures.

The killer appears to be targeting rich, white women in the Upper East Side region. His aim is unclear, but is sure to strike terror into one of the world's wealthiest and most established communities.

Harper sat up straight in his chair. Everyone had absorbed the information. There was a long silence. Every one of the cops in the room who'd worked a high-profile case knew the impact the story would have. It was like standing in front of a derelict building, with the wrecking ball about to fall. 'They're going to print it?' he asked. 'That's the bottom line?'

'That's the bottom line, Tom. This goes to press in the next couple of hours. It'll be on the newsstands tomorrow first thing, then the world and his nephew is going to come calling. And you know what they're going to say, don't you? They're going to start pointing and asking why the hell didn't Homicide let anyone know?'

'Who the fuck is Erin Nash? And how has she got this information?'

'We don't know, Tom. We have no idea. The paper is keeping her well protected. We haven't been able to speak to her.'

'Do we even know this shit?' said Tom. 'It says the victim had cherry blossom in her throat.'

'Yeah, it's true. The Medical Examiner confirmed it. The report went up to Williamson this morning.'

'Who did you share it with, Nate?'

'Not a soul,' said Nate. 'Soon as it came in, I got pulled out and taken down to headquarters to try to talk these newspapers into sense.'

'So how many people knew about the cherry blossom?' asked Tom.

'The Medical Examiner and her team. Me and the captain. A couple of other administrative staff.'

'You think one of us is briefing the gutter press, Nate?'

'No. No one in Blue Team would piss on his own floor. Either this is a very good investigative reporter piecing together fragments, or else I don't know how she knows.'

'They're going to be all over this now,' said Eddie. 'She's called him a serial killer, she's given him a moniker. Hell, where did that name come from? The American Devil?'

'She probably made it up,' said Williamson. 'Creative types do that. Make up names to scare people.'

'What's the plan?' Harper asked.

'We got a few hours to put out our own story. That's all. We've got to take the initiative and roll this out ourselves. We've got a press conference in a couple of hours.'

'And what about the scale of the operation we're going to need?'

'It's being agreed,' said Lafayette. 'We're going to double the team, keep the press pack away from you guys. I want you to keep working the case, not the fucking media.'

Harper *was* working the case, but his question was all about Erin Nash and where she got that privileged information. He looked at the apprehension in the faces around him. The investigation had just entered phase two. Phase one was the quiet time, when you tried to get a lead. Now it was the public phase. And the media would be hunting for every scrap of information and raising fear levels by a factor of about a thousand.

Chapter Sixteen

Ward's Island
November 18, 8.35 a.m.

From a distance, the killer watched the release. They always threw them out early in the day. Winston Carlisle was a sad case. He was thirty-six years old, his family had abandoned him at an early age and he had stalked and attacked pretty young girls once too often. He'd never actually raped any of the girls. He liked following them and had groped them, pushed them to the ground, threatened them with a knife and exposed himself to them. He didn't seem able to go further. His records showed that he was arrested for attempted rape at the ages of twelve and fourteen, twenty-two and twenty-nine. However, not one of these attacks resulted in a court case. Instead, because he was delusional, Winston was given treatment. He'd been in and out of institutions his whole life.

And now Winston Carlisle was on the sidewalk outside Manhattan Psychiatric Center with a small brown case, an address he didn't recognize and a look of profound confusion on his face.

The killer followed him as he walked from the hospital towards the bus stop. He took the bus into the city and the killer got on behind him and sat there. He enjoyed the feeling of following people. It was like being in a movie. You had real purpose when you were scoping out a victim. Winston got off the cross-town bus and struggled to work out the right way to go. He stared at the scrap of paper the orderly had given him and then up at the street signs. He finally just started walking.

At the first burger joint he came to, Winston stopped and ate three hamburgers, one after the other. It was the only time he looked content. He got on his way again soon enough and even asked a passer-by about the address. Eventually he found the discreet halfway house that would be his new home.

It didn't surprise the killer much that characters like Winston spent their whole lives in horrible anonymity and bewilderment – moving between the ordered cleanliness of a psychiatric unit and the profound confusion of the outside world. Winston needed an escape, that was for sure. The killer just knew it.

He was going to make Winston famous. He was going to give this nobody a profound legacy. Winston Carlisle, another nobody from nowhere, was going to be remembered, just like his victims. The killer smiled at the thought as he watched Winston enter the halfway house. Winston looked just right for the part he was going to play. But he would need some very close direction.

The killer noted the address and went on his way. A sprinkle of New York rain was beginning to fall. He smiled. He liked the rain. It called to him. He walked down the street and hailed a cab. He spoke through the glass.

'Kinsley Memorial Church.'

He sat back, leaving his seatbelt undone. A recorded voice suddenly cut in, telling him to belt up and proudly exclaiming, 'That's the law in New York City.' He pulled the belt across his chest. This was one law he was happy to oblige.

The cab took thirty minutes to travel three blocks through a snarl-up on Second Avenue. As it passed the big yellow diggers and two blocks of orange and white plastic bollards and vehicle barriers, the cabbie complained, 'Can you see a fucking construction worker? They close off the street and then go for a three-hour cup of coffee. No one works any more.' The passenger in the back seat checked his watch again and nodded silently. It was ten minutes before ten.

They turned into East 61st Street and the cab pulled up. The passenger slipped the driver a twenty-dollar bill. It was a nice neighbourhood – a quiet, residential tree-lined street. He got out and stood on the sidewalk, a man in his prime, tall, angular and athletic. He was feeling his passion now as he came closer to the girl who was number four on his list. Her time was up. She didn't know it, but this was her last day on earth. The killer breathed deeply with the thought. There was no limit to what he could do. The gift of life or death was in his hands. God had no more power than he did. He just had different uses for it.

The Baptist church was a surprisingly large and ornate stone building, dating back to the mid-1850s, when someone built it in honour of Wesley Kinsley, a philanthropist of vast industrial means. It was a well-attended church with a good choir, a healthy smattering of young people and a very liberal bias – they accepted everything and anything at the Kinsley Memorial and were devoutly opposed to violence, which was a shame. It was homosexual liberals against Iraq at the Kinsley.

The morning service crowd was already sauntering through the large wooden doors. The organ inside was playing a modern hymn and the Reverend Angela Timms was greeting her flock with a smile and a wink.

In his disguise, the killer went inside and sat, as he always did, as far from the altar as possible. From the very back row, he scanned the heads of the flock, looking for the girl he'd grown attached to, but he couldn't see her.

This was bad. He didn't like disappointment. He'd already waited too long and his patience was beginning to snap. He needed someone soon. He couldn't bear another day of imagining girl number four contorted and weeping under his hands – even one more day would be an unimaginable cruelty to himself. He needed her image. He needed her, period. The rain had whetted his appetite. Fat raindrops appeared on the dry sidewalk like drops of blood. *The American Devil,* he thought. He liked that. He was the sidewalk Satan. He smiled towards the altar. Would they guess that the devil was there in their flock? *Sometimes, everything made sense.*

The killer had been interacting with the girl even more in the last month. She was such a prudish type, he liked to shock her. He'd Photoshopped an image of her head on a nude by Manet and stuck it to her apartment door. It was at a Manet lecture he'd first spotted her. She had long blond hair and always sat very still, listening intently to the lecturer. He liked to think they were made for each other, a prudish virgin Baptist and the American Devil. It felt perfect. She was an exceptionally pretty girl who smiled too easily at strangers and did voluntary work. Her eyes were so brightly blue that he thought she might be wearing coloured lenses – but her outfits suggested that vanity wasn't her thing at all.

He waited. He knew how to wait. He was concentrating on the exquisite feel of the girl's arm as it brushed against him the previous week. He liked to get close when the time was nearing. It heightened his pleasure. He'd stepped in against her body. She'd apologized, but it was he who'd leaned in for a touch. He couldn't contain his passion for beauty. He was a poet. He was an artist. He was doing the devil's work. He turned as girl number four walked through the door. She looked heavenly. The killer smiled. *She was just perfect.*

Chapter Seventeen

Dr Levene's Office
November 18, 10.00 a.m.

Denise Levene had caught the stark headline on her way to One PP. Several people on the subway were reading a story headlined 'Serial Killer Strikes New York'. She hadn't heard the press conference the previous evening, so she was in the dark as she travelled in to work.

She wasn't usually a reader of the *Daily Echo*, but any mention of a serial killer got her attention and so she bought the paper from a newsstand outside the subway and read it as she walked up the street.

The killings were suddenly being tied together. Denise felt flushed. For years, her research had sought to find a link between childhood neglect, specifically in pre-verbal children, and the propensity for violence. It wasn't that serial killers were the only examples, but it was sometimes the extreme cases that brought new information to light. The American Devil, if this article was to be believed, was the type of killer she'd looked at many times before. A man who was clever, organized and focused, but who put all of these qualities to evil use because he lacked the sphere of influence that Freud called the superego, which she understood as the neurological pathways between empathy, self and consequence.

She re-read the news story several more times in her office, but the details were frustratingly sketchy. A quick search of the internet led her to several other reports. She read them avidly, but there was nothing more than she'd found in Erin Nash's article. She looked down at her watch. Tom Harper was due any minute and he would have all the detail she craved. However, she couldn't ask. It was wrong. She was there for him, not the other way round. She'd just have to bite her lip and put it to the back of her mind.

The day was brightening up when Harper arrived. The sun sneaked through the gaps in the dark clouds and as he sat down a sunbeam hit him directly in the eye and danced around the edges of Dr Levene's hair, silhouetting her like an arty photograph. Harper threw another gum in his mouth and shifted in his seat.

'Thanks for coming back,' said Denise.

'It wasn't from choice.'

'You looked wasted,' she said.

'Is that a pick-up line?' said Harper. 'I'm feeling a warm glow of appreciation.'

Denise smiled. 'You sleep at all?'

'No.'

'What's keeping you up?'

'Same thing that's got you wired.'

'What do you mean?'

'There's a glint in your eye the size of a two-carat diamond.'

'I'm fine,' she said.

'The story's got to you, too, hasn't it? Everyone's wired.'

'No, not me,' she lied. 'I'm just good in the mornings.'

'So tell me how a well-presented woman like yourself got her fingertips so grubby.'

Denise looked down at the newsprint on her fingers. 'Okay, I took a look.'

'You took a look? I bet. I looked you up, Dr Levene. I know your research interests. Must've felt like your lucky day.'

'Don't insult me, Detective.'

'You saying your little heart didn't do a flip?'

'I'm interested, all right? I've worked these cases.'

'Worked or studied them? There's a big difference between tracking a live killer and reading the court reports.'

'I know that.'

'Sure you do, you know everything.'

'Stop busting my balls, Harper. I'm on your side.'

'No, Doctor, you're on your own side. If you were on mine, you'd let me get out there. There are a thousand places I'd rather be than wasting both of our time pretending you can fix people's brains.'

'You like being angry, don't you?'

'I don't think about it.'

'Lisa did, is my guess. I bet she thought about it a lot. Women do.'

'What's that supposed to mean?'

'You lost your wife. Are you not curious as to why she fell out of love with you?'

'No, I know why. My job came first, and she didn't like that.'

'That's a nice clean theory, isn't it? Your wife left you because you're a dedicated public servant.'

'Cop work stinks, everybody knows that.'

'You buy that yourself or is it just for my consumption?'

'Jesus, you don't let up, do you? Does your husband get a word in?'

'A good detective would know I'm not married.'

'A great one wouldn't give a rat's ass about your marital status.'

'And what are you, good or great?'

'I'm neither, but sometimes I get lucky.'

'Modest too?'

'We're a team. You don't solve a murder as a lone wolf. There's over a hundred detectives working the case.'

'Let's get back to the case of Tom Harper. I've got him down as a hero-fantasist, how does that feel?'

'Like an insult that fell flat on the floor.'

'Okay, we can keep this going all day, but you've got a problem with aggression and I can help you.'

'Boxing helped me. It gave me an outlet, but I'm too old for the ring now.'

'So you start on your superiors?'

'He went for me first.'

'Because?'

'Because he made fun of Lisa.'

'And that got to you?'

'Sure.'

'Why did it matter what he thought?'

'You don't know? Come on. I loved Lisa. She left without warning. I was blown wide open. I was an explosion looking for a detonator. Cracking the Romario case should've been the best moment of my life, but all I got was an empty apartment and a phone message telling me not to call.'

'You must've seen it coming?'

'Every couple argues. You never know it's terminal until too late. I thought the arguments were part of the working out, but they were more than that for her.'

'And now? Angry still?'

'It makes less sense the clearer I see it, so the anger seems to get worse.'

'Would you like to know why she left?'

'Sure would, and what she says sounds like a load of soft soap.'

'What does she tell you?'

'She tells me that she's not good enough. She tells me that she can't live up to my expectations. She tells me she thinks she makes me unhappy.'

'They're well-considered explanations. Sounds like she doesn't want to hurt you.'

'Well, she's not doing so well at that.'

'More to the point, she doesn't know how to tell you the truth.'

'So what's the truth, Doctor?'

'I don't think you're angry because Lisa left. I think she left because you're always angry.'

Tom paused. He let the idea work around his head for a moment. 'She was scared of me?'

'You're a tough guy, you have high expectations, you work in a highly stressful environment and you don't give yourself an inch. I'd say you were so caught up in that cycle that she became one of the wheels in your life that needed ordering about. Maybe she wasn't scared, maybe she just felt like a piece of shit.'

Tom's face drained of colour. This was worse than he had imagined. He had thought the good psychologist might gently prise some truths from beneath his skin, not land a knock-out combination on his second visit. 'She felt like shit?'

'I don't know. I'm guessing, but your reaction tells me something important. You felt like you treated her badly, didn't you?'

Tom looked at the floor. Shit, Levene was good at this. Against his will, he nodded to the floor.

'What triggers the anger, Tom? You have an idea, or you just feel it late on and it catches you out? You've got a quick mind, and that means you're good at hiding the signs from yourself.'

Tom chewed the idea over for a moment. 'Maybe I just don't like the way people talk about things that matter.'

'You don't think they're free to say what the hell they like?'

'No, I don't. Not at all.'

'Well, I got news for you, they are. They can say any damn thing they like, but it isn't what they say that riles you.'

'What is it?'

'You like watching birds, don't you? You ever see a hawk trying to get a lure from his flyer?'

'Sure.'

'You see how the hawk will use all kinds of strategies to surprise the flyer so that he's not seen until the last moment?'

'Yeah.'

'That's how the mind works. It catches you out, and the anger keeps you from seeing what's really there.'

'And what's really there?'

'That's what we've got to find out. But we've got to do it together.' Dr Levene let the silence hang in the air. 'You want to be helped or are you seriously just here because you need to be?'

Harper had been thinking. He looked up at her. 'You think you can help?'

'I can try, if you'll let me.'

'I never thought I'd say this, but okay, I'll give it a go.'

'You've surprised me,' said Dr Levene. 'Why the change of heart?'

'I need help.'

'That's a serious admission. I'm impressed.'

'Not for me, Doctor, for chrissake, for the case. You're good at what you do, I can see that right away. You've also done more research on serial killers than I've ever heard of and if I need to do one thing it's to get to understand this killer's mind. I don't think I can do it alone.'

'What are you saying? You're asking for my help on the case?' Denise couldn't disguise the excitement she felt and her voice lifted an octave.

'Calm down and listen. From the moment this story went to press, this just got a whole lot more difficult. The American Devil is going to be reacting to his own drives and, also, the way the press report it. And on top of that, it gets very messy with the media and politics involved, but if this guy's going to be caught I need to see things clearly. I think you can help, Doctor – you've got good eyes for how people tick.'

'Coming from you, that's a real compliment.'

'So the deal is, I'll talk about myself and do what I'm told, if you let me talk about this killer's behaviour and tell me if I'm on the right lines, psychologically speaking.'

Denise nodded slowly. 'So tell me, how's the investigation going? You got anything to go on?'

Harper shot her a sidelong glance. 'This won't be a nice conversation. There's a bitch of a killer out there and he's beginning to feel confident. He took out a woman on a Saturday afternoon. That's quite some self-belief he's got. The thing is, he looks uncontrolled and random but he's left nothing for us to go on at all. He's actually very well organized and very smart. He seems to know exactly what a cop would look for.'

Denise was taking notes as he spoke. Harper paused and stared at her pen. She looked up. 'You want help, this is how I do it, on paper.'

'Okay,' said Harper. 'Now the thing for me is that he's focusing on rich society girls. We got a hell of a lot more groundwork to do to find out why, and time's running short.'

'What's his motive?'

'Good question.' Harper looked up from the glass he was twisting in his hand. 'I think his motive isn't just to hurt these women. I don't know. I think he wants to make a hell of a statement about something. He wants attention and he's going to get it now Erin Nash is feeding the public, but there's so much groundwork to do. There are hundreds of patients from Manhattan State who need to be assessed and interviewed and there are hundreds of witness statements that we're not getting through properly. They don't correlate. The whole thing is swimming in detail and I got to figure out one or two angles.'

'What about a profile?'

'Yeah, we've tried that. We've sent the packages over to the Feds for Mary-Jane and Grace and they came up with a pen portrait based on the first two victims. Then the MO changed – you know, he took someone out by day, he changed his trophy from eyes and hair to heart – and the Feds got nervous and withdrew the profile. They don't know which way to jump, so they're just sitting on it, afraid of getting it wrong and getting the blame. Now the press is breathing fire they'll be even more careful.'

'I think the profile looks stable to me – three similar victims, three similar attacks. Don't you think that the change reflects changed circumstances rather than a change of personality?'

Harper looked up from the glass again. 'Yeah, I think so. Anyhow, you've got a head full of good questions there, Dr Levene, but now I got to go. I've got to see how this Nash lady got her information.'

'Okay,' said Levene. 'I'll help with the investigation, but if I'm also going to help you, then the first thing you've got to do for me is notice just how many times you get riled. You keep a note of that and I can begin to work.'

'How the hell do I monitor that?'

Denise took out a small green elastic wrist strap. 'You wear this on your wrist and whenever you have an angry thought just give it a twang. I just want you to see how often your mind takes a walk down that particular avenue.' She handed him the band. He took it and looked at it suspiciously.

'You are fucking kidding me.'

'Think of it as an investigation into your own psyche. It's not medicine, it's a form of information-gathering.'

Harper stood up and pocketed the elastic strap. 'I'll see what I can do, Doctor.'

Chapter Eighteen

Blue Team
November 18, 3.48 p.m.

Mark Garcia hurried across to Harper as he walked into the Major Investigation Room and handed him a blue manila folder. 'Report you wanted, Harper. They just completed the walkabout. It tallies with Amy's credit card records. Nothing unusual that we could see. But I know you wanted it soon as.'

'Thanks, I appreciate it.' Harper took the folder and returned to his desk. There was a little postcard sitting on his keyboard. Harper picked it up. It had a picture of Muhammad Ali in his younger days and a quotation below it.

> Champions aren't made in gyms. Champions are made from something they have deep inside them – a desire, a dream, a vision. They have to have last-minute stamina, they have to be a little faster, they have to have the skill and the will. But the will must be stronger than the skill.

Harper turned over the card. He read the scrawl of black ink. *Good to have you back, champ. We know you have the will but we hope the skill will come later. Eddie.*

Harper smiled and stuck the postcard on his monitor. 'Nice to be back, Eddie,' he said aloud.

He poured himself a coffee and caught up with the latest

news coming in from the various arms of the investigation. With three kills, they had hundreds of interviews to get through, as well as a wealth of forensic data to process. Harper looked in at the office set up to deal with tip-offs from the public. A team of five men and women were sitting with headphones speaking into their mics. Harper caught one girl's eye. 'How's it going?' he mouthed. The girl pointed to the whiteboard by the door. They'd set up a tally for day one. Three columns. *Confessions*, *Leads* and *Irrelevant*. They had 132 irrelevants, 207 confessions and zero leads. Harper nodded. It was always the way. But still, if the cops were honest, a case like this needed a tip-off from a member of the public. Someone somewhere must've seen something.

Down the hallway, the press team were putting together information for the public. This would lead to a reconstruction of each murder for TV. The more people knew about each crime the more likely it was the cops would get valuable information. As yet, the public didn't know enough, so the only people who called were geeks and freaks.

Harper took out the report on Amy Lloyd-Gardner's last hour on earth. They had traced her through a number of shops, all expensive designer boutiques. They had her purchases down one side. She'd bought two pairs of shoes. One from Christian Louboutin, one from Prada. She had bought a handbag and a silver Versace dress. The overall bill came to $3,900. That was a hell of a shopping trip. Harper knew that the killer might keep these items so it was important to get photographs of them for the media. Someone somewhere might see them, even be wearing them. He wrote a note on the file and tried to find anything else of value, but he couldn't. Everyone had been interviewed but no one had spotted a guy following her. Harper wanted them to go through them all again until they had a sighting. He wrote a second note and closed the file. He took it across to Kasper.

'I need these two things, Eddie. I need shots of all the items she bought sent through to the press and I want these interviews repeated.'

'Repeated?'

'Yeah, repeated.'

'You want me to square it with Williamson?'

'Sure, if he's around. If not, take a couple of guys and start yourself. Last two or three shops would be the best place to start.'

'Okay, I'm on it.'

'And thanks for the card, Eddie. It's good to be back.'

'How's the shrink?'

'She's not as bad as I thought.'

'High praise.'

'You get anywhere on Erin Nash?'

'You bet . . . I got her home address for you.' Eddie handed him a scrap of paper. Harper read it and nodded.

'Thanks, Eddie. That's quick work.'

Harper arrived at Erin Nash's apartment block still feeling wired. He hadn't asked anyone's permission to go talk to this upstart reporter, simply because he knew he'd be refused. Up at the top of the tree, they were doing political deals and giving Nash a midnight call wouldn't smooth proceedings. But Harper wasn't interested in the next mayoral elections. He wanted to meet the bright spark who'd fucked up the investigation for her own personal gain. Harper got out of his car and walked to her brownstone down near Greenwich Village feeling a mixture of emotions – or two separate feelings, rather: hungry and pissed off. He'd not had a bite to eat all day, and it wasn't improving his mood. It was not a great combination but he wanted to know her source: a source who somehow knew too much and might be the key to unlock the case.

Harper went to the door and buzzed her apartment.

A bright, crisp voice replied. 'How ya doing? Come on up!' The door buzzed open.

Tom took a half-second to consider his actions. He went for dishonesty and the next moment was inside the building. This was further than he imagined he would get. But luck or something similar seemed to be on his side.

What was he going to do? He had no idea. He wanted the source but didn't really know how he was going to get it.

He took the stairs up four storeys. The corridor was deserted. A little gold sign pointed him in the direction of her apartment. His back was sweating. He was more nervous than he should be. Why was that?

He got to her apartment and knocked on the door. Erin Nash, dressed in a big blue-flowered kimono, opened the door wide. 'Hey, there,' she said with a nice big smile. Then she saw it wasn't the man she was expecting and her big smile vanished. 'Who are you?'

'I'm Detective Harper of NYPD North Homicide. I want to talk to you, Miss Nash.'

'You've all talked to the legal team at the paper. I'm not saying anything.'

'Well, unfortunately, that's not possible, Miss Nash. You're the journalist with the source and I want to know who you've been talking to.'

Erin smiled sweetly and tried to slam the door shut. Tom reacted immediately and pushed the door so hard it bounced off the wall and back against his outstretched hand. He was surprised by the pent-up energy. Erin stood in the doorway. She was about five foot two with jet black hair and pale skin. In her blue robe she looked scared and vulnerable.

'Get out of here!' she shouted, but she was moving backwards as she did.

Harper took a step across the threshold. 'Can we speak, please, Miss Nash? Lives might depend on it.'

'I told you! Get the fuck out of my apartment!' Erin screamed. 'How fucking dare you!' Her hand rose instinctively as Harper stepped towards her. She was cat-like, good at self-preservation and good at lashing out. She hit Tom hard across the face.

That was the second thing he wasn't expecting. This wasn't going well. As a cop, he didn't ever want to meet the unexpected so he thought things through. He hadn't thought any of this through. Not a single thing.

Tom's reaction was automatic. Eleven years of police work dealing with dangerous criminals left no room for thought. He had her wrist in a tight grip and she was on the floor. The two bones in her forearm moved one over the other and then hit the point where there was no more give.

This was the point where movement translated into pain. In less than a half-second Erin Nash was on her knees, her right arm held firmly above her by Tom, her chest cavity heaving. It was a basic arrest technique, but she wasn't under arrest and he had no right to be in her apartment.

Tom released her arm and stepped back. 'You hit a cop, he'll disarm you. Sorry, Miss Nash.'

She looked up at him and rubbed her wrist. 'Get the fuck out of here! How the hell do I know who you are? You haven't even shown me your shield.'

'Who were you expecting, Erin? Your source? Look, there's a killer out there and we need to know everything you got.'

'Do you think I'd give up access to my exclusive stories because some thug came calling? Grow up, Detective. People got a right to know what you're not telling them. It's a big bad world out there, and we all gotta get by. This is my moment.'

'This isn't some game. Real women are getting killed. Your source knows something. If you stand in the way of this investigation, we'll throw everything at you.'

'Can I get my notebook, so that I can write down what you say when you're intimidating, harassing and threatening me? It's going to make a great sub-story. What was your name again?'

'Fuck you,' said Tom. 'I just want a name. Who is it? Is it a

113

cop? Someone from the coroner's office? Some wife of one of the team? Give it up.'

'I'll tell you who it is, it's my fairy godmother and she's just sealed my reputation. What are you offering me? Moral satisfaction? Get real, Detective.'

Erin Nash was still not afraid. She had a reporter's lack of fear and, deeper still, the sense of a story. It was even half forming in her mind. 'Hero Cop Knocked Me to the Floor and Threatened Me.'

Tom had nowhere else to go. He saw the glint in her eye and knew this was a battle he couldn't win. 'If you get a change of heart, call me. My name is Tom Harper.' He backed away from her.

'What? Lost your balls?' she called out.

'You don't mind that your story just kicked a house-sized hole in our investigation? We had a means to find out who was telling us the truth and who was lying. Now we got to spend double the time on every witness and confession. You've just given this killer a two-week lead.'

'If a few hundred words can do that to your investigation, I'd question your approach. Sounds like it's already full of holes.'

Tom knew there was nothing to say. She had out-thought him. Beaten him. But that last line was too much. He took a step towards her, his face intense with emotion. 'You aren't worth the trouble,' he said. 'You've fucked things up enough. But we'll be back with a warrant and we'll tear this place to pieces.'

'You know that won't work. What I reported is a matter of record, isn't it? It's in your reports. What you going to get a warrant for? Telling the truth?'

'You need to think about what you're doing and why you're doing it.'

'Nice little speech. Now get the hell out of here.'

Tom turned and walked out. He'd just have to hope there was some part of her that was still human, but he doubted it.

Chapter Nineteen

Yorkville
November 18, 8.48 p.m.

Jessica Pascal nodded and sipped slowly from her vodka and cranberry juice. Her eyes were calm but her heart was racing – she had just realized that the man sitting across from her was going to kill her.

From the outset, Jessica had known that there was something not quite right about her date, but she'd only just realized why. He was too good to be true. She felt caught in a way that she'd never experienced before and all she could do was watch him and hope. When would he realize that she knew? Did he know already? What if she got up to go to the bathroom and made a run for it?

What did he want from her? She had liked him anyway. If it was about sex, why force it? She'd made it clear that she liked him, hadn't she? She hadn't ever felt that before. Never.

The ice in her glass had long ago melted. Jessica was now scared deep inside – a white fear that shut out everything else. She felt it somewhere so primal that she didn't even recognize what it was at first.

He was talking and talking, though. His ideas getting crazier and crazier.

Jessica listened and nodded attentively. Her hands clasped

the cold glass. It was hard to concentrate on exactly what he was saying.

The man in the black suit and white shirt had been charming and funny too. She had had the best time. There was no way, otherwise, that she'd have invited him up to her apartment. And anyway, he'd been reluctant, hadn't he? She'd had to ask him if he wanted to come in for a cup of coffee. That's how you did it, right? Didn't mean she was promising anything. She just wanted his company a little longer. Life should be happy, right? We should trust people, right?

'Right!' he'd said, flashing a knowing look.

They'd gone in. He locked the apartment door. Yes, she'd thought that was odd. He turned and locked all three locks – the double cylinder deadbolt, the vertical deadbolt and the sliding bolt.

'It's a rough neighbourhood,' he said.

Was she just feeling too distracted to notice? She'd made the vodka cranberries, lowered the lights, put Philip Glass on the stereo and for good measure even put on the ambi-light – which glowed in various seductive shades and gradually moved across the spectrum.

He was now bathed in green. She was definitely scared.

When did it hit her? He didn't make a move on her at all. He could've sat next to her on the long red sofa her parents had bought her as a leaving home present, but he chose the black fake-leather armchair. Maybe he was just trying not to be presumptuous. He's shy, she thought. I like that. Just like me.

She was drinking and they were chatting about . . . what was it? Art. That was it. He looked at her print of Giorgione's *Sleeping Venus* – a painting she just absolutely loved – and was telling her about the artist. She knew next to nothing about the artist. She just loved the erotically charged nude lying seductive and self-assured in a mystical landscape.

'He was an enigma,' her date had said. 'His name was

Giorgio Barbarelli da Castelfranco. Only six works are fully attributed to him.'

She had flip-flopped at that one. Speaking Italian! A sudden shudder of electric pulses had shot up and down her spine. 'What you say his name is again?'

He'd smiled. He was dark-eyed with dark eyebrows and dark hair streaked with grey. Glamorous looks, great smile and confident. He looked at her directly. 'Giorgio Barbarelli da Castelfranco.'

Yeah, that was it all right! That hit the spot. Now ravish me, she was thinking. She couldn't help herself. Maybe it was him. Maybe it was the vodka. She was thinking: *Castelfranco me right up against the wall.* It must've been the vodka speaking. Something was getting her giddy.

But he didn't move. He continued to stare at her. She laughed, but he just stared. Suddenly it was disconcerting.

'You can stop looking now,' she said. 'I'm a shy girl at heart. You might not believe it, but I am.'

'Why? Does it make you feel uncomfortable being looked at?'

She looked back at him in silence. Her knees pressed together.

That was it, wasn't it? Where it changed? He had changed. The Prince Charming had somehow evaporated in that stubborn, intense stare. She could see his eyes. But his eyes weren't full of lust. They were quite cold. He was observing her second by second as her simple open-eyed horniness slowly faded to incomprehension and then, as he still wouldn't avert his gaze, to fear.

That's what he wanted all along. He wanted to see fear in her eyes, not lust.

'Weren't you making sheep's eyes at me, Jessica? Didn't you flash that smile at the church? Didn't you invite me up here? What were you anticipating? A nice Baptist girl like yourself. Girls like you look like butter wouldn't melt, but then here we are – and all on a first date. You know what that makes you?'

She shook her head.

'A whore, Jessica.'

The killer felt a twinge. They were locked in her apartment. It was many hours before dawn and there were things he wanted to do that she would not consent to.

Jessica was just realizing that she didn't know him at all. He'd come on to her at the Baptist church, smiled, made her laugh out loud.

As she stared, still holding her glass, he put a hand to his inside pocket. He took out a brown leather case. He opened the popper and pulled out a small old-fashioned switchblade with a black handle and a small curved blade. He opened it and looked at her.

'There was a double murder back in the sixties in an apartment just like this one. Two college girls. Don't know what happened exactly. I mean, the autopsy showed what had happened – the killer had stabbed one of the girls sixty-three times. Can you imagine that? Sixty-three times. And they weren't rapid, violent stabs. No, siree, these were slow and considered. He pushed the knife in real carefully. They think he was watching her face as he did it. You know, like he was interested to see what happened? You know what they call people like that, Jessica?'

Jessica's voice trembled. 'No, I don't.'

'They call them sadists because they enjoy other people's pain. Sadist. Do you know where the word sadist comes from, Jessica?'

She shook her head. Her knuckles were white on her glass. Her eyes were rimmed with red. She knew she mustn't cry, but she kept sniffing and the glass was now trembling.

'From a French gentleman called the Marquis de Sade who enjoyed inflicting pain on his lovers and anyone else for that matter. But the young man who was operating that night wasn't

118

just an over-enthusiastic lover, Jessica – he was something else entirely. Sixty-three times. In and out, that's one hundred and twenty-six individual movements. In and out.'

Jessica was praying now. She was hoping her prayers could somehow help her as they had always done before. *Help me, Lord Jesus.*

'Seriously. Is that sick or what?' The killer breathed deeply. 'Do you think, Jessica, that he was enjoying the sensation? Why do you think he stopped? Do you think he got excited watching the knife go in and out?'

'I don't know.'

'Are you scared, Jessica?'

'Yes, I'm scared.'

'What do you say, Jessica? Would you like to go to bed with me now or have you changed your mind?'

She shook her head. 'No, thank you.'

'I think that's a wise choice. I don't think you'd like it at all.'

The man stood up and walked over to her; he flicked open the top button of her blouse. A small silver crucifix caught the light.

'Do you believe in God, Jessica?'

She nodded.

'Do you think he'd come and save one of his own if she needed his help?'

'I don't know.'

'How about we test him out? Or do you think it's wrong to tempt him?'

'Please. I'm sorry. I'm so sorry. I don't know what I've done,' she said, the tears now falling.

The man moved to the door. 'Be careful who you invite into your home, Jessica.'

'Yes,' she said. 'I will be.'

'You know what might save you?'

'No.'

'Maybe God. Let's see, shall we?'

The man turned and unbolted the three bolts on the door. Then he opened it and stood there.

'Today's special number is sixty-three. You think you can count to sixty-three? Count to sixty-three before you move and you can go free. God has sixty-three seconds to save you. And you just need sixty-three seconds of faith. Do you have that much faith?'

Jessica nodded and the killer smiled. He didn't really think she'd get past five or six, but he wanted to give her a chance. Everyone deserved a chance – even God.

He walked out, leaving the door slightly ajar. Jessica sat and suddenly started to shake uncontrollably. She counted as she stared at the door.

'One, two, three, four . . .'

But she kept imagining that the door would fly open and he'd return.

'Five . . .'

She felt so vulnerable.

'Six.'

So scared, so terribly scared. It was too much. She was terrified. Suddenly, she ran at the door and closed it with the full force of her body. Her trembling hand reached for the dead bolt.

But she wasn't quite quick enough. Or strong enough.

The door burst open and Jessica fell to the floor, her wet, terrified eyes staring up. He was back. Not the bright, witty guy she'd met at church, but a sinister figure weaving the curled edge of the knife in the air.

'They call me the American Devil, Jessica. Do you want to know why? I want you to call out my name. I want to hear you say it.'

Jessica did as she was told, but the words trembled on her lips.

'You only had to do what I told you and you'd live. Faith is hard, isn't it? It was that simple, but you couldn't resist, could you?'

He took her by an ankle and pulled her towards the centre of the room.

'Shall we start counting again, Jessica?' he said. 'Let's see what we can get to. But this time, each number comes with a price.' He put the point of the blade against the sole of her foot.

'One,' he said, loud and firm as the point of the knife pressed into her flesh.

She closed her eyes and wished for an angel.

None arrived.

Chapter Twenty

East Harlem
November 19, 5.58 A.M.

Either someone was putting something in his coffee or Harper woke up feeling better after his first two sessions with Denise. In truth, he had unloaded almost nothing of his feelings about Lisa, but it was enough just to hear Denise put them in some kind of order. He liked her hard edge and her lack of sentimentality. Maybe that was exactly what he needed.

From his drab apartment he looked out on the new day. The morning was grey all the way across the city and a light rain was falling. Harper was up before first light and at 6 a.m. headed out to Central Park with his binoculars. He needed to spend a simple hour in the park. It was the walking that did it: somehow it released his mind and got him thinking. The American Devil was interacting with his victims, and had been for years. Then suddenly, out of nowhere, he started to kill. There was nothing similar on the Federal database. Why did a man start to kill? What was it about Mary-Jane that triggered this terrible spree?

Harper walked along the wet street and ran the thought over and over in his mind. Maybe he hadn't intended to kill her? The killer was in her room, wasn't he? Maybe he was there before Mary-Jane. Yeah, he thought, it just might be. He'd have to look at the case information, see if his idea had any weight.

He looked up. Even early in the morning, the poor of Harlem seemed to leak out of the pores of the city. Harper stopped in a doorway and looked down on a woman in her fifties, lying on her side underneath a hard sheet of cardboard. She was wearing a pair of old tennis shoes without socks and her legs were swollen and glowing with a bluish tinge. Harper knelt down beside her and put his hand on her forehead. There was still heat under the skin. She wasn't dead, just right next door. Harper stood up and walked on. Then he stopped and turned back. He walked across and put a couple of twenties into the woman's hand. It was a cold day: the weather had turned again.

Eddie Kasper was walking up the block and caught sight of Harper leaning over the homeless woman. He shook his head and shouted up the street, 'Why don't you leave the poor woman to sleep? If you want a date, Tom, I can sort you out.'

Harper looked up. Kasper being up at 6 a.m. wasn't a good sign. 'What's up?'

Eddie Kasper was shaking his head. 'Are you looking to be sainted or have you lost your sub-prime mortgage and are sorting out alternative accommodation with the homeless doorway rentals?'

'I'm just connecting, like my psychoanalyst tells me to.'

'She does, does she?'

'This is a type A behaviour, for which I get a reward. Type A is the kind of behaviour I'm supposed to do more of, so I'm doing more of it. And you know what, crazy as Dr Levene is, she's right. It makes me feel a whole lot happier.'

'Are you thinking of fucking her, is that it?'

'Your mind is a sewer, Eddie. There are other motivations in life.'

'So you're just being good for goodness' sake?'

'Goodness is its own reward,' said Harper.

'I fucking hate those kinds of rewards.'

'Cut to the chase, Eddie. What's happened? What the hell got you out of bed at dawn?'

Eddie shook his head, 'Sorry, man, they found another body. A girl in Yorkville.'

Harper felt his stomach clench. 'Damn this bastard. He's like a machine.'

The two of them walked in silence from the darkness of the doorway into the flurry of New York City. The rain started to fall harder, causing the few people who were out to rush about, covering their heads with any objects to hand. Harper stared at the ground as he walked alongside Kasper, his chin down in his collar.

Eddie's car was round the corner, so they walked through the rain getting soaked to the sound of tyres ripping up surface water. Harper noticed the changing colour of the asphalt under the rain and the dawn light – it was almost purple. He thought of the water on the rocks at Ward's Island. He remembered the wet ground by the corpse in the parking lot. Did this killer like water? The waves must've kept coming up over Grace Frazer's body. One more piece of the illogical that would make some kind of sick sense in the killer's mind.

Eddie pulled a pastrami and mustard sandwich from his deep jacket pocket, held it tightly in his left paw and started eating hungrily. 'Anyhow, Harps, I'm sorry to break up the do-gooding, but this one looks bad.'

Kasper's red 1996 Pontiac was parked at an angle, half on the kerb. They both looked at it. 'What?' asked Kasper. 'I was rushing to get you.'

Inside the car, Harper finally spoke. 'What's the situation? Fill me in.'

'A college kid, Jessica Pascal, living in the dorm district. One of the students found her. The door of her apartment was left wide open. She was just lying there in the entrance, just like Mary-Jane.'

'Dead?'

Eddie looked at Tom. 'Yeah, it looks like it. We're homicide, right? That's when we get the call, when people are dead. Did you just think it was bad luck?'

'Is it the same killer?' said Harper.

'If this is his, he's on some roll. Three kills in a week.'

'He's in heat.' Harper slipped on the seatbelt. The old leather seats crunched under his weight. 'Any details?'

'I ain't got no more details, Church-boy, so don't do your questions.'

Eddie pulled the car into gear and slipped into the traffic, causing another car to slam on the brakes and honk.

'Any indication of the method?'

'Bloody.'

'How so?'

'Don't know. They said we gonna need to get overtime for the cleaners on this one.'

Harper stared ahead. Speeding headlong towards a bloody crime scene hadn't figured in his plans. He'd wanted to check out his theory on Mary-Jane. He felt the whole case dragging him in.

Harper closed his eyes and rested his head back on the seat. He had already started to prepare himself for what was waiting for them in Yorkville. He was clearing his mind, trying to create a space for what was to come, a place inside his head where he kept all the bloody images and case materials. A room he could close and lock at the end of the day. A fresh murder room.

Chapter Twenty-One

Yorkville Crime Scene
November 19, 6.45 a.m.

The car took forty minutes to pass through the snarl-up and continued noisily towards the crime scene with some mid-range R&B that Harper couldn't identify. They arrived at the corner of York Avenue and East 82nd Street. Two uniforms were taping off the entrance to the building and a small crowd of seven or eight civilians were hanging round to watch the action. Two Dodge Chargers had cut off the street with their flickering lights, but there wasn't an ambulance in sight and the Crime Scene Unit hadn't yet showed up.

'It's just the start of the day,' said Kasper. 'Everyone works slow for a couple of hours.'

On the fourth floor, Harper and Kasper entered the hallway and saw the entrance to the apartment. It was one of the better buildings in the area, much more expensive than the usual student could afford. They moved past the officer on the door and signed the log.

'Watch out,' he said. 'It jumps right out at you.'

Tom flicked a smile towards him. 'Thanks for the warning.'

Together, they turned the corner and looked into the interior of a smart and well-kept apartment.

'Anyone been in yet?' Tom called to the officer.

The man appeared at the door. 'No one yet. We just got here, called it in and taped it off. The cavalry are on their way, Detective.'

Tom Harper and Eddie Kasper felt the icy breeze coming through the open sash window at the end of the hall. Someone had already been feeling queasy. The smell of a corpse could choke you, but the sight was worse. They looked down at the body.

The stark glare of a naked 100-watt bulb illuminated the grainy early-morning darkness of the room. Below it, the bloody remains of a sweet college kid, her future now brutally crossed out with yellow police tape: college, life, marriage, career, kids, grandkids – nada. No entrance.

Both men felt their nerves jangle. The girl's body was directly in the doorway, her legs close together, a white cloth covering just her groin as if hiding her modesty. She was cut to pieces.

Eddie grimaced and popped a strong mint into his mouth. He offered one to Harper, who declined and pressed his palm to the door frame. 'This bastard wanted that to be the first thing anyone saw.'

They had to step over the body to get into the apartment. The floor was red and slimy throughout with large bloody footprints all over the carpet and linoleum. This killer didn't care enough to cover his traces.

The victim's body was lying cruciform and naked, posed like a dead Christ. Harper looked down across the body. Small cuts all over the arms, down the thighs and calves, and even in the feet. The Medical Examiner called them torture cuts. Too shallow to kill, deep enough to really hurt and always on the veins so there was enough blood to cause fear.

'He's taken another trophy,' said Harper. 'See?'

Kasper was looking round at the room. 'I ain't sure I could say what organs you're supposed to have.'

'He's cut off her breasts,' said Harper.

It was their man again. It had all the savagery of the three earlier kills and the body was again strangely posed. She was a young blond-haired student who had started the day with her whole life ahead of her and ended it cut to ribbons. Tom saw the two highball glasses on the small side table and leaned in. He smelt the vodka and cranberry. 'Seems like the kid here had a guest.'

'A date?'

'Yeah, maybe. They had a drink and then he put enough holes in her to make a sieve. Some date. He likes to cause pain, doesn't he? And he likes to shock. You see any flowers anywhere?'

Eddie shook his head and then pointed at the white loincloth and screwed up his face.

'Maybe. You want to take a look?' said Harper.

'No. You?'

Harper pulled on a latex glove and reached across. The white gauze lifted easily from the corpse. 'What you see?' said Eddie.

Tom replaced the gauze, shook his head and looked closely at the victim's hands and arms. 'So many cuts. Jesus.'

'It's the American Devil again,' said Kasper. He clicked on the CD player. 'Hound Dog' by Elvis erupted into the room. The two men looked at each other. 'You thinking what I'm thinking?' said Eddie.

'Music you can torture by – loud enough to hide the screams.' Tom kept looking at the corpse, counting the small black knife slits. 'There's a lot of work gone on here. Upward of fifty individual wounds.'

'What are you thinking?'

'She's got a similar look to the others. He likes them fair-haired, wide-eyed and pretty. And if she's a student, then she's got a helluva place. Wealthy parents, no doubt.'

'I got something else, Tom.'

Harper looked up. 'What?'

Eddie Kasper was standing further into the room. From

behind, Tom could see the tension in his shoulders as he kept himself from throwing up. 'He's left a picture.'

Harper rose slowly and moved to the window. He felt the horrible anticipation from the slight quiver in Kasper's usually deep and robust voice.

On the window was a photograph printed out on a sheet of plain white paper. It was a picture of the victim before she was dead. She was sitting on the floor in an old dress, staring up. Both her feet and her hands had already been cut but she was smiling a horrible forced smile and staring up at the camera.

Below the photograph, there was a quotation. *Subtle he needs must be, who could seduce Angels.*

The two men remained speechless. They found somewhere inside themselves to hide as they stared at the photograph. Her eyes were so full of pain and fear, yet she thought she was going to live if she behaved. This killer was enjoying the feeling of absolute control.

'What's your reading?' said Kasper. 'He's some kind of religious nut? Maybe it's some kind of revenge attack.'

'No damage – look at the place. Nothing turned over. No struggle.'

Harper had a strong sense of pitiless evil. He looked at Kasper. 'This is going to get worse before it gets better. He's a well organized killer with a plan and he has all the features of your all-American psychopath – sex, religion and violence.'

The two cops walked out of the room to wait for Crime Scene to arrive. They both headed straight for the open window in the corridor and gulped the cold air.

Chapter Twenty-Two

OCME
November 19, 2.02 p.m.

Out in East Manhattan later that day, at the Office of the Chief Medical Examiner, Tom Harper and Eddie Kasper were led into the blue-tiled morgue for Jessica Pascal's autopsy. It was windowless and claustrophobic, with great banks of white and steel drawers.

Closets of the dead.

Robert Toumi, the diener, had worked for the OCME for twelve years. He pointed across to the autopsy room. 'We've not even got her on the slab, gentlemen. Laura's scrubbing up. You're welcome to watch me work, but it ain't pretty.' He went across to a body bag on a gurney. 'I've weighed her and she's had an X-ray. Pretty busted up by the look of it. Gangbangers, was it?'

Kasper shook his head as Toumi wheeled the gurney through to the autopsy room. The two detectives followed silently. It was never nice being inside the morgue. Dead or alive.

In the centre of the room, the stainless steel autopsy table shone clean and bright. Kasper took a sideways glance at the instrument table and began to feel less than comfortable. Bone saws, hammers, scalpel. Kasper suddenly jumped.

'Jesus, man, that's a fucking pair of garden secateurs!'

Toumi laughed. 'Gardening equipment is cheaper than

surgical stuff, often better too. The ribs can be a little tough.'

'That's not right,' Kasper said and took out his shades. He put them on. He would be able to close his eyes if it got too much.

Toumi rolled the gurney beside the autopsy table and unzipped the body bag. 'Seeing as you're so quick on the case, I'm figuring this ain't your average murder. What's the situation? She been cut down by the new psychopath in town?'

'That's what we want you guys to tell us,' said Kasper, watching intently as Toumi lifted and dropped the corpse's feet on to the steel and then humped the upper body half on to the slab.

'You got to roughhouse these babies,' the diener said, yanking the torso across and letting it drop unceremoniously. 'This one's only a hundred twenty-two pounds. You should see how I get the obese ones on the slab. I played football in my younger days – you ever watched a linebacker sack a corpse?'

'I imagine it ain't like watching the salsa,' said Harper.

The floor, like the dissection table, was sloped slightly towards a drain. A hose in the corner indicated how they did their cleaning. The whole room smelled of disinfectant. On the gurney, Jessica's naked pale blue corpse glowed under the strong lamps.

Harper hadn't seen a corpse on the slab for a while. He felt a stab of anger and breathed deeply. There was nothing more liable to make you question your belief in the soul than a lifeless, mutilated corpse.

Dr Laura Pense entered dressed like someone about to do a spot of riot control. She was wearing a plastic face shield, surgical scrubs and gloves. She'd worked with Manhattan North for five years, and knew the team well.

'How you doing, guys? You want to watch some theatre? I understand this is an important one for you.' She looked at the corpse. 'Is this our American Devil? I've had three of his girls through here already. You get to know the work. You in a hurry?'

Harper nodded. 'We're pushed, yeah. I was just about to go see if there's anything like this on ViCAP. I don't know what to input: I've no idea how they died. Just wondered if you could give me a sense of what happened.'

'I will in about four hours, Detective.'

'We'll be back in four, Laura, but if there's anything you can tell us now, we'd appreciate it.'

Laura Pense turned and winked at them. 'Let's see what I can do.' She looked at the corpse. 'This is quite some overkill, I can tell you that.' Toumi handed her the X-rays in an envelope. She opened them and flicked through them quickly. 'Someone's been tossing this body around like a rag doll. Jesus, that would take some strength.'

Harper looked down at the red-stained corpse of Jessica Pascal. Kasper was looking at the floor, his eyes concealed by his shades.

'What happened?' asked Laura.

'A nice apartment in Yorkville out near the East River. The victim was left at the door, just like a cat leaves a dead bird. You can see what the killer did to her.' Harper looked down at the woman again. Her face was blood-splattered, her body a strange livid purple with slits the colour of eggplant. What kind of monster could do this?

'You think it was just one killer?' asked Laura.

'We aren't making any assumptions.'

Deputy CME Laura Pense was sharp and to the point. She was a first-rate forensic pathologist and destined for any job she wanted in the city.

'Right, ready for your four-minute autopsy?'

Laura turned on her Dictaphone, checked the microphone at her lapel, then read the tag on the corpse's toe.

'Dr Laura Pense, November 19, OCME, New York City. Body number CNZ14135. In attendance, Robert Toumi and Detectives

Harper and Kasper from the NYPD Homicide. Initial inspection of the body.'

Laura did a quick once-over, took the plastic bags off the corpse's hands and looked closely under the fingernails. She examined the scratches, and started to mark wounds.

'This is going to take some unravelling, gentlemen. But she's got upward of sixty stab wounds. Deep wounds on the right side of her neck. Breasts sliced upward through the pectoral muscle and removed. He must've used a variety of knives. Finger-shaped bruising on the cheek. Several lacerations to the heart area with shallow striations – slash marks. Several deep wounds to the abdomen. But the majority of the wounds are shallow. Teaser wounds. And a number of torture wounds crossing the veins. He was probably cutting her for a good while. She probably died from the neck wound, but he continued. He's getting to enjoy time with these bodies.'

She leaned in and looked closely at the corpse's arm, then looked up at both men. 'There's a print of his lips here and here. Looks like he was sipping at the wounds – or kissing them. We need to get Latent Prints down here.' She examined the woman's lower abdomen. 'Open her legs for me, Robert. Foreign object inserted into the vagina. He's been working down here too. Robert, get me the forceps. Okay. Okay. Yes, I think I know what this is.'

Laura attached the forceps to the end of the object and slowly pulled it out. Harper watched closely, his face impassive. Kasper's eyes were shut tight.

'Petals. It's a flower of some kind,' said the doctor and pulled the forceps out. She placed the bloody cherry blossom on the autopsy table.

'That's not nice,' she said. 'That's no way to give a girl flowers.'

Chapter Twenty-Three

East Harlem
November 19, 2.13 p.m.

The killer was disguised as a doctor and had assumed the name Dr Mark Keys. He was feeling good about life and was smiling as he parked up and got out of his car. He looked at the worn-out building ahead. It was a flat-roofed, unimpressive two-storey building that must've housed between twenty and thirty rehabilitating inmates. A halfway house for the half insane.

The killer looked at his hands and noticed a line of blood under his fingernails. He suddenly felt his stomach tingle with excitement again. He'd spent the morning with his girls. He'd been working on *The Progression of Love*. He'd be a world-famous artist one day. His works would last for centuries.

Four clear glass vitrines were already complete, the first containing the eyes of girl number one, the second with the hair of girl number two, the third containing the heart of girl number three, the fourth the breasts of girl number four, which the police had just discovered were missing.

His photographs and news stories were pasted up behind the vitrines. The latest was a large photograph of Jessica Pascal, smiling, staring right at him. She was wearing an old dress he had taken to the scene and looked just like a girl he once knew. The killer felt he had perfected his art. It was just as he dreamed.

He could bring her back to life, love her again and, more important, kill her all over again.

The man disguised as Dr Keys shuffled his shiny black shoes in the dirt and walked across to the green front door. It had metal bars across it, but it was wedged open. Dr Keys walked right in and up to the small reception desk.

A black lady at the counter didn't look up. Not nice, thought Keys – doesn't matter who you are, you ought to be polite. He slapped his ID down in front of her. He hadn't intended to, but her arrogance annoyed him.

'Dr Mark Keys, senior investigator for the Joint Commission on the Accreditation of Healthcare Organizations. Do you always ignore your guests, miss?'

Her eyes rose to meet his. 'We ain't under your jurisdiction, Doctor, and the name is Felicity Adams.'

'No, but your patients are. You recently admitted a psychiatric patient released from Manhattan State.' He looked at her. 'Yes or no, Miss Adams?'

'Yes. I'm sure we have.'

'Under the revised release accreditation guidance, halfway units need to ensure secure monitoring arrangements for category three releases.'

'We don't worry about curfews and in-and-outs. They look after themselves.'

'I need to see Mr Carlisle's room and access arrangements.'

'Well, he's in Room 52, so go and help yourself. The access arrangements are right there.' Her eyes fell to the desk and her extended arm pointed to the door which seemed to be permanently wedged open.

'The *National Enquirer* more important to you than the rehabilitation of your residents?'

Miss Adams looked up. 'Yeah, just about in every way, Doctor.' She turned over the page.

Dr Keys was genuinely angry with her, but he wanted to keep his anger from getting spoiled, so he looked around for something. He saw her open bag and a faded Volvo key fob. He had information now. She drove an old Volvo. Information was useful. He walked to the stairs and followed a series of green plastic signs leading the way to the rooms.

At Room 52, Dr Keys stopped. Winston Carlisle's door was wide open and he was lying on the bed staring ahead. Dr Keys entered without knocking.

'Hello, Winston. I'm Dr Keys from the Manhattan Psychiatric Center. I need to have a conversation with you. We need to do a little work on your rehabilitation.'

Winston held out his hand without looking and Dr Keys shook it. He then leaned forward and handed Winston a small plastic vial.

'I need a sample, Winston.'

Winston stood up without question and took the small bottle. 'You gonna let me go back to the hospital?' he asked as he unzipped himself and urinated into the small bottle.

'If you're good I will,' said Dr Keys.

'I'm invisible out here. No one sees me. I can just walk right through them.'

'Well, I can make you visible again, Winston. Don't you worry.'

Winston nodded. Dr Keys sat down on a small side table and took out a notebook. 'I've got some things I need to go through with you. It's all in the name of rehabilitation. It's a new approach to help guys like you reintegrate. What we do, Winston, is ask you to follow some of those urges of yours under close supervision. We monitor your testosterone levels each week and see if there's a pattern.'

'You want me to follow my urges?'

'That's right, Winston. What we will try to do is watch you and monitor how you act out here in the real world. Then we can see if we understand you a little better. Are you interested?'

Winston stared for a moment and then nodded. 'I guess.'

Forty minutes later, Dr Keys walked out of the halfway house and took a quick turn around the perimeter of the building. Winston was an obedient patient. He would do as he was told. It was looking like a very good choice. Dr Keys was pleased. Before he left, he had enough time to find the only Volvo in the parking lot and, therefore, the car belonging to Miss Adams.

He took out a small thin blade from his pocket, slipped it under the hood then yanked the engine cover open. He quickly identified the brake feed and cut a nick in the pipe. That would give her perhaps another three hours of driving before, hopefully, she paralysed herself driving across a red light.

Chapter Twenty-Four

Dr Levene's Office
November 19, 5.30 p.m.

Harper and Eddie took the news from the Medical Examiner back to Williamson and the team. The cherry blossom hidden in Amy's throat and now inside Jessica showed the killer was enjoying setting a little puzzle for the cops. Harper wondered if the killer was starting his next phase. He had started to communicate with the police and media by posing the corpse and hiding his signature cherry blossom.

Harper took the Mary-Jane file from Williamson's desk and began looking for some evidence to back up his idea that her killing had not been planned. It took him about an hour to read through the key documents and they seemed to confirm what he'd thought. He took out the interview with Mary-Jane's school principal. She said that Mary-Jane had left school at 1 p.m. that day, just after the end of the morning session, as she'd forgotten an essay. The killer could not have known that, could he? If he didn't know that she was going to be home then it might have been a chance meeting. He might have been scoping out her apartment. Harper took out the report from A–Z Security, the company responsible for the elaborate entry procedure at the Samuelson building. It showed that someone entered the apartment on Mrs Samuelson's card at 12.30 p.m., half an hour before Mary-Jane left for home.

That was the evidence he needed. The killer was in her apartment. He hadn't followed her in. He didn't expect her to return. This guy was an obsessive stalker with multiple targets who needed to get closer and closer to his victims just to keep the buzz alive. He felt the need to get so close that he touched them up in the street, took things they owned and even tried to snoop around where they lived and get intimate shots. Then, he took it one step further. He wanted to be in Mary-Jane's bedroom. He needed to be there, so he broke in. Harper let the situation come to life in his mind. He had been wrong to think that the killer was stalking her that day. How else would the killer know she'd left school early? He didn't know, did he? She came back early, he was in her room. He saw her. She screamed. He panicked and grabbed her. She had no idea he was a killer and fought hard, but he'd held her easily. He was strong. Nothing was overturned in her apartment, but she had bruises all over her body. The autopsy had found his skin under her fingernails. She had fought him.

He had to stop her or his whole plan would fail. He put his hands round her neck. He just kept them there until she stopped breathing.

Harper knew he was right. That was what happened. An accident. An unfortunate coincidence that he chose to steal into her room on the day she had forgotten her homework and slipped back at lunchtime.

An accident had triggered all his fantasies. And he'd liked it. Christ, he'd really got a taste for it.

Harper had an idea about what they might do. A long shot, but he needed to talk this through with someone who understood criminal behaviour. He needed Dr Levene's input.

Forty minutes later, Harper hurried up the corridor towards Denise Levene's office. He needed someone to show him how to unlock the symbols. He pushed straight through the office door and looked directly at her. 'He didn't mean to kill

Mary-Jane. She disturbed him. I want to know the implications for his behaviour.'

Denise stared up at Harper with a look of surprise. She pointed across to the chair in the middle of the room. 'I'm with a client, Tom.'

'Did you not hear me? We need to talk now. He's killing every couple of days. Grace Frazer on November 14, Amy Lloyd-Gardner on November 16. He killed again last night.'

'Yeah, I heard it on the radio this morning. Can you give me a moment, Tom? I'm with someone.'

Tom moved towards her desk. 'How is he keeping up the pace? Psychologically? Is it possible? I've never known anything like it.'

Denise stood up and walked round her desk. She smiled at her client, a rookie officer who was now looking more terrified than ever, and put her hand softly on Tom's shoulder. 'Can you just step outside for a moment and let me wrap up here?'

Tom only then noticed the cowering figure looking lost in the big black leather chair. He apologized and retreated.

Outside her office, Tom paced. The need to move was more powerful than anything else. He needed to do something. The killer needed to be engaged or flushed out. With the profiler at the New York field office going cold on the case and refusing to take a line, the team was left with old-fashioned detective work – piecing together every piece of available information and looking for something that linked the bodies and crime scenes with the identity of the unsub. But Harper knew, just as the rest of the team knew, that that took time and it was just dawning on them that time was something the killer was using against them. He was leaving them no time to assimilate and process the details before he struck again.

Harper picked up a magazine, flicked through it absently and then threw it back down on the glass table. He looked at his watch, and then, right beside it, the thick green attitude band that Denise Levene had somehow got him to agree to wear at the end of the last session. He put it on after the fiasco at Erin Nash's apartment. Denise was right, he got angry a lot. Now he was feeling the anger burning up inside him, so he pulled the elastic back and let it slap hard against his wrist. It twanged and stung. He did it once more. Yeah, it distracted him momentarily.

Denise appeared at the door of her office with the rookie, who made a big detour as he walked away to avoid Tom Harper's great brooding figure. Denise was feeling excited rather than annoyed. The case had been keeping her awake since Tom had talked about it the previous morning and now he was here unprompted. She'd pieced together what she knew about the killer but she needed detailed crime scene information if she was going to be able to help. Maybe Tom Harper would fill in some of the missing pieces.

She beckoned him into her office. She saw his right hand twisting the attitude band and smiled. 'How's the anger management?'

'I'm still angry,' he said.

She shook her head with mock disapproval. 'I know what you're going to tell me.'

'What?'

'You didn't twang.'

'I feel stupid twanging.'

'But if you don't twang, there's no psychological movement. There's no learning. Listen . . .'

Tom smiled broadly. He couldn't help it. He liked it when she was earnest, even if he didn't buy into all the CBT shit. Still smiling, he twanged, looking directly into her eyes. Then he twanged again.

'Yeah, yeah, I get it, you're thinking I'm just a quack with stupid ideas.'

'I need to talk about the case, not myself,' he said.

'Okay. Talk me through the victims.'

'He disempowers them by force or fear, then he rapes them

141

and tortures them. His preferred method of killing them is asphyxiation. Then he takes something.' Tom paused. 'He took Mary-Jane Samuelson's eyes, Grace Frazer's hair, Amy Lloyd-Gardner's heart, Jessica Pascal's breasts. He poses them. Mary and Grace were posed to humiliate, with their legs apart. He posed Amy and Jessica in quasi-religious poses and added a line of poetry to each. He leaves cherry blossom at every scene. Sorry. It's not nice.'

Levene pulled her Powerbook across the glass table and clicked a couple of times. 'Listen,' she said. 'I want to help you get back out there and catch this monster. You know my research. We were trying to detect early neurological signs in these killers, so I spent time working with these guys.'

'What happened?'

'If I'm honest, I couldn't handle seeing them close up. Hey, Tom, just so you know – I've got baggage that would put yours to shame. I'm just better at the makeover than you are. All I'm saying is that I got to know a thing or two about profiling killers. That's why I took this job, to find out more about them from you guys.'

'A profile can't work in all cases. This guy defies profiling.'

'Maybe, maybe not. The key is, Tom, to isolate the important points from the noise.'

'How?'

'Look, your killer is working on all kinds of different levels. He's taking psychological reminders, he's hiding himself from the victims, he's sexualizing and degrading them, he's also romancing them and then giving them some afterlife. It's a lot of detail.'

'Don't we know it.'

'Look, we just got to work facts and deductions from facts. Deductions, you know – necessary factual conclusions, not guesses.'

'I get you. If you can work up a profile, we can see if we can use it. But I need something else.'

'What?'

'I got a strong feeling that Mary-Jane wasn't premeditated.' He paused and looked across to her. 'I think he's been getting closer to these women and he broke into Mary-Jane's apartment to be near to her stuff, maybe even take something. But she came back unexpectedly, and then I think things went bad.'

'In many cases I've studied, the killer isn't sure what he's going to do until he interacts with the victim. It depends on the victim's reaction. Sometimes the killer sees no way out except by silencing them, especially if they struggle. It can trigger a very aggressive reaction. It's self-protection.'

'But he got a taste. He liked it.'

'Yeah, this guy really liked it.'

'The thing I'm thinking, Denise, is this. If I'm right, then we've got a piece of useful information about him. You know, something that we might use to lure him in, maybe even get him to speak to us. You think that's possible?'

'You want to interact with him?'

'There's a greater chance of finding him if we can get him to talk to us. I want to know if he's responding to what we say. Can you help with this?'

'Yeah, but I've got to understand him a little better.'

'Okay, what do you need?'

She smiled thinly. 'You give me the case files and as a quid pro quo I will try my damnedest to resolve your aggression against women. Not, of course, your aggression against me, which is textbook defensiveness for your psychological weakness. By the look on your face, you'd say that isn't what's wrong with you, but I'm here to tell you that's what you've done with all that sadness. Turned it to something hard and unpleasant.'

Tom stared at her. It felt like a relief to hear someone identify things he didn't dare identify for himself. 'Okay. We have a deal. I'll get you the files, but based on what you've heard so far, how do you read him?'

'Well, first off, your killer is focusing on the key romantic symbols from his women. Eyes, hair, heart, breasts – they all have romantic symbolism. He's afraid of the power that women – or a particular woman – have over him. What they make him feel. He's afraid of the effect they have on him. If he's a stalker, then he needs to control not only the women, but the way they excite him. He can go to them or their artefacts or pictures whenever he wants. He wants to neutralize the real threat, though, because he's been hurt and humiliated by them. You're looking for someone with a problem relating to strong women. If he's in a long-term relationship it'll be with someone weak. He's smart, too. He's someone who would be able to hide all of this from the person he lives with.'

'Will he kill again?'

'Yes. He's compulsive. It might be his weakness. Now he's been triggered, he might just keep on going until you stop him.'

'What else?'

'Here're the thoughts I've been having. Forget trying to work out all the noise. Let's focus on one or two things. Here goes. He attacks women he has stalked, right?'

'I think so, yes; there's evidence he'd been stalking. Jessica Pascal was spotted with a tall, handsome guy and Grace Frazer reported a stalker.'

'He photographs them and takes their clothes. He wants to know them intimately and they're all quite refined and educated girls. Forget all the symbols. He likes these girls. In his head, he might believe they like him. He might even believe he loves them. My first profile note would be this – your killer is building a relationship with these girls and he also feels bad about what he's done. The religious posing suggested, to me, a kind of naive attempt at forgiveness. He can't help what he wants to do, but he tries to absolve himself from it with romance and religion.'

'So how does that help?'

'Well, you lost Lisa, didn't you – what did you do, after she'd gone? Move on and forget?'

'No.'

'What?'

'Visited places that reminded me of her.'

'One thing I can be sure of, he will return to the scenes. He'll want to continue the buzz it all gives him. That's why he takes the trophies, to relive the kill.'

'Yeah. But what can we do? Surveillance? We do that at the crime scenes anyway. It's standard.'

'No, not surveillance. You asked me how you could interact, based on your information about Mary-Jane. You need a set-up.'

'That's what I was thinking. Tell him we know Mary-Jane was a mistake, that he can get out of this ... that kind of thing.'

'Maybe, but if you want him to talk to you, give him something to talk about. You need to press his buttons.'

'Go on.'

'He's a control freak. How do I know? Because he doesn't mind hurting these women when they're alive. A disorganized type would kill them first because he'd be too afraid. This guy can communicate okay. Perhaps he's even charming. But the point is, he likes to control everything – including, I'm guessing, his reputation. Part of this is about making society notice him.'

'I don't think I follow you,' said Harper.

'What we might do is release a statement live on air or through a newspaper and say something that undermines him and makes him look weak or even uncontrolled. Piss him off.'

Harper's mind started to work on the idea. 'Maybe we could get Erin Nash to run the story, if we promise to give her Williamson for an exclusive. What do you recommend, Doctor?'

'Go with the paper, but it needs TV too. He needs to see someone bad-mouthing him. He'll need it to be personal. Let's set up a press conference and follow it up with an article from Nash. That covers all bases. Can you get it cleared?'

'I can try. I could do the press conference myself. I'd love to bad-mouth this bastard.'

'A couple of other things, then. First, tell him you understand the pseudo-intellectual messages he left at the corpses, the kind of messages an uneducated halfwit would leave to make himself look like someone he's not. You got those poems, didn't you?'

'Yeah, random poetry.'

'You can say this is a message to the poetry-loving American Devil. Say you know where to expect the next kill and when. Say that he's making errors and leaving a trail and that it's only a matter of time. Tell him that the NYPD found something at the last crime scene that is central to the investigation and likely to lead to an arrest. Say that he can't control his emotions and that's the problem, that's why he's making elementary mistakes. And then you've got to make that all seem real to him.'

'How?'

'By releasing a piece of information about him that will surprise him.'

Harper nodded. Who knew if it would work, but it was worth a go. 'What do we reveal?'

'You can reveal the Mary-Jane information. Say that you know what happened. Or else tell him you know that he drives a blue car. A premium brand. Probably a classic model.'

'And how the hell do you know that?'

Denise raised an eyebrow. 'Think like him. He's a low-status guy who wants to look like he's made it big. He can't afford a new high-status model because he works in a low income or commission job, but he doesn't want to be seen to have an old model – what do you do? You go for a classic premium brand: low cost but high status.'

'Why blue?'

'That's the serial killer's colour of choice. You didn't know that?'

'I didn't know that.' They both smiled. 'I like it,' said Harper. 'Don't know if it'll work but it beats sitting around and waiting. I'll sell it hard to Lafayette.'

'Yeah. If you front this up, Harper, remember, he'll take it personally. And he's going to be hard pressed to avoid speaking to you. He'll need to know what you know. You gonna do this?'

It was the first time since the start of the case that someone had spoken any sense about this killer. Tom smiled. 'Consider it done,' he said.

Chapter Twenty-Five

Blue Team Major Investigation Room
November 20, 2.23 p.m.

Harper took the script from the printer and held it up. He felt a sense of pride. He and Denise Levene had sent the draft backwards and forwards all morning, trying to get every word right on the button. And now it was ready. What's more, it was going to be used, live on air. Harper and Levene's long shot was nearly set up and ready to go.

It was going to be a difficult day. Harper had put his reputation on the line by insisting the department try this technique to lure the killer into speaking to them. It had taken every second of his time to make sure it happened. Everyone needed convincing.

The previous day, Harper had worked until midnight putting together the operation they were now calling 'Janus'. The most difficult person to convince had been Williamson. He didn't believe it was right to put out a false report. It wasn't in the spirit of the homicide squad. It smacked of the kind of thing the Feds would do and boast about endlessly.

In the end, Lafayette overruled Williamson and sanctioned it at Homicide. He knew that even if it failed, it gave the executives down at headquarters a sense that something was happening. He gave Harper the green light and that gave

Harper only a few hours to put together the operation, get it approved and set up a press conference.

The idea of putting the same thing out to the press via Erin Nash died at the first phone call. The *Daily Echo* wasn't going to lie to its readers. End of story.

Everyone in the homicide bureau knew that they had to be quick. Since the murder of Grace Frazer, the killer had struck every second day; if he was consistent, he'd be planning to hit again.

Harper took the script across to Nate Williamson. 'Do you want to see it, Nate?'

'No.'

'If it doesn't work, we've lost nothing,' said Harper.

'I'm okay with it, Tom,' said Williamson. 'I'm just not the innovative type, but you're right to try. I've been going over the autopsy protocols again, seeing if we've missed anything. Looking at what this guy did to these kids. He's evil. You understood that straight away, didn't you? You saw it.'

Tom reached out and put his arm on Williamson's shoulder. The man was fifty-four. His own daughter must be in her mid-twenties. 'We'll screw this bastard into the ground, Nate.'

'Yeah, well I hope I'm there to see it. I want to put my heel in.'

'Listen, Nate, I think I ought to do the press conference.'

'Fuck that, Tom.'

'This is going to rile him. He might react. It's dangerous. It was my idea, I'm happy to front it.'

'I'm lead, Tom, I lead. No question. If he wants to come and get me, I'll be ready for him.'

Harper worked until the press release was ready to go, then he sat down alone in the bunkhouse and tried to get a few minutes of sleep before the evening sitting by the phone lines.

In the cold, drab room, Harper felt a sudden loneliness. For three months, there hadn't been anyone to open up to. Lisa had been the only person he'd confided in, and now he didn't know where to turn. He pulled out his phone and scrolled down to her name. He looked at it for a moment, then pressed call. She picked up.

'Lisa. It's Tom, you got a moment?'

'I'm on my way out, Tom.'

'Where are you?'

'Not your business, remember.'

'I just . . .'

'What, Tom? How is this going to help?'

Welcome to my life, he thought. He loved Lisa, sure. And he knew he'd messed the whole thing up. It had gone wrong so slowly, almost invisibly, and then suddenly they didn't know each other.

'I love you,' Harper said. There was a pause. 'Don't be angry.'

Lisa's voice came back all calm and slow: 'Tom, I know you think you do, but you don't. You just don't like to lose, Tom, and that's ego – not love.'

It didn't matter what she was saying. For a moment, it was just good to hear the way she spoke in nice neat sentences.

'I'll prove it to you.'

'No. Listen. I don't want you to prove it to me. It's not the point. Listen to me. It's hard. I know it is, and we've been doing this the hard way. You know. Love you, love this – just wrong time, wrong place . . . whatever.'

'What are you saying?'

'Tom, I don't love you. This isn't hard for me. This is good for me. I'm happy. I don't have to go through it with you any more. I'm not in love with you. I don't think about you. I'm not waiting. I'm not looking to move backwards. And another thing . . . I don't think you can love . . .'

There was a silence. Lisa knew she had hit out but she knew the big hit was to come. That was all just padding. He knew it too. He sensed what was coming. He'd known for some time now. But he wasn't going to let it happen.

'Right,' said Tom. 'I'll get off. Sorry I called. I gotta—'

She interrupted. A second later and he'd have ended the call.

'I'm seeing someone, Tom. I'm seeing a guy I met. He's a nice guy.'

'Don't lie to me, Lisa. You're not seeing anyone.'

'It's goodbye, Tom.'

She hung up. He threw his phone hard across the room.

Chapter Twenty-Six

Fullerton Lounge
November 20, 6.23 P.M.

The man in the black suit and white shirt was drinking a martini in the Fullerton Lounge. He was dog-tired. Like someone had drugged him or something. He needed a pick-me-up. Killing wasn't as easy as some people contended. It had its costs as well as its benefits.

The Fullerton Lounge on Lexington was an over-expensive and self-important bar that aimed to extract as many dollars as possible from people too self-consciously rich to dare to ask the price of things.

The man in the black suit liked it because it was quiet and dark. He had three newspapers from the last few days spread out in front of him. He picked up the *Daily Echo* and started to read the account of Jessica's murder.

It was front-page news in all of the papers. It was page one to five in the *Post*. The headline in the *Daily Echo* read: 'Devil Kills Fourth Angel'. He liked that. He opened the other papers. They'd all caught on now. They understood. This was serious. He was the main attraction. The killer smiled. It was in the detail that the horror lay. None of them had the level of detail that the *Daily Echo* reporter had got. He read Erin Nash's exclusive with particular glee. She even had the nice touch of his with the cherry blossom. The public would be terrified and secretly excited by it all.

It was good to be the only man in the world worthy of the media attention. At 6.25 p.m., he asked the bartender to put on the news. He watched as they trawled through the political nonsense and finally, towards the end, they got round to the latest on his story.

A cop from the old school was speaking at a press conference about Jessica's murder, telling the city that it was all under control. He was lying. They had nothing under control. They just didn't know it yet. The cop said little more than had already been in the majority of the papers: a student had been murdered by her date. He said that it was a vicious attack and that the police were doing everything they could.

The killer sneered. He didn't like the cop's attitude. It was disrespectful. He'd murdered an entirely innocent, moral young woman in an apartment block full of residents and they didn't have a single lead. Give the American Devil his due. He looked at the cop's name: Detective Williamson. He made a mental note. He had a head full of mental notes. Then the cop's face came right up close and personal. He wanted to make a statement to the public. The killer watched and listened.

Williamson cleared his throat. The statement he was about to read out was designed to prick the killer's pride. 'We are seeking help in finding this killer. The following information will help us to identify major suspects. We are looking for a man too weak to control his own temper, a man who routinely sees himself as inadequate. He always preys on weakness and is a confused and random opportunist. We are looking for a frightened individual who has difficulty holding down relationships or speaking to women. He only picks on defenceless victims because he is weak himself, weak and afraid. Further to that, he attacks these bright young women from behind with lethal force so that they are absolutely no threat to him. These are all symptoms of a deranged and fearful psyche. He will be unable to have normal sexual relations and will rely on fantasy to fuel his own self-hatred. He is not careful. He leaves a great deal of evidence, both physical and behavioural, at the scene. However, he does work and drive. At the last crime scene the killer left behind a very telling clue to his identity. We also know he drives a blue car. A premium brand classic car. We have a number of sightings of his car and his face. We need the public to help identify this killer. But we'd prefer to speak to the American Devil himself. This is a direct appeal. We know you did not intend to kill these girls. We know what happened at the first murder scene and that it was a mistake. You need help. We need you to get in touch with the NYPD on the number below to discuss the case. If you don't, we are close to homing in on you, and you will be brought to justice by force. Please call the number below if you want to talk to us.'

The killer's jaw was wide open. He looked left and right to see if anyone else was shocked and confused. He wasn't anything like the portrait they'd painted. They were fucking idiots. They were the fucking incompetents. He had not left evidence and his victims had all been wide awake. The killer downed his shot and ordered another. The indignant anger was rising in his chest. He had to put this right. He had to make sure people knew what he was really like. He felt a pulse throb in his temples. He looked into the mirror behind the bottles on the bar. He was handsome, wasn't he? Not a snivelling incompetent. He was the American Devil. And he was strong and capable. He tried to calm himself but for some reason it wouldn't stop circling in his mind. He was offended. He was also curious about the evidence left in Jessica's apartment and how they knew what'd happened with Mary-Jane. He licked his lips. Maybe Williamson knew too much. He wanted to know. He wanted to know right now. He drank another shot and started to think.

*

At seven his next girl, Elizabeth, entered the bar. He knew she would: he had access to her electronic diary. She was meeting Kyra, a colleague and fellow intern. He stared at her. She was more beautiful in the flesh than in the photographs he kept of her. He'd come across her by chance at a city function three years earlier. She'd been standing by her old man, smiling and playing the pure, dutiful, all-American daughter. He'd liked her then. He liked her more now. But she'd not stayed pure, that was the problem, and now he had to act. She needed to be snuffed out. They all did.

He went up to the bar and stood next to Elizabeth. He ordered a Black Russian and turned to her. 'Can I get you something?'

She smiled and shook her head. Polite but firm. He tried again.

'You had a tough day?'

'I'm just waiting for my friend. Thanks.'

He nodded as the barman put his drink in front of him, not taking his eyes from Elizabeth. She didn't dare look up, but she knew he was staring.

'Listen,' he continued, 'I'm sorry, I'm just a little nervous. I have to admit, I've seen you before. Your father's the TV preacher, right? A real puritan. Just what this country needs.'

At the realization that he might be genuine, her lifelong training in good manners kicked in.

'Hey, sorry, I just . . . I hope you didn't think I was being rude.'

'No, it must be hard – you walk into a bar and want a bit of peace and some asshole hits on you.'

'It can be,' she said and smiled sweetly.

His eye was watching her little silver crucifix oscillate in the beautiful dip of her neckline.

'You wouldn't mind . . . I mean, I know it's odd, but you wouldn't mind sharing a beer with an admirer?'

'Of me or my dad?' she said.

'A little bit of both, maybe,' he said and smiled broadly.

She was flattered. She couldn't help it. 'Maybe one beer until my friend arrives,' she said.

He called the barman. 'Can you get this woman a cool one?' He smiled at her. It was a great smile, and she felt a little frisson of something in her stomach.

'What do you do?' she asked.

'Me? I work in art. I buy and sell paintings.' The man laughed. 'Nothing as beautiful as you, though.'

Elizabeth smiled. 'Please. You can cut the corny lines.'

The man in the black suit watched her take her beer and sip the white foam off the top. He leaned in slightly to catch her perfume. 'You know which painting you remind me of? Manet's *Olympia*.'

'I don't know it,' she said.

'Well, maybe I'll show you sometime. But it's in Paris. Or perhaps you wouldn't mind a European adventure? The thing with Manet's painting is that it's a nude of a prostitute. It offended the public taste. I sometimes do that myself, you know, offend the public taste. All great artists do.'

She smiled. *This guy was a little too intense.* 'You're a great artist?'

'I do a little sculpture,' he said. 'I've not been discovered yet. But who knows.'

She smiled again. He was just drinking her in, letting his imagination run away with him. He was starting to feel slightly delirious. He needed to get away from her. It was not the right time. More than that, her friend would be in soon and that would be the end of the chase. He had to keep the lines clean. No residues. He finished his drink and thanked her, leaning in and kissing her cheek. As he did so, his hand passed quickly into her handbag. He left quickly.

He would've liked it to rain now. He looked up to the autumn sky. It looked good for a shower.

And now he had her entrance card, he could begin his plan.

She'd change her entrance card soon, sure, but would soon be soon enough? He didn't think so – she was girl number five and tonight was her night.

She just didn't know it yet.

Chapter Twenty-Seven

Blue Team MIR
November 20, 10.30 p.m.

Down at Blue Team, the day turned into evening and everyone was waiting. Williamson had got the team to set up the big blue boards in the basement room. They had three photographs each of Mary-Jane, Grace Frazer and Amy Lloyd-Gardner, and now Jessica Pascal's face stared out innocently alongside the others. Williamson wanted no mistakes. He wanted to hurt this guy.

Tom Harper and Eddie Kasper walked into the basement. The other detectives of Blue Team were all sitting around facing Nate Williamson, who was talking to them in low tones.

They'd been talking about the lead detective's performance live on air. Everyone agreed that he'd done a good job. Williamson wasn't happy with it, but that was his character. He was at least pleased that he'd fronted it. He'd insisted, he told his guys, even though Harper had offered to do it himself.

The team went quiet as Harper approached. Everyone was hoping this would work, but they all knew it was a hell of a long shot. Harper was looking tired and sat on the desk at the front. He nodded to the guys and wiped his nose with his forefinger. 'That was a great job out there, Nate. If he's listening, then that's gotta sting.'

'Yeah, well, I did what I said I would. Let's just hope it pays off – administration want every report on these murders to go in triplicate right up to the deputy commissioner, so if this fucks up, then everyone in the fucking city knows it. How about that?'

'High stakes,' said Harper, 'but I hope it pays off for you.'

'He can only do two things, call or not call. That's evens. This is a good bet. I'd back it myself, but I'm saving up for retirement.'

Harper felt a smile cross his lips. It was good to hear someone being less than cynical, a rare thing at Homicide.

Williamson moved off to the coffee pot at the back of the basement room, then came back with a steaming cup. He turned to the rest of Blue Team. 'Let's focus on our killer. How we doing out there?'

'Still nothing on ViCAP,' said Kasper. 'I've been trying to get the FBI profile coordinator to give us something concrete, but they're still reluctant to make a judgement.'

Lol Edwards chimed in from the soft seats at the back of the room. 'My view, for what it's worth, is that he's from out of state.'

'Opinions are fine, Lol, but we need evidence. Nothing else? What's the autopsy report looking like, Garcia?'

'Everyone's got a copy. Details worthy of note are as follows: the cause of death in the case of Jessica Pascal was asphyxiation. Plastic bag was found at the scene. The wounds mostly occurred before death. The victim had recently had sexual intercourse. Traces of semen on the body. Impossible to tell whether it was rape or they had sex and then the killer went ape. Get this – there were sixty-four separate shallow knife wounds.'

Lol Edwards sniffed for attention. 'ME called, she overlooked a bite mark on the left buttock. Pretty deep, too. We've got another teeth print. It's the same mouth. And the lip print matches as much as they can tell.'

'How did he get in?'

'We've got sightings of Jessica in Joe's Bar with a grey-haired man in his late thirties. We've also got an ID of the same guy at the girl's Baptist church. We're working them into sketches.'

'What do you say, Tom? What are we looking at?' said Eddie.

'Well, don't let the fake profile fool you. This is an aggressive sexual predator. Organized and ruthless. He enjoys hurting and humiliating. There's a religious element that I don't understand yet but he already likes to communicate. He left quotations with Amy and Jessica. The quotations are both poets, Rilke and John Milton. I've been up to Columbia University so we've got a little background. They were both visionary poets. Milton was also blind. Rilke was a radical. God knows what he's getting at.'

'Maybe he just likes poetry,' said Eddie. 'You know, hobbies – walking, poetry, serial killing.'

The guys laughed as Williamson edged away from the circle with his coffee and turned to Rick Swanson. 'How about the progress on Amy, our angel?'

'We got a hit on the nail art. There's a salon up in Harlem. Quite a low rent affair, not the kind of place a banker's wife would be in, except, in nail art circles, it's got Harlem kudos. Anyway, they claim the designs are theirs, but they don't recognize her photo. So we're still digging. They say that sometimes these high society girls get their maids to come in for designs, get a one-off and then repeat them themselves in their more upmarket beauticians.'

'So, what we can conclude is that we got nothing,' said Mark Garcia. 'You want me to do the press release? A guy goes out on a date with a church-going virgin, doesn't get his way so he kills the poor kid.'

'Garcia, fucking button it,' said Eddie.

'Fuck you! That's all we got.'

The captain had entered the room during their intense conversation. No one had noticed him, but he was watching them all closely. He had some news.

'Williamson, we had a caller wanting to speak to you.' The room stopped dead.

Williamson stood up. 'Was it our guy?'

'He said he's got a handful of cherry blossom that he wants to shove up your ass.'

There was a murmur of laughter throughout the room but the captain wasn't smiling at all. The room went still for a moment.

'He hung up real quick,' said Lafayette. 'He said he was busy, but he'd call back when he had a moment.'

'Was it him?' said Harper.

'He said he'd cut Jessica sixty-four times. He said the career girl murderer only managed sixty-three. He wanted to see if he could go one better.'

'No one knew that detail,' said Harper. 'It's got to be him.'

Chapter Twenty-Eight

Blue Team Major Incident Room
November 20, 10.55 p.m.

The detectives from Blue Team were all crushed into the small interview room and had been ever since the news of the first call. At 10.55 p.m., the phone rang again. Williamson signalled through the big glass window into the observation room which was set up with the technical team. They patched through the call and started the trace.

'Hello, this is Detective Williamson, lead detective on the American Devil murder case. How can I help?'

There was a crackle and a pause on the line. The seven police officers in the room all held their breath.

'Hello? This is Detective Williamson. Are you the man we want to speak to? You want to talk about your mistakes? You want to know how we know all about you?'

Again there was silence. Williamson looked up at the window and shrugged. The technical guys rolled their fingers. Whoever it was, he was still on the line and Williamson needed to keep talking.

The silence from the other end continued. Williamson started up again. 'If you want to keep me talking, let me know you're not just another timewaster. I get a hundred calls a days claiming to be this guy and every one is a fake. So give me something or get back into your hole and stop wasting police time.'

The men waited. Taking a harsh position could go either way. Harper glanced at the clock. A minute had elapsed. It was good, but they hadn't traced the call so Harper presumed it was a cell phone, probably unregistered. The only hope of getting anything was by triangulating the call. The technical guys had set it all up. They just needed to get the signal of the cell phone transmitter received by two or three base stations, then they could work out the location based on the time difference from each station. But it needed more time than tracing a traditional phone and it was fallible.

Keep going, mouthed Harper.

'Okay, Mr Silent, let's get one or two things straight: this is my investigation.'

'Shut . . . the . . . fuck . . . up.' Bingo. The killer had replied. The first time they'd heard the voice. It was deep, slow and considered. A frightening voice. A voice you didn't want to find in your apartment after dark.

'You're talking to me, then,' said Williamson.

'First things first, you fucking loser. You make claims about me in public like that again and I'll kill two a day. I can do it and you know it. I don't need to do all the embellishments, I can just cut and go. You get me? So less of the disrespect and lies. I have got you boys pissing your pants and sucking your fucking thumbs because you don't know who the hell you're dealing with. Well, let me tell you who I am. I'm not no trailer park inadequate with a fucking speech impediment. I'm an artist. One day you'll see my grand work, *The Progression of Love*. It's taken years and years to put together. Some day soon I'm going to reveal it to you all. My name's Sebastian, and I'm an artist. I'm the American Devil. I'm Abaddon – that's where I am. But you'll never find me. Open the door and I'll be gone.'

The seven detectives stared at the small speaker. Williamson was not coming back. You could see that his head was empty. He drew some saliva back into his dry mouth. 'Fuck you, you asshole,' he said. It was his standard reply when he felt threatened. It was not a good move.

'Okay, Detective, let's be quite clear what we're dealing with now. I'm in her apartment already. She is probably walking home as we speak. You can't stop her, you can't warn her, you can't stop me, but you know it's going to happen, as inevitable as the sun rising. I've got a blade here sitting on my lap and I'm going to dedicate this one to you boys. I'm going to give you a real show, but then again you only ever turn up after the show's over. Like the cleaner in the movie house with your brush and scoop.'

'Who is she?' said Williamson.

'I'm looking at her picture right now. Pretty girl, blue eyes, skin fine as silk. Her name, in case you're interested, is Elizabeth. I'm going to pull her apart and put her back together again. When you see her, she'll be transformed. It's just the way of the world – angels become whores, whores become angels. It's a damn shame you can't save her. She's going to be mine by the end of tonight. Sealed with a kiss. You know I like to do that, don't you?'

Tom Harper was copying out every word into his small black notebook, under the previous note, which read: *Connecticut warbler, Red-eyed vireo, long-eared owl.*

It was bad news – the killer was active again. Every two days. He was in there. There was a woman returning home with no idea of what was waiting for her and there wasn't anything they could do. Harper looked at the technical staff. One guy was holding up ten fingers. They had to keep him on the line.

Harper grabbed the phone from Williamson. 'Sebastian, it's Detective Harper here. Sorry for the lack of courtesy. Truth is, we haven't got a clue who or what you are. You've stumped every one of us and we're scratching our heads. We don't know how in hell you do it. You've got to give us something, or you're just pissing on us from a great height. Tell me something, you feel bad afterwards, don't you? You pose them because you regret it and you feel bad about hurting these girls.'

'Bad?'

'You feel bad for hurting these girls, don't you?'

'A curious word, Detective, but no, I never feel bad. They feel bad, not me. They feel fucking terrible, in fact.'

Suddenly, the dialling tone cut in. He had gone. The four technical staff could be seen leaving their seats in the next room and rushing out into the corridor. In a moment they entered the small interview room.

'Did you get it?' shouted Harper.

The lead guy was nodding. They were all nodding.

'Well, what the hell have you got?'

'We've triangulated the signal. We've got an apartment block on the Upper East Side.'

'Okay, let's move,' said Williamson.

'Any more information?' said Harper.

'The trace takes us right to the Laker Building, but we can't get any more definite. The phone's unregistered.'

The lead technical officer passed the read-out and address to Williamson. 'Right,' the detective said. 'We've got an address and no time, let's make like it matters.'

The team bustled out of the interview room and down to the station house parking lot. The bait had worked. They had the killer on the end of their line.

Chapter Twenty-Nine

Upper East Side
November 20, 10.56 p.m.

Elizabeth was just turning into Roma Avenue. A daddy's girl through and through. It paid to be a daddy's girl in her family. It got her the Upper East Side apartment, the Mercedes, and the expense account, as Daddy called it. It got her expensive clothes, expensive treatments and all the trappings of wealth – just as long as she played the virgin daughter to her preacher father.

Hey, but she was also doing well on her own, wasn't she? Never put a foot wrong. Straight-A student. Graduated top of her class at Princeton. But it was love she really craved tonight. Firelight, candles and strong arms. Love she wanted and love, she thought, she was going to get.

She fished in her handbag for her entrance card, but couldn't find it. Damn. When she reached the apartment building she signalled to Marvin, the concierge, and waited for him to release the heavy door for her, rewarding him with a smile. Marvin turned and followed her with his eyes as she headed for the lift. Elizabeth was used to attention. The elevator travelled quickly to the twenty-second floor.

Elizabeth was thinking about Anthony. He was an investment banker. All gaunt cheeks, awkwardness and sparkling eyes.

Gorgeous. And he made love like a man who wanted you to remember it.

She walked up the thickly carpeted corridor to the door of her apartment and took out her keys. They were on a little Tiffany lock charm shaped as the letter E.

She looked at the lock. It was covered in small scratch marks. She put in her key but the door was not locked. The killer heard the key in the lock. She opened the door and was surprised by the sudden scent of flowers. She raised her eyebrows, tossed her handbag aside.

Anthony had got in somehow. Maybe he was planning something special. 'Is that you?' she called.

She walked towards the bedroom. The phone started ringing and she hesitated, but then she saw it. The bed had been turned down and a small box lay on the pillow. It looked like the kind of box you'd put a ring in. A dress was all laid out. Was this Anthony's big secret? Was he going to propose?

From inside the wardrobe, the killer watched her. Beauty and wealth were so strange, so very strange. You could see them, but you couldn't ever grasp them in your hand. They were in her, somewhere. He was going to find out where.

She opened the lid of the black velvet box, and her smile drained away. An eye stared back at her. He had decided to use one of Mary-Jane's eyeballs. Elizabeth suddenly felt terribly vulnerable, a feeling she'd not experienced before. Her legs began to shake. She couldn't move as the door of the wardrobe opened. She couldn't move at all. He appeared and stood before her. Over six feet and holding something that shimmered and caught the light. She held up her hand, open-palmed in a gesture of conciliation, as if that tiny little protest would be enough to stop the American Devil.

He walked up to her and put his other hand out to touch her golden hair.

'Remember me?' he said.

Elizabeth recoiled from his touch, her body frozen in shock, her eyes staring at the blade he held by her cheek.

'You're just perfect,' said the killer. 'I watched you for a long, long time, Elizabeth. I need you to cooperate with me. We haven't got much time.'

Chapter Thirty

The Laker Building
November 20, 11.16 p.m.

The crossroads outside the Laker Building were burning with flashing light, but there wasn't a siren going. The dispatcher had called all patrol cars to go silent to the glitzy building overlooking Central Park. There were seventeen cars parked at angles within ten minutes of the call. Several squad cars, Dodges and Chevrolets were kerb-parked forming a semicircle around the entrance to the building. The Emergency Service Unit Hummers were just beyond. Uniforms were keeping the civilians away. This was the one. The big endgame.

As Harper and Kasper pulled up, the enormous SWAT trucks arrived. They'd got a team together in advance, just in case, and the squad was jumping out of the back of each truck in their black armour and helmets. They were about as well armed as a man could be.

Williamson was directing the operation from a TARU truck. The concierge was in the truck with him already and they had a list of the registered owners of the apartments within minutes. Williamson ran his finger down the list. 'Here we go,' he spat excitedly. 'There's only one Elizabeth in the building, thank God. We've found her.' He took the map of the layout of each floor and circled the apartment, then called it through to the rest of the team over the shortwave.

The captain of the SWAT team moved close to the map and then looked up at the building. 'We got to hit this quick,' he said. 'No telling what he's done already.'

'Then get going!' shouted Williamson.

Outside, the patrol started cutting off the scene, several officers skirting the edge of the building from both sides, making sure no one left and no one got in. Harper looked round at the flashing lights and then up at the windows. He turned to Eddie. 'Well, if he didn't know we were coming he does now.'

'What do you think? You don't look convinced,' said Eddie.

Harper was reading through the notes of the phone call. 'He's not stupid, is he?'

'No, he's smart.'

'Does a smart guy let us know his location with a cell phone?'

'No, he'd be mad to do that.'

'Yeah, so what's his game?'

'I don't know. You think this is just a red herring? He's gone already?'

Harper took off his jacket and pulled on a Kevlar vest. Kasper started getting kitted up too. 'No. I think he's here. But if he's up there with her, they need to go in now.'

Kasper looked across to the first SWAT team. They had assembled at the great marble entrance to the Laker Building. Six black-clad officers in body armour were heading in the door. Each one had a face mask, Kevlar helmet and either a Heckler and Koch sub-machine gun, a Benelli M3 shotgun or a semi-automatic rifle. They looked formidable. The SWAT teams worked as small units with a leader taking the team forward: two assaulters with the heavy weapons, a scout to go on ahead and a rearguard. The team entered the building.

Harper and Kasper ran across to Williamson at the TARU truck. 'What you got? What's the plan?'

'We got one Elizabeth in the building,' said Williamson, breathing heavily. 'Elizabeth Constantine. We're lucky this time.

I've sent the SWAT team to storm the apartment. We're going to get this bastard. I just hope he's not got to the girl yet.'

'What's the layout look like?' asked Harper.

'The building's got an elevator and two stairwells. They make their way to the apartment up the stairs, take the door off its hinges, then take him down.'

'Simple as that,' Harper said.

'That's how it's going to be. What's the problem?'

'I don't like it,' said Harper.

'What? That I'm going to take him down?'

'No, Nate, I don't like the situation. He's too smart to give us such an easy lead.'

'He's not smart, he's spooked – the press statement panicked him. He doesn't know we can trace his cell phone. He thinks he's indestructible.'

'Maybe, but he didn't sound like it. Give me a look at the residents' list.'

'Sure, look all you like, but there's only one Elizabeth living in this building. I'm going into the lobby,' said Williamson. 'I need to be there when they bring the bastard out.'

Harper leaned over the list of residents. He called the concierge to his side. 'Hey, what's your name?'

'Marvin,' said the concierge.

'Is this list up to date?'

'Sure is,' said Marvin. 'I only just got the latest list yesterday.'

Harper stared down the list. He was working through the angles. The killer's call had been triangulated and he'd given them a name, Elizabeth, but maybe the name was phoney. They couldn't know for sure. The triangulation meant only one thing and that was that twenty minutes earlier the killer had been somewhere in the building. But that was all they knew.

He turned to Marvin. 'Tell me about Elizabeth Constantine.'

Marvin sucked his teeth. 'Like I told Detective Williamson,

she's pretty, all right. About twenty-four. Nice lady. Quite a small woman, but she's very polite.'

'What colour hair?'

'She's blonde.'

Harper nodded. Williamson's instincts seemed to be right. 'Well, I hope she's all right.'

'So do I,' said Marvin. 'She's a real nice addition to the family.'

'What did you say?' said Harper.

'We're like one big family here.'

'No,' said Harper, 'you said she was a nice addition.'

'Yeah,' said Marvin. 'She's only been here a couple of weeks.'

'Where did she live before?'

'I don't know that kind of stuff, but it'd be on her registration documents. You'll have to see the building manager.'

Harper's finger stopped halfway down the resident list. Elizabeth Constantine was new to the building. The question troubling Harper was whether she was also new to the city. 'Get yourself back to the building and find me those documents,' he said.

Marvin jogged back towards the Laker Building. Harper looked up at the building. Eddie sidled up. 'You've got that look on your face, Harps.'

'Elizabeth Constantine moved in two weeks ago.'

'Does that matter?'

'I don't know. He's a careful bastard. We know he stalks them for a long time, sometimes years. If she's just moved here, he's not had long to get to know this building. I don't know. And if she's from out of town, how the hell has he been stalking her?'

'Maybe he's killed all the girls he's been stalking,' said Eddie.

'Yeah, or it means he might be setting us up. Get across to Williamson and get him to call the SWAT teams, let them know we're less than a hundred per cent on this. Tell them to be cautious. I don't want anyone hurt. We need to be certain.'

'Got you,' said Eddie, and he ran towards the building.

Harper needed to check his thinking. He couldn't afford to be wrong if he was going to get Williamson to back off. He called Denise Levene. 'Listen up, Denise. I've got no time to explain but I've got a major situation here. Can you speak?'

Denise shook off her tiredness and sat up in bed. Fahrenheit, her spaniel, lay between Daniel and her on the big double, blissfully asleep. 'Go ahead,' she said as Daniel stirred in his sleep.

'The killer called us. He identified himself as Sebastian. He said he's going to kill a girl called Elizabeth and we traced the call to a building here full of wealthy residents. So we've got the killer located somewhere inside the building, except we're not sure which apartment.'

'Is this Elizabeth in the building?'

'Well, there's only one Elizabeth listed. We're about to go in. Except this Elizabeth is new to the building. She moved in a couple of weeks ago. She's maybe even new to the city. What do you make of it?'

Denise let it float around her mind for a moment. 'He likes to know things inside out. I'd say it's improbable if she's new to the city, but I'm not sure it matters if she's moved apartment.'

'Except that we're pretty sure all his locations have been thoroughly scoped and he wouldn't have been able to get to know how this building works in two weeks. You can never be a hundred per cent, but if he doesn't know this building, then this is high risk.'

'You might be right, Tom. You got the residents' list?'

'Right here,' said Harper. 'But it doesn't have any other Elizabeth on it.'

'Okay, this isn't absolute but his type is likely to be late teens to mid-twenties. She will live alone. She will probably work in a people profession. She'll be fair or blonde. You got anyone else like that? Keep looking. Maybe it's someone's daughter.'

'I'll look into it. Thanks.' Denise was about to reply but Harper had already switched off the phone and was sprinting towards the building.

Chapter Thirty-One

The Laker Building
November 20, 11.27 p.m.

The hallway was pitch dark and the SWAT team wouldn't switch the lights on. They put some patrol on the lift but scaled the stairs on foot, all seventeen storeys. It was quiet as hell in the building. The halls, exits, roof, lift and fire escapes had all been sealed and manned. They were the only way up or down. The rise up the stairs went quickly. They pushed through into the hall, three men arriving from each side. They kept in contact with hand gestures. Again, it was pitch dark in the hall at their request and the team felt their way along in torchlight. Then they were there at the apartment.

Down below, Williamson was listening on his headset. His heart was thumping. Through the headset, he could hear breathing and footsteps, but nothing else. Suddenly Harper appeared at his side. Eddie was already there with his arms out, palms upwards, pleading. 'He's not listening!' he yelled to Tom.

'Williamson, I've got to speak to you. This killer wouldn't use an apartment building he doesn't know. He wouldn't make a mistake like that. He's not going for Elizabeth Constantine. He's set you up. You've got to call them off.'

'The call located him in this building, her name's Elizabeth, she's blonde, I checked. Hey, Harper, I'm following the evidence, not you.'

'They didn't locate him in her apartment. Look at the detail. The only reason you think he's up with Elizabeth Constantine is because of her name and he gave us the name. There might be another Elizabeth or another girl altogether. Do the math, Nate. If she's been here for two weeks, then he can't have worked out how to do this.'

For a moment, Williamson felt doubt well up in his chest. He looked at Harper and cocked his head. 'What is it with you?'

'Fuck that, this is about saving someone's life. Call off the SWAT teams. He's not after Elizabeth Constantine, so we've got to keep looking. Call them down.'

Williamson breathed into his mouthpiece. 'Proceed,' he said and turned his back on Harper.

Harper took Eddie by the shoulder and they ran to the small concierge office. They were going to have to work this out by themselves.

Outside Elizabeth Constantine's apartment, the SWAT team could hear the TV going. One of the team pushed a tiny camera through the gap at the bottom of the door. He looked down on the monitor. The living area appeared to be empty, but there was no telling what was on the sofa. They could only see the back of it.

The lead gave the signal and they checked their weapons. The door had a shotgun, assault rifle and two pistols pointing at it. The rearguard moved in with the jamb spreader. They'd decided to go in quiet. Ramming the door would allow the killer the few seconds he might need.

The hydraulic jamb spreader was inserted against the door jambs and the rear guard started to gently crank the pump arm. The idea was simple. Up to three tons of pressure pushed the door jambs until the lock was no longer sitting in its carriage and the door could be quietly pushed open.

The team watched as the pressure began to build up.

Down in the concierge's office, Harper was questioning the building manager over the phone. He'd already told Harper that Elizabeth Constantine had moved from another apartment on the Upper East Side. 'Listen,' Harper said. 'We're looking for a woman called Elizabeth, but we've got no one else registered in that name. You got any ideas?'

'I don't know all the residents,' the manager said.

'Well, this one will be a single woman in her early twenties. She'll be pretty and blond-haired, slender build. Have you got anyone like that?'

'I wouldn't know. I don't spy on them. Look, I'm sorry,' said the manager.

Marvin had hung back during the conversation but he was nodding even before Harper had finished the call.

'What is it, Marvin?' Harper asked.

'I know a girl like that up in 146. Miss Seale. She's a real beauty.'

'Her name's not on the list,' said Harper. 'What's her first name?'

'I don't know her name. It's her father's apartment. Here it is.' Marvin pointed to a name on the list.

Harper looked down at the name Seale. Miss Seale. He remembered the curious line the killer had used on the phone. 'Sealed with a kiss.' Could this be the one? He felt a surge of energy. 'Describe her to me, Marvin.'

'Beautiful, blonde, slim, just like you said.'

This had to be her. Harper was sure. He got back on the radio to Williamson.

'I think her name's Elizabeth Seale. He's set us up with the wrong apartment. We should be going for 146.'

'It's too late, Harper, we're going in,' said Williamson.

Seventeen floors above the SWAT team held steady as the door loosened. The lead gently pushed the door open. The first officer crouched and moved into the room. In less than two seconds, he whispered 'Room clear' and pointed to the bedroom. The team of six black-suited officers moved forward into the room. They could hear faint noises from the bedroom. All six firearms were raised. The lead turned the handle and pushed the door.

'Freeze or I shoot!' shouted the captain, and six weapons pointed into the room.

On the bed, a man was writhing naked on top of a woman.

The man turned and stared at the six monsters in black, a look of panic frozen on his face. 'What the hell is going on?'

The next few seconds were brutal. The team floored the naked man and had him cuffed in moments.

'Are you Elizabeth Constantine?' asked the rearguard. The woman on the bed nodded, her face terrified.

Down below, Williamson listened. This was not a dead end, this was the fucking guy. He waited for the words. Then he heard them. 'We apprehended the suspect. Threat nullified. She's alive.'

'Is the suspect in the apartment?' asked Williamson.

'Yes. He's on the ground, sir. Victim is unharmed, Detective.'

Williamson felt a surge of pride. He ran to the stairwell and started up the stairs. His heart was beating with joy. He had come good. Harper was wrong. Williamson had backed the right horse for once.

Five floors up, Harper and Eddie arrived at the door to Elizabeth Seale's apartment. Harper put his head to the door. 'We've got no choice.'

'No.'

'How do we get in?'

'Lucky I thought ahead,' said Eddie. He held up his shotgun.

'Well, what are you waiting for?'

Eddie crouched in front of Elizabeth Seale's apartment door. He swung the shotgun butt to and fro and then let the full force smash against the lock. It split and shattered at once and the door yawned open. Harper and Kasper threw themselves to the floor and looked into the apartment. The first room was clear. They looked to the bedroom. The door was ajar and a light was on. The muzzles of a Glock 19 and a SIG pointed towards the door.

'What are you waiting for?' said Eddie.

Harper breathed in deeply. 'Wait a moment.'

'Why, you see something?' said Eddie.

Harper shook his head. 'Breathe in.'

Eddie sniffed and turned back to Harper. 'What is it? I got nothing.'

'I can smell blossom,' said Harper. 'We're too late.'

Williamson's voice came through on the radio. 'We've got the bastard, boys, we've got him. And Elizabeth is alive.'

Eddie looked at Harper. They stood up and walked slowly to the door of the bedroom. The whooping continued on the shortwave as the cops below congratulated each other. Harper pushed open the bedroom door with the muzzle of his Glock. The door swung open and they stared at the body of Elizabeth Seale, who was propped up on some pillows, staring right back at them with cold dead eyes. Harper rushed across and put his fingers to her pulse.

'She's dead,' he said, turning to Kasper, 'but she's warm. The killer might still be in the building.' He went out on the shortwave. 'Nate, this is Detective Harper. We've got a dead woman in Apartment 146. Elizabeth Seale. She's only just died, Nate. He could still be in the building.'

'There was no Elizabeth Seale,' said Williamson. 'There was no such girl.'

'Thing is, she wasn't registered. It was her father's apartment. He fucked us, Nate. We need to get the CSU crew here soon as we can and get the whole area sealed. We need to search this building. He could still be here.'

There was no response from Nate Williamson, just the crackle of static.

Chapter Thirty-Two

The Laker Building
November 21, 1.47 a.m.

The proud, glass-fronted lobby of the Laker Building reflected a massive light show of flashing red and blues. It looked like carnival time, but it wasn't. Not even close.

The small crowd that had started to form a couple of hours earlier as seventeen patrol cars swooped, full of authority and optimism, had swollen to a great sea of wide-eyed gawping faces, all flickering with the dancing lights of the NYPD.

Harper looked out at the crowd. He knew that the killer may well be out there watching them all, enjoying the scene he'd created. They liked to do that sometimes. Watch their own show. They couldn't resist. Harper scanned left to right. It could've been any of them.

Harper had just walked the perimeter. He had yet to figure out how the killer had left the building. He knew damn well that the killer had duped them, and that made him doubly dangerous. This killer had sidestepped a SWAT team and executed a young woman, then walked out of a murder scene. He would be walking tall, feeling supercharged and invulnerable.

The two partners went across to the concierge, who was talking to a uniformed cop. Tom wanted to know one thing only. 'How many ways can a guy get out of here?'

'Two ways,' said Marvin. 'Out through the front, or through the service doors, but they're electronically sealed. We don't open them until seven a.m.'

'So this is the only way out?'

'Yeah.'

'And no one saw a thing? Not one of the patrol? There were thirty to forty guys out there. How did he do it?'

The concierge shook his head. 'I ain't the detective.'

Elizabeth Seale's apartment overlooked Central Park. It was a stunning apartment. Worth a fortune. At the door, two uniformed officers stepped aside. They knew Harper from the Romario case and nodded respectfully.

There was something different about this crime scene and Harper was trying to pin it down. Two officers were still there hanging just inside the apartment talking to CSU detectives. The crime scene had been secured and no one had moved the body.

The patrol supervisor nodded across to Eddie. The two detectives walked over.

'You been in yet?' the broad-backed, silver-haired supervisor asked. Both Eddie and Harper nodded. 'We should've protected this girl better,' the big guy sighed.

Harper looked at him directly. 'We tried, we were just too late this time. The truth is, he was probably watching us all arrive as he killed her. Bastard. He was torturing her as we were running around like headless chickens. That was his plan. Kill her with the cops in the building. Another buzz.'

'We'll know more later,' said Eddie, 'but as yet it's as clear as Mississippi mud.'

Harper shuffled past into the living room where Williamson was waiting. It was bad. He felt it. He wished he had something to say.

The supervisor called out, 'Williamson has the reins, Detective. We're waiting on next steps.'

Williamson was staring at Harper. 'I messed this up, Harper. I should've listened.'

Williamson was granite hard and chewed constantly, but his cold grey eyes were full of sadness. Harper shook his head. 'He was playing us, Nate. It made no difference. He knew what he was doing. He knew that there was only one Elizabeth on that resident list. He knew what we would do, too.'

'How did you know my guess wasn't right?'

'He's an obsessive planner, Nate. He wouldn't have dared to do this if she'd moved in two weeks ago. She had to be a phoney.' Harper looked about him, embarrassed with Williamson's awkwardness. Finally he walked away and opened the bedroom door. Garcia was already inside. 'We've got a crime scene to get through. Let's make like it matters.'

The crime scene detectives were combing the scene, taking photographs, sketching and lifting prints. Detective Williamson called to Garcia.

'Anything gives?'

'No, sir, nothing.'

Williamson lowered his head and slipped out the living room. The bureau chief, Ged Rainer, moved through to the bedroom. He was shaking his head as he passed Harper and Eddie at the door.

The two detectives looked at each other. Whoever Elizabeth Seale was, she clearly mattered. The top guys were already there. That's what felt so strange. A crime scene was usually a lonelier place.

'Who is she?' Harper asked Ged Rainer.

'Patty Seale's little girl. The evangelist preacher – Mr Moral Outrage. This is going to be bad. That's all I know.'

Harper felt nervy. The whine and flash of the cameras. The smell of death. Not good when you're already about to puke your guts. And death scenes always smelled of shit. He didn't feel ready for a lungful of putrid air and an eyeful of the grotesque. The things you never forget about a crime scene.

Reluctantly, he led Eddie back into the bedroom. It felt harder second time round.

Elizabeth Seale was lying on her side on the bed, facing the door. It was like a film set in the perfect little room, like some sick fairy tale gone wrong. Her body was full of knife cuts. Harper felt the emotion but he went cold, like you have to. You either go cold or you lose your focus.

He stared at the vision of death. Except it was strange. From the door, her naked body was posed in a carefully arranged S-shape, upper torso upright, her arm modestly over her pudenda. Her mouth was closed in a smile and a black ribbon was tied around her neck. She had a scarf around her hair. It was crimson with a gold design. She looked like she was posing for a painting.

The body shocked you with its nakedness and direct stare. Harper felt as though he was looking at an exhibit in some sinister museum. On the white carpet beside the bed, the girl's clothes were laid out, the dress, the brassiere, the panties, the nylons, the jewellery and the shoes. Each item was perfectly spaced.

Harper couldn't do any more. He needed air. He walked out of the building. On the street, the crowds and the press had all come out. It was a mass of lights and cameras and perverts and people, all there to soak up the gruesome glamour of murder. Harper knew what this killer was doing, all right. He was showing off and this was just the beginning. He had started his show, the lights were bright, the audience was set.

The circus animals were all in town.

Chapter Thirty-Three

The Bronx
November 21, 3.31 a.m.

After the main work was over, Nate Williamson left the scene. He was depressed by the whole thing and wanted to go home and hang his head. The truth was, he had nothing. There was a looming fear in his mind. He'd worked the Romario case dry and left the way open for a slick-looking hero to come in and clean up. If he came up with nothing on this one, with the city in a state of fear and the eyes of the nation on his back, then his whole career would have meant nothing. Retirement was getting closer and closer. Maybe it felt like this to everyone: time came calling and you weren't the man you once were.

Maybe that's all it was, the progression of time. Even so, Nate didn't like it. Every day, the investigation grew more complex and he felt he was failing. He wasn't just failing himself, though – that wasn't the thing that shot him that look of hate he saw in the mirror each morning. He was failing the city. His city. He'd loved her his whole life long. He'd never once moved from the Bronx or wanted to. But now his city was turning her back. He felt it like a personal slight, like a lover saying no, like your own child pushing you away.

That's what was eating Nate Williamson.

It was dark in the drive when he got home. Lillian, his wife, was out in Michigan visiting their daughter so the house was dark and unwelcoming. Nate thought of his daughter, Rose, a large girl with red hair. She always made him smile. She was just like him. Except she was six months pregnant. He was going to be a grandfather. Maybe that new role would save him. Maybe he should throw in the towel before the final round. He would've loved to drive through the night to see them both. He was smiling as he searched his pocket for his keys. The outside porch light had been broken for months. Williamson fumbled for the right key, but he couldn't find it. He took out a small flashlight from his hip pocket and shone it into his hand.

The light hit the ground just by his feet. There was a line of small droplets on the stone. Williamson crouched and looked closer. The droplets were a dark red colour. He dipped his forefinger in one of the drops and then smoothed the liquid between his thumb and forefinger. He held his finger under the light. Blood.

Nate stood up straight and listened. The night was still. The rumble of traffic continued in the background, but closer to home he could hear nothing. He shone the torch to the left and right. The droplets continued to the right along the path that led to the side gate to the back yard. Nate moved towards the gate. Whatever it was, it was hurt. Probably a small animal, by the look of the droplets. There was a small copse behind the houses and sometimes small rodents or cats got injured on the road. But Nate feared something more. His wife's precious cat. The droplets went directly to his front door, suggesting that the animal had tried to get in.

His wife's cat, Emerald, was an eighteen-year-old Exotic Shorthair. She was the laziest cat you ever did see and rarely moved, but she had the kindest nature and a small grumpy face that everyone seemed to love. Lillian doted on the cat and the cat doted on Lillian. If something had happened to Emerald, it was real bad news.

The torchlight shone up towards the wooden gate. It was

ajar, which was unusual, and the drops of blood continued on through the gate and beyond.

The backyard was dark, lit only by a bright, cold moon. The light wind was shaking the tops of the trees. Williamson shone the light across the lawn. At the centre was a small apple tree. The drops of blood carried on across the grass but were harder to detect. Williamson shone his light into the trees at the back of the garden. He felt suddenly alone in his own yard. Then the bright green eyes of a cat lit up in the torchlight.

'Emerald,' he called. He felt his heart warm to the small pudgy face of his wife's pet. She was sitting close to the tree trembling and looking terrified, but she was alive. That's what mattered. Nate strode across the lawn towards her. She might have been in a fight with some local cat who had no idea that Emerald wouldn't raise a paw for a treat let alone to defend herself. She was real class. You even had to take the food out of her bowl to feed her. A true Williamson.

The grass by the tree was thick with leaves. They crunched under his feet. That was another of Nate's failures. He hadn't swept up the fall leaves and now they were heaped all over the yard. 'Come here, baby,' Nate called out but the cat didn't move.

Nate padded round towards the tree trunk. It was very silent, but Nate could hear some creature noises and shuffling in the trees.

He took the final step to reach Emerald. His foot landed on a soft bedding of leaves, almost a small mound – not flattened like the rest. His head had just sensed this as his foot came down through the soft leaves and on to something hard. Not earth, but metal. His foot touched a wide plate.

A low creak rose from the ground followed by a horrifying clash of metal and a sudden snap as a great iron jaw sprang up and butchered his right calf like a shark bite – two huge tooth-filled jaws and a massive force.

The pain was explosive. It sent splinters into every part of his brain – horrific pain as the flesh split and the bone crushed and cracked. Nate buckled, his great weight thrown forward, and his fibula snapped at the weakest point. As his weight was falling, the bone ripped through the front of his shin. Williamson's wild scream echoed along the back yards.

Williamson grabbed onto the tree. Against the pain, he lifted himself and looked up. He was panting. He gazed down at his leg, but was near to passing out.

What the fuck was it? Two great iron jaws clamped fast to his leg. A mantrap? A bear trap? Was this left here by accident? Surely not.

And if not, then what? Against the flood of pain from the injury and his body's own pain-relieving releases, he managed to take out his gun. He searched around. Emerald was a foot away. He scooped her up in his arms and pointed his gun at the trees. In the corner of his eyes he saw lights flicker on in the adjacent houses. His scream had woken them.

'Call the police!' shouted Williamson. 'Call 911!' He turned back to the woods. 'Come out and face me, you coward bastard, whoever you are!' His courage had not faltered. He hid Emerald in the crook of his arm and stared ahead, feeling the surges of pain hit him in sudden waves, over and over.

'Ready to die?' a voice called from the copse.

'Who are you? What the hell do you want?'

'You're a detective. Work it out.'

Williamson had heard enough. He raised his pistol and unleashed two rounds towards the voice. There was silence. Maybe he'd hit the bastard. He looked up. There was a long pause.

Then Williamson heard a strange noise. It was hardly a sound at all. Like a piece of wood twanging on a desktop. A wooden thrum. A moment later, an aluminium bolt thumped into Williamson's chest. He cried out again. The guy had a crossbow. Williamson managed to lift his gun hand and let off another two rounds.

Then he heard a swish of air again and felt the thud of something landing in his thigh. He looked down, shocked. Another bolt was lodged deep in his leg.

'You're a fucking dead man!' Nate screamed. 'You're fucking dead. They know I'm here, so screw you! This place will be crawling with cops.' Williamson fired until his gun was empty, but the rounds zipped into the trees and no one screamed.

Again, the deep thrum of wood and an arrow hit him hard in the stomach. Then another hit his shoulder and threw his upper body backwards. Williamson was almost out. The pain and blood loss were taking his mind away. He was going to die.

Vvv-dumm, sounded the crossbow. The thrumming of the shot echoed across the backs of the houses and the bolt ripped hard into Williamson's arm. He hardly felt it. Then he heard something moving towards him and another bolt hit him in the stomach.

The killer emerged from the shadows, his face illuminated by the white light of the moon. Williamson focused his eyes and furrowed his brow in confusion. He saw the face of his killer silhouetted against a beautiful spread of stars. He opened his mouth to speak, to plead, to talk to this man, but before he could utter a word an arrow entered his brain through the roof of his open mouth.

The American Devil smiled down at his victim. 'You're just not good enough, Detective Williamson. I want a better challenge. I want Tom Harper.'

PART TWO
November 21–24

'In each human heart terror survives
The ravin it has gorged'
P. B. Shelley, *Prometheus Unbound*

Chapter Thirty-Four

East 71st Street
November 21, 10.00 a.m.

Marty Fox wore plaid suits and still smoked, which almost no one else in the world did. He was forty-one, chronically unfaithful to his wife and wanted life just as it was – comfortable. Why he slept around was because he liked it. Why else do people do things? And he liked the sensation of new flesh better than flesh he knew. What was so odd about that? It was a proven fact that new experiences produced more serotonin than habitual ones. Man was hard-wired to go somewhere new for his fun and games, and the truth was Marty was just not strong enough to override the temptation.

Man, Marty maintained, is a primitive beast wearing a civilized coat. At times, the coat must come off or man cannot operate. It was his release valve, that was all.

He'd married his wife some long-ago distant time in the past, for hell's sake. She had been pretty and vivacious. She was a bombshell, as they used to call it in the good old days of black and white TV. All platinum blond hair and squeeze-me tits. He smiled when he thought about her back then. She could excite a man from four hundred paces. Beautiful and dirty with wide hips and a come-to-bed smile.

Yeah, he loved her still. Hell, yes, he did. He stubbed his cigarette out on the back of the packet and watched the smoke twirl in a dying flourish. He felt the scab on his lip with his tongue. It was still cracking every time he moved.

You fall in love with your libido, whatever anyone says. You want the proof? How many young bucks go head-over for an old woman? None. Only with women they want to bed. Is that coincidence or is that just the basic fact?

No one disagreed with him. He was alone in his little office, but he liked to talk to himself. He found himself interesting. He knew that he'd fallen in love with his wife because she was the woman he most wanted to screw. But he didn't fall in love with a 45-year-old woman and that's what he had at home now, while in his own head he was not a day older than twenty-five.

He still wanted to stay married to her, no question. Life was easy and comfortable. Like his job. His motto was: don't succeed, as success brought responsibilities and even more work. Be a nobody and enjoy it. He lived with his wife but just had his fun elsewhere. And anyhow, women liked him. They smiled at him in the street, they giggled when he joked, they had a whole battery of alluring and suggestive looks to make it clear to him how they felt. God knows why. He was an egotistical womanizing pig and he knew it. An old-fashioned tits-and-ass guy. But it was the simplicity they liked. No messing about, no new man tagging along for the emotions and philosophical discussion. He liked them, showed them he wanted them and that was all it took – everyone wants to be wanted, right?

He also had classic good looks and knew how to make a woman howl with pleasure, so they could live with the old-fashioned attitude. When it came to a flat choice between a man who could empathize or a good time, he knew what women chose every time.

His latest affair was a 26-year-old semi-depressive office manager with nice looks, an underused libido, a quiet urban desperation and a need for self-esteem. She was a real annoying date but good in bed. What he called a dilemma-lay. You like the afters but will you sit through the main course?

It was all fine and dandy in the life of Marty Fox. All fine and dandy except for one small fact. And that was that his dear wife had caught him in bed with the office manager.

The thing was, psychologically speaking, his wife had known about his affairs for years, but they existed in some strange shadowland that she could pretend didn't exist. The previous day she had been confronted by the sight of her loving husband slap-bang in between some strange woman's thighs. It was a confrontation with reality that she couldn't ignore.

This was a whole other fucking ball game. No way could she switch off the image in her head or what it released inside her. Pure, red-blooded fury. She'd punched Marty. It was the first time in her life she'd hit anything. His lip split with a dramatic flood of blood. Then she went one better and grabbed the depressed office manager by her hair and threw her out of the house. She pushed her naked into the street and threw her clothes out after her. It wasn't going to help the poor girl's depression or self-esteem a whole lot. Then his wife returned indoors. As Marty nursed his lip in the bathroom, she locked herself in the den and took Marty's rare vinyl jazz records and smashed his entire collection one by one. Marty was outside scratching and pleading at the door as his cherished Art Tatum albums met the 22-ounce hammer.

The day had started nice and ended like a car wreck. All in all, it wasn't a satisfying day. And now his wife had given him the ultimatum he'd dreaded. One more strike and you're out.

He lit another cigarette. Was this as far as he had come in his life? From an overeager sexual teen to an overeager sexual mid-lifer? Maybe Freud was right. Sex was about it, really. All else was footnotes. He was a prize jerk. His wife was the one thing in his life not open to his child-like whims. Without her, he'd fucking die – he knew it.

A buzzer screeched on his desk. He leaned back and pressed the intercom.

'Go ahead, Keren.'

Outside his office, his receptionist smiled up at the tall gentleman in the lobby. He smiled back, nervous and twitchy. She could tell he wasn't used to coming to see a therapist.

'Your ten o'clock, Dr Fox.'

'Well, send him in,' said Marty with a mock Southern accent. He hadn't ever bagged his secretary and now it didn't look as though he would. His world was turning from a land of endless opportunity to a sad landscape of things he couldn't have. There was silence on the other end of the intercom.

Marty stood up. God, he hated clients. He wanted to drown them all. He often sat there listening to their long rambling self-indulgent diatribes imagining terrible fates for them. He pulled Nick's file out of his in-tray and opened it.

'Oh, yeah, Mr Nick *Smith*, the fantasist! Lucky me.'

As a rule, Marty preferred female clients; at least he could distract himself from their tedious problems by imagining some sordid sexual adventure. Not so with Nick with his little domestic issues and his fake surname. The tall gentleman entered. He was wearing a smart black suit. They'd had two previous sessions and were yet to feel comfortable with each other.

'How you been, Nick?'

Nick looked up. 'I've not been feeling so good, Doctor.' He sat down heavily in the leather chair. He fidgeted with his hands as he stared out of the window in silence. It wasn't easy for him to be there at all, really. He felt a sense of betrayal as well as fear, but he wanted to get down to business. He wanted to know what was happening to him. His visions and dreams were so vivid they terrified him. 'Will you sit down, Doctor? I don't know where I am. I'm feeling down and confused. I need your help.'

'I like to float, Nick. I need to keep my mind active.'

'Please *sit down*.'

Marty hadn't heard this tone before. It was different. Military almost. He looked at his client. 'Okay, Nick, you're feeling fragile. That's no problem. I'll sit down for you. So, last week we touched on a problem you felt you have with women. Your wife and you have been having some domestic issues. You want to pick it up at that point?'

'I have a problem respecting women. I know that.'

'I do too, Nick.'

'Not like me,' said Nick.

'I wouldn't be so sure,' smiled Marty.

'I'm very sure, but that's not what I want to talk about.'

The two men looked at each other. Marty decided to let the guy twist himself up in his little world of self-importance if that's what he wanted. The only psychological cure Marty ever really believed in was not taking yourself so goddamn seriously – but his jokes were never appreciated. Clients wanted to know that even the colour of their shit was psychologically relevant and pertinent to their current position in the world. 'Go on, Nick, I'm listening,' he said, smooth as silk.

'I woke up in my car. I'd passed out again like I said happened before. I get this drumming in my head like I'm dying and then I just feel my brain squeezing tighter and tighter. The pain is too much, I guess. It's killing me.'

'You had this checked out with a doctor?'

'You're my doctor.'

'I mean a medical doctor.'

'No. Got no insurance or nothing like that.'

'You have intense pain and then you black out?'

'Yeah. Pain and white lights all across my eyes.'

'How often do you pass out?'

'Been happening for years but it's worse now, I think. I can't remember too well any more. I just don't seem to remember much for long. I really can't. I just feel drained. Look at me.'

Marty looked. Nick's skin was pale and his eyes were

sunken. He looked like he'd had a few rough weeks. 'What started it? Do you remember that?'

'Listen, Doctor, I haven't even told Dee this, but I lost my job. They locked me out of the office, left my things in a box on the sidewalk. A woman was staring from the window. She was wearing pink. I dropped the box on the way to the car. She was laughing.'

'When did this happen?'

'About a month ago.'

'Found nothing else?'

'Not a thing. I've just been wandering around, driving my car, waiting. Then I got into arguments with Dee.'

'What kind?'

'I love Dee. I love my kids, but I wasn't nice to her. I'm so sorry. I was so sorry. I told her about a hundred times, but she still looks at me strange.'

'What happened with Dee?'

'I hurt her, Doctor. I think I really hurt her.'

'Why?'

'I get the feeling she doesn't love me.'

'You feel pretty bad about it?'

'Yeah, then I have to go out and drive and wait. I wait until she's asleep, but sometimes I bring her presents. She likes the presents I bring her. She likes pretty things.'

'You have bad dreams again?'

'I dreamed of Bethany again.'

'Your sister?'

'She wasn't my real sister, Doctor. I was fostered. She was nice to me but I never was part of that family. Bethany was so beautiful, though, she'd make me ache just to look at her. In the dream I was still just a boy.'

'What happened?' said Marty.

'I watched her crossing the meadow again, her little frock blowing in the breeze. I remember that dress so clearly. Strawberry pattern all over it. She was such a perfect thing.'

Marty nodded. His own daughter was fifteen and a money-hungry, promiscuous little rock monster who left condoms on her bedroom floor to show Mom and Dad how mature she was. Still, if purity and innocence was Nick's ideal then yeah, if the archetype works for you, run with it. 'What happened this time?'

'I was being beaten as I watched her. Held upside down and beaten.'

'Who beat you?'

'A man. Her father, I think.'

'What for?'

'Looking at his girl.'

'He didn't like you looking or you looked with your hands?'

Nick stared, fierce and unnerving.

'What did I say?' Marty asked.

'I didn't ever touch her, I told him I didn't. I never did.'

Marty squinted. 'Sure you didn't. I'm just searching around. I need to find out why you're fixated on Bethany.'

Nick rose to his feet. 'Leave her alone. No one touched her. You gotta try to help me.'

'I don't get your problem, Nick. You want to stop the dreams or stop hurting your wife?'

'I want my life back, Doctor Fox.'

Marty paused and looked up. 'How so?'

'I don't know what's happening to me. I'm falling apart. I think about killing her.'

'Your wife?'

'Yeah, Dee. I think about it a lot.'

'You want to kill her?'

'Sometimes I can't think of anything else. Sometimes I see Dee's body all bloody and cut all over the floor.'

'In your dreams, right?'

'Not dreams like that, no. I daydream about it.' Nick paused and stared towards the window. 'But I get excited when I'm imagining it. I'm sick, Doctor. I'm so sick it scares me. I ain't going to go home any more, in case I hurt them. I love them. I love my two kids. I love Dee, but I told her to hide all the knives in the house, put them away so I couldn't get to them. If I find one, I don't know if I can stop myself.'

'She must be frightened.'

'She made me come to see you, Doctor. She's using her savings to pay for these sessions. She says if I don't get better, she'll have to go away.'

There was a pause as Nick let the thoughts fill his mind and float away. 'I've got a little place in my head where I put these bad things, you know. All the blood and all the noise go there.'

'Where do you put them?'

'In a little glass cage inside my head. Where I can't hear them scream and I can't feel their hatred.'

'You're going to have to open that glass cage there, Nick, if you want to get better, you know. Get in touch with those feelings.'

'Don't be stupid, Doctor, you can't open the glass cage. You gotta keep it locked up all the time.'

A cloud passed over the bright sun and the room darkened. 'Why do you think you're dreaming about Bethany?' asked Marty.

'Maybe I was in love with her. She was just about as beautiful as you could imagine. Like a cherub with a beautiful face and golden hair.'

'Did something happen with your sister, Nick?'

'What do you mean?'

'Did anything happen with you and your sister?'

Nick stared coldly at Marty. 'No, nothing happened to my sister. What do you mean?'

Marty Fox poured Nick a glass of water and passed it to him. Nick was staring up at him. 'What's wrong with me? Am I losing my mind?'

Marty put his hand on Nick's shoulder. This poor American

nobody was like a lot of people he saw. Their home lives were degenerating because they hadn't become the people they imagined they would and they started to fall apart, lose their jobs and turn on their families. They were desperate to get some attention, but Nick was worse than most. He seemed close to the edge.

'I can try to help you, Nick. It's good you came. If you keep coming, I can help. Do you think you can do that?'

'I think so,' said Nick, looking up with hopeful grey eyes.

'I know,' said Marty. 'Keep talking, Nick. The talk is good. It helps the brain to process the traumatic details. Let it flow.'

Chapter Thirty-Five

Academy Lecture Hall
November 21, 10.30 a.m.

First thing in the morning, Captain Lafayette got the message out that he wanted to get together the task force and everyone else in the team. He pulled in the detectives from North Manhattan Homicide, all the precinct homicide detectives, the back office staff, everyone involved in the case.

Bringing everyone together unexpectedly brought a locker-room camaraderie to the room. In the large academy lecture hall, the air was thick with jokes, insults and testosterone. They'd managed to keep Williamson's death from the news crews, but that meant that most of the team were still in the dark.

Lafayette walked in. He wasn't looking either solemn or jovial. The deputy commissioner and Ged Rainer walked in by his side. A chorus of whistles went up. This was the main man coming down to see his troops.

Lafayette mounted the platform. He introduced Lenny Elwood and invited him to speak.

'Ladies and gentlemen,' Elwood said, 'a while back, Blue Team took down Eric Romario, one of the most repulsive killers we've seen in this great city. They took him down with perseverance, good old-fashioned police work and great leadership.' He paused. 'Great, great leadership. I'd hoped to come here to encourage you to redouble your efforts to catch the American Devil, but I'm here as the carrier of bad news.'

The lecture hall dropped to silence. Bad news in the NYPD always meant that somebody had died. The teams started looking across their ranks, thinking it might be someone close to them. Lenny Elwood looked left to right, top to bottom, his eyes trying to meet every person in the room.

'Nathan Alexander Williamson, Detective First Grade, North Manhattan Homicide Squad, was found dead early this morning in the back yard of his own home. He'd been murdered. Details are unclear at the moment, but it looks like the American Devil is responsible. He has just made this very personal. But I wanted you to know that Nate died fighting. He was a fighter through and through. Nate leaves behind his wife and daughter. I'm very sorry for you all. It's a terrible thing to lose a great detective, for a family to lose a father and for each of you to lose a friend. My heartfelt condolences.'

Lenny Elwood stepped back from the podium and Ged Rainer moved in close to the mic. 'Detectives and police officers of North Manhattan, your job is one of the most dangerous and demanding there is. Make no mistake, you're all heroes out there, but you've got no superpowers to protect you. When you get shot, you bleed, just like the rest of us; but that only goes to prove what real heroes look like in our day and age. They are not made of iron, they cannot fly, they do not have supernatural strength or amazing powers of recovery. Detective Williamson was an everyday, made-of-flesh hero, just like yourselves. Your job is to protect this great city and keep her from harm, to make America as safe for others as we want it to be for our own children. That is what Detective Williamson spent his life doing. That is what he died doing. Ladies and gentlemen, he gave his life in the line of duty, he died keeping our city safe, I salute him. God bless him and God bless America.'

A round of applause broke out in one corner of the room and

quickly moved through the audience. Captain Lafayette was emotional as he rose to the platform.

'Sorry, guys, that's all we have. We will all miss a cynical old bastard, a good friend and a great cop. Nothing to add. We've got a lot of police work to do to find out what happened. Dismissed.'

Lafayette left a silent hall stunned and confused.

Directly after the briefing, Lafayette called the Blue Team together. He had already told his close associates an hour before the briefing and they'd had time to absorb the horrific truth that the American Devil had gone after one of their own.

Tom Harper was devastated by the news, but he didn't show it to the other guys. The false profile had been his idea. He had forced it through and now Nate Williamson was dead, cut down outside his own home. He looked each of them in the eye solemnly as they listened to Lafayette going through the next steps. Then Lafayette turned to Harper. Harper was feeling bruised by his own guilt, but most of all he felt angry. He'd watched Nate walk away from the scene with his head bowed. He could have gone after him. He stared back at Lafayette.

'Detective Harper, we need you to step up to the plate on this. I want you as the lead. Nate would've wanted it too. I know what you must be feeling, but bottle it. This guy has killed six people, none of which is anybody's fault but his. Listen to me, Harper, I want you to take this bastard down for all of us. What do you say?'

Harper moved his weight from one foot to the other. He wasn't worthy of it. He gritted his teeth and looked up. 'I'll do it if the team wants me to, otherwise you gotta find another guy.'

Lafayette looked around the room, and each member of Blue Team nodded the signal that it was okay by them. 'Okay, I'm in,' said Harper. 'Let's get to work. He's a cop-killer now: we're all targets.'

Chapter Thirty-Six

Blue Team
November 21, 1.00 p.m.

Lead Detective Tom Harper knocked back his fifth cup of strong black coffee. He hadn't slept at all since he walked in on Elizabeth Seale's still-warm corpse and now he didn't want to sleep. Williamson had been dead less than twelve hours and someone needed to focus the investigation. There were so many people involved now, the leads were in danger of getting lost in the mass of detail.

'We can count on this being private until tomorrow morning,' said Harper to Captain Lafayette and Eddie Kasper. 'Then, if she's true to form, Erin Nash will tell the world that the American Devil took out the lead detective.'

'You want us to put the frighteners on her, Tom?' said Eddie.

'I tried that and she doesn't frighten easy. I think I might have even strengthened her resolve. But maybe we could try to get the DA to agree to get her put under surveillance. What do you think, Captain?'

'You want the District Attorney to agree to the NYPD spying on journalists? Are you out of your mind?'

'Look, Captain, did you read her account of Elizabeth Seale's murder? It's just gone up on the website. She's got everything. She knows about the false arrest in the wrong apartment and another piece of information that we only got back from the autopsy this morning.'

'What was that?'

'That the killer took another trophy. Elizabeth Seale's uterus had been removed from the body.'

'I didn't know. How the hell did she get that information?'

'Only Blue Team and the Medical Examiner's office knew that her uterus was taken,' said Harper.

'You think it's someone on the team?' asked Lafayette.

'I'd hate to think that, but where else? And if not, then we've got to pin her source down. Can't you do anything at all, Captain?'

'After what you tried with her, you're lucky we're not facing a lawsuit. Her editor made it clear that he'll run with a harassment and assault suit if Erin gets any more heat.'

'It was self-defence,' said Harper.

'Always is with you, but even if they make the complaint, you're out. You made her untouchable.'

Harper shot looks between them both. 'Look, if the DA won't sanction it, Eddie, how about you see what you can get done unofficially.'

'Will do, boss.'

'And one more thing, Captain. Can you at least get us some peace? Guys are getting hammered as they go in and out of the building. The press have been camping outside since Erin Nash called this guy a serial killer. Now we've got news crews running hourly updates. If I've got a grimace on my face, they'll report it.'

'I can move them away from the building, but it's a free country.'

'Well, get them across the street, at least. Give our guys a chance.'

'I'll see what I can do.'

Harper had been sifting through the files for an hour and he wasn't at all impressed with Williamson's approach to systematic logging and filing of case information. In fact, the dead man's approach stank. Harper could see what was wrong immediately. Due to the speed of the kills, each murder hadn't been fully investigated and the information hadn't been cross-referenced with any of the other victims or even logged centrally. Williamson was leaving too much to chance and old-fashioned thinking. This all meant that they were walking blind through the case, hoping to stumble on something. With Harper in the lead spot, it had to be different.

At 1.15 p.m. Tom Harper called the investigation team together for a briefing. Along with the core members of Blue Team, he had over a hundred detectives working the case, but he only wanted his top people. He had six members of Blue Team, another six members of Manhattan North, four detectives drafted in from Manhattan South, and another six from the precinct detective squads. These experienced homicide detectives made up his core team. Along with his administrative team, there were twenty-five faces looking up at him, all angry and expectant.

'Good morning to you all. I'm Detective Harper and this is Detective Kasper. Nate Williamson was a good cop and he didn't deserve to die. So we've got to nail this creep for Nate. We're here to take down the American Devil, but we're not going to do it unless we're organized. So far, as far as we know, this guy has killed five women in New York and one cop. Around the room, we've got five boards. I'm putting a team of six detectives on each woman. I need their lives fully investigated. We've got another team working Williamson's murder. I want to know everything these women did for the last month of their lives. I want to know every person they spoke to, every phone call they made, every shop they visited. I want a moment-by-moment account with nothing left out. I want to see photographs and names of their boyfriends, dates, family, and friends. I want their computer records searched. I want everything back here. This killer has been interacting with them and he will have left traces.

'So listen up, we will work two systems. The boards for all the visuals and key incidents, people and places. The database for absolutely everything. Every name, number, location and event. We're working six different murders here, gentlemen, and it'll be easy to miss something, but the computer won't. It'll flag up any similarities. Got that? The boards for basic facts, key leads and suspects, the database for everything. All clear?'

The room nodded its approval. Harper continued. 'Secondly, I'm putting three teams, round the clock, to respond to information from the public. I don't want to be swamped by this shit and I don't want to miss anything. Again, all names, numbers, details logged and cross-referenced to crime scene details – if anyone is authentic it should flag it up. We meet every day to give a brief report, we see what the computer flags up and we see if anything on the boards throws up an idea. We haven't been doing the ground work, gentlemen, and it's not good enough. He's one man, we're many. We've got over a thousand hours a day of detective time pouring into this case, so let's not waste any of it.

'And one more thing. We're getting serious heat from One PP and I don't want anyone, and that means anyone, talking to the press. Someone is briefing Erin Nash and it's ripping big holes in our investigation. They're hyping this up enough as it is. I trust you, so be trustworthy. Now, let's go to.'

'Amen!' shouted Kasper and the room laughed in response.

Harper dismissed the detectives to set up their teams and then started calling in the advisers he'd identified as necessary. First he called the FBI at the New York field office and asked for two special agents to join the task force and offer advice. As far as Harper could see, they needed every bit of help they could get.

By the end of his first few hours in the lead spot, Harper returned with Kasper to find the boards were already filling up. They had three full-time administrative staff and it was finally beginning to look like a serious operation.

Harper looked at the photographs of the five female victims. They had a lot of overkill and they were all posed. He looked slowly at each in turn: Mary-Jane Samuelson with her legs apart in the hallway of her own home; Grace Frazer, hands together, on the rocks off Ward's Island; Amy Lloyd-Gardner posed like an angel in an underground parking lot; Jessica Pascal posed like Christ in the doorway of her apartment; and Elizabeth Seale posed like a nude in a painting on her own bed.

Each of the victims had their most recent photograph next to their crime scene shots. They looked undeniably similar. All had the same blond hair, but more interestingly they all had similar features. It took a while for Harper to see, but there was definitely a 'look' the killer went for. They all had long hair and thin, angular faces. And, of course, they were all very rich and very beautiful. But it was more than that. Harper called Eddie to his side.

'What do you think? It must take him quite a while to find the particular type,' he said.

Eddie moved over to the boards. 'Yeah. Rich, blonde and – well, if I saw them in a club, I'd call them stuck-up. No, not even that. They've got a quality to them. I don't know. Innocent. Not ones I'd pick out for a one-night stand.'

Their eyes fell from the five bright smiling faces to the corpses. It was a terrible contrast. Harper's eyes scanned across the women in quick succession. The horror jumped right out, but so did something else. The five corpses were sexual to different degrees.

The victims, Elizabeth Seale, Jessica Pascal, and Amy Lloyd-Gardner were posed with their genitals covered; the others were posed pornographically. Kasper put it a lot more plainly. 'Open legs, shut legs.'

Harper jumped down his throat. 'Okay, I like the jokes, but do some thinking too. Why are they like that?'

Kasper looked again at the corpses. 'Some got him hot, some didn't.'

'Try harder,' said Harper.

'I don't know, Tom, that's not my area.'

Harper paced up and down in front of the boards. 'Maybe he thought some were whores, some were angels. Maybe it depends on how they responded to him. It's still a feature that we can't explain, so we ought to look into it.'

'I'll put it on the list for the briefing,' said Eddie.

Harper thought about calling Denise Levene. He picked up the phone and then put it down. He needed clarity. He'd think through this himself.

Thirty minutes later, after reaching no conclusions whatsoever, he called Levene directly. He admitted to himself that he didn't know what the symbols meant. Maybe this was Levene's area. He heard her voice on the line. They hadn't spoken since Nate's death.

'How is it going up there?' she asked. 'I wanted to call. I didn't know if I should.'

'Well, it's been hard, but we're all focusing on the investigation. It's all we can do.'

Denise held her breath for a moment. 'I'm sorry, Tom.'

'We're all sorry.'

'My profile backfired, badly. I don't know what to say.'

'It wasn't the profile, Denise. This guy had been stalking Nate for a good few days. We've got eyewitnesses.'

'You sure?'

'Don't beat yourself up. The killer wanted to show us what he's capable of.'

'I thought it was my fault.'

'Well, you can't take the credit this time.'

'You shouldn't joke.'

'What else can I do? No time for feeling. I've got to cut to the chase here.'

'Fire away. What you got?'

Harper gathered his thoughts. 'Our killer is a compulsive sexual predator, right? We've just got the crime scene photos of all five women in front of us. Amy, Elizabeth and Jessica are posed with their genitals covered, but Grace and Mary-Jane are posed explicitly. What do you think? Anything might help.'

Denise thought for a moment. 'It's a difficult one to call, Tom. Research says that if a killer poses them graphically and hides or mutilates their faces, then it's likely that he knows the victim. Hiding the face and exposing the genitals is an act of depersonalizing the victim and, some say, blaming her.'

'What about the other type?'

'Well, the other type suggests that he doesn't know them, so they aren't personal to him.'

'Can I conclude from what you're saying that this killer might have known Mary-Jane and Grace?'

'Well, it's possible.'

'But that's important. That's real important. How would he know them?'

'It's possible, if – as you say – the killer is stalking these women, that they are women he knows and has become obsessed by. Sometimes killers start with people they know. Then they move on to the unknowns.'

'Okay, Denise, that's a great help. We need to have a look at that. What the hell kind of job might this guy have to meet this kind of woman?'

'Might not be his job. Maybe he knows them socially?'

'What, like this guy is an upper-class madman?'

'I don't know, Tom, but it could be anything, that's all.'

'We'll follow it up.'

'I'll try to work up some ideas.'

Harper nodded. 'Keep thinking, Denise. We've got until tomorrow. If he's keeping to his two-day cycle, then we're expecting another body to show up.' He put the phone down, his head spinning.

'What she say?' said Kasper.

'Maybe the killer knew the first three victims.'

'Okay, that's worth a look,' said Kasper. 'We need to cross-reference every place they come into contact with others and see if there're any points of connection.'

'Exactly. Let the teams working Mary-Jane, Grace and Amy know about this.'

Eddie shrugged. 'Will do, Harps. And listen, we've already got news coming in from the teams. You want the headlines?'

'Sure, run it.'

'They found out that Elizabeth Seale was drinking in the Fullerton Lounge yesterday. We got a pretty firm memory from the bartender that she was talking to a man in the bar before she met a friend. The bartender said the guy hit on her so he didn't know her. The guy drank a Black Russian, wore a black suit. He was also good-looking with a touch of grey hair. It could be him.'

'Just like he did with Jessica Pascal. So let's say Denise is right and he knew the first three, then ran out of victims or maybe he tried to date the next two and that changed things for him. He likes to interact with them. He gets a buzz out of it.' Harper went across to the board. 'Listen, Eddie, we need to know where he got to meet these three women, which might be where he's scoping the next victims. We need to find out where he does his stalking.'

Chapter Thirty-Seven

The Frick
November 21, 4.30 p.m.

Across town, after the day shift, Tom met Denise at the Frick. He wasn't sure whether she thought he was uncultured and needed an injection of art or whether she was keen to pick his brains about the job.

Walking the east side of Central Park in the fall dusk was a pleasure anyway. The wealth of New York had lined these avenues with grand houses, beautiful gardens and a peacefulness that you couldn't often find in the city.

The Frick was a New York treasure. A beautiful house that was now a museum and art gallery. Harper stood around staring at the visitors, trying to guess at their lives. It was hard to know. Creative types, rich types, students – people who didn't do nine to five or shift work to make ends meet.

Denise arrived in a yellow cab. She was dressed in a long black coat with her fair hair loose about her shoulders.

'You not tried dyeing your hair like the rest of New York?' asked Harper. He'd read that morning that New Yorkers had given up being blonde since news of the killings had come out. Everyone was turning brunette.

'Mine's natural and I like not being taken seriously.'

Harper laughed. 'What's the idea with the museum?'

211

'I was thinking about things. Thinking about Williamson's murder.'

'I was going over it myself. It's cruel.'

'Then I remembered something. Something I want to show you.'

They talked low as they went into the museum. It was quiet and hushed inside the beautifully ornate rooms. It was obvious that Denise spent some of her spare time in the Frick, as she moved purposefully through the rooms to one in particular.

'Here,' she said. 'See if you can spot it.'

Harper looked around the room. Lots of pictures hung closely together. Harper didn't know what he was looking for, so he moved slowly from picture to picture. Denise watched him closely. She was comfortable with Harper. He had a rare commodity: he didn't interfere, he let you be. It was just a quality he had and it was something she liked about him.

Suddenly, Harper shouted out, 'Fuck!'

A guard took a step into the room and hushed him severely. Harper apologized. He turned to Denise. 'Is this why you brought me here?'

She nodded and moved over to his shoulder. They stared together at the picture.

A classical figure, muscled and toned, tied to a tree, stripped naked except for a loincloth. His face was turned upward towards the sky, his eyes transfixed in pain and hope.

Harper's eyes dropped down his body. The first arrow went through his neck, there were two in his chest and another in his shoulder. His stomach was peppered with three and then one in his thigh.

'You think the guy who killed Williamson was an art connoisseur?'

'Dunno,' said Denise. 'I count seven arrows and I don't like coincidences.'

'You think there's a connection?'

'Read the label.'

Harper read the title and sucked in his breath. Sebastian was the name the American Devil gave himself on the phone. 'You think he was making a reference?'

'I think that an arrow is a strange way to kill someone.'

'Good work, Denise. But what does it mean? You think he's into art?'

'He killed Williamson as if he was a martyred saint, he posed Elizabeth Seale like a nude. Amy and Jessica might reference paintings we don't recognize.'

'It's worth looking into,' said Harper. 'If your idea is right and he knew the first three girls better than Jessica and Amy, then this might be something. We need to check up on their interest in art.'

They stood there shoulder to shoulder, staring at the Renaissance images of the martyred saint.

'What's the significance of St Sebastian?' said Harper after a while.

'His motto is *Beauty constant under torture*. Our killer thinks he's a martyr. He thinks he's the one who suffers most of all.'

Chapter Thirty-Eight

Dr Levene's Apartment
November 22, 6.00 a.m.

Denise was woken at 6 a.m. by a persistent knocking at the door. She was dreaming of a prairie. A huge open prairie. Her father was visible but only at a distance. He was calling something that she couldn't understand. As she squinted into the sunlight to discern what he was saying, his image zoomed with frightening suddenness and she could see that he was calling her name and sinking into the ground.

'Denise, Denise, Denise.'

Her eyes opened. Her left arm moved out to her bedside cabinet and hit Daniel as she flicked the switch. A low orange glow lit a corner of the room. Daniel groaned and shrugged. Fahrenheit was lying flat out across the foot of the bed and hadn't stirred. A great guard dog he'd turned out to be. Denise got up and stood in a vest and shorts, on the carpet. She could hear the voice at her door now. It was difficult to discern, but her name was being repeated in a loud whisper.

'Denise, Denise, Denise.'

At her door, she took the red towelling robe and put it on. She wasn't afraid for her safety. How could she be? Her man was asleep in the bedroom and her guard dog was slumbering beside him.

As she reached the narrow corridor that led from her living

room to the apartment door, she thought she recognized the voice.

She relaxed. Who else would it be? The door opened and she looked down at the crouching figure of Tom Harper calling through the keyhole. Behind her, Fahrenheit appeared around the door of the bedroom, walked across and stared quizzically at Tom.

Tom saw Denise's legs first, a glimpse of her smooth tanned thigh between the ruby of her gown. He looked up. Her hair was forward on her face, messy from sleep. She had a cross look on her face.

'Are you having a crisis?' she asked.

'No.'

'You want to come in?'

'Sure.'

Denise turned and walked to the kitchen, leaving Tom to stand and enter by himself. He watched her walk. She was more graceful without her heels, a softer, slightly longer stride – more confident. Then his eyes looked around her apartment. Her office was a temple of order, this was not – clothes and bags and shoes lay all over the room.

'I've heard this happens to some therapists,' she said, a coffee pot in one hand. 'You know, guys getting fixated, calling after hours for a chat. I didn't figure you for the type, but if you need me, you need me.'

'I need you,' said Tom, watching her closely. He liked her off-duty attitude.

Denise nodded, but decided not to follow it. 'How did you get in?' she asked. 'And while you're there, how did you know where I lived?'

Tom shrugged.

'You're a cop, right.'

He nodded.

'So, you like Colombian or Ethiopian?'

'I'll leave the decision to you.'

'Very wise, Detective. I care about my coffee.'

Tom watched her take a small steel scoop and extract some bright brown beans from a jar. She whizzed them in a grinder, then filled her espresso machine with the grind. She was on automatic the whole time. Her eyes were hardly open. In her living room, there was a collection of framed photographs on the sideboard. He picked one up. A lanky guy with a cheesy smile had his arm draped around her shoulder. He was in several of the pictures, but one particular photograph had a spot in the centre. It was a picture of a rugged-looking man with a little girl on his knee. She was smiling like a sunbeam and so was he.

'I get all my beans from a specialist delicatessen in Little Italy. I recommend a visit,' Denise called through. She appeared with the coffee. 'I guess this isn't social, so what's up?'

'I've been working through the night. This killer's working a two-day cycle, which means that today he strikes again. Some poor blonde woke up this morning and she won't go to sleep tonight.'

'That's quite a burden to carry.'

'Erin Nash still won't speak. Eddie saw her yesterday. She knew all about Elizabeth Seale. She knew he took her uterus. No one knew that. You read it?'

'Yeah, course I did. Horrible. She said nothing?'

'Not a thing. Says she just has a good source. If it's one of my own team!'

'You don't know that.'

'There just aren't that many people who know the details. You know he posed Elizabeth like a painting. Like the painting on the wall of Jessica Pascal's apartment. A nude. She looked beautiful from the front. He'd kept her all nice there, but behind, yeah, he'd gone to work.'

'Calm down, Tom.'

'Nate's death has got to us all. After that picture in the Frick, I've been trying to track down any art links with the victims.

Ten hours solid and nothing. It's not art. Sorry. I'm wired.'

'Yeah, me too.'

'Listen, I've been thinking all night. Going over the fiasco at the Laker Building. The killer knew what we were up to, he knew it was a set-up and he set us up. Made fools of us. But he had Williamson's home scoped already. He was seen parked in his road twice in the past week. I think he was going to kill Nate anyway.'

'And now you're the lead detective. You thinking that he's after you?'

'I don't know.'

'Maybe he went for Nate because he thought he wasn't high-profile enough.'

'Yeah, I thought of that.'

'I guess he wants to prove he's the best. Or maybe he wants you all to know you're not invulnerable.'

'The one thing that keeps coming up in my mind is the fact that you knew how he'd react. You were able to predict his behaviour. No one else has got close to this guy, but you got him. I know he played us, but you got him to speak to us. How the hell did you do that?'

'I trained in psychology; you know that.'

'No, this was special. You were able to think like him, think how he felt. Where did you learn to think like a killer?'

Denise shuffled in her seat. 'My research meant I spent time interviewing killers. I went to training sessions at Quantico. I picked it up.'

Harper looked at her suspiciously. 'I don't believe you. There's more, isn't there? I've been to those training sessions with the FBI and I couldn't have predicted his behaviour like you did.'

'It was a lucky shot.'

'Bullshit.' Tom looked into her eyes. 'I'm sorry to call so early, but if we can't track down how these women knew the killer then we need to work out where he stalks his victims.

I want to do a reconstruction. I want to run through the murder at the Elizabeth Seale crime scene and I need you there. I need that talented head of yours. You might see something everyone else has missed. What do you think? Might help? Would you?'

Denise's eyes widened. 'Get out of here, Tom.'

'Come on. I need some fresh thoughts. You predicted his behaviour. You understand him. I'll keep you safe. It'll be okay.'

'Visiting a murdered girl's apartment at dawn with a cop I'm supposed to be treating – are you kidding?'

The door to the bedroom opened and Daniel walked in. 'Lot of commotion for six a.m. Are we in trouble?'

'Sorry,' said Denise. 'We'll try to keep it down.'

'Is that coffee I smell?'

'Yeah. I'll get you some. This is Detective Harper, North Manhattan Homicide. Tom, this is Daniel Mercer.'

'Morning,' said Tom. 'I'm sorry I disturbed you.'

Denise walked through to the kitchen to fetch the coffee. Daniel stood looking at Harper. 'My girlfriend under arrest, Detective?'

'No.'

'Early for a house call, isn't it?'

'Yeah.'

'You're talkative, aren't you?'

'I'm on police business, sir. Got nothing to say.'

'What do you want with Denise? She's a psychotherapist, not a cop.'

'It's confidential business, sir. I can't say.'

Denise arrived back with the coffee. 'Daniel, we're kind of in the middle of something. Would you give us a minute?'

'Sure, but it all sounds very secretive to me. Hope you're not getting in too deep, Denise.'

'Hey, if I wanted a handler, I'd be wearing a collar.'

Daniel took his coffee and left the room. Harper looked

across to Denise. 'I'm sorry, I didn't know you had someone here. I'll go. I'm just not thinking straight. My apologies.'

'What about your reconstruction?'

'I can go through it alone. We can talk later.'

'You think I can help?'

'It might make the difference.'

'It's a long shot,' she said, breathing in the aroma of her coffee. 'I've never even been to a crime scene.'

'It's worth a shot, isn't it?'

'And what do I do?'

'You're the victim.'

'Oh, that's just terrific. I'm typecast on my first case.'

'I'm not much good in heels. And I need to walk in his shoes a while. I got to feel this guy think. But don't feel you ought to.'

'Don't you worry about me. I'm coming,' Denise said. 'But no weird shit. Give me ten minutes.' She drank the espresso down in one.

Chapter Thirty-Nine

The Laker Building
November 22, 6.48 a.m.

Denise and Tom drove over to the Laker Building in silence. Daniel had not been in a good mood when she went back into the bedroom to dress, but she just ignored it. It was the only way to deal with his unfounded jealousy. She put on her jacket, and then, as an afterthought, took a little photograph of her father and put it in her pocket. He'd come with her. She might need some moral support.

There were reasons why Denise knew the criminal mind and it wasn't from anything she'd learned at Quantico. Throughout her childhood, she had come to know the inside of a prison well. She had come to know about the dangerous criminals who inhabited the same strange rooms as her father. He told her the stories. No lies from her old man. He told his little girl, straight. Never romance or euphemism. He pointed them out – the rapists, the murderers, the child molesters he did time with. He told her what they'd done, why they'd done it and what they were like. He told her that's why they were locked up. Her father had told her everything she ever needed to know about the criminal mind from behind a perspex screen.

He also told her that he never meant to kill Albert Mack and she believed him. He told her he regretted it every day, but you had to live with your mistakes.

Her mother was long gone by the time Denise got to know her father. The little girl lived with a collection of relatives in a small tenement building. It was not bad. It was limited, sure, they had nothing, but they were good people, all of them. And they looked after her.

When Denise Levene got a scholarship to university, she was the pride of her family. Her old man cried for the first time in his adult life. It was the only time they'd ever got sentimental with each other and it didn't last long. Cancer was burrowing up through his gut by then and he only had a year to live.

So Denise was left with a legacy. She was not afraid of criminals or their mental states. She was fascinated by the darkness that took those lives and destroyed them. She was just about brilliant enough to end up at Quantico, but her family's criminal background meant that she didn't get through the first round of interviews.

But you pick yourself up and try again. And then again and then again. And that was her philosophy: get off your knees.

She looked across at Harper, firmly gripping the wheel. She could see from his eyes, his attitude, that he could easily have been on the other side – some maverick, hard-ass criminal. She thought he maybe saw something in her too. Some basic recognition. You know it when you meet someone who's actually lived. You see it. You just have to look down a little to catch it. People with scuffed knees.

They arrived at Elizabeth Seale's apartment just before 6.50 a.m. Harper's police shield got him through the doors, and Marvin was still sitting on the desk.

Tom flicked on the lights. Denise was feeling her heart beat heavily in her chest. 'Kind of spooky to think the poor girl came in like this and was dead an hour later.'

'Medical report says he kept her breathing for as long as he could. He sat there and held a plastic bag round her neck until she nearly died, then he opened up the bag. Over and over again, just playing with her life like it's some toy.' Tom walked further into the apartment. 'I like to do reconstructions. Run through the scene, see if it brings anything to light.'

Denise looked around. The apartment was cold. It already had the feel of an abandoned place. She shrugged. 'What do I do?'

'I'll hide in the wardrobe, just like he was. You come in, put your bag down. Come into the bedroom.'

'Got it. Then you kill me, right? It's just like a first date.'

Tom nodded and went into the bedroom. He moved inside the wardrobe. The chair that the killer had used was still there. Tom sat down. He tried to calm his breathing. It was definitely spooky. He could see through the thin gap between the wardrobe doors. A thin line of light. This was how the killer had seen his victim. This was where he sat, excited and demonic. What was he doing in the wardrobe? Was he daydreaming? Anticipating? Thinking of how he was going to kill her?

Denise went outside the apartment. Half of her was thinking, what the hell am I doing? Still, if it might help, she was willing to try it. She wondered if the hardnosed Detective Harper was just plain old-fashioned lonely and needed a good excuse for company. She suspected that he was.

She re-entered Elizabeth Seale's apartment, but this time she was on her own. She looked into the dark and silent room and switched on the lights. She felt the apprehension that Elizabeth Seale would not have felt and tried to act casual. She did what she would've done, which was to toss her bag on the polished mahogany side table in the small hallway. Elizabeth was probably a lot more refined. She probably had a handbag storage system. Denise shivered. She shouldn't make light of it. Poor Elizabeth Seale had no idea that there was a killer lurking in her home. A killer who had been tracking her movements for months, who was waiting in the shadows, waiting not only to kill her but to slowly torture her to death.

'Perhaps he was taking things from his victims for months,'

she called out. Harper heard her but didn't reply. The silence made Denise feel doubly scared. Suddenly she felt really alone.

'Tom!' she said quietly, trying to stop her hand shaking. Pretending to be a murder victim was just plain wrong in every way. She felt the fear soak through her. She knew it was irrational, but she felt it just the same. A thin line of perspiration formed on her upper lip. Her skin was tingling, her pulse drumming a fast beat. The room was still cordoned off and sealed. In the early morning, it was an eerie place to be.

'Bastard,' she mouthed as she walked through the living room and kicked off her shoes. She then walked into the bedroom. 'Okay, I'm in the bedroom.' Still no reply from the guy in the closet, who was taking this way too seriously. It wasn't nice. Not long ago, in this very room, the American Devil had been waiting in the wardrobe with a seven-inch blade and a plastic bag. He'd killed Elizabeth slowly, slit open her side, taken out her uterus and probably photographed her in all kinds of poses.

Denise shivered. Her eyes were on the wardrobe. On the bed, she saw that Tom had placed a dress. She walked over and looked at it. Then, from behind, she heard the door of the wardrobe creak open. She turned quickly.

For a moment, it was not Tom coming out of the wardrobe but a stranger in the shadows and her heart thumped. 'Tom,' she called out. There was no answer. He was staring hard, trying to feel the killer's movements.

'Tom, you're scaring the fuck out of me, you shit!'

'Shut up. I'm concentrating. The killer approaches the victim. She freezes and he shows her his knife. He tells her not to cry out or he'll hurt her. She asks him what he wants. She says she can get him anything he wants. He shakes his head. Nothing is knocked over, so I guess she doesn't run. He walks over. He's holding the knife. Then he takes hold of her.'

Tom walked over to Denise. He suddenly realized that she

wasn't joking. Her hands were shaking. He pulled up and smiled. 'Are you all right?' he said.

'I'm okay. But, no, I don't like it. I don't like it. Why did he do that to her? In here. God. She was alone and terrified and there was nothing she could do. How can anyone put someone through that?'

Tom moved forward. He put his arms round Denise and she let herself fall against his body. 'It's just like you say in your theories,' he said. 'He desires them as objects, but doesn't see them as people. Are you okay?' Just a second more, she thought, resting her head on his shoulder. It felt safe against his chest, with his arms around her. And then she felt herself resenting her own weakness and pushed him away from her.

'We've got to catch him out, Tom. What can we do?'

Tom put his hands in his pockets. 'We'll forget the reconstruction. I'll go through it on my own. I'm sorry. Let's look around. How about that?' Denise stared at him. Something she didn't understand yet. Was it intimacy Tom didn't like? Or was he being sensitive?

'He scopes them for a long time. That's got to leave some tracks. Look at this place. Open her wardrobe.'

Denise walked to the wardrobe and opened it. Tom stood where the killer had stood and looked out of the window. The city was just waking up.

'She's got a lot of clothes,' Denise called. The walk-in wardrobe was expansive, with racks of outfits and shoes.

'Yeah,' Tom confirmed. 'She was a big shopper.'

Denise came back. 'What does it mean?'

'Maybe he likes well-dressed women. Maybe he likes clothes. Maybe all rich women shop a lot.'

Denise looked around. 'Maybe he finds these women at the upmarket stores.'

Tom looked up. 'That might go somewhere. If we want to find this killer, we've got to find out where he stalks them. What's the link? We're guessing he's after rich blondes. So he finds one. He follows her. He seems intrigued. We found Amy Lloyd-Gardner's SUV; the new clothes she'd just bought from Madison Avenue were missing.'

'Take a look at Elizabeth's shoe collection,' said Denise.

Tom walked to the wardrobe. It was neat and organized, in colours and styles. The shoes had their own little shelves and there were upwards of a hundred pairs. Tom looked at the shoes. There were spaces on the shelves where two pairs were missing. One, no doubt, was the pair she died in, but the other pair? Had he taken them?

'Denise, take a look here. Why would she be missing two pairs of shoes? One pair she was wearing, but the others, how does that work?'

Denise stared into the wardrobe for a moment. 'He fetishizes objects, maybe shoes too. Maybe he took them. They all take little reminders, don't they?'

'Yeah, but a second pair of shoes is strange. We ought to go back to the other murders and see if any clothes were missing. We wouldn't have spotted this if she wasn't so organized.'

Tom looked again and noticed a bright chiffon scarf hanging with several others. He called Denise over and pulled it off the hanger. It was crimson with a gold design. Very distinctive.

'What do you make of this, Denise?'

'Silk scarf. What of it?'

'Elizabeth Seale had a scarf wrapped round her head. Just like this. I'll have to check it, but I'd say it was identical. This is a pretty distinctive design.'

'So what are you saying, Tom?'

'Elizabeth had this scarf around her head. Exact same design.'

Denise just stared. 'She had two scarves. She's a woman, she's got a hundred pairs of shoes.'

'How many pairs of shoes the same?'

Denise took a few seconds to look. 'None.'

'Expensive scarves. You don't buy two of them, do you?'

'Maybe one was a gift.'

'Maybe,' said Tom.

Denise clicked. 'Or maybe, he doesn't just follow the women. Maybe he's doing more than just following.'

'That's right. We've got evidence from every victim now that showed he was either stalking or interacting, but this is different.'

'Okay,' said Denise. 'Let's say he's scoping his target, getting closer, but he's not quite ready to go the next step and talk to her or touch her, so what does he do? He breaks in like he did with Mary-Jane or he starts to buy the same things that they buy. You know, mimicking them and taking the same item home. It could have a kind of totem value to him.'

'Psychologically, is that possible? That buying the same thing could give him a buzz?'

'Yeah. I think so. Imagine it, he's watched her for a few days. He follows her into a store, sees her buy something, then he goes up and buys the same thing. He's walking right behind her with the same item that she has. It's a kind of weird way of connecting.'

'Very weird,' said Tom.

'You're not getting it, are you? Listen, he bought the scarf, Tom. He bought the scarf, brought it to her apartment and strangled her with it.' She trailed off.

Harper let the idea travel once round his mind, then he nodded. 'Yes, I get it. I think you're right. I think he did buy it. That means we've got a potential point of contact. We need to find out where she bought this. But why does he do it? What's he after, Denise?'

'Intimacy,' said Denise and held Tom's stare. They both suddenly got it.

'We've got to hunt the stalker, not the killer,' said Tom 'And now we know where he's been stalking. The killer is very careful. But maybe the stalker isn't.'

226

Chapter Forty

Dr Fox's Office
November 22, 11.00 a.m.

Nick looked up at the cream ceiling of Dr Fox's office and closed his eyes. He'd been sitting opposite his psychoanalyst for just under an hour and was feeling no better. He'd spilled his sick nightmares all over Marty's lap but that just left him feeling confused and angry. He looked across at Marty with wide eyes.

Marty was drumming on his desk. Nick hadn't answered his question so he repeated it. 'How often do you dream about hurting people, Nick?'

Nick had felt bad for so long, he'd forgotten what feeling normal was like. He didn't enjoy the dreams, no question about it. He wasn't himself. The thing was to keep tight. When the feelings came on him, he had to concentrate real hard, but he was scared. He looked up at Marty. 'The thing is, Doctor, I think maybe there's a devil in us all, wanting to get out there and destroy, you know. My wife, Dee, she says I'm possessed some-times.' Nick turned his eyes to the psychologist. They were rimmed with red. He had a real strange look to him sometimes. 'It doesn't feel like I've got a lot of control left. I used to be able to stop it, you know, hold it off.'

'Hold what off, Nick?'

'The pain in my head. I used to be able to run clear through it. Now it just continues until I just . . . I can't stop it any more.'

'Then what happens?'

'I told you. I can't remember what happens next. I black out. I wake up and I don't know what I've been doing. I don't know where I am. Sometimes, I'm wet all over. My clothes, you know, are dripping wet like I've been standing in a shower. What am I?'

'I don't know, Nick, you've got to tell me.'

'I sometimes find things in my car.'

'What kind of things?'

Nick turned away from Marty. 'Can I tell you?'

'Sure you can tell me.'

'I won't get into trouble?'

'I can't tell anyone anything, Nick. Not a thing.'

'Sometimes I find things I must've stolen.'

'Like what?'

'Jewellery, clothes, shoes. Money sometimes.'

'Where do they come from?'

'I'm some sick bastard, aren't I? Ever since I lost my job, I've been blacking out and stealing things. Haven't I, Doctor?'

'I don't know.'

'Well, where in the hell do these things come from?'

Nick's right hand slipped into his trouser pocket and pulled out a necklace. He held it up. A small silver crucifix studded with diamonds glinted in the light. 'I found it yesterday. Along with over a thousand dollars in cash. I'm burglarizing people, aren't I?'

Marty picked the necklace from Nick's hand and held it up. 'Looks expensive.'

'I know I'm doing something, Doctor. Sometimes, I got scratches on my face and hands. Is it possible to rob people like that? What am I, some monster? But I don't remember any of it. Only sometimes I see the inside of people's cars or apartments. I guess that's where I must steal these things.'

Marty Fox wrote *Dissociative Identity Disorder* on his pad.

This guy was a potential multiple personality. Memory loss. Flashbacks. It was possible Nick had invented an alter ego. A man who gave an outlet to whatever Nick couldn't face about himself. From Nick's dreams, Marty guessed that this alter ego stole what he could and maybe stalked women and even mugged them. He didn't know. This was beyond his expertise. He leaned in to Nick and spoke as quietly as he could.

'You're confused, Nick. Listen, it is possible that you're suffering some kind of split personality. Sometimes a traumatic event can trigger things off, and the mind creates these alternative personalities to protect you from whatever is too difficult for you to see.' Nick stared ahead. 'You ever have a traumatic time, Nick, somewhere in the past?'

'I was in love once, Doctor.'

Marty's eyes glanced down at the personal column. He had been searching the dating ads. He couldn't act on them any more, but he still couldn't help himself looking. Then he looked up. 'I like love stories, Nick – who was she?'

Nick twisted his body in his seat. 'My first love. I was only a boy. I knew her as a friend, you know. I was a real quiet one back then. She didn't love me, Doctor. I loved her from a distance.'

'All sounds pretty normal to me, Nick. She was hot, was she?'

'Like a perfect doll. But she was untouchable.'

'So what happened with this girl?'

'I wanted her so badly, it drove me crazy. She was just a kid, but then she started growing up herself. I couldn't take seeing her with other boys.'

'You were jealous?'

'I'd say I was pretty jealous. I watched from a distance but kept it all tucked deep inside. See, she was a goddess to me. Nothing in my life was pure and perfect, Doctor. But she was.'

'Not easy when you're smitten.'

'I knew the day would come. I'm not stupid. I knew that she

would flower and the insects would come and feed on her. Have you ever seen how insects crawl over beautiful blossoms? I knew it would with her. I watched and things happened inside me. I couldn't bear it.'

'Did she date someone else, Nick?'

Nick lowered his eyes. Marty was intrigued. He liked a little *je ne sais quoi* in his sessions.

'Someone took her. A young man who didn't really care about her.'

'What happened?'

'On a summer day, he took her to the local spot. He charmed her. She was reluctant and scared. They were walking in the valley and I was following on the ridge above. Then he pressed her to the ground, kissing her. His hands started to touch her. All inside and out and where you shouldn't. I watched like I was behind glass. He touched her. She called out for him to stop but he didn't. He wouldn't. He lifted her skirt and he put his hand right inside her skirt. She cried out "No". She screamed it. She said "No" over and over but he said, "You want to make me happy, don't you?" I wanted to help her. I couldn't move. Why couldn't I move, Doctor?'

'Why do you think you couldn't move, Nick?'

'I was paralysed on the spot like some dumb staring animal. They wouldn't call it rape, Doctor, but it was rape. It was . . .'

'What?'

'After that, I couldn't sleep. I went off the rails.'

Marty Fox liked the story. Girl and boy making out in the grass with a fierce rival staring from the ridge. The girl gets a little hands-off when it starts looking serious. Yeah, he got that story. It was a TV movie kind of story. Marty imagined it easily. Except he didn't identify with the boy on the ridge. He identified with the boy with his hands inside the girl's jeans. That's where he was in the story, not with the loser. He looked at Nick.

'The boy who raped her, Nick. Was that you?'

Nick turned his head suddenly. 'Me? I was watching. How could it be me?'

'Sometimes, we do things we regret. Bad things. Sometimes, we get confused over what happened because we feel so damn guilty. Sometimes we build great big barriers and when we look at the situation again, we don't really know what happened.'

'I loved her. I didn't do that. I didn't ever do that to her.'

'Okay, let's calm down. Why don't we talk about processing these past events. There are details there that need drawing out. I think we need closure on the girl.'

Nick was clenching his fists and staring down at his feet. 'What would you do, Marty? Someone killed the girl you loved?'

'He didn't kill her, Nick.'

'He did kill her, Doctor. God, I miss her. When they die, you don't half miss them.'

Marty looked at his patient. He was shaking and holding himself. It was time to refer him. Marty didn't like serious problems and this one was beginning to feel outside his comfort zone. He drew two red lines under the session notes and wrote a note to his PA: *Transfer to Dr Bartholomew with immediate effect.*

Chapter Forty-One

Upper East Side
November 22, 12.12 p.m.

The first full freeze hit the city and coated it in a fine grainy dust. It was Thanksgiving and no one felt like celebrating. The trees and street furniture were already filling up with Christmas lights all down the avenues and the shop fronts grew brighter each day. New York looked like a child's toy sparkling with colour and light.

Harper returned home at 8 a.m. and slept for a few hours. He woke from dreams he couldn't remember and chose to walk down towards Madison Avenue via the meer. He had a bagful of bird seed and a growing sense that he was finally getting somewhere. The birds were skating around on the surface of the frozen lake, looking confused and lost, as if waiting for someone to come and put their world right. Harper took a handful of seed and tossed it across to the stranded ducks. In the frosted branches of the trees, the blackbirds and finches looked on with interest. Harper wandered around the circumference, breathing in the chill air and crunching the icy blades of grass beneath his feet.

He recalled that Lisa had never really liked Central Park. He sensed that she was just uncomfortable in places where people's actions weren't predetermined. She liked order. A cop's life was anything but, it was reactive and random. It must've driven her half mad. Tom realized that it was the first thought about Lisa for nearly two days. It seemed a good sign. He looked out at the frozen landscape. There were times when he could've never imagined letting go of her. The connection had been too deep, but now, somehow, she was starting to fade away.

He threw the last few handfuls of seeds to the birds and made his way down through the centre of the park. It was so beautiful and peaceful that his pace slowed. At around 82nd Street he peeled off and joined Madison Avenue just above the Museum of Modern Art. After the reconstruction with Denise, he'd hit the precinct and given the task of finding the shop which sold the two gold and crimson Vivienne Laurec scarves to the two FBI agents. By the time he woke up just after 11.30 a.m., they'd called. They had found the right store. It was simple, they said, but Harper didn't mind them showing off their skills.

Two Vivienne Laurec scarves seemed such a flimsy and weightless hook to hang an entire murder investigation on, but it was all he had. There was still, in his analytical mind, a nagging doubt about the scarves and he couldn't quite understand why he was less than a hundred per cent about what they were telling him. Maybe it felt too easy.

The team was focused more than ever after Williamson's murder. Whatever the captain had tried with the media, it hadn't worked. Around the precinct, there was an hourly barrage of questions from a seemingly endless stream of newspaper journalists and TV reporters. The story was being drip-fed emotion daily with new stories from the families of the bereaved, new theories about the poems and the posed corpses. There were websites and blogs dedicated to the killer and everything about him. Whoever this killer was, Harper guessed that this was all part of his need.

Asa Shelton and Isaac Spencer, the two special agents from the FBI's New York field office, had spent a couple of hours talking to distributors for Vivienne Laurec, then they got through to Vivienne Laurec itself. The scarf Harper had taken from Elizabeth Seale's apartment had its own identity code, and once they had sent this over to Vivienne Laurec's head office the company could give the Feds the life story of the scarf, from production through distribution to sale. They not only knew the store, they knew when the scarf had arrived and when it had sold.

Harper called Denise to let her know and arrived at the store about ten minutes later than he'd arranged. Denise Levene was standing at the window admiring the luxury goods. Inside the store, the two special agents were already talking to the young sales girl at the counter. Harper crossed and took up the questioning. The girl confirmed within minutes that they had sold that particular scarf. She took out the store records, which were still written down by hand in a large ledger before they were logged on the database.

'So what's in the big book?' said Harper.

The girl leafed slowly though the pages. 'Okay, I've got five sold this month. The gold and crimson only came in at the end of October, so that's the whole story. Five sales.'

'Do you have names down there?'

'Yes, sir, they all leave their names,' she said, and smiled. 'That's what we do at a store like ours.'

'Well, I'll know where to come next time I've got a hundred to spare.'

She smiled thinly and read out the names. The fourth name was male.

'Bingo,' said Harper as the name John Sebastian was read out. 'Okay, let me check I've got this right. On November 17, Elizabeth Seale buys a crimson and gold scarf. She pays with a credit card. Right?'

'Yes, sir.'

'Then, on the same day, a "John Sebastian" comes in. What does he pay with?'

'It was a cash purchase.'

'No records, right.'

'No.'

'What do you think, boys?'

Asa Shelton and Isaac Spencer both nodded. 'We'll check the name, but he's not going to pay with cash just to leave his real name. Obviously Sebastian is some kind of alias.'

'You remember the cash buyer?' asked Harper.

The sales girl nodded. 'Yeah, pretty much. It was only a few days ago. People don't use cash any more, so he made a joke about it. Said his wife checked his credit card bills so he had to use cash for presents and affairs. I didn't laugh. Why would I? Affairs aren't that funny. He had glasses, greying a little. He had a nice smile, but he was a bit intense.'

Harper clenched his fist. They had something. The killer had purchased the Vivienne Laurec scarf the same day Elizabeth had bought hers – the sales girls had seen him. Then he had killed her with it.

It was unravelling. The killer had made a mistake. They always did at some point. He'd not been able to resist. He'd stepped off the path. He'd thought himself clever enough to get away with it. He'd coveted her possessions. And for Harper it meant that there were now two links to the stores on Madison Avenue. First with Amy Lloyd-Gardner and now with Elizabeth Seale. He needed more precise information, but he was beginning to see where the killer stalked his victims and that would give him a chance to set a trap. He looked at Denise.

'I think you've got something,' she said.

'Yeah, I got something, but it's gone midday already, and he could be on his way to kill any time now.'

Chapter Forty-Two

Blue Team
November 22, 3.00 p.m.

Harper went direct from Madison Avenue to Captain Lafayette. He pushed open the glass door and stood there in the doorway.

'I can see that look on your face, Harper. What is it?'

Harper sat down on the one chair facing the desk and looked across at Lafayette. 'We think he's going to kill again. If he's working a two-day cycle, then it's going to be today. We can't just sit on our hands.'

'What are you suggesting?'

'I want you to throw every officer you can on to the Upper East Side. I want to saturate the place. I want to see uniforms on every street corner. I want to make it look like there isn't a square inch over there that we're not watching.'

'Shit, Harper, that's a big ask. Overtime city. How we going to sell that?'

'Tell City Hall that it's got two benefits. The first is that we look like we're doing something and it'll give people a little peace of mind. The second is, there's a chance it will spook him and put him off his stride. It might just save someone's life.'

Lafayette picked up the phone. 'OK. Let me see what I can do.'

The new information about the scarf had caused a surge of

optimism and activity at Blue Team. The two federal agents, Shelton and Spencer, had already been painstakingly piecing together the movements of the women, Mary-Jane, Grace, Amy, Jessica and Elizabeth, in the last months of their lives. Using the information gathered by the team regarding cell phones and credit cards, they were able to plot an intricate and detailed picture of the women's movements.

From the victims' bank details and phone records alone, they could create a pretty good idea of what they were doing on any one day. There were garage receipts showing when they parked, café, shop and restaurant receipts showing where they'd been, and phone records showing who they had called. Putting it all together, along with statements from their friends and families, the Feds produced a document that showed their movements at almost every hour of their last two months.

Harper gathered Blue Team together to listen to the special agents' report. Despite the recent developments, it was still sombre in the windowless investigation room and the ominous blue board with the stark and chilling pictures of the dead sat as a reminder of the need to break through.

They listened intently to the geographical profile of the victims' movements. Spencer and Shelton stood up front and talked through their findings in a slow, methodical fashion, showing such impressive attention to detail that Blue Team was ready to give them a standing ovation.

As they concluded, Asa Shelton moved to the front spot. 'Gentlemen, the point of all our investigation is this. We now have a geo-profile of the victims. We know that your killer was stalking them in the weeks before they died. We know, for instance, that the killer watched Elizabeth Seale buy a Vivienne Laurec scarf and then purchased an identical one which he used to decorate her dead body. We know that he watched her go into the Fullerton Lounge on at least one occasion because he knew where she was going to sit and placed himself right beside her.

'What we have here, therefore, is not only their movements, but, somewhere, the movements of the killer. The question we have to ask ourselves is this: what is the pattern here? Where is he most at home stalking?'

Asa clicked the small control in his hand and the next slide flew in. It was a close-up of Madison Avenue. 'These spots, highlighted in red, are the intersections of movement of three of the five women. A killer like the American Devil will probably have different phases. In the trolling phase, the killer will visit places he is likely to see victims to his taste. Trolling is a fishing term: the killer is sitting in his boat with the net out, seeing what comes his way. Now, while it's possible that a killer will come across a victim in a place that they don't usually frequent, it's more likely that he'll spot them in a place they and he go to repeatedly. You all follow? If we plotted your geo-profile, about ninety-five per cent of your movements within a set period would be repetitions. It's likely, therefore, that the trolling spot is also the place where he stalks. Now, even if, as Detective Harper suggests, our killer knew victims one through three, it makes no difference. We want to know where he stalks so we can set a trap. Our best bet, therefore, is public locations that these women visited frequently. So, for Amy Lloyd-Gardner, we've got Madison Avenue. She was a shopper through and through. Jessica Pascal went to two places most frequently, the Baptist church and the campus at Columbia University, but she walked home via Madison Avenue. We'd suggest the Baptist church is not a good trolling area, although he certainly stalked her there, so with her we red-spot Columbia and Madison. Elizabeth Seale has the widest geo-profile. She's all over the city, but she was, on three occasions, on Madison Avenue. Her most frequent spot, though, was the airport, LaGuardia. Grace was at LaGuardia four times and also at a shop on Park Avenue, just around the corner from Madison. Even Mary-Jane travelled via LaGuardia once. See the two red spots? Madison and LaGuardia. It may be, gentlemen, that this is a map of your killer's trolling and stalking zones.'

He continued. 'We also came up with something interesting. The Triborough Bridge toll road that runs through Ward's Island connects in the north to the Major Deegan Freeway, which takes you up to the Bronx, and in the south to Grand Central Parkway, which takes you direct to LaGuardia. The east side of Manhattan is only a few minutes' ride. That's the killer's stretch of road.'

'That's interesting, guys. That's great work,' said Harper. 'Did you find any place they might have met the same employees? We're guessing that the first three knew him through his work. Is there anything to connect them?'

'Not a single place. Every victim in the last month visited numerous clothes stores, coffee shops, hairdressers and beauticians, but we know which stores they went into and there's no crossover at all. Unless the killer himself moves between these stores.'

'Is that possible?'

'Well, we can look into it, Detective, but it'll take a little time.'

'Do that. That's good. So what do we do with this information?'

'Given our two points of fixed information, the proximity to his primary route and the crossover of victims, I'd suggest we set up observation posts at Madison Avenue and LaGuardia.'

'Stakeout?' said Kasper. 'In New York City? At LaGuardia Airport? In Madison Avenue on Thanksgiving?'

'Yes, sir.'

'How the fuck are we going to find a nondescript man like that? He's clever; we don't know if he's going to show. It'll be like searching for a snake in a snakepit.'

'Any action we take that might find this killer is likely to be high-risk, labour-intensive and painstaking,' said Harper. 'I think we've got to do it.'

It felt like something. Harper went straight back up to see

Captain Lafayette. Lafayette smiled. 'They went for it, Harper. And they want you to get out there and brief the press. They won't saturate the area, but they've given us an extra forty patrolmen, so it's going to feel different.'

'That's great, Captain. Let's hope it works, but I need you to make another call.'

'Shit, Harper, what now?'

'We got his stalking areas outlined and we want to put up a full surveillance operation on the two red dots on the map – Madison and LaGuardia.'

Lafayette stared across, trying to judge the seriousness of Harper's suggestion, but Harper didn't blink. 'Jesus. Set it up, Harper. But set it up with the manpower you've got. I'm not asking for more men. We've got to have something to show before we call in another favour.'

'That's fine. We've got the capacity. I'll go ahead.'

Harper left Lafayette's office feeling good. He looked at his watch. Time was running short and putting together an operation like this would take at least twenty-four hours. He had a hell of a lot of work to do. He just hoped to God that something would interrupt the killer's cycle in time.

Chapter Forty-Three

Marty Fox's Office
November 23, 12.15 p.m.

Marty Fox was already late and the elevator seemed to be stuck on the sixteenth. He looked up, rolling his shoulders back as he felt the clammy sweat on his silk shirt. He shouldn't have run. Rushing through the crowds in a cashmere overcoat really could crease a nice shirt. He was thinking about dollar signs on his credit card bill and how he was going to transfer a thousand bucks without his wife's persistent questions. He'd park the car two streets away on his way home and tell her it was in for a service. The idea pleased him, and he suddenly looked happier. He had promised his wife that he would never have another affair, but it hadn't quite worked yet. Some temptations were once-in-a-lifetime and Joanna Anderson was one of them.

He knew he had spent too much money on impressing Joanna Anderson with a first-date lunch. Over four hundred bucks for a piece of poultry with some salty sauce and no fries. Still, French cuisine impressed women; no wonder it was so expensive. Joanna was a rich man's mistress and looked like it. Hell, he knew she was a totally economically unviable fuck. He could maybe afford getting one night out of her, but he'd have to make it a memorable one. After that, the till was closed and he knew a burger joint wouldn't spring Joanna's locks. She was about eight levels out of his league.

The elevator finally arrived and a family of four identical overweight individuals in velour tracksuits came out, all holding hands. Marty thought that family therapy should be deemed illegal as a matter of course. Nothing worse for a family than a psychologist. He was standing in the lift, his back to the shining fake gold interior, when he saw Nick Smith striding towards him. Marty felt uncomfortable. He'd taken Nick off his books and not even told him. He always preferred the coward's way. Nick put out his hand to hold the door, and entered the lift. He looked at Marty but didn't speak.

The doors shut and the lift started to climb. Finally, Marty couldn't bear it any more. 'Hey, Nick, I passed you to Dr Bartholomew because he's trained in DID. It's a specialist area and I'm worried I can't help you. He's a great doctor.'

Nick remained silent.

'Are you going to see Dr B. now, Nick?'

Nick shook his head. 'I'm coming to see you, Dr Fox. You're my doctor.'

'That's not possible, Nick, I've transferred your file. I've spoken to Dr Bartholomew. It's all set up.'

'I'd prefer to stick with you, thanks,' said Nick.

'You don't quite understand. I'm not willing to treat you. I can't help.'

'You are helping, Dr Fox. I rang your PA and got her to transfer me back over to you. I told her it was a mistake. She was happy to oblige.'

Marty was open-mouthed as the two men stood side by side, waiting for the lift door to open on Marty's floor. Marty decided that small talk with a guy like Nick was pointless and might as well wait for the couch where at least he got paid for it. He looked down, and his eyes focused on Nick's black leather shoes. They were covered in mud. He looked up to his hand. It was shaking.

In the office, Marty pulled off his coat and watched Nick prowl around the room. He was going to throttle his fucking PA as soon as he got a spare moment. He turned to his unwelcome client. 'You want to take the weight off your feet there, Nick?'

'I don't feel good,' said Nick.

He didn't look good, either. His face was pale, his body was shaking more obviously and Marty could see panic in his eyes.

'Calm yourself down, Nick. It's a panic attack. It's not real. Let me get you a glass of water. Just sit down.'

But Nick wasn't listening. He was shaking and shivering more violently now. His eyes were staring ahead, fixed on some point in the distance. Marty went across and put a hand on his shoulder. 'Sit, my friend.'

Nick cried out as the pain in his head increased. Marty sprang back, frightened, and looked around his office as if there might be someone there to help. Nick started to crouch down, wailing, his head swaying. Marty wanted to run out of there. This guy was seriously strange.

Nick continued to shake for a few more seconds, more and more violently. His eyes closed and he squeezed his fists hard against his temples until, after a minute, the shaking subsided and his body went still. Marty walked over and sat next to him on the floor. He felt for his pulse. It was still high and erratic. 'What just happened?'

The patient opened his eyes and stared at Marty. His stare was cold and intense. 'He tries to stop me, Doctor. He tries all the time. I know what he wants. He wants me to leave the girls alone.'

'What are you talking about, Nick? What girls?'

He turned his head sideways and his eyes rested on Marty's. 'They used to call it demonic possession, Doctor.'

Marty got up from the floor and moved back. 'You seem all right now, Nick. Speak to me. You went into a fit. Are you okay? Is this how the DID comes on? Should I call emergency?'

He smiled. *'My name is Legion, for we are many.* Isn't that how the old book goes?'

'Yeah, I'm sure it is. Listen, I'd like to be able to help you,

Nick, but I'm not sure I can. You got to explain to me what just happened.' Marty Fox was at his desk. He wanted to be close to the phone in case anything else erupted. He imagined living with this man, this poor broken specimen, torn apart by his own demons. He imagined what the man's wife must be going through. He suddenly thought of his own wife and felt a pang of guilt.

'Can I have another drink of water?'

Fox moved across to the water cooler. 'Sure, sure. So what just happened? Can you go through it?'

Suddenly, Nick pulled his legs close together and rested his forehead on his knees. 'I don't know if I can tell you.'

Marty Fox handed him a glass of ice-cold mineral water. Nick sipped slowly and stared up at him.

'Sure you can tell me, why not? Come on, Nick, that was some weird shit.'

'I think I hurt people,' he said.

Marty sat down, feeling the power of his patient's gaze. 'How do you know?'

'I was trying to explain it to you in the last session. It's not my fault, I can't control it. I wake up sometimes and I find blood on my hands. I can't say any more.'

'I won't tell anyone else, you know. Physician-patient privilege, Nick. I can't tell anyone. We've got a confidentiality and liability clause.' Marty was trying to figure out if Nick was just deluded or whether something serious had happened. It was difficult to tell.

'I'm afraid, you know that? I'm afraid of what I'm going to do. I'm afraid of what I've done.'

'What do you mean?'

'That girl I told you about. You remember her?'

'Yes, I do.'

There was an awkward silence. Nick started to push his cuticles back. 'The girl in the dell,' he said, 'the one I loved, Chloe.'

'Yes?'

'Her name was Chloe Mestella. She was found dead.'

'Dead?'

'Yes. A week after I saw her in the dell.'

'What was it? Automobile accident?'

'No, Marty, she was cut to pieces in her own bed.'

Marty's face went pale.

'Someone got into her house after dark and raped her and killed her.'

Marty was trying to work out what was going on. His arm twitched. He put it on his desk to steady himself.

'Her heart was missing. It was a gruesome thing to happen to a young girl.'

'I don't know the case—'

'When someone dies, Doctor,' Nick went on, putting his arms tight around his own waist, 'you truly miss them. You truly miss them. It's like nothing else, the way you miss them.'

'It's okay. You're safe here,' said Marty. The beeper on his desk went off and Nick looked up automatically.

'I want to know if you can stop it,' said Nick. 'Is it possible?'

'What?'

'That I killed her? That I killed Chloe?'

'No, Nick, that's just the guilt. You feel responsible. It doesn't mean you did it.'

'I can't take much more.'

'I can't stop the delusions, Nick, but maybe I can help to find their source. We have to find out what you're feeling so guilty about.'

'I think he's after someone else,' Nick said. 'I want to stop him before he hurts her.'

'Who is he? What's he after?'

'I don't know. But on my phone there're photographs. Lots of photographs. She's blonde. I don't know who she is.' Nick

245

pulled out his phone and pressed a couple of buttons. He held up a picture of a beautiful, rich-looking girl outside a shop.

'It doesn't mean anything,' said Marty. 'It's just a photograph.'

'Why did he take it?'

'I don't know, Nick. I don't know.'

Nick stood up. 'I'll tell you why. I'll damn well tell you why. She looks like Chloe, that's why. She's looks the spitting image of Chloe.'

Chapter Forty-Four

Madison Avenue
November 23, 12.42 p.m.

Since 3 p.m. the previous day, Harper had been busting everyone's gut trying to get the operation up and running. There were many upscale stores on Madison Avenue on the Upper East Side, but the victims had made purchases at only four of the stores. They were all big, fancy names – shops where a handbag would set you back near enough a thousand dollars.

Harper made contact with the department chief of the Technical Assistance Response Unit. They needed the best support for a covert operation of this size and TARU had the capabilities. It was a difficult set-up. First, they didn't know who they were looking for, and second they didn't know if the killer would show up. Pattern killers worked in heat cycles. The American Devil had killed five women in quick succession, but he might have been stalking them for weeks or even longer. No one knew his range or the duration of his stalking.

There were two composite images of the killer. Both agreed that he was in his thirties or early forties and had a good smile and grey hair. The killer might be disguised, but the one thing in their favour was that he was a man and not many men visited Prada, Versace, Christian Louboutin or Jimmy Choo.

Harper set up seven teams with three mobile units sited

between the stores around Madison Avenue and Park Avenue. Each team consisted of a female undercover cop and a support officer. Harper put Mark Garcia in charge of the other stakeout. Garcia set up three teams around Arrivals at LaGuardia and headed the operation at the airport. TARU's mobile trucks could beam any video images right back to HQ.

In the precinct, there was plenty of interest in spending time pretending to shop on Madison Avenue, but Harper didn't want a bunch of low-salaried cops scaring the killer away, so he brought in some advisers. They worked with the cops on the kind of look they needed and the kind of attitude that would help them not to stand out.

Up in the main investigation room, at eleven o'clock the previous evening, Harper had stood looking at his teams. Seven cops looking severely out of place in designer outfits and heels. He was pleased. The advisers had done a great job. Kasper stood at the side and nodded his cynical approval.

The operation was ready to get going at 12.30 p.m., and Harper and Kasper drove to where a white van was parked in the heart of the Upper East Side. Inside, Ali Maakam, the technical supervisor, nodded a hello and showed them the control centre. There was a bank of nine screens. Ali flicked a row of switches on the console and the monitors flickered into life.

'As requested, Detective Harper, we've got seven mobile CCTV units covering the streets. At the moment, they're focusing on the store entrances. Each unit can be contacted here. Just press the button and let them know what you want. They can trace individuals, zoom, or move location.'

'That's great, Ali, thanks.'

'Well, I hope you find something. This is a bad one. We all want to see him taken down.'

Ali took his seat at the far end of the truck and took out a newspaper. Harper and Kasper looked at him. 'It's all about waiting, guys. This could be a long haul.'

A quiet rap on the door preceded the entrance of Captain Lafayette. He huffed his bulk up into the van. 'You move quickly, Harper. I just hope you know what you're doing.'

'We're watching, that's all. If he comes we'll see him, if he doesn't, we won't.'

'It's Zen policing, Captain,' said Eddie. 'Harper's got this new world philosophy and we're gonna really try to pick up any negative karma.'

'Does he never get tired?' said Lafayette to Harper.

'Not yet, he hasn't.'

'We should get us some orange robes, Captain. Imagine the NYPD patrolling like that, offering blessing and talking youngsters out of crime. You think City Hall would go for it?'

'You know, Kasper, the problem is, I think they might.'

Harper laughed, then looked up at Lafayette. 'No kills yesterday? Looks like the extra patrols worked.'

'Sure, they worked on the Upper East Side.'

'Meaning what?'

'Meaning, we took a lot of men out of East Harlem. We found a body this morning. Some poor hooker by the look of her. You plug one hole and another opens up somewhere else.'

'No one told me.'

'This isn't one of yours.'

'How was she killed?'

'We only just got the call. She was found in a dumpster.'

'I should take a look. Maybe he got put off the Upper East Side by the extra cops and headed north.'

'You just sit tight down here. If there's anything to report, you'll know about it.' Lafayette patted Harper's shoulder, said his goodbyes and headed back to the precinct.

'What do you think, Eddie?' said Harper, staring at the feeds from the CCTV.

'About the homicide? Not his style, dumping a hooker.'

'Just the right day, that's what's bugging me. No kills on the Upper East Side. Maybe he couldn't get to his target. Maybe he wandered uptown feeling hungry.'

'It's possible. Anything's possible.'

'I don't know.' Harper took out his cell phone and called Denise Levene. 'Guess who?'

'I should be on your payroll, Harper,' said Denise.

'Listen, last night there was a kill up in East Harlem.'

'He's struck again?'

'We don't think so. I just heard about it, but it looks like a prostitute was murdered. Look, Denise, is there any way a guy like this could change victim type?'

'Difficult to say. We don't know this guy's capabilities. He killed Williamson. He might have killed before. I can't say. Tell me more about it.'

'Got nothing more. Just a body in a dumpster.'

'It's your call, Harper. I can't be certain.'

'I want to take a look,' said Harper. 'Can you get up to Madison?'

'Sure. I'll be thirty minutes.'

Harper hung up and turned to Eddie. 'I'm going to shoot up to the crime scene. You hold the fort here.'

'No problem. Watching TV is my specialist area.'

Tom waited outside the van. The sidewalks bustled with shoppers jostling for space in their thick coats. It was almost impossible for the Blue Team to keep an eye on everyone and Harper hoped the stakeout wasn't going to be an expensive waste of time.

Denise Levene pulled up twenty-five minutes after the call. She'd been working up a profile of the killer and was keen to share it with Harper. As a starting point, she had reduced the profile to seven characteristics. She could've given more detail but Harper had insisted that the only words he could share with the team had to be as hard as facts.

Harper was getting bustled around the crowds of rich shoppers as he headed for her car. Blue Team was just up and running at LaGuardia and Madison and the cops weren't yet feeling the cold. But they would soon, after working all through Thanksgiving and spending hour after hour standing on the street in the ice staring at Christmas presents they couldn't afford.

They transferred to Harper's Buick and drove back up through the forgotten streets of Harlem. Harper was going over the case in his mind and feeling the adrenalin kick of anticipation.

'You said you know a thing or two about this killer. Why don't you take me through it,' he said.

'Okay, but I can do without the cynicism. This is my first attempt.'

'I know you're a rookie, that's why I trust you. You don't know what it feels like to be wrong yet.'

'Well, that's a vote of confidence I could do without.'

'Hey, look,' said Harper, 'I've not been suspended once since I started your treatment.'

'Yeah, and don't think I haven't noticed that we're doing a lot of case work and nothing on you.'

'I'm healed. You work quick. Take it as a compliment.'

'Yeah, well, don't compliment me, just listen to me. I think I've got seven incontrovertible facts about the killer. You want to hear them?'

'Sure, go ahead.'

'He's white, mid-thirties, married, high school educated, self-controlled, and works in a sales or marketing job with some background in police or military work.'

Harper listened to the brief summary and then nodded. 'I hope you're right. I'll share it with the team.'

'You don't want to ask questions?'

'I figured this guy had a stable background, or at least something that appears stable on the surface. If not, he would've been found out years ago.' He turned to her. 'How are you feeling about this?'

'More curious than scared, I think,' said Levene.

'Well, just hang back. A corpse can hang on your retina for a long time. Some stay for years.'

'Yeah, I'll do that. Thanks for the warning.'

They arrived at the near-deserted street in East Harlem and got out of the car, seeing the first officer slowly tying off a parking lot and talking into his shortwave. It was a quiet crime scene, with no traffic around – just a dirty street of unused warehouses and old abandoned shops. They could hear the pervasive roar of traffic and the echoing shouts of distant arguments, but here it was still and silent. There were a couple of detectives on the scene and a single crime scene officer.

'What's the story?' asked Harper as he approached the detectives.

'Nothing, yet. Precinct got a call about a body in a municipal dumpster, so we showed up.'

'Who called?'

'No name. Just gave us the location. Patrol came by about two hours ago, had a look and called us in. Might be a gangbanger, a shooting or some crack whore sleeping off her debts for the rest of eternity. Who knows?'

Tom took a look around. This was a real quiet one. Someone getting rid of a body quickly. No showmanship, wealth or extravagance like they'd been dealing with on the Upper East Side. This body was hidden. It wasn't the American Devil's style at all.

Denise leaned forward. 'What's your feeling, Tom?'

Tom shrugged his shoulders and shook his head. 'It's nothing like the others. The killer always left the naked body visible. He likes to show, to shock. This is off his track, too. I don't know. Maybe it's got nothing to do with him. Just another sad life coming to an end.'

He didn't want to go over to the dumpster and look at the

252

body. He breathed deeply as he took a step forward towards the crime scene detective in her whites.

'Detective Harper, Homicide. What have you got?'

She didn't look up. There was an expression of fierce concentration on her face.

'Can't see much. Strangled by the look of it. Raped, probably – at least, her pants and jeans are round her ankles. It's difficult to tell.'

It wasn't the answer Harper wanted. The American Devil raped and strangled his victims. Tom just wanted to be sure he could strike this one from his list. 'Can I take a look?'

'You want bad dreams? Go ahead.'

Tom walked over to the side of the big steel dumpster and looked in. The woman in white handed him a torch.

The beam of light caught the flat, smooth skin of the girl's stomach. Tom passed the light over the rest of her body. A poor young life thrown out with the trash. He didn't want Denise to see it. How can you look at the destruction that human hands can wreak and show it to someone else? That's why cops got cynical. You had to keep it to yourself. Crime scenes were usually peopled by those who had been desensitized, and together they created a community of objective observers that protected everyone at the scene. Seeing Denise at the edge of the lot made him realize it was a good thing to keep outsiders away. They bring emotions and emotions create cracks in your own defences.

It brutalizes you, no doubt about it. You see things that take you down notch by notch until all you see around you is the human animal – an aggressive and dangerous beast.

Harper went over to Denise and took her to one side. He told her not to look.

'What did you see? At least tell me.' Her hand gripped his arm.

'Caucasian female. Late teens. Bruising on the neck. Half undressed. Not a lot else.'

'A sad end,' said Denise. Then her mind started working. 'Why did you think it might be him?'

Harper walked with her to the edge of the car park. He looked up at the grey fall sky splintered with dark slashes of storm clouds and wished he had faith in something. 'I just can't put my finger on it. But I don't like the similarities.'

'It's not his signature, is it?'

'No. It doesn't look like it. It's not his ritual. We'll wait for the DNA analysis, see what this looks like. But he might change his style. He took out Williamson with arrows. He's capable of anything.'

'What's your gut say?'

'It's telling me that I'm hungry.'

'Mine too.'

Harper moved Denise across the parking lot as a CSU van pulled up. His eyes scanned the graffiti tags all over the dumpster as he passed by. 'There's no posing, no poem,' he said, 'but I want to look around a little more.'

Harper put Denise in a patrol car and sent her back to her car on Madison, while he watched the team arrive at the scene. Was it his elusive serial killer? He couldn't tell. If it was, he'd suddenly taken a different approach. That didn't help. Patterns caught killers.

Harper spent an hour walking around the scene trying to figure out what had happened. They should be able to ID her pretty quickly on the street if she was a hooker.

The car park was covered in a thin layer of sand and dust. He looked all over it, but there weren't any car tracks at all. It was strange. How do you hump a dead body around one of the most populated cities in the world without getting seen? Then he saw something that could easily have been overlooked. Leading up to the dumpster were two small tracks about ten inches apart. Harper knelt by the tracks. A small trolley of some kind? He called the CSU detective across and asked her to get the tracks mapped and photographed.

As Harper was walking back to his car, he spotted something else so small that it might easily have been missed. Something on the ground in the dirt, caught in the wet along with the trash. Harper crossed and knelt by the kerb. He pulled on a latex glove and then reached down into the gutter and picked the thing up carefully between his thumb and forefinger. He put it to his eye and turned it. He knew what it was. It was a single pale pink petal. Harper felt the hairs on his neck prickle. Cherry blossom.

He scrambled to his feet and called Captain Lafayette. He was about to give him the whole scenario, but Lafayette broke in real fast. 'Save it and get your ass back here. I'm watching the Madison Avenue feeds and I think we got ourselves a situation developing. We've got a high-heeled blonde and some guy in a black suit is following her.'

Chapter Forty-Five

Madison Avenue
November 23, 2.33 p.m.

On the Upper East Side, Kitty Hunyardi entered Lush & Low on East 67th Street. It was her weekly appointment. A salesman was blocking the entrance as he tried to get to speak to the manager. Kitty tutted loudly until he moved his large case out of the way. She moved across and sat in her favourite leather chair without speaking to anyone, placed her Gucci lizard clutch bag on her lap and clicked her bright blue snakeskin Mary Janes on the chrome foot rail. She had only to wait a few seconds before Antonio appeared behind her, his hands on her head, letting her long blond hair fall through his fingers.

The salesman turned and stared at her. It was hard not to. Kitty was the beautiful twenty-three-year-old daughter of some dead line of Hungarian aristocracy. Her family had lost its title in the forties, but they had emigrated and invested in rubber. And rubber had come good.

Across the street, a man in a black suit with grey hair stared in at the salon. Kitty didn't notice him at first. He was just part of the background, part of the noise that she needn't bother herself about. But there was something about him that caused her to turn and look.

As she did so he turned and walked away. Kitty had noticed some guy a couple of times now. She thought she was being followed. The night before, someone had been overly interested in her in a cocktail bar. She was sure that the same guy followed her outside and tried to get his hand in her bag as she waited for a cab in the road, but a couple of cops had been close and the guy just walked by. A week earlier, someone had been waiting around near her apartment. The first time, she'd just let it go, but now it was three times and Kitty was superstitious. She didn't like threes. Especially not if it meant someone was stalking her.

Kitty's instinctive reaction was that it was her father's protectiveness again. The man in the suit was probably hired to look out for her, make sure she walked in safety at all times.

But he wasn't quite like the bodyguards she'd known before and bodyguards didn't swoop in so close you could smell their cologne. What was it about him? When a guy won't let go of you with his eyes? That was it. He stared at her. She could feel it. Drilling into her. Anger? Hatred? Something that just felt wrong.

Kitty left the salon forty minutes later with her hair trimmed and blow-dried. She looked up and down the street but the black-suited man was nowhere to be seen. She looked at her diamond-encrusted watch, checked her lips in the window of the salon and walked across the street to Madison Avenue. She was due at her mother's in an hour, enough time to see if anything caught her eye.

Kitty walked up Madison, her eyes fixed ahead, her long legs moving with practised precision and her mind far away in some fantasy land of her own making. She always imagined that the paparazzi were trailing her and she acted with the exaggerated gestures and look of disdain she'd seen in so many magazines. Only Kitty Hunyardi wasn't famous. Not yet, anyhow. She'd talked to her PR firm that morning and they'd found a producer willing to give her a meeting. It was the first step. That's all you ever needed. Just one step.

A distance behind her, the grey-haired man in the black suit appeared from a doorway and started to follow her. Kitty turned into the Versace store. The man in black walked straight past the boutique and stopped on the corner of East 69th Street. He waited for about ten minutes. This was how it was supposed to be. He pulled out his schedule. Following the plan was important. Keeping exactly to the plan. He knew exactly how long Kitty would spend in each shop and he waited accordingly. When people kept such rigid routines, it was easy to track them.

Across the street from Versace, the mobile CCTV unit filmed the store entrance. Kitty was an obvious target for the American Devil. In the van, Kasper was watching her closely.

'Zoom,' he called into the microphone. The camera caught Kitty swaggering into the store. She was stunning to look at. Film star looks and attitude too. Plastic bottle beauty. Kasper raised his eyebrows in appreciation and ordered one of his undercover agents into the store.

The report came back quickly. Subject was in visual contact. No suspects. Kasper sighed and kept scanning all seven screens. Kitty appeared again on the screen. She was carrying a Versace bag and turned right. She walked about a block and then entered the Prada store. Kasper watched her, camera to camera.

Inside the Prada store, Kitty flicked through the rails, half interested, and picked out a zip-fronted silver dress. The man in black was already in the store, as the plan dictated, and he was on her in an instant.

'Can I help, madam?'

Kitty didn't even look up. The staff always crowded her. 'No, go away,' she said absently.

The man picked out another silver dress and held it up. 'I should think Madam would look fantastic in this.' Kitty looked up at the dress. 'What do you think?' said the man in black.

'I think you didn't hear me,' said Kitty and turned away.

The undercover cop strolled into the store on Kasper's

command. 'Nothing to report. Female shopper and male shop assistant. That's it.'

In the van, Kasper sat back. Maybe it was going to be another day with nothing to show.

'I think it's gorgeous,' said the man at her shoulder. 'You've got a hint of silver in your eyes, a kind of stone colour.' He smiled broadly. 'I'd love to talk about them over lunch.'

Kitty reacted to his tone. She didn't like his attitude or his smell. She suddenly realized what she could smell on him, too. It was the cologne from the night before. She turned and looked at him. It was the guy who'd been following her. If he was following her, he was taking things too far. She would get out quick, get home and tell Daddy. Daddy was real mean when he wanted to be. 'I don't need advice or a lunch date from the hired help,' she said. She pushed the dress into the man's chest and shot him a look of disdain. Then she left the store in a hurry, feeling the anxiety rise in her chest. Inside, the man in black replaced the dress with slow, careful movements. She'd had her chance. He always gave people a chance. Funny, they never took it.

Kasper watched Kitty leave Prada alone and head up East 68th Street, away from their surveillance towards Park Avenue. It was another three minutes before he caught a glimpse of the figure of the man in black leaving Prada. He sat up.

'Where did he come from?'

The team on the street responded. 'He's been in there a while. He's the shop assistant.'

'When the blonde was in there?'

The cop confirmed it. Kasper watched the figure with the grey hair move past the final camera. He zoomed in. 'Get me closer, Ali.' Ali shot across to the control desk and moved the zoom. The face was partly obscured but Kasper thought it was similar to that in the photofit. This was a grey-haired man. He whispered through his radio to the team, 'We got a visual on a possible suspect. Male, six foot plus, black suit, greying hair, walking south down Madison.' He looked back at the screen. 'Shit! Have we lost the blonde?' He called across to Lol Edwards, 'Get her ID from Prada or Versace – wherever she made a purchase. We need to know who she is.'

'We're on it,' said Edwards.

The last team to follow her reported in. 'She went straight past us. She's out of shot on Park Avenue.'

Tom arrived in his Buick and parked half on the sidewalk on East 68th Street. He had the killer's profile from Denise on his knee, and had been listening to the radio conversations as he drove. As he picked up the latest thread, he saw the blonde woman with the shopping bags hurry past. She was uneasy and even glanced behind her. Tom looked right down the street and saw the man in black.

Tom felt his nerves prick up and slowly opened the car door. 'Kasper, this is Harper. I'm going to get in tight and see if I can follow him,' he said on his radio.

Camera Three zoomed in, but the blonde and now the man in black had gone out of range. It was difficult to tell anything about the latter's intentions. He was doing nothing but walking up the street. He walked out of shot and out of the range of the final camera just as Tom stepped on to the sidewalk and crossed the street.

Kasper thought for a moment. 'Team Four, the blonde in Prada was talking to a male shop assistant. Can you give me a brief description?'

Detective Elaine Fittas came back over the airwaves. 'Yeah, boss. We've got a guy, mid-thirties, greying hair, black suit.'

Kasper stood up. 'Team Four, one more thing. Is he or isn't he on the staff of Prada?' He waited as Elaine went to check.

Her voice crackled back. 'Negative, boss. They've never seen him before.'

That was all Kasper needed. He had to make a quick decision. 'I think it's him. Put the teams on standby, we've got to follow on foot. Team Four – get going. Has anyone got a visual?'

Team Four couldn't get near the suspect. The crowds were so thick that they couldn't progress. Harper was closest, only a few yards behind, watching the man in black as he closed in on the gorgeous blonde. What was he planning? A public execution? Or was he in the stalking phase? This guy was capable of anything. Was the American Devil on a busy Manhattan street about to do serious damage? Harper started to run.

Chapter Forty-Six

Upper East Side
November 23, 3.58 p.m.

The killer could see Kitty on the street, walking in her perfect bright red coat and dress. He wanted to taste her blood so much he could feel the sweet metallic flavour already rolling around his mouth. He wondered when he became a killer. Was it the first time he held someone's throat and watched them pass from life to death? Or was it long before that? Was it some time way back in the past?

Perhaps it was just an art, like poetry, but with human blood and human remains to be savoured. Or perhaps he became a killer at high school. He had strange thoughts sitting in those classrooms.

He knew every action had consequences. These things went deep. But did they make him kill? He didn't know. And he so wanted to know, to solve the problem of himself. Like everyone did. He was just a regular guy trying to solve his particular set of problems. The devil had come to rescue him. Slipped into his skin. He was a devil now – a real-life, walking, talking son of Satan.

He had been reflective all morning, as he showered, as he shaved, as he pissed. He knew why, too. He'd wanted Kitty the night before. He'd been ready. He'd been really ready. And he had to go away empty-handed. Not today. Not at all. The heat was still on. Deep within him, he felt the surge of lust that he knew would swamp him and drag him down to hell.

He strode towards Kitty as she walked up the street. The air was peculiarly stark and bright. It felt incredibly vivid to him. It always did when he was out hunting. He stopped to look at the bursting colours of the sky. It was absolutely magical. He knew that the devil was here. It was only when the devil woke that the world changed so quickly and everything looked like a Technicolor extravaganza. Such a strange night, it was, when the devil killed for the first time.

The killer was now a few yards behind Kitty, who'd crossed Park Avenue and was heading towards Lexington on East 68th Street. He stared at her back as he approached. Then, out of some deep animal awareness, she felt his eyes and turned to look.

'Hello, Kitty. I've been watching you.'

Tom Harper was about ten feet behind the man in the black suit. He lost him for a second in the crowd and then, seemingly from the other side of the sidewalk, saw him swoop towards the blonde. 'How the fuck did he get so close?' Harper started to push through the crowd. He saw the man get right up to the blonde and then he saw her turn and shudder.

Kitty swung round and stared into the eyes of the tall figure who towered above her. She couldn't catch her breath as she felt his hand grab her thigh and squeeze. He was smiling as he did so. Christ! What was he going to do to her?

His hand was grabbing her crotch and pulling at her as he watched her face. Her heart beat hard in her chest and her hands gripped her shopping bags with such force that her knuckles turned white. Her scream was automatic. She felt his fingers dig into her and just freaked. When her eyes opened again, he was gone. He'd moved into the crowd. Where was he? What did he want? Kitty looked round. Then she saw him coming back from the opposite direction. The same black suit surging towards her through the crowds, his head bowed low and purposeful. She saw the Hunter College subway and moved quickly towards it.

Harper knew something was wrong. He yelled, 'Police! Move, move!' He was shouldering through the crowds but he was advancing slowly. Then he heard her shriek. The high-pitched squeal rose above the low hum of the crowd. 'Police!' shouted Harper again, pushing the shoppers aside. 'Get out of my way.' He looked ahead. The blonde had disappeared from view. Maybe the killer had taken her out in the crowd. He was capable of it. Of anything.

Harper had lost both the blonde and the man in black. It was no good. He climbed on top of a trash can and scanned around.

He spotted the blonde heading into the subway, her bright red coat easily visible in the crowd now he had the height. About two hundred yards down the street, the rest of the surveillance operation were heading towards him, but there wasn't time to wait. Then he caught sight of a man dressed in black at the subway entrance. He was following the blonde.

Kitty's heart was pounding so much she could hear it loud in her ears. Her heels clipped quickly across the crowded subway station towards the gates. She didn't have a card or a ticket and looked around, but there was no time, the man was there again. Or was it another man in black? She was confused, but he was heading right for her. She kicked off her Mary Janes and left all nine hundred dollars' worth of designer shoes behind her as she bundled through the barriers on someone else's metro card and ran to the escalators.

She took out her cell phone, but as she was dialling 911 she reached the escalator and reception died on her. She looked back. He was still there – putting his card in the gate and staring at her intently. She was terrified. He was a predator. Now she understood. She was being hunted.

The man in the black suit didn't hurry. There was nowhere for her to run. He made a move towards her, increasing his step. The great thing about the blonde hair was that he could spot it from a distance.

Tom Harper appeared at the subway entrance just as the blonde and the man in black were getting off the escalator down below.

Harper ran and vaulted the gates, then stopped and looked at the crowds. He wouldn't make it in time. Down the side of the escalator was a wide aluminium slide. Harper jumped and slid the length of the drop, keeping himself from falling by using the shoulders of the shoppers as he passed.

At the bottom of the escalator Harper shoved the crowds out of the way and darted down into the subway. He started to sprint towards the platforms, craning his neck to look ahead. The blonde disappeared down one of the tunnels: behind her and closing in was the killer. If Harper allowed the killer to get on a train, he might lose him for good. He followed their route and came out into another large, central tunnel. He kept his eye on the tunnels leading left and right from the main thoroughfare. Which way?

About fifty yards ahead, he caught a fleeting glimpse of the man taking the southern line. Tom darted left and found himself on a packed platform.

By the time he'd got halfway along the platform, a train had pulled in and opened its doors. He scanned the crowd quickly, letting them get on the train, moving up the platform in the space behind them. As the doors were about to shut, he caught sight of the man in black getting on about four carriages up. There was a flash of red inside the carriage and Tom jumped aboard just as the heavy metal doors skidded shut.

The train pulled away into the darkness of the tunnel ahead.

With no way through the packed carriage, Tom knew he'd never reach them in the short time he had and he'd lose them at the next station. He looked at the emergency stop handle for an instant, then pulled it.

The train started to screech to a halt, the lights flickering on and off. The crowds began to look around, worry and annoyance more than fear crossing their faces. Slowly, Tom began to move through each cabin. The lights kept flickering as his eyes scanned ahead.

As soon as the train jolted to a stop, Tom's quarry panicked. He could see Kitty up ahead, but he knew the cops must've stopped the train. He scanned down through the carriages. He couldn't see anything, but he had to go. He had to escape. He couldn't bear the crowds, the claustrophobia, the police on his tail. He felt sweat pouring down his face as he pushed through the throng to get to the driver's cab.

Ahead of him, Kitty was rushing through the carriages as fast as she could, terrified now and shouting as she pulled herself through the crowds. She could hear the commotion her attacker was making behind her as she reached the end of the train. She saw the man coming through the last carriage, sweat pouring down his face. The driver's door was shut and locked. Kitty smashed her flat hand hard against it and started screaming, but the door didn't open. She rattled the handle and pleaded, but she knew the driver wouldn't open it. It was against all regulations. He had to sit tight and wait.

As her pursuer approached, Kitty gave up. She turned towards him with her back hard against the driver's door, slid down the door and pulled herself into a tight little ball. She closed her eyes and bent her head as far as possible into her knees.

The man in black had nowhere to go. He turned and looked back down the train. He could see someone moving towards him, close now. He looked down at Kitty. He had no option. He smashed a window with his heel and clambered out. He hooked himself on to the side wall of the tunnel and moved to the front of the train, dropped down, and sprinted into the darkness.

Tom arrived and knelt by Kitty. 'You're okay now,' he said softly. 'We've got him trapped. He's out in the tunnel. I'm going after him. You're safe now.' Kitty didn't even open her eyes and Tom climbed out of the broken window. He was less than a minute behind his quarry: near enough to hear his footsteps as he sprinted ahead in the pitch dark. Tom started to run, fearing the live electric rail and trying to find a rhythm on the track.

At the next station, the cops had cleared the crowds from the platform and were waiting, staring into the dark tunnel. They heard footsteps in the tunnel and a man appeared in the opening of the station, running from something or someone. Then Harper appeared behind him.

The man tried to get up on the platform but cops spanned its length, their guns pointing down at him. Panicking, not knowing which way to turn, he turned and rushed straight at Harper.

Harper sidestepped him, caught him by the neck and threw him to the ground. A knife clattered across the rails and the man scrambled away from Harper, his heels digging into the dirt.

'Who are you?' said Tom.

The man looked up. 'I don't know who I am!' he shouted. Harper saw the manic look in his eyes and watched as his right arm reached out towards the live rail. If he touched the line, over six hundred volts would course through his body, killing him instantly. Harper grabbed hold of his ankle and tried to pull him back, but it was too dangerous: if the man touched the rail while Harper was holding him they would both die. He looked up. Three officers were staring down their sights at them. Harper didn't want this killer dead, either punched full of holes or fried on a train line. With one last effort, he threw himself on top of him, caught his right arm and rolled him towards the platform. The two bodies rolled twice and then the killer went limp. There was no fight left in him. Harper turned him in the dirt and stared at his face. The fucking guy was weeping. Harper wanted to break his jaw. He jammed his forearm under his chin and pulled his head up. He had the American Devil in his control on the ground. It felt good. Real good.

'Who the fuck are you?' he shouted. 'Who the fuck are you, you sick bastard?'

The man was crying even harder now. 'I'm nobody. Nobody at all. I was just following her. I wasn't going to touch her or hurt her.'

'I want your name,' Harper screamed. 'Your name!'

The man looked up. 'Carlisle,' he said. 'Winston Carlisle.'

Chapter Forty-Seven

East Harlem
November 23, 6.22 p.m.

A few hours after the man in black had been rolled away from certain death, a cavalcade of red and blues screeched across the car park of the desolate halfway house up in East Harlem. The guy wouldn't tell them where he lived, but they'd run his name through the system and in less than an hour his file came up on a screen at the NYPD database. Winston Carlisle had a record and he'd just been released into an adult housing block. The address was called through directly to Harper. He gave the order and Blue Team set off.

Winston Carlisle had been a patient at Kirby Psychiatric and Manhattan Psychiatric Center. He lived in a halfway house in East Harlem. Things were fitting together. The killings started about a month after he was moved to a non-secured room in MPC. He was free to come and go, and that's when the killing began: a few weeks after his release from a secure ward.

The quiet parking lot up in the Heights was ripped up by the arrival of Blue Team and the rest of the task force. The halfway house was a low-roofed municipal building. The green barred door was wedged open and a nervous-looking woman sat in reception, eyes wide at the chaos of lights and activity. She'd only been in the job a week – the previous receptionist had died in a traffic accident – and was not yet used to dealing with cops.

Harper led the team through the door. The killer probably went under any number of aliases as he stalked and dated these women. He probably wore disguises. He was probably a lot smarter than he made out.

'We're looking for Winston Carlisle's room,' said Harper. The receptionist's arm pointed towards the stairs. 'Room fifty-two, gentlemen.'

The team made their way up to the second floor and down the corridor to the small room where Winston Carlisle lived. Eddie Kasper was at Tom Harper's side. They'd spent the last few weeks hunting this man, terrified by his capabilities, and now they were looking at a urine-soaked bed in a six-by-nine room at the end of nowhere street. Winston Carlisle had been right. He was a nobody. A nobody who wanted to be somebody.

The two men looked at the small single bedroom and couldn't believe that it had all started in that tiny, pathetic space.

'So this is the home of the American Devil,' said Kasper.

'Looks like it,' said Harper. He opened the brown file and read out the report from the hospital. 'He was a patient at Kirby Psychiatric. He's got a long record of treatment for paranoia. Get this. Numerous counts of attempted rape against young women going back a long way.'

'Sad little bastard,' said Eddie.

'It's not what I expected,' said Harper. 'It's nothing like Dr Levene's profile. She had him down as a successful guy living with someone. This is a no-self-esteem loner with a history of mental illness. Shit. He must have gone haywire. Probably stopped his medication or something. He was released from the Kirby a month before the first murder. Jesus, we should've checked this.'

'That's too cruel, man. Someone should've been monitoring this guy,' said Kasper.

Harper pulled back an orange curtain that formed a makeshift wardrobe. The two detectives looked at the hoard. A tin bucket with four bloody knives. Clothes covered in blood. Enough evidence to condemn the man. It was all so casual, so pointless. So fucking avoidable.

'He wasn't the clinical, terrifying mastermind I'd suspected. He was a lowlife,' said Harper. 'How did we miss this one? Somehow, this man went under the radar. Who was checking out recently released prisoners and patients? They should've interviewed this man in the first few days of the investigation. What was Williamson playing at?'

Catching a killer never felt great, but it usually felt good. But this felt really bad. It just seemed so empty. Harper stood at the threshold of the room staring at the bookshelf.

'What you thinking?'

He looked across at the graphic novels and airport trash and shook his head. 'Nothing.'

'What do you mean?'

'I mean, no poetry, no art, nothing.'

'Well, at least the women of the Upper East Side can sleep easy.'

'Yeah,' said Harper. 'Did anyone make contact with Kitty Hunyardi as yet?'

'Yeah, we got her off the subway train. She's being debriefed by Victim Support. She's fine, just shaken. It's good we can tell her we've got the killer behind bars. She'll be going home soon.'

'Good work, Eddie.'

'Press are all over the precinct, Tom. You need to avoid the front entrance.'

'What did Lafayette tell them?'

'We've arrested a suspect, nothing more, but they're hungry as wolves out there so they're running with any comment they can get from us.'

'As long as that's all they've got, that's fine until we charge him.'

271

Harper and Kasper walked out of Winston Carlisle's room. The forensics team were there ready to collect the evidence that would condemn him.

They were all exhausted by the events of the day as they headed back to the precinct. Most of the detectives would go home, but not Harper. He wanted to interrogate this killer until he understood what the hell had happened over the past few weeks.

It was the end of November and the team were all ready for a break. Catching the devil felt hollow now, but in a day or two the feeling of relief would come, the blondes would emerge from the shadows and New York would start to glimmer again. Glimmer and forget the horror.

On his return to the precinct, Harper got straight down to the darkened observation room. Denise Levene had been called in and she stood there with Lafayette and a couple of Blue Team, all crowding round the window watching the interview room and Winston Carlisle through the mirror. Two detectives were still going at him. Soon, it would be Harper and Kasper's turn again.

'Hard to believe when you get them in captivity, isn't it?' said Captain Lafayette. 'He's admitting he followed the girl, but he says he didn't hurt anyone. He's smart.'

Harper's eyes found Denise. 'What do *you* think, Doctor?'

'My profile said seven things about this killer. This guy only ticks two boxes, so you know what I think. He doesn't fit the profile. You sure it's him?'

'I've just been to his room in the halfway house. We found bloody knives in his room, the girls' bloody clothes. Looks like it was him, Denise.'

'Well, he doesn't fit the usual pattern. Either I'm way off or this guy is not who he appears to be.'

'He's got a history of sexual assault but no murders. This seemed to come out of all those years inside Kirby.'

'Minor sexual assault and long periods of incarceration doesn't make a killer, does it?'

'It could've been in his head a long time. You just don't know what's inside these guys.'

'I do,' said Denise. 'I've spent ten years finding out.' She walked closer to the glass and stared into the frightened face of Winston Carlisle. It wasn't nice to be wrong, and ten years of interviewing killers was telling her she wasn't.

Chapter Forty-Eight

Downtown Restaurant
November 23, 8.28 p.m.

Across town, Erin Nash of the *New York Daily Echo* was sitting in a plush restaurant dining with a deputy editor from a rival paper. Short-haired, slim and wiry, Erin was pure-bred New York stock. Her father was still a barber in Brooklyn. Her favourite colour was gunmetal grey; her favourite drink was a shot and one day she would be an editor. For now, she was intent on just getting up the first few rungs of the ladder. The editor sitting opposite thought she looked cute, like an angry little elf with big brown eyes. The *Daily Post* had been impressed with her crime coverage. The *Echo*'s circulation was up 32 per cent on the basis of her exclusives and this impressed the editor even more.

Jed Brown was leathery-skinned but his hands were soft from daily moisturizer. He looked across at Erin's fierce concentration. 'What do you make of the arrest? You got any inside information?'

'No, just what everyone's got. Some guy was pulled out of the subway and they're interrogating.'

'Could be it's him.'

'Could be. We'll have to wait and see.'

'If it is, that means your little goldmine comes to an end.'

'There's a book in this, if I can get access to the killer.'

'How will you do that?'

'Give up my source to the NYPD in exchange for access. If they've got the killer, I don't need my source any more.'

'You're quite a determined player,' Jed said, and smiled. 'Who is he?'

'A cop on the homicide team with a liking for reporters.'

'You've got no scruples about that?'

'I do what I got to do,' she replied, her spoon about to enter the little bowl of Roquefort and asparagus soup.

'You want to play a numbers game?' asked Jed. His blue eyes were clear and attractive, but he was too old for Erin. And she'd never gone for the perma-tan look.

'No harm playing,' she replied.

Jed let his top lip crinkle up into a reptile smile and wrote six figures on the linen napkin in blue biro.

'Want to wipe your mouth on that?'

Erin picked up the napkin and moved it to her mouth. She read the number. 'My,' she said. 'That's a big one.'

Jed laughed with an overexcited bullet-like rattle and nodded. 'Is that a yes, Miss Nash?'

'A yes to what?' she replied. God, this was so easy.

She didn't have time to hear his answer. Her cell phone lit up with a flash and she picked it up. She listened to the voice on the line, her face bright and animated as the caller revealed his story. As she listened, her face drained of colour. Jed watched with interest as she wrote down everything in her notebook and ended the call. She looked up at her host. She needed to get back to the office.

'Sorry, Mr Brown. That was my friend in the NYPD. I've just had a real interesting breaking news story on this American Devil and I've got some urgent copy to file.'

'What is it? Everyone's waiting for confirmation that they've caught him.'

'But I got something extra to offer our readers,' said Erin.

'I wish you were mine, Erin.'

She smiled and rose. 'I'll consider your offer very carefully.'

'Which one?' he asked and let his hand slide down over her dress as he kissed her cheek.

Erin raced back to the *Daily Echo* and started to write up the story. It was another terrific exclusive, and on the basis of her recent track record her editor took the decision to run it without further verification. It was too late for any detailed checks and Erin's source had been reliable so far. It was too good to miss. The latest news would sell thousands of papers. Murder was big business.

Erin filed her copy at 9.30 p.m. and then took a moment to think about her future. This was the time she had to make a choice. It might not come again. Which way was she going to go? She smiled. It was nice to have a choice for once; she'd never really had that kind of luxury before.

Chapter Forty-Nine

Blue Team
November 24, 4.00 a.m.

Tom Harper was unshaved and smelled like he looked. He hadn't washed since the arrest and didn't intend to. He'd worked until midnight interrogating the suspect, reviewing the CCTV images, putting together the team report and briefing his senior and executive officers. He finally laid his head down on the grey blanket of the precinct bunk at 2 a.m. and slept in his clothes for two hours. He woke suddenly at four with a terrible premonition that the killer had escaped him and disappeared down the subway tunnel, laughing like a madman in a film.

He sat up on the edge of the bunk. His head ached and his big hands were still stinging. He looked down at the deep cuts running across both palms from the struggle in the subway and tried to close his fists, but the wounds had started to crack open. He could hear it now – the footsteps in the dark, his own heavy breathing. His hands were still dark with dust and soot. He could even smell the tunnel fumes in his hair and see the arch of light ahead and the silhouette of the killer moving towards it. He sighed long and hard. In the bunk room, four other officers lay flat out, snoring and stinking. Tom pushed himself to his feet and dragged his body towards the coffee pot.

There was no one around in the large investigation room. It

glowed pale and ghostly with pre-dawn light. Tom's eyes scanned the five blue boards with their photographs of pointless slaughter. There wouldn't be another. Thank God for that. He felt the emotion rising from his thoughts and breathed in quickly. Hundreds of officers had slugged through these past days, working overtime and trying to do something about these killings in their muted, sarcastic, smart-assed but none the less caring way – enough to go home empty, with no energy or emotion for their own lives and families. He nodded his thanks and respect to the empty room. They'd nailed the bastard and now he was sitting in a cell some fifty feet below him, surrounded by cold steel and concrete.

In his right hand, Harper picked up the previous day's *New York Daily Echo*. The headline was 'Serial Killer Turns Cop Killer'. Harper had been right. Erin Nash had been told about the Williamson murder by someone on the team. One day he'd find out who it was and that person would be very sorry. Underneath the headline, there was a composite image of the five female victims with Detective Williamson in the middle, looking more like the killer than one of his victims. Erin Nash didn't need to try to make this sensational; the grainy print of the photographs was enough of a headline – it gave the faces the aura of tragedy.

Tom walked up to his profile board. Denise Levene had constructed her vision of the killer. He read slowly, sipping scalding coffee slowly over his lips so it burned the tip of his tongue. She'd written seven single traits: *High school educated, White, Mid-thirties, Self-controlled, Police/military background, Living with someone, Employed in sales*.

Tom took up a blue marker pen and circled two words: *White, Thirties*. He looked at the rest and crossed a line through the other five traits. It was hard to get a profile right when the killer was as deranged as someone like Winston Carlisle. Even though Denise had been so sure and he'd been convinced himself, it wasn't a perfect science. It was all guesswork really and profiles were often hit and miss. He took a cloth and scrubbed the profile off the board. No need for recriminations: they had their man.

Harper took the stairs down to the cells. His shoes tapped out a quick beat on the concrete steps.

He walked down the corridor, past the thick steel doors painted in cream enamel, as if this touch of softness could disguise the need to incarcerate untamed human evil. He stood outside the cell. His heart was beating hard in his chest. He read the board. *Carlisle, W.* He pulled back the bolt, which clinked loudly in the quiet of the cell. He lowered the flap. He felt like a man in a fairground who'd paid to see a monster. He put his eyes to the gap and stared in at the figure sitting on a bunk, staring silently at the floor. This was the Devil – this grey-haired snivelling piece of humanity was the American Devil, but it just didn't feel right.

All of a sudden, out of the silence Harper heard Captain Lafayette shouting. He listened but couldn't make out what was being said. He shut the steel flap and hurried upstairs.

Captain Lafayette was sitting in the investigation room. The rest of Blue Team were struggling in from the bunkroom. Lafayette looked deadly serious. He had been woken himself forty minutes earlier when the first copy hit the street. The mayor's office had been in touch directly. Their words were to the point – 'What the fuck is happening?'

The men looked at each other in the dark room. Lafayette looked at his men. All of them looked tired. Well, they were going to feel a lot worse in a minute or two. Lafayette threw down a copy of the *New York Daily Echo*.

'Read it for yourself.'

Harper moved towards the table and turned the paper round so that the headline faced him. The byline name under the subheading was Erin Nash. He took up the paper and read the report out loud.

279

AMERICAN DEVIL STILL AT LARGE
PSYCHO SLAUGHTERS BLONDE HEIRESS AS COPS CLAIM CAPTURE

Manhattan's notoriously sadistic pattern killer, the 'American Devil', struck again on the Upper East Side yesterday evening as cops were interviewing the man they believed to be the killer, a source said.

The stripped and mutilated remains of the rubber heiress, Katrina Hunyardi, 23, were found in her apartment an hour after she had been released by the NYPD. She had been raped and stabbed repeatedly with a thin-bladed knife.

The American Devil, who poses his dead victims in macabre and artistic ways, again left his horrifying signature. Kitty Hunyardi was posed like an angel and covered with cherry blossom. As with all his previous kills, the Devil took a trophy – this time, he removed the victim's hands.

The NYPD yesterday were confident that they had the killer behind bars. So confident, in fact, that only hours after being identified as a target for the killer, Kitty Hunyardi was left without police protection. That mistake cost her life.

Lafayette stared at the team. 'What the fuck's going on? I thought we had Katrina Hunyardi? She was in the fucking station yesterday afternoon. Two cops took her home. She ID'd Winston Carlisle. What's going on?'

Blue Team had no idea. They looked around at each other. 'It's got to be some prank,' said Eddie. 'Or maybe a copycat.'

'Have we had any reports? Any homicides yesterday or last night?' asked Harper. 'Have we called Kitty? What do we know?'

Lafayette sat down. He was looking close to a coronary. 'Nothing. No reports, no homicides, but we've been calling

Kitty and there's no reply. We're sending someone over now. Jesus. If something's happened to her!'

Harper was remembering Denise Levene's words. All day, they hadn't heard one fact directly from Winston Carlisle.

'We've got to see this reporter, right now,' he said.

'If this is all bullshit, then she's going to pay,' said Eddie.

'She's been running this story from day one,' said Harper. 'Someone's been leaking to her. We've interviewed everyone, but we got nothing.'

'You sure this wasn't a little bit of revenge?' said Lol Edwards. 'She maybe stopped giving her source what he wanted and he leaked her this false information?'

'Could be,' said Tom, 'but I'd feel a whole lot better if we could get in touch with Kitty Hunyardi.'

'I think someone's playing games with Erin Nash,' said Eddie. 'It's gotta be that.'

'We got to go and see Erin Nash, Captain.'

'That's exactly where you're all going, right now.'

The previous afternoon, Kitty Hunyardi had spent three hours at the precinct while her story was checked and she identified Winston Carlisle in a line-up as the man in the subway. Two officers took her back to her building. She didn't want to spend any longer than she had to in the company of cops and dismissed them at the door. The whole dirty business was something she wanted to erase from her brain, including the acrid coffee breath that all cops seemed to have.

Inside her apartment Kitty crouched down under the hot stream of the shower and cried. It had been a hell of a couple of days. The worst she'd ever experienced. It was too much. She wanted to be strong and independent but she needed someone. It was hard, knowing a killer had been stalking you for weeks. That's what the cops had said. That he tended to scope his victims and even take their clothes and shoes. The idea was terrifying. She felt violated and it dragged her out of the privilege and safety of her wealth and into a place she didn't recognize.

Worse still, the killer had got close enough to her to kill her. He could have put a knife into her right there in the street. He had grabbed her crotch. All her life, she'd been safe and protected. Now she remembered his hand on her, her fear. She felt sickness starting to rise in her stomach and ran to the lavatory. Her wet blond hair flopped over the white bowl of the toilet as she retched up her guts.

Kitty walked out of the bathroom feeling weak and tired. She had promised herself that she'd never ask for her father's help. She'd made it a point of honour that she would be able to cope in her own apartment. She wouldn't ask for his help now, either. She had to get through this alone. It was over. She just had to sleep. She lay down on her bed and closed her eyes, feeling a little calmer. She hugged herself. In truth, she wanted to be eight years old again, far away from the present, back in a time when everything was safe and secure and men didn't grab you on the street. The line-up had been horrible, but there he was, that face, that disturbed face. That horrible, ragged, miserable face.

Warmth. Forgetfulness. She drifted into sleep. Sleep was its own world. Soon enough, Kitty Hunyardi was finally dreaming peacefully again.

An hour ticked by. The still and regular sounds of the night slowly slipped through the apartment.

Just after 4 a.m., the door to the bedroom opened. A man stood there in the doorway, a silhouette in the darkness of a silent apartment. He was tall and wearing a black suit.

Sebastian was smiling. His plan had worked. He'd fooled the cops and now he was five steps away from girl number six. Winston had played his part like a professional. He'd get his fifteen minutes of fame, but the real fame would come to Sebastian. He was better than them all. In his hand he held the morning's *Daily Echo*.

'Kitty,' he whispered. She didn't stir. He looked around her room. It was very clean. There was a faint smell of perfume. It was all tastefully done. Homely. You know. In an artless and decadent way.

He shivered. He hated happiness. He had always hated it. Her arms and legs were splayed across the bed, enjoying the space. He wanted her now. Kitty Hunyardi. He took a seat and stared at her, his head tilted to one side. Nice lips, nice skin, nice low relaxed breathing.

These moments lived with him. They were the only moments of quiet he had ever known, the moments before his innocent women became his victims, when he felt a serene sense of power. He was a god now, looking down on his beautiful creations, blissfully unaware they were being watched. Blissfully unaware the devil had come to take away God's gift.

He shook her shoulder. Her eyes opened. She screamed loud and high-pitched. Sebastian smiled and a gloved hand smacked hard against her mouth. 'Shh, now, princess, shh and all will be well.'

He watched her eyes. He was waiting until she calmed, until reason returned. 'I've just come to deliver the morning paper,' he said. 'But don't scream. If you stay quiet, I'll let you live. Do you understand?'

Kitty nodded. She didn't understand anything at all. A newspaper was placed in front of her. The gloved hand slowly slipped from her mouth and the bedside light flicked on. 'Read all about it,' Sebastian said. 'It's not often we can see how we're going to be remembered.'

Kitty's eyes glanced over the headline.

AMERICAN DEVIL STILL AT LARGE
PSYCHO SLAUGHTERS BLONDE HEIRESS AS COPS CLAIM CAPTURE

She started to read but tears were streaming from her eyes and the paper was shaking so hard, she couldn't take in the words.

Sebastian smiled as he watched her. His right hand moved to his pocket and pulled out a neat little surgical bone saw. It was only about six inches long. He snapped the handle into place as he looked down at Kitty's shaking hands. He loved her. He always had. She had such beautiful hands.

Chapter Fifty

Blue Team
November 24, 4.38 a.m.

Forty minutes later, a buzzer screeched in the darkness. Erin Nash's hand had reached out to stop the alarm when she realized that it was the door. She was naked in her large pale pink bed, a leathery-skinned naked body asleep at her side. She'd chosen Jed Brown after all. Shit. Her head was barely functioning. It had been a late night. She'd filed the copy and then gone back to see Jed to celebrate. She had an exclusive on the sixth victim of a multiple killer – this was going to get her everything she wanted. Every other paper was screaming about the killer's capture, but she knew better. He had killed again: her source had said so.

The paper was paying her well for the inside track on the serial murders. Very well. But Jed Brown had offered to double her salary, then he'd offered her a ride home in a limo, then he'd offered himself.

The buzzer screeched again and didn't stop. Erin rose and pulled on a gown and then walked to the intercom.

'Hey, what's so fucking important?'

'NYPD, open up. Is that Erin Nash? You've just reported a murder that no one knows about but you. Open your fucking door. NOW!'

The news hit her like a wave of cold water and woke up her

mind quicker than a double espresso. She buzzed the door and sat back in a lazy chair, her body fizzing with fear. *Shit and fuck and fuck again!* Had someone sold her a dud story? Was it her source following some weird agenda of his own? What the fuck was happening?

Tom Harper, Eddie Kasper, Lol Edwards and Mark Garcia appeared at the door of her apartment. All four faces were angry and tired.

Eddie Kasper moved closer to her. 'Is your name Erin Nash?' She nodded slowly and looked from man to man.

Harper moved in. 'You remember me, I hope. My name is Detective Tom Harper, NYPD. Let me just make this clear for you. You've reported the death of a woman called Kitty Hunyardi. Is that true?'

'I filed the story late last night. What's happened?'

'The murder you reported has not been notified to the NYPD. We know nothing about it. Not a thing, but you're telling us Kitty Hunyardi is dead. What do you know? Someone's screwed you. Who's your source?'

'I don't reveal my sources,' said Erin, defiant even though her limbs felt like jelly.

'I know you claim that, but this is different.'

'Why?'

'Because we're going to bust you for obstructing an investigation and Katrina Hunyardi's family is going to sue your paper for so much money that it'll have to shut down. Ms Hunyardi was in the station yesterday afternoon. Now you tell us she's dead. You got any facts, Erin?'

She shook her head. Harper continued: 'You just might be an accessory after the fact. Anyone who receives, relieves, comforts or assists an offender in order to hinder or prevent his apprehension, trial or punishment is an accessory after the fact. Do you understand? We're going to arrest you, Erin. Now open your mouth. Who is it? Where did you get this? We need to know, Erin.'

'Okay. I've been briefed by a cop in Homicide. One of your team, Detective Harper. One of your own fucking team.'

'Who?'

'A guy. We had a drink.' She was twisting in her seat. How the fuck did she get out of this one? She had no idea. Maybe last night had marked the end of her career, not the beginning.

'Sleep with him, did you, Erin?'

'That's not against the law, is it?'

'Is that how you got the information? Sexual favours?'

'Fuck you, I'm a grown-up, I can sleep with who I like.'

As he was about to speak, Harper's cell phone buzzed. He picked up and listened. The room went deadly silent as Harper's face tensed, and then his eyes closed momentarily. The duty sergeant on the line had just got a call from the patrol at Kitty's apartment. It wasn't good news. They'd found Kitty Hunyardi's body and she was posed just like Erin Nash's article said, with her hands removed. But there was one important fact that Erin had missed. Kitty's body was still warm and a copy of the *Daily Echo* was sitting by her head. She'd been killed after the paper had come out. Harper listened and then hung up. Kitty had only just died. Harper turned to Erin, his face very harsh.

'Who's your source, Erin? Believe me, this just got fucking serious.'

'He said he worked on your team.'

'I want a name, Erin.'

'Mark Garcia. I looked him up. He's authentic. He works your team.'

Harper pointed to the shocked cop standing at his side. 'This is Mark Garcia. Was this the guy?'

'No,' Erin said, her voice trembling. 'That's not Mark Garcia. He was much taller, dark-haired, slightly grey.' She stared at Harper's face. 'What is it? What's with the look? You look like you've seen a ghost. What's happened?'

'You slept with this guy? This fake cop? You let him in your apartment?'

'Yes.'

'When?'

'About three weeks ago? We spent the night together a few times. He gets in touch by phone. We talk. He didn't seem that interested in me. Who is it? Who the fuck is it?'

'When did he last call?'

'Yesterday evening. He told me all about Kitty's murder. I just had to run with it.'

'What can you tell us about him?'

'It was a while ago. Like I said, he was nice-looking, had salt-and-pepper hair and was about six foot one or two. Tell me what the fuck's going on, please!'

'That call was from the precinct. Kitty Hunyardi has just been found murdered in her apartment. Her body's still warm. How the hell did your source know about a murder before it had even been committed? How did you know?'

'I don't know. I can't think.'

'Then let me spell it out for you, Erin – there's only one person in the world who can know about a murder before it's been committed.'

Erin was shivering and shaking her head. It wasn't true. It couldn't be true. She'd kissed the guy, slept with him. Jesus!

'Your source, Erin, the man you brought back here to fuck around with. The man you let into your apartment. The man you've been helping all along.'

'No, please!' Erin Nash's face drained of colour. She was completely still. Shock was paralysing her. She couldn't speak.

'It wasn't Mark Garcia feeding you the information. It was the killer – the American Devil – he's your fucking source, Erin. You've been sleeping with the American Devil.'

PART THREE
November 26–December 1

'For each man kills the thing he loves.'
Oscar Wilde, *The Ballad of Reading Gaol*

Chapter Fifty-One

Rockaway Beach, Long Island
November 26, 3.12 p.m.

Out on Rockaway Beach, the Atlantic winds snapped across the two walkers' faces in sharp icy bursts. Up above, the sky spread out bright and cloudless. 'It's cold as hell,' shouted Denise Levene as she struggled along with her chin deep in her collar. Ahead, the athletic figure of Tom Harper continued to push its way along the edge of the surf, binoculars scanning left to right.

Kitty Hunyardi's death had knocked everybody off their feet, including Harper. The investigation went from elation to sudden meltdown. Then it got worse. The press had been primed by the police commissioner to hunt for their victim down at North Manhattan Homicide and they descended like a swarm of angry bees. And Harper got stung, along with everyone else who worked Homicide that day. The public were frightened, the press were stoking the sense of outrage and wouldn't let up. Winston Carlisle was not the American Devil. He was a set-up.

It had been a tough time for Tom, but worst of all was the horrible realization that the American Devil was still out there, planning his next kill. Harper found himself wishing that the battle-hardened Nate Williamson was at his side as they fielded press questions. Nate would've told it how it was. No soft soap, no apologies, just iron with a sprinkling of lead. *He's a maniac killer who's trying to fuck the city up, confuse us and throw us patsies. It's a fucking game to him – what do you think he would do, hand himself in?* Tom heard Williamson's voice in his head and couldn't believe he missed the guy as much as he did.

And there was one other piece of bad news that Harper hadn't yet told Denise. At the end of the twelve-to-four shift the previous day, Captain Lafayette had called Harper into his small glass office on the fourth floor and twisted his mouth sympathetically. That wasn't a good sign. Harper saw it and shook his head. He was off the case. He was off Homicide. He was off active duty. Harper was asked to hand his shield and gun over. He did so in silence, the two men awkward and clumsy.

They needed a carcass to throw to the press pack and it was the lead detective first. They needed to say that a new lead was being given the ball. If that didn't calm the situation down, the commissioner would just keep humping bodies out the door. Lafayette would be next. 'I'm sorry,' the captain had said. Harper had smiled thinly and walked out.

The long white sands reached out as far as they could see. From Jacob Riis Park all the way to Atlantic Beach, the sea rolled white crests over and over with a relentless crashing beat. The two friends were buttoned up against the wind, their hair flapping wildly. Denise's spaniel was running all over the beach, his big soft ears flopping around in the wind. Denise had heard about the murder of Kitty Hunyardi on the news but could only guess how Harper was feeling. She tried to contact him all through Sunday, but he'd gone for a long walk.

'I thought you wanted to talk,' said Denise.

'Yeah, but walking is better.'

'Better to keep it all inside till it ruins you. Just what I would've recommended, as your psychologist. It's a surefire way to mental health.'

'Not much to say, Denise. I'm here for some R and R – and I want to show you something.'

'There's nothing here that could possibly be worth seeing.'

They walked up the low dunes that reached towards the streets running across Long Island. Tom stopped by a low sign cautioning against the tide.

'The great unknown,' said Tom, staring out across the vast ocean.

The grey water was churning and beating the shore with a frightening regularity. Denise pushed her hands into her coat and sat down. 'You got a hat or something? My ears are gonna fall off.' Fahrenheit appeared between Denise's legs and placed his muzzle on her lap. She stroked his warm fur.

Harper reached into his backpack and handed her a green hunting hat with ear flaps. Denise pulled the hat over her head and tied it under her chin, then turned to Harper. He nodded in approval. 'You look like Kyle from *South Park*.'

'God, you know how to make a woman feel special,' said Denise.

He raised his eyebrows and looked out to the ocean.

'Listen, Tom, at least tell me what happened,' she said, reaching out and putting her hand on his arm for comfort.

'I got moved off the case. That's it. I got moved off the damn case.'

Denise felt a lump in her throat but controlled it. 'Remember what I taught you about revealing the detail, Tom?'

Harper's head shook slowly. 'The detail is I failed. The detail is that this maniac killer just duped us all and got me and half the team canned. So they're going to start again with a new lead. Someone from Manhattan South. It'll take them weeks to catch up. The killer's going to be laughing. I feel so fucking useless, Denise, if you want the truth. So fucking impotent. And more women will die because of this.'

'The killer set you up?'

'Yeah, but we don't know how, exactly. It looks like Winston

293

Carlisle was being controlled and manipulated by someone. Witnesses saw another man visiting Carlisle on several occasions. Winston is a little vague himself but said he thought he was a doctor from the hospital. This guy, who we presume is the American Devil, sent Winston this list of instructions about how and when to stalk Kitty. Winston followed them to the letter. Let's face it, I called the chase at the subway and it was the wrong guy.'

'You didn't fail, you took a chance. What do they want, police by numbers?'

'That's exactly what they want. Statistics don't lie. We've got a serial killer in Manhattan, they asked me to catch him and I didn't close the deal. I'm embarrassing some serious players up at the top of the tree.'

'They want him caught in under three weeks? What the hell do they expect?'

'Kitty Hunyardi died when we were busy interrogating an innocent man. The way it looks, we went way, way down the wrong track.'

'You don't know that.'

'I made a mistake. I've been going over it in my head. I don't know where it happened.' Tom looked across at Denise. 'I'm sorry for what I said about the profile. You were right to doubt Carlisle. I was pumped up. I saw what Sebastian wanted me to see.'

Levene stared up to catch his expression. 'How did this Carlisle guy get caught up with Sebastian?'

'Carlisle had a history of minor sexual assaults, and my guess is he made a good ringer. The killer must've come across him in the hospital on Ward's Island somehow. They're looking into it, but Winston said that the first time he saw this guy was at the halfway house. Sebastian chose him to make us look like fools. He could've left us to stew for a while, but he went for Kitty as soon as he could. I think he got jealous of all the attention Winston was getting. Maybe he had to show the world that the great killer was still top dog. And that the cops had fucked up.'

'What was Erin Nash's part?'

'Sebastian met her in a bar, told her he was a cop, fed her information and ended up in her bed. He set that up too. He wanted the world to know what he was doing in all the detail.'

'How is she? Quite a shock to discover you've been sleeping with a killer.'

'Yeah, the shock lasted a good ten minutes, then she realized that she was sitting on a gold mine. You could see the book title running before her eyes: *My Nights With a Killer* by Erin Nash.'

Denise shook her head and started to pound her feet on the ground to keep warm. 'Is there a café around here?'

'Not at this time of year.'

'Hell, it's freezing.' She stood up and they began moving on. 'My thoughts on the profile have changed a little, Tom. He's not going to be like the statistical norm, he's one of the pathfinders. An original.'

'It's not my case any more, Denise. You'll have to find another cop.'

'Come on. Don't give in so easily. What about the girl in the dumpster? Any leads on her?'

'We identified her as far as we could. She had two tattoos that people recognized. We think her name is Lottie Bixley. She was a hooker. She went missing for four days and then turned up dead. No one thinks it's his kill. It's not his style. There's no prints, no DNA, nothing.'

'What about you, what do you think?'

'I can't quite believe it's nothing to do with Sebastian. I found a cherry blossom petal in the dirt by the dumpster. You don't find much cherry blossom in New York in November. Everyone else thinks I've lost it.'

'It needs explaining.'

'I know, and it's one of three things. Either it's one of life's strange but random coincidences, one of us contaminated the scene or Sebastian was somehow involved in her death.'

'Where would you put your money?'

'She's a hooker and there are no other similarities, but I would bet on Sebastian's involvement.'

'She was missing for four days. He's not done that before, has he?' Denise said.

'Well, maybe I'm just reading too much into things. It's only a petal.'

'Unless Sebastian changed his MO radically because of some changed circumstance, like his wife and family were away for a few days and he couldn't let himself miss the opportunity. It's worth a look, isn't it? Maybe he had an opportunity to keep one at his house for a while. Maybe he dumped her quickly because something disturbed him.'

'I'd look at it, Denise, but, as I said, it's not my case.'

'You can't give up, Tom.'

They walked along the sand until Tom stopped and his arm reached across to halt Denise. 'Wait up one second.' He put his binoculars to his eyes and felt a warm thrill reach right down to his stomach. 'She's a damn beauty. Take a look at that.'

Denise took the binoculars. It took her a second to find what Harper wanted her to see. There it was, sitting on a heap of white rocks, the wind buffeting its white feathers.

'That's what I came for. Isn't it the finest thing you ever saw?' said Harper, taking the glasses back.

'What is it?' said Denise.

Harper laughed. 'That city-girl act is no act, is it?' Denise shook her head. 'It's a snowy owl,' he said and stared again at the yellow eyes, the ripple of black markings and the end of its hooked beak. 'Looks beautiful, but it's got some serious talons under those pretty feathers.'

Chapter Fifty-Two

The Jersey Bar, Harlem
November 26, 10.35 p.m.

The interior of the Jersey Bar looked just like Harper felt and that was how he wanted it. He sat on a red velvet barstool with a rip right across the centre and looked into the dim lights peering from beneath old yellowing shades. There wasn't a barman in sight, only the streaks of dried beer running the length of the counter. Up back, a small wooden dance floor stood empty and looked as sad as a three-legged dog. Four other customers in various shades of lonely were stowed away in darkened booths and none of them looked like they wanted to talk, which was just about perfect. Tom slumped his whole weight against the bar and waited for someone to serve him.

They'd driven back over from Long Island in the warmth of her little Honda with the dog licking his neck the whole way. They'd talked a little more about the case in sentences that seemed to get lost in the sound of the traffic, and at some point she realized that he wasn't listening and the case drifted away into the darkness. She let him out just over the Triborough Bridge, but he only managed two or three steps towards his apartment before he felt the old familiar sense of dread. The horrible fact of being alone was that you went home dog tired but as soon as you were through the door the bright lights in your heart flickered on and you were trapped with your own carousel of memories. Home was a place you sometimes didn't want to get to.

Four beers in and Harper was drumming his fingers to the country music and letting his memories pitch and recede like the tide. He watched the oddballs come and go with little curiosity and sometimes managed a smile of acknowledgement. Patsy Cline was soon drowning out all else in the bar with her sad stories. She'd just started an old song, 'I Don't Wanna'.

Tom sipped his beer. He didn't need memories now. He listened to Patsy Cline singing about love and the lack of it. The beer and music were doing all the work his heart needed.

Love felt like a hollow echo of some once perfect time and place. Perhaps it was just a fantasy that kept emerging from the deep to ruin your life. He felt so mad at Lisa, his teeth clenched. It wouldn't happen again. He'd keep things tight and impersonal. His eyes lifted. A couple danced in the gloom. He watched their hands clasp and their hips touch.

Sometimes it was hard to admit that it wasn't anger eating him up, but something else entirely. Levene had it right. It was plain old loneliness. It was never easy to open the door to need, but the beer was helping and Harper knew that what he wanted was nothing more than to hug up close to someone and let the world drift away. He drained his glass and listened.

As the song finished, an attractive brunette who'd been catching his glances sidled up to him at the bar and pulled up a stool. She was mid-thirties, wore tight denims and a top with a deep neckline.

'You mind if I join you for a conversation?'

'I never mind a conversation,' Harper said.

She sat. For a moment, Harper wondered where she was from and what she did. He took in the heavy perfume, the lack of a ring on her wedding finger and the tired look in her eyes.

'What you thinking about tonight?' she asked.

'Why love passes us by.'

'My, that's a big topic.'

'How about you? Love pass you by?'

She smiled. It was nice. 'Well, it stopped in the station a day or two.'

'Same here,' Harper said. 'What's your name?'

'Samantha. You?'

'Tom.'

'What do you do, Tom?'

'Me, I don't know. I really don't know any more.'

She laughed. 'Me neither.'

They talked for an hour – he told her all about Lisa; he heard all about her Frank. Then Tammy Wynette came on the jukebox, singing 'Help me make it through the night', and Samantha took his hand and led him out from the seat. She came up close to him on the dance floor and they slow-danced to the sentimental old song, her warm body comfortable against his.

It'd been years since Harper had felt another's skin next to his own apart from Lisa's. He felt strange, like a man doing something he shouldn't. He was moving like a wooden marionette, and Samantha felt it.

'It's no big deal, Tom, just a dance: she's not watching.' She pulled him back towards her and leaned her head on his shoulder. Tom felt her hair brush against his skin. He remembered something Denise had once said to him. *You want to get to somewhere new, let go of the ledge.* Tom slowly moved his hand on to her back and let it lie flat against her shoulder.

'Let's enjoy tonight just for itself,' she whispered.

That seemed the right thing to do. One hand off the ledge at a time. The two of them held each other tight and danced into the New York City night, momentarily parted from their loneliness.

Chapter Fifty-Three

Outside, snow had started to fall. The thick white flakes turned black as soon as they hit the wet street, but the tops of cars were gathering a blanket of thick snow. Inside the one lit all-night shop on a narrow and dilapidated row, wet footprints trailed from the door to the counter. A path made of ripped-up brown boxes continued around the two aisles. In the back room of the 7-Eleven, Maurice Macy danced from one foot to the other like he was desperate for a leak. He picked up a large stack of boxes of tinned meat without breaking sweat.

Benny Marconi looked up from the old black leather La-Z-Boy in the corner of the back room and nodded his approval. Mo had only been with him a few weeks but he was the best worker Benny'd ever had – strong, silent and able to work fourteen-hour shifts, seven days a week for minimum wage without a single complaint. Mo, aka 'Redtop', was the perfect employee. Benny leaned out of his seat and slapped his back as he passed. 'Way to go, Kong!'

Maurice placed the three boxes on the floor of the shop and took out a knife. He ripped open the first box. Tins of prime cooked mince. He more or less lived on tinned mince and tinned stew. He smiled and licked his lips. But his mind was a simple one and had very few avenues for thought. The idea of mince made him think of dinner, dinner made him think of home.

And home made him shiver and sweat.

It had been like that for days now. Half the time, he had too much to do and could forget all about it. Put it out of his mind. He was normal old reliable Mo. Smiling, forgetful, helpful Mo. Serving the coffee, sweeping the store, helping an old lady get something off the high shelves.

Then it'd come to mind like a sudden vision and he'd shake. He'd shake because he suddenly remembered. And it was hard to remember. Too hard. All his life he'd been cold. He didn't want to be cold again. He didn't want that. He wanted to be warm now. Good and warm.

He left the boxes of mince and walked over to the till. The only way to stop his anxiety was counting. He liked to count. Counting was his best thing. He opened the till.

'Just counting up, Mr Marconi.'

Benny Marconi mouthed something under his breath, but let the big guy do his thing. Redtop cashed up about eight, nine times a day. He was compulsive like that. But in the short time he'd worked there, Maurice hadn't lost a cent.

Now he was cashing up, but little Lottie was still coming to mind. She'd been strong. She'd cried all night long. Low horrible sobs. All night long. Even when he warned her. Even when he held his hand over her mouth and really pleaded with her to be quiet.

'Don't be making me do this. Please don't be making me do this.'

He didn't like it when they got emotional. He liked just talking to them and holding them sometimes. Looking after them was nice. His hands started trembling. He liked to pet them, that was all. A sweat formed on his brow. He knew there would be trouble if she didn't shut up.

Now Lottie was gone and he missed her something terrible. His boss, Benny Marconi, was jabbering on from the back room. Something about cockroach suppliers and some whore he'd heard would give head for eighty-five cents. Benny's truck was busted. When the truck was working, Mo would go up to the Bronx and get the good cheap supplies, but what they were getting delivered now was expensive shit. Benny moaned every day about it.

Mo counted the nickels and dimes slowly and methodically – he didn't want to have to start again. He would cash up and leave. He wanted to be out on the street. Feel the night air in his lungs. He needed someone warm, that was all. He couldn't live alone any longer. Not any more. For years he'd been alone, locked up in those small white cells on Ward's Island. He'd told the psychiatrists that he didn't want to touch the girls any more and he thought he would be all right. But once he was out again, he saw them on the street and the old feelings came back. He wanted one. He wanted one of his own to keep. Lottie was so nice and warm. But she had gone now and he needed more.

He wrote the total in the final column in pencil. He added across the columns. He added up thirty-five figures in each of seven rows and totalled them. It took him eight seconds. He checked the number against the till read-out.

Bingo. Not a cent out.

He liked it like that. Not a cent more or less. He worked all day making sure that not a mistake was made. All fourteen hours.

Benny emerged from the back. 'You get that, Redtop? Eighty-five cents. She'll take an IOU too, they tell me. It's cheaper to get your dick sucked than get a cup of coffee in this city.'

Maurice looked up from the books. 'It's all correct, Mr Marconi. All exact.'

'Just like always, Redtop. You're a fucking marvel. You know that. A fucking counting machine. My big lump of the world's stupidest genius!'

'Just like to get it right for you, Mr Marconi.'

Redtop took off his blue apron and hat. He hung them carefully on a hook labelled *Mo*. He put on his jacket, over one of the bright red rollneck sweaters which had given him his nickname.

Maurice was one of life's sad stories. The kind of guy that little guys like to take a pop at in the street. He was six foot one, clean-cut and strong. It was only the look in his eye that told you something inside wasn't quite right.

As he got to the door he picked up the large brown suitcase that he used to carry laundry to and from the launderette.

'You washing again, you dirty old dog? What've you been up to?'

'Just like clean sheets, Mr Marconi.'

Maurice nodded his goodbye and opened the glass door. It was snowing.

'Here,' called Benny and flicked him a dollar as he was leaving. 'Get your dick sucked on me.'

'Sure will, Mr Marconi.'

'You just make sure you bring me the change.'

Chapter Fifty-Four

Central Park
November 27, 12.40 a.m.

It was the perfect evening for young love to blossom – to explode even. The snow had started falling on the city again. New York City in the snow – the air chill on your face and hands and the tall buildings of the city rising up to the deep dark sky.

East Drive was so quiet you could hear owls from Central Park either side. It was almost deserted. Just a happy young couple weaving along the empty cycle path, laughing as they walked.

Lucy James was twenty years old with long dark hair and a playful smile. She was dressed in a short denim skirt with a big puffa jacket. Seth McAllister walked by her side listening to her glorious ramblings. She was such an extrovert, such a force of nature. An arts major to his love of the sciences. She jumped, skipped and turned as she walked and talked. He just loved to watch her like she was some effervescent experiment and she just loved to be watched.

They'd spent the last few hours drinking and flirting together in a bar looking out over the city – a romantic view, alcohol, mutual attraction . . . his hand brushing against her thigh, her hand touching his arm. It was going to happen tonight. They'd waited months to get this far. Oh, and didn't the wait make it all so worthwhile. Christ, it was going to be good.

They were so obviously desperate that they could see it in each other's eyes. They would enter his college room so full of pent-up passion that they would tear at each other's clothes, kiss deeply and wrestle each other to the floor before they even reached the bed.

They entered the twisting path of the park. It was so beautiful to see the huge snowflakes falling over the trees. They passed a man in a red top sitting strangely still on a bench with a suitcase beside him.

'On holiday?' Lucy asked with a giggle. The man on the bench just looked at her. He looked at her short denim skirt. She was the type. She looked like a hooker. Hookers you could take. Hookers didn't cause a fuss like those rich girls. No one missed a hooker. They all wore clothes like that. Lucy's laughter floated by. There was no one else around. The couple walked further into the park. Lucy was a risk-taker and a romantic. Seth was getting nervous.

'Where are you taking me, Lucy?'

'Somewhere private!' she called out. She'd got this idea in her head that it would be pretty fucking amazing to do it al fresco with snowflakes falling on your face, in your open mouth.

They came to some low evergreen shrubs and left the path. Seth heard something to the side. A crack. 'What was that?'

'An escaped lion!' shouted Lucy. 'Coming to get you!'

'Listen,' said Seth. 'It's getting closer.' They both stayed silent. They could hear something, or someone, walking close by. But they couldn't see through the dense shrubbery. Lucy pulled up close to Seth. Why not use it as an excuse? She held him firmly. Seth was keen to listen, though.

'It's moving away now. What do you think it is?'

'Don't know, don't care,' Lucy said and ran ahead. 'Follow me, Seth!'

Seth laughed. She was so impetuous. He called after her.

'Let's get back to my place. I've got an old bottle of Amaretto and a Neil Diamond CD!'

She stopped, winked and flashed him a cheeky smile. 'Why wait till we get back to your place?'

Now it was a different game she was playing. She darted into the bushes. 'If you can catch me!' she called out.

Seth saw her disappear and he felt a sudden surge of adrenalin as he imagined her body against his in the cool snow. He didn't follow her, though. No, he would surprise her. He would come round behind her and make her jump.

Lucy ran a little distance and then stopped. She could hear Seth moving now, coming through a tree with low-hanging branches. He was only a few steps away from her, but the light from the paths had disappeared and the park was suddenly very dark.

Lucy could no longer hear his footsteps. She felt strangely excited by the secrecy of the darkness and didn't want to wait any longer. Why not make their first time memorable. Right here – in the heart of the city they both loved. Under the city sky!

She was feeling pretty adventurous after several Malibu and Cokes. She rested against a tree. Her chest was heaving with excitement. She called out: 'Oh, Seth! I'm here! Come and get me!'

He didn't reply. She walked a few steps back through the shrubs. There was a thin sliver of pale light from the path. It seemed a long way away all of a sudden. The night seemed unnaturally quiet.

Out of the stillness, a shuffling noise. Then she heard the shrubs rustle. She jumped. 'Seth, you bastard.' A figure appeared in the clearing, covered in snow.

'Is that you?' she called out. Again no reply. Lucy suddenly felt fear tighten around her. She wanted to run, but she managed to calm herself.

It had to be Seth playing one of his jokes! She screamed out,

'Seth! Stop it. Stop it now. I'm scared.' He was approaching. She could see there was something wrong. His size, his movement, was all wrong.

The guy in the red top rushed at her and Lucy started to scream but the sound was quickly cut short as a heavy cosh landed on the side of her head. She fell on to the snow and Maurice quickly opened the suitcase and put her in it. He clipped the clasp shut and lifted the case with one hand.

Then he was gone. He was smiling now. A great big excited smile.

Chapter Fifty-Five

East Harlem
November 27, 1.20 a.m.

The suitcase had been light as a feather with this one. He reckoned that she could be no more than ninety-five pounds. He lugged the suitcase up the street and no one batted an eyelid. He was just simple old Mo and no one cared enough to get involved.

His small apartment was a stinking hole in a disused schoolhouse. At one time the whole building had been alive with people. But the school had shut down and now the building was in a state of progressive decay. Each day it seemed that more windows were broken and boarded.

Once in his apartment, he had a fixed routine. He used chloroform, which meant you could bathe them without having to restrain them.

He opened the case and the curled body of Lucy James lay inside like a little snail in a shell. Maurice stroked her cheek. She did look different from his previous girls. She looked younger, and clean too. Much more healthy than the others. Maybe she was new to the game. Still, it didn't matter much to him. She'd be just as nice to take care of and hug up to.

He picked her up and put her on the bed. Lying flat out, she was probably only just five foot three inches tall. A real little 'un, he thought. He liked her, though. He liked her little button nose and her straight shiny hair. Her skin smelled of cream.

He was light as air as he tiptoed into the bathroom to run a bath. He put in some special nice bubbles that he bought from the store and opened his bathroom cabinet. It was stocked with things he thought his girls might like. Anything a girl could want.

He returned to the girl with a bottle of disinfectant and some cotton wool. He dabbed the dried blood from her head. There was an inch-long gash from the cosh, but it would heal real soon.

Then he undressed her, took her denim skirt off, her black pantyhose and black panties. Her jacket came next and a large pink woolly sweater and a T-shirt. No brassiere. That was new, but it was good if she didn't wear one. Buying brassieres was not easy. The girl lay naked on his bed. Mo looked on, scared by his own trembling excitement.

Maurice took her clothes to his little desk and took out a notebook. He flicked through the pages. He came to the next blank page. He wrote her name real neat. It was Lucy. He liked that, too. Lucy with the button nose. Yes.

He took each item of clothes one at a time and wrote the details in his notebook. The size, the colour and anything else. He just liked to know so that when he went to the department store he could get something right for her. He wanted to keep her for a good long time.

He wrote down:

Skirt – blue, denim, short, petite

Sweater – pink, wool, small

T-shirt – orange, cotton, Jeff Beck logo, petite

Pantyhose – black, opaque

Panties – black, size six, polyester and cotton

Now he knew the girl liked different colours and was size small or petite. It felt good to know a little more about her.

The trickle of water from the hot faucet had filled the bath and Maurice lifted the girl into it. He liked the washing and cleaning and looking after. He soaped her all up with a sponge and got her all clean and soft. Then he put her in a nightdress and laid her back on the bed.

The restraints were not strictly necessary as the room had no window and the only door was locked with a single key Maurice kept on a string round his neck. But still, it was best at the start in case they went crazy at you.

He had a really good set of bed restraints straight from a mental hospital that a guy gave him for nothing. The bracelets were leather on the outside and a soft material inside so it didn't hurt their wrists and ankles. There were four body restraints but he left these untied. She was only a little thing. He couldn't imagine she'd need them.

When the job was finished, Maurice sat and turned on the TV. He liked TV. He liked to watch it with his girlfriends. It was like being married, sitting there together with the TV on, and it made him feel safe and happy.

He couldn't wait to go to bed and hug up close to her and smell her hair. He reckoned she might be a stayer if only he could keep her alive. It was hard to keep them alive, just like the rabbits he used to be allowed to keep. Sometimes they just died on you. Maybe it was the cold, maybe they were scared or maybe Mo just wasn't feeding them right.

Chapter Fifty-Six

The red display on the bedside clock in Tom's apartment read 6.14 a.m. A crumpled cotton quilt lay half across his outstretched body. The room smelled of sweat and whisky. In the hour-before-dawn stillness, a sharp knock rang out. Four hard and fast raps on the apartment door.

Harper stirred slowly and listened. Again, he heard four short knocks. He flicked the lamp on. He certainly wasn't expecting visitors. Whoever it was knocked again. Tom stood up and nearly reeled over on unsteady legs. The room was still coming together out of hazy grey dots. He didn't like this. Who wanted him at this time of day? Perhaps it was just Eddie with a new story to tell him. He hoped.

In the living room, Harper quietly pulled on his jeans and stared out into the darkness. He could see the light in the hallway under his door. He could see the shadow of two feet. He edged round the room, keeping out of the line of the door, and took up a position low to the floor. The knocking continued. It was a careful, precise knock. He suddenly imagined it was Lisa standing in the corridor and felt his heart hammer in his chest.

'Who is it?' he called out.

'It's me,' replied the voice quietly. It was Denise. Harper felt

311

his anxiety begin to recede. He'd left Denise hours earlier. Plenty of time to get drunk. He remembered slow-dancing long into the early hours. He pulled on a T-shirt and opened the door.

She stood there in a long black coat. It had snowed again on her way over. Her hair was wet and she was holding a black and red notebook.

'Denise.'

'You can't give up on this one, Tom. Not just yet. Not now. Listen, I went through my notes. I've been working on the profile. I know you say you're not working the case, but we can still help. We've already done some good work, but there are some errors and our analysis doesn't go far enough.'

'Denise.'

'If we use my earlier profile, we're looking for a married salesman with a high school education. Too many people. We need to be more precise. Until we're precise, no one's going to recognize this guy.'

'Denise,' he said for the third time.

'I know who I am, Tom. Now put some coffee on, we've got work to do here. You and I could get somewhere on this one. We can pass our profile to Blue Team and see if it helps. Then we leave it, all right? We can call it quits and walk away. But we've got to give them what we know.'

Harper smiled. She was sure determined and he liked it. And what's more, she was right. He went to the kitchen and put the kettle on. He stood at the door and watched as she took off her coat. It sparkled with melting snowflakes.

He put the coffee on the table and she sat down. 'I've been up all night, but we're going to have to go through this line by line. I want a perfect picture of the killer. By the time we finish, we need to be able to determine where he buys his socks. You ready?'

'I'm ready,' Harper said. He had a sceptical smile on his face but Denise was more than ready for his attitude.

She opened her notebook. 'My profile was all right, but it's general. I've tried to add some specifics. Let's see what you think.'

Tom nodded.

'To begin with,' she said, 'we're dealing with an SSSK: a sexually sadistic serial killer. That tells us one important thing – SSSKs don't stop until they're caught or killed. The ultimate fantasy for the SSSK is control. The collection of trophies is an example of possession and the expression of the fantasy. The taking of the body parts indicates a need to possess the dead as well as the living. The killer needs trophies because he does not feel adequate with women. And we'll see this in his work and home life.'

Tom sat down next to her. She was a scientist, but she was homing in on the kind of person the killer might appear to be from the perspective of his wife or colleagues. It was promising.

'These are my profile notes,' said Denise, and handed him her notebook. Tom flicked over the pages.

'He's a man with two sides, a kind considerate man who has violent mood swings. He might even hit his wife, but be overly sentimental with children. He has a fixation with being loved because it's the only way to fulfil his needs, but he will not be sexually active with his wife.'

Tom smiled. 'You're describing Average Joe, Denise. He's a good guy who sometimes gets angry, he loves his wife but loses his temper, and they've lost touch with each other.'

'It's not Average Joe,' said Denise. 'Listen carefully. His mood swings are violent. He will be sentimental with his wife at times and then get angry. He will enjoy hurting her. Enjoy it because it allows him to control how she thinks and feels. That's what he wants. He wants to own the narrative. He sees himself as a martyr who loves too much, too intensely, who is not loved enough in return. The unusual feature of this case is that he's gone for sophisticated victim types – maybe prostitutes as well, but we'll leave that for now. These high society girls are the unobtainable angels. Either this is because he's got this whore/Madonna thing going on or it's something practical. My thinking is that he indulges himself with these girls to prove he's not the loser he inwardly knows he is. He's living out some fantasy life in which he is a part of these women's lives. If Lottie Bixley is his, then it indicates that there is a strong need to feed the impulse to kill. He might have two modes – an organized mode and a disorganized mode. I've never seen that in the same killer before.'

'Or he's just trying to fuck with the profilers,' said Tom, sipping coffee.

'It's not out of the question after what he did to set up Winston Carlisle. Or it could be more banal than that. If I'm right about Lottie Bixley, then he also had access to a house for four days in November when the family were away. He might have been alone at home and needed someone quick – so he took a hooker.'

Harper nodded. 'The Lottie connection is very slight, but you might have something, Denise, so go on.'

'Okay. He drives a car, possibly a blue car. He's in his late thirties or early forties and is clean shaven with dark or greying hair. He has an interest in poetry and art, again because it makes him feel like less of a loser. He likes going to museums like the Frick and MoMA. They make him feel intelligent and sophisticated. He lives somewhere off the Triborough Bridge, possibly in the North Queens area, and works in and around North Manhattan, but he's on the move. That's why he's less worried about being identified. I think he sees lots of different people all the time. He owns a garage or workshop of some sort and is often away from home for extended periods in the evening. He needs to be in East Harlem and on Ward's Island more frequently than other locations. There's a reason for that. I don't know what it is, but it needs looking at. He buys expensive fashion gifts for his wife. Shoes, scarves, jewellery.

She will not know where these items come from. His childhood was somewhere rural, but he will rarely speak about it. He also has a problem with the police. He wants to prove himself better than all of you, so I would suggest that at some point he will likely have applied for the police department, either in New York or elsewhere. He will have been rejected at the psychological assessment. He will sometimes come home in different clothes from the ones he was wearing in the morning. He may leave items of women's jewellery or underwear in his car. In the last month his strange behaviour will have escalated rapidly. His family will have noticed his preoccupation. He will clean his car thoroughly at the weekend. He will vacuum the boot of the car and shampoo the interior. His shoes will sometimes have mud on them. There may be small scratches on his face, neck or hands. He may come home with a smell of unfamiliar perfume. He will have dirt under his fingernails. He has hunted and skinned and gutted animals before, so he's not afraid of cutting. My guess, Tom, is that his wife will know who he is. She must know.'

Harper listened intently. Denise was wired. This was far beyond anything she'd done before. And it was compelling. 'Where did it all come from, Denise?'

'It takes a while to come together. It's all based on evidence. Your evidence. All the stuff that came back from each team. I just painted a picture – the kind of picture that his wife would see. You were wrong about my interests, Tom. I don't care about his psychology, I care that he gets caught. This might help. What do you think?'

'It's very good.'

'Even though it's written by a civilian?'

'Even so. It reads good. Shit, Denise, it's very good. You've brought him to life.'

'You're not going to call this a load of psychobabble?'

'Not this time.'

'You think they'll use it?'

'I guess that they will.'

'So,' said Denise, 'do we know where he buy his socks?'

Tom looked at her. 'Yeah, we know. He doesn't buy them – his wife does.'

Chapter Fifty-Seven

The Met
November 27, 10.35 a.m.

Straight after they agreed all aspects of the profile, Denise and Tom left his apartment and continued their conversation over breakfast in a coffee house for another couple of hours. By the end of that time Tom was convinced he should do something with Denise's profile.

He called Eddie Kasper. He couldn't meet him at the station house, so they agreed to meet on the steps of the Met, a short walk from Harper's apartment and a shorter walk to the murder sites on the Upper East Side.

When Denise and Harper arrived at the elegant steps leading up to the stone façade of the Metropolitan Museum of Art they stood for a moment and looked at each other in the winter sunlight. Tom was preoccupied. He felt guilty about his late night dance, the subsequent kissing. It was supposed to show him he was over Lisa, but it had just brought her back to life. He still felt connected. He needed to get out of the deep tracks in his own mind and there was only one way he knew – Denise Levene's way: an elastic band. He snapped it hard against his wrist and looked up at the cool grey façade of the museum. A text message interrupted him.

'It's Eddie,' he said.
'Where is he?'

'He's inside pretending he loves art. It's a surefire way to get a date.'

'What happened to the last love of his life?'

'Like a firework – they burn bright, but die out quick.'

Tom and Denise waited in the lobby until Eddie Kasper drifted across in a sports jacket. He was smiling.

'Look the fuck at this,' he said, holding up a small piece of paper. 'I got three numbers here inside of ten minutes. This place is like some secret garden of available hotties. Why you never tell me about this place, Harps?'

'Just as long as they didn't ask you about the paintings,' said Tom.

'Fuck that, I've got that critical look down to a fine art. I suck my cheeks and say, well, you know, you got to ask yourself, what was the artist trying to say, you know, we got to throw our minds way back to understand all of this.'

'Nice threads,' said Denise, smiling at the jacket.

'You offering your number too?' Eddie held out his scrap of paper.

'Only when you need therapy, which is going to be soon.'

They walked across the polished stone floors until they found a quiet room, where they sat in a line on the bench.

Harper shuffled for a moment. 'Thanks for hearing me out a moment. Denise has been researching and working up a profile.'

Kasper nodded, 'Least someone has. FBI profilers say that our pattern killer is too indistinct. They won't give us a line in case it's wrong and we point the finger their way. There's nothing they say we can go public on. And we've got nothing new on the case down at the station house. The new lead, Detective Lassiter, is still clearing his throat.'

Harper half smiled. 'Listen, they're wrong. Denise has a profile of the guy. It's very good. It's based on his behaviour patterns. Imagine what his wife would see and you'll get the picture. She'll see a violent, preoccupied and secretive husband who shows small signs of the kills. He'll have dirty fingernails, scratches, blood stains, and he'll make frequent changes of clothes and stay away from home.'

Eddie looked hard at Tom. 'You serious, Tom?'

'Yeah, it's a good profile.'

'No, I mean about praising someone else for casework? Are you ill or something?'

'Hey, I praise when it's due, which isn't often.'

'Denise,' said Eddie, 'you need a medal for getting a good word out of this sonofabitch. Can I be the first to congratulate you?'

'Knock it off, Eddie. Just tell us – do you think you can get Lafayette and Lassiter to go public with this? The killer's wife knows him. She'll recognize him. It's a chance.'

'We publish these telltale signs of the killer and wait until she calls? Is that what you're saying?' said Eddie.

'Yeah. Exactly.'

'I'll try for you both. You know Lafayette thinks Denise is a good thing and Lassiter will want to look like he's making a difference, so it might be okay.'

'We also think that there's more to find out about where Lottie was held for four days before she was murdered. I want to look into it,' said Tom.

'Why? Lottie Bixley's got nothing to do with Sebastian.'

'We don't know that for sure. I found cherry blossom at the scene, which is something. In the profile, we suggest that maybe the family were away from home for the four days Lottie was held.'

'That's a long shot,' said Eddie.

'Just go with it,' said Tom. 'Listen, I went back through the case in my mind and we didn't even start to do work on Lottie's murder. We were preoccupied with the Kitty situation. Things got messy and then I was off the case. We need to speak to some people who knew Lottie. There might be some play in checking out her last movements.'

'Maybe,' said Eddie. 'Denise, what do you think?'

'We need to look into it,' said Denise. 'My take is that Lottie might have been an opportunity he couldn't bear to miss, so he may have made mistakes there that we haven't spotted.'

'Okay,' said Kasper. 'I get it that Lottie is a different package. You're saying it's like someone likes real fine food but sometimes they just want a good old hamburger.'

'Yeah, something like that,' said Denise.

'For some reason,' said Tom, 'whoever killed Lottie held her for four days and then discarded her quickly. We got to figure what happened.'

'So we need to go speak to some hookers,' said Eddie. 'See if we can get anyone talking.'

On the way over to Lottie Bixley's last known location, Eddie Kasper stopped at the station house to pass Denise's profile to Lafayette at Blue Team. Captain Lafayette looked at it gratefully and promised to consider it carefully. He agreed that they needed something to big-up the department's efforts after the débâcle with Winston Carlisle and this would keep the hungry mouths at One Police Plaza quiet for a day or two.

If Lafayette could get the executives to agree to the profile, every newspaper would run the short 500-word description covering her key points. The headline would read: 'Is This Your Husband Or Boyfriend?' There would be many across New York having sleepless nights.

Chapter Fifty-Eight

Marty Fox's Home
November 27, 2.05 p.m.

Marty Fox sat in his bedroom waiting for his wife to emerge from the bathroom. He'd set up a nice early lunch for them both in a quiet restaurant that he knew she liked and now they were going to do something they hadn't done in about ten years – slip off into bed for the afternoon. Marty drank a few glasses of good wine with his meal and their conversation had turned all nostalgic – there was a time when the only woman he wanted was her, and somehow he'd remembered it as they sipped their red wine and talked about the years of struggle and good fun. Good years. Very good years. Just a little distant now.

Sitting alone, Marty was finding it difficult to concentrate. The photograph in the paper shocked the life out of him. Kitty Hunyardi, her name was, but Marty was sure it was the same girl that he'd seen on Nick's cell phone. What the hell did it mean? He felt terrified by the prospect that Nick was involved in Kitty's death somehow, but he kept on trying to convince himself he was mistaken. The last session with his patient, Nick had been too fucking weird. Maybe his memory was confused. Marty didn't like weird. He liked categories so that he could file these things away, far away from his conscious mind. But he couldn't file Nick. All that stuff about the girl called Chloe and her apparent murder. The photographs of Kitty. It was too much for Marty. Way too much. Fantasy or reality? Marty didn't know. And then the reports of Kitty's murder in the papers and on the news, and suddenly everywhere he fucking looked, he could see the news about a guy who stalked and followed women. A guy who was unstable. A guy who could be Nick.

Marty Fox stroked his forehead slowly. The word 'coincidence' was a very reassuring one in these circumstances. Yeah, he'd been running that same word around his head for a few days now. Sure, a coincidence: two unrelated events that seem connected but are only similar by chance. That's all it was. An alignment of unconnected events. They must happen a million times a day. It was nothing at all to worry about. Nothing.

Marty started to yank off his socks. His feet had that yellowing look of a life spent too long in the dark. He looked up at the décor. Wallpaper borders of twisting roses and fake brass wall lamps. His wife's taste was not his own, for sure, but he'd let her indulge herself. He'd passed on the responsibility. Maybe he shouldn't have given up like that – let her have the house. Maybe that was where they began going their separate ways. Sitting there with his yellow feet, and the dizzy feeling of being overfed under the light of fake brass lamps, he felt like a failed car salesman having a bad day at a cheap motel.

Life had become a series of disappointments welded together with the hope of an affair. That's what Marty had done to himself. Sure, for a long time he'd thought he was a smart ass to be getting so much off-limits sex, he'd even enjoyed fooling his wife, but all he was doing was pouring good old gasoline into a leaking tank.

He'd loved her so much, too. She'd been able to funnel the idiot inside him somewhere good. Without her, there was no way he would've got his qualifications let alone set up his practice in New York City.

Why had he thrown it away? Or, moreover, when had he thrown it away? The shock of Nick had made Marty melancholy.

It'd also made him run to the one place he'd only ever wanted to be.

'I never was good enough for you, babe,' he said to himself in the room. 'Maybe I just became the asshole I always thought I was.'

Marty wondered for a moment if anything in life was really and truly redeemable. If the betrayals could be undone, somehow, his failures and mistakes wiped away with a gleaming new beginning. He pulled off his trousers. He didn't think so.

The worst thing was the fact that while his beautiful, far-too-good-for-him wife was refreshing herself in the bathroom, approaching their promised intimacy without bitterness or recriminations, all he could think of was Nick and a girl called Kitty.

Maybe Nick just happened to be around the same Kitty, maybe he wasn't a psycho killer. Marty had even considered going to the cops. Yeah, and getting caught up in a whole world of shit he'd rather keep clear of. Instead of going to the cops, he did a little research. He wanted to know more about the girl called Chloe. He didn't know whether Nick had somehow been involved in Chloe's murder or if he'd grown up near to it and kind of fantasized about it. His curiosity had got the better of him, though. He'd spent a few hours looking up the case on the internet. He wished he hadn't. It took him a while to track it down, but he found it in the archives of the *New York Times*. The story had hit the nationals it was so gruesome. And that was when the tension really started to get to Marty.

The murder of Chloe Mestella was real all right. She was a beautiful young West Virginian prom queen from a wealthy farming family and she'd been raped and murdered in her own bedroom while her parents entertained downstairs. It was a savage murder. Marty had read the details and winced. She was real. Chloe was a real girl, not a character from Nick's imagination. She was real and she was dead and Nick was still not over it. Marty had to consider why that might be.

He tried to forget about it, but his curiosity and the media's obsession with a rubber heiress called Kitty who was stalked on the day that Nick turned up with her photograph on his phone wouldn't let him. He couldn't get to grips with what he was thinking. Maybe, Nick had killed Chloe out of rage and jealousy. Maybe Nick had killed Kitty. He couldn't be sure: Nick was a delusional paranoid – fantasy was his modus operandi. It was all just coincidence, right?

Marty felt better when Nick didn't turn up for his session. But later even that got to him. What if Nick was watching him? Marty was a self-confessed, T-shirt-wearing coward. He wanted to run away and hide. He wanted to tell his wife. He wanted her to look after him again, to sort out the big problems.

His wife appeared from the bathroom. She was smiling as she struck a pose in her underwear. She was still gorgeous to look at – all dark eyes and lush dark hair. He'd just stopped seeing it. Somehow, the woman that all other men would still drool over had become too available to him. His eyes had glazed over.

He smiled up at her and put his arm round her waist. She moaned a little as he moved his hands over her soft skin. This was just what he needed, a little afternoon of relaxation. He kissed her stomach as she ran her fingers through his thinning hair.

She pushed him back on the bed. She wanted to please him. That had been her undoing. Wanting to please a guy like Marty. It had spoiled him, no question. She unbuckled his belt with a flourish and unzipped him. A minute passed and her expression changed from that of a sultry mistress to sadness and disappointment. Marty lay there feeling a sweat form on his brow. *What the fuck is happening*, he was thinking as he tried to bring to mind all the sexy things he'd ever thought, but all he could see was Chloe and Kitty Hunyardi. *Fuck!* This hadn't happened before. Not ever! *Fuck me*, he pleaded, *not with her, it's not fair.*

His wife raised her head. Her face was a picture of self-loathing. 'I just don't attract you any more, do I, Marty? I'm sorry.'

Marty looked at her in despair and shook his head. 'You do, I promise you, you do. I'm just . . .' He reached out to her and tried to hug her, but she pulled away.

'I bet this doesn't happen with your lovers, does it?' She stared at him and he had nothing to say. The look of disgust on her face would remain with him for life.

Chapter Fifty-Nine

East Harlem, 7-Eleven
November 27, 2.23 p.m.

The air outside had dipped a few degrees and the sky had darkened. In the gloom, Harlem looked more deserted than ever. Only a few stragglers were about, propped up by steel fencing posts and drinking direct from the bottle.

Tom Harper and Eddie Kasper drove to the 7-Eleven. This was Lottie Bixley's last known location. According to the statement of Lottie's brother, she had left her two young children in the apartment while she went out to get cigarettes. It was only a five-minute walk on foot, through some dangerous territory if you were the wrong type of person or just happened to meet the wrong type of person. If Lottie Bixley had been in a hurry, she might have taken one of the many side alleys and who knows who she might've met.

'What do you make of it, Eddie? How did Lottie's killer take her? What's his style?' asked Harper, tapping on the Buick's cheap plastic dash.

'Posed as a john, probably.'

'Dangerous for the kids, isn't it?' said Harper. 'Given that she wanted to clean up her act. She would've returned home if she could have. The 7-Eleven was a short walk. If she's going to jump in a car with a trick, she's going to make sure someone is with the kids, and she'd thrown Carl out.'

'Maybe,' said Kasper, nodding to some tune in his head.

'If she's not going to get in with a john, either someone took her by force, or maybe she knew him.'

'That's a big jump, Tom. You got any evidence on that piece of bread or you just going to eat that big surmise sandwich all by itself?'

'I'm just casting around, Eddie.'

'We've taken one big fucking leap from a walk home to a known associate.'

'Hey, that ain't such a big leap.'

The sedan drew up outside the worn-out 7-Eleven store. An old white van was parked right across the kerb. 'Parks like you do, Eddie.'

'Sure does, but I got a shield says I got a right to do it.'

Graffiti was scrawled across the metal shutters, tagged by hundreds of young artists. In the centre was a cartoon of a half-naked blonde, winking. The legend on her panties read *The only Bush you can rely on*.

The detectives approached the store. The door jangled. A small intense-looking guy in a Hawaiian shirt and khaki pants was sitting on a box of tinned peaches, pricing some tubes of syrup. A big guy in a red top was standing at the counter counting coins.

'How you doing, bro?' said Kasper. 'You in charge here?'

The big guy shook his head. 'I ain't in charge. Mr Marconi is the man.' He pointed at the guy in the Hawaiian.

'Mr Marconi?' called Eddie.

The short man stood up and looked Eddie up and down. 'What the fuck do you want – fashion advice?'

Kasper smiled. 'Calm down, feller. We're cops. Just want to ask a question or two.'

At the mention of cops, Mo shivered and stepped back from the counter. They had found him out once before, all those years ago. But he had been careful this time. He edged backwards as

327

Benny Marconi gave the two cops a wide sardonic smile. 'Just what I fucking need, a couple of New York's finest.'

Kasper laughed and turned to Harper. 'See, he likes us.'

Harper didn't smile. 'Sorry to bother you, sir. Can I ask you a couple of questions?'

'Sure. What else do I have to do? This is my store – you get it?'

'We get it, Mr Marconi,' said Harper. 'Listen, we're investigating the disappearance of a woman by the name of Lottie Bixley. She was on her way to this store around Thanksgiving, early morning. Do you work Thursday nights?'

Benny nodded sarcastically. 'Monday, Tuesday, Wednesday, Thursday, Friday, Saturday, Sunday.'

'Well, maybe you can help us. Have you seen this hooker around and about?' Tom Harper handed him the photograph of Lottie Bixley. It showed a smiling woman about 110 pounds, blue eyes, aged eighteen – beautiful.

Benny looked at the photograph. The detectives waited. He continued to look. 'Pretty girl. It's a fucking shame,' said Benny, handing the photograph back.

'Did she come and buy anything?' Kasper went in so close that Benny could smell his breath.

'Back off and I might give you something. Anyway, the answer's no. I never saw the girl. Or maybe I did. I see girls like that all the time. I got nothing to say.'

'How about the big guy?' said Harper.

'Try him. He's slow, but if he saw her he'll remember all right.'

Tom Harper walked across to the big guy. Redtop was visibly shaking and standing with his back hard against the wall. 'Hey there, no need to worry. What's your name?'

'Mo.'

'Okay, Mo, I just want to show you a picture.' He handed him the photograph he'd taken from Lottie's brother.

Mo looked at the photograph. The detectives waited. Mo

continued to look. Harper looked at the suitcase beside the till. It was a large brown leather case. 'What's the case for?' he asked.

'Laundry,' said Mo.

'Do you know her?' said Harper.

'Pretty,' said Mo, handing the photograph back.

Kasper went in close and put an arm round the big guy. 'Did she come and buy anything?'

'Sure, yeah, that's right. She came in one night. Don't know what day it was. Nearly two a.m. We're a 7-Eleven, but we never shut.'

'You got a good memory there.'

'Sure. She bought a box of Viceroy Kings.'

'Anything else?'

'A box of Viceroy Kings. She gave me a five-dollar bill.'

'What was she wearing?' asked Harper.

'Pink dress. White shoes.'

'She say anything to you, big guy? Mention anyone following her?'

Mo shook his head.

'She just left?'

Mo nodded.

'Think some more, Mo. Did she have anyone with her?'

Mo shook his head. Benny appeared by his side. 'Are you this slow on the uptake all the fucking time, gentlemen? She bought cigarettes and left. What more do you want? Now let this guy earn his living.'

'Just one more thing,' said Harper. 'Is that your van outside blocking half the sidewalk, the one with MARCONI all along the side?'

'Hey, you going to ticket me? The fucking axle broke.'

'Get it off the sidewalk or I'll have it towed.'

'Tow the thing, you'll be doing me a favour.'

It was all they were going to get. So they knew she got the cigarettes, left the store alive and headed home. And then, in the five-minute walk, something happened to her and she ended up four days later in a dumpster.

Eddie looked across at Harper. 'What next, boss? You think we should take the big guy in for questioning? Not that we'd get much, by the looks of him.'

'You should, but it's not my call any more. You back on duty tomorrow?'

'Yeah.'

'Keep me posted, will you? Anything come up, I'd like to know.'

'What about you?'

'Missing persons have a database and she might have been logged. I want to check it out. I'll catch up tomorrow. And Eddie.'

'Yeah, man?'

'Thanks.'

Chapter Sixty

There were about 70 million hits for the word 'Viagra'. Marty Fox raised an eyebrow. *Thank shit, I'm not alone,* he thought. It was terrible news that his stresses since the last meeting with Nick had hit the bedroom. But there were different approaches to problems in life: one was to face them head-on and talk to someone, the other was to try to hide from them and hope a quick fix with some strong drugs would help.

Marty was going for the quick fix. *What am I going to do if I lose my one talent?* He put in an order and hoped that this would solve his problem. God, he was sorry about his wife. He'd insulted her in a way he hated himself for. Never again, he declared, typing in his credit card details.

He had also done what he could to get rid of his disturbing client. He'd asked his PA to cancel the next session with Nick and, in fact, cancel all sessions. He told her if she re-booked him this time he'd fire her. That would do it, he thought. Refuse to see Nick, bury his head in the sand and buy Viagra for the droop. Welcome back to normality.

He smiled. He was beginning to feel himself again. He picked up a carton of cigarettes and lit one, leaning back in his leather chair. So what if he was breaking the law. It felt good.

He inhaled deeply and felt the tingle of nicotine ripple through his veins. *Sweet heaven!*

At that moment, the door opened and Nick entered the room.

'What the hell do you want?'

His PA ran in after him. 'Sorry, Dr Fox, he just pushed past.'

'I need help, Doctor. It's urgent.'

Marty leaned forward. His problem had just come back. He waved his PA out of the office. 'It's okay. I'll handle this.'

'I need to see you, Doctor. You saw the news in the paper. Do you know what that means? You saw the photograph of the girl. Kitty Hunyardi. You must've thought what I thought. I've been terrified. Do you think I had anything to do with it?'

'Nick, Nick,' said Marty, taking control. 'I reflected on our last session. Therapy needs trust and confidence and objectivity. I don't think I can provide you with those elements. I have a list of other therapists you might want to see. I'm not a specialist in this area. They will be able to help you. Unfortunately, I can't. I'm sorry.'

Nick was wearing a cheap suit with a faint pinstripe. He looked like he'd slept in his car or something. 'I have to know. I have some more information for you.'

'Information?' said Marty. 'What kind of information?'

'Can I sit down?'

'No! I told you . . . Nick, you've gotta listen . . .'

Nick sat. 'I can't tell anyone else. What I'm about to tell you, Marty, will shock you. I've thought about telling you before but I've been afraid. But we have a connection. I feel that I can tell you. I can trust you.'

'Whatever it is, Nick, I don't want to know. I'm not going to listen.' Marty got up and walked to his desk. 'This session is over. You need to leave.'

There was a silence. Marty was hoping that the lunatic

would lose interest, but Nick just sat there. If he doesn't move, thought Marty, I'll just get up and go myself.

'Okay, Marty, have it your way.'

'Yeah, I will.'

Nick stood and approached Marty's desk. He took out a photograph and laid it on the desk before Marty. It was a picture of a beautiful girl.

Marty didn't recognize the picture. He looked at Nick. 'What?'

'Just after I heard about Kitty, I went home. I downloaded pictures from my camera to see some shots of my kids and I found several pictures of this girl. I've never seen her before.'

'Who is she?'

'Her name's Rose Stanhope. That's all I know.'

'How do you know her name, Nick?'

'There's a picture of her at a conference of some kind. Her name's on a label on her lapel. Rose Stanhope.'

'Oh, my God,' said Marty. 'You think she's next?'

'I don't know. I don't know anything.'

'Then who took the pictures?'

'This is who Sebastian wants,' said Nick, almost in a whisper. 'This is his next girl. I think he scopes them and then attacks. Sebastian always sees the worst in people. He killed Kitty, what's he going to do next? I don't know what to think.'

Marty felt the warmth drain from his skin. 'Hey, Nick, this has to stop. This is a fantasy you've got. Kitty was a coincidence. These are just photographs. You're not a killer, you're just disturbed. You live in a fantasy. You're projecting your feelings into these strange murders. You're from West Virginia, right?'

'Yeah,' said Nick.

'And you were around, right, when this terrible thing happened to Chloe. Am I right?'

'Yeah, of course.'

'But you didn't know Chloe yourself, did you?'

Nick thought for a moment. 'I wasn't lucky enough to know Chloe, not me, no. She was at my high school. In the year above.'

'That's right. It wasn't you. It was someone else, wasn't it? But for some reason, you felt guilty for it because you had a crush on her.'

'That's right, Doc, I did feel guilty. But it doesn't matter. It was Sebastian who killed her.'

'Why?'

'Chloe was my angel. He doesn't like me having angels. He likes to destroy them.'

'What or who is Sebastian?'

'I don't know.'

'It's just a fantasy, Nick. You're projecting all your fears on to this killer.'

'I just know I've stood by while Sebastian has done these things. I can't any more.'

'No, you didn't, Nick. You've just got yourself caught up in some fantasy. You need proper help. We need to get you to see Dr Bartholomew. This is a fantasy. He can help.'

'No, it's you I need. I'm trying to get help here. Sebastian . . .'

'What?'

'I can't tell you any more. I don't know any more. You can help me to stop him. Help me to stop him taking over.'

Marty's mind was a white sheet of fear. He couldn't think at all. He was scared for himself now. Perhaps this man had killed Kitty Hunyardi. He stared at him hard.

'Shocking, isn't it, Dr Fox? I'm as shocked as you. Please help me.'

'What do you want? I can't help. Go to the cops. You need to get yourself sectioned or locked up.'

'I want to know what I am. I want to know why something happened to Chloe. I want to know what the hell is going on. I want it to stop.' He pulled out an envelope and poured the contents on to the glass table. 'A diamond necklace. I found it in my pocket. Where the hell would I get a necklace like this?'

Marty didn't know what to think.

'The American Devil has killed rich girls. Why do I have a rich girl's necklace in my pocket? What am I going to do?'

'Listen,' Marty said, 'we've got to get you some serious help.'

'I'll be put away for the rest of my life. Please help me.'

Nick was a pathetic, weak figure on the couch. Marty looked across. 'Look, I can't help you. Have you not fucking noticed? I'm a fake, a flake, a pathetic excuse for a therapist. I know nothing about how to heal people. I just talk to them. I just want an easy life. We'll just say goodbye and forget all about it. How about that?'

'Then Sebastian wins,' said Nick.

Marty reached for his cigarettes and lit another. 'I can't help that. I really can't.'

'You know that those things will kill you, don't you?'

Marty looked up at Nick. 'Yeah, I know.'

Nick felt someone or something move within the corridors of his mind. Footsteps, heavy and distant. He was coming now. Nick looked up to Marty, his face contorted with fear. 'He's coming, Doctor. I can feel him.'

Nick's voice suddenly dropped an octave and a deep baritone voice said, 'You know what the motto of St Sebastian is, Doctor? *Beauty constant under torture*. Show nothing, remain beautiful, whatever the pain.'

Nick removed his hand from his pocket and raised a clenched fist up before him. 'I can sometimes keep him away. Sometimes I can.' Marty looked across – dark red blood was streaming from his hand, through the fingers and knuckles and on to the table and carpet. Marty rushed across and took hold of Nick's arm. 'Stop it! What the hell are you doing? Jesus!'

He pulled open Nick's bloody fist and a handful of sharp flat-headed nails clattered on to the glass table and across the floor, peppering the pale carpet with spots of blood. 'What the fuck are you doing, Nick?' Marty said, staring hard at Nick, who was concentrating with all his strength. 'What the fuck are you doing?'

'Resisting,' said Nick. 'Resisting him.'

Chapter Sixty-One

Marty Fox's Suite
November 28, 11.45 a.m.

Marty waited until he saw Nick disappear across the street, then he stood up. His shirt was sticking to him. He pulled off his tie and unbuttoned his shirt. He pulled it off and threw it in the trash. Then he pulled the *New York Times* out of the trash. He'd seen the killer's profile that morning in the paper but ignored it. Now he wanted to know. He read the 500-word description. His pulse started racing. Nick was a good match.

He pressed through to his PA. 'Get me a new shirt, will you, Jane.'

'I'm sorry, Dr Fox, he pushed right past me.'

'Yeah. I... Don't worry. And put me through to the police.'

'The police?'

Jane paused and then she said she would do as he asked.

Just then, Marty's cell phone vibrated. He took his jacket and searched the pocket. He pulled out his phone and pressed to read the text. An image appeared on his screen. He stared at it in confusion. What did she do that for? It was a picture of his wife. She was outside their house, getting into her car. It was earlier that day, he was sure of it. She was wearing what she had on that morning. White trousers and a purple blouse. What did she send that for? He looked at the message details – it wasn't from her cell.

Marty put his phone down on the desk and tried to think. Then the cell vibrated again and clicked against the glass. Another text arrived. Marty opened it. It was another picture. His wife, getting out of her car at her office. Again, it was a picture taken earlier in the day. A fear was dawning on Marty as he looked at the screen. Then another text arrived. There was his lovely wife at work. Another text came quickly after. This time she was looking directly into the camera and smiling. Marty's hand was shaking. His phone was vibrating constantly as photograph after photograph appeared. All of his wife, all from earlier in the day. All from someone standing close to her.

Jane called back through. 'I've got the police on the line. Can I patch you through?'

'Jane, that guy who just left; the guy who calls himself Nick Smith – he didn't say anything to you, did he?'

'Nothing.'

'You ever give him my cell phone number?'

'Sure. At the first session. Just your work phone, not your private number.'

'Thank you, Jane.'

'Can I patch you through now?'

'Sure.'

Marty looked down at his wife's smiling face then put his cell phone down. It continued to buzz with a life of its own. He picked up the office phone, his voice catching dry in his throat. 'Sorry, officer, I've made a mistake. It's fine. I had a client who was refusing to leave, but he's gone now. Sorry for wasting your time.' He put the phone down quickly.

Five more photographs arrived. Nick Smith had been following her right until he started out to Marty's office. Marty's heart was pounding. Nick or, worse, Sebastian had been stalking his wife. And he was feeling the guilt himself. Marty felt his cowardice leaching the colour from his skin.

He looked down at the last photograph of his wife, a woman

he'd lied to and betrayed for fifteen years. And now someone was threatening her life. Tears formed in Marty's eyes like long-lost relatives arriving at a funeral. He was a cheap, lying, adulterous bastard, but his heart yearned for her like a dog. He wanted to howl. He looked at her familiar face and realized why he was crying. He was looking at the only thing on earth that he really loved and wondering why the hell he was killing her.

Chapter Sixty-Two

Dresden Home
November 28, 11.55 a.m.

Dee had never meant to get married. It was always part of her long-term idea of what she'd do, but she'd never meant to marry Nick. Somehow, she'd found herself at an altar standing in front of a priest knowing both that this was her destiny and that she didn't want it at all. She cried all through her wedding night. Women like her just didn't have the heart to fight against it. She presumed that these doubts were normal, that marriage was, for all women, a compromise between personal dreams and the needs of men.

Her problem over the years, as she saw it, was that she was loyal. Faithfulness was her cardinal virtue. It was worth more to her than love. Faith was her gold standard and she expected it from herself.

And faith was a good thing, wasn't it? Faith was good in itself. Dee felt that her faith was tested every day after the children were born. She spoke to her priest and he agreed that faith was a good thing. He saw her bruised arms, he saw her hurt. 'Have faith,' he said. 'Stick with it.'

On the morning that the papers arrived, Nick was out with the children. There was a cherry tree wood a cycle ride away and Nick sometimes liked to spend time with them there. Dee had sat in the kitchen with the weak wintry sun touching her hair and her face. The paper lay open on the table as she sipped her tea. That was when she came across the police profile of the man they called the American Devil, and her faith finally slipped.

The thoughts that flew about her head seemed terrible and impossible. Dee stood at the window, her face taut with pain, biting her nails off one by one. Her hand encircled her waist and gripped her skin until her nails were embedded deep in her side. In her head, she went through every detail of the profile. It all fit.

It all fit so closely that it might've been written by her. She went through the details again and again, doubt springing up in accusation, denial breathing fire on every new memory. Her mind was a rush of tiny fragments – tiny blood spots, dirt under his fingernails, mood swings, long absences, violence and senti mentality, perversion, rape, manipulation, drinking, cleaning the car. He was ticking every box.

Every box, that was, except the four-day absence from home. Dee checked her calendar. She had been at home and so had Nick. It was a doubt large enough to make her feel stupid, large enough to make an excuse for herself.

For two hours, while Nick was out chasing his two children through the woods, Dee bit her nails, grabbed her skin and felt her mind contort. One detail didn't fit, but several did. She had to call the police number just to check, just to be reassured. Dee picked up the phone and began to dial. Her mind was still uncertain. Faith was turning somersaults in her heart. The line started to ring and she felt like a guilty child, her pulse racing, her breath short. In fact, Dee was terrified.

Then she saw Nick appear at the end of the driveway. He was carrying Michael under one arm. Michael was giggling and laughing with his father. Susan was on his shoulders, thumping his head as though he was a monster. She was screaming with delight and Nick was roaring like a troll.

Dee broke out a smile. She felt the muscles in her face ache from the tension. There he was, playing with his children. William and Susan with their father. He wasn't a killer, he wasn't a bad man, he was her children's father. Nick was right, sometimes she did get all confused in her head. Maybe she was going mad. The line rang once more and Dee replaced the handset. Once again in Dee's life, faith won.

Chapter Sixty-Three

Missing Persons Unit
November 28, 12.05 p.m.

A hooker somehow disappeared and her kids had half starved in a project that housed 3,500 people. So much for neighbours looking out for each other. So much for equal opportunity policing. The neighbours even said they heard crying and screaming from the girls, but that was normal in the projects. No need to interfere and find yourself facing a teenager with a gun. Shut your own door and block your ears.

Tom stared again at the image of Lottie Bixley's face. For four days, her children suffered on their own. For those four days, she was a missing person, not a murder victim. He logged on to the National Missing Persons database. He was looking for something. Anything at all. He typed in Lottie's details. Within about half an hour, he'd found another missing girl called Elisa Dale. He opened her details.

Female, 110 pounds, Caucasian, nineteen years old, brown hair. Suspected prostitute.

He scrolled down to her address and considered it for a moment. The date was June 14, 2006. Nearly eighteen months before Lottie went missing. He looked at the brief description. She went out to work the street and never returned. That was it. No investigation. Case closed.

Tom's curiosity clicked into gear. He narrowed his search

location and dates and began to find other young women.

Within an hour, Harper had pulled together three photographs of young women in front of him. Two Caucasian, one Hispanic, all in their late teens or early twenties, all of a slight build. All hookers living in East Harlem. All missing without a trace in the last twenty-four months.

None of these cases ever reached the homicide squad. None were investigated. Hookers were not considered high priority. Somebody somewhere just wrote a report and filed it. What the hell had happened to all these young women?

Harper wanted to push on with this missing persons thing further. He got a map up on the internet and started to pinpoint the addresses and the points at which the three girls went missing. He looked at the pattern in front of him. If these were homicides and not missing persons, this would be a major investigation. Maybe something went wrong with Lottie. Maybe her killer never intended to dump her. A body causes problems.

Deep into the database, staring at face after face of lost people, Harper felt suddenly very lonely. But something was bothering him. Missing hookers got shit while the rich girls had hundreds of detectives assigned to their cases. No one gave a damn about the girls up in the projects who made up the numbers.

Women who just seemed to disappear.

It took hours of going through the files to try to piece the jigsaw together. He had all the last known locations of five missing hookers across several different precincts going back four years pinned on a map. The missing hookers obviously congregated around the areas of poverty and prostitution. They couldn't all be just missing, could they? These girls were disappearing. Slowly, silently, invisibly – one after the other. And no one gave a damn. Deep in his gut was the churning feeling that this was somehow connected to the American Devil. The single cherry blossom petal was enough to keep him going.

Harper clicked on to open cases. The face of Lucy James stared out at him. He read the report.

Lucy James was not a hooker, but she had gone missing in Central Park late at night, just like Lottie Bixley. Tom read the details. She had been with her boyfriend in the park. Then she had been abducted. He read the boyfriend's statement. He said that they were out walking. She ran away from him into the bushes as some kind of tease and she was snatched. There was blood on the ground. Then something sprang out at Harper and he felt a rush of adrenalin. He re-read the boyfriend's statement and there it was.

'Along East Drive, we passed a guy sitting on a bench. He was a regular guy, tall, strong-looking, wearing a red rollneck and a black coat. He had a suitcase by his side. I remember that because Lucy asked him if he was going on vacation.'

Harper called Eddie directly. His voice sounded wired. 'Eddie, did you pull that guy from the 7-Eleven yet?'

'Just about to. Why?'

'I was looking into the missing persons angle. I found a young college girl who's disappeared. Last seen two nights ago. She's not a hooker like Lottie, but she went missing in Central Park.'

'Not from Harlem?' asked Eddie

'This girl was near enough to Lottie's last known location down on East Drive.'

'Any details? What's her name?'

'Lucy James.'

'So what's the connection?'

'The boyfriend saw a guy sitting on a bench just before Lucy disappeared. And guess what? He was wearing a red rollneck and had a suitcase with him. That spark any memories for you?'

'A fucking suitcase! He said he kept his laundry in it. He was also the last person to see Lottie alive.'

'The scene at Lottie's dump site had wheel marks,' said Harper. 'About the width of a suitcase. That's how he did it! How he moves these girls from one place to another without being seen. He puts the girls in a suitcase. Shit. A fucking suitcase.'

'I'll call the team,' said Eddie. 'Maybe it'll cross-reference with some sightings we've had for the American Devil. We've got thousands and thousands of statements but we weren't ever looking for a suitcase.'

'We've got to get back to the 7-Eleven, right now.'

Harper grabbed his coat and made for the door.

Chapter Sixty-Four

7-Eleven
November 28, 12.45 p.m.

The wipers on Eddie's red Pontiac struggled against a scuzzy grey sleet as they drove at high speed up to Harlem through the post-vacation traffic. Shoppers laden with bags from the pre-Christmas sales hunkered down into their coats, carelessly stepping into the stream of cars and cabs as they hurried to the subway.

Up in East Harlem, Eddie slammed the car hard against the kerbstone and both cops rushed out towards the 7-Eleven. The door jangled and hit a wire stack of magazines but no one appeared at the counter. 'Police! Can we get someone out here now!'

Benny Marconi, in a different coloured Hawaiian shirt and khaki pants, appeared from the back, pushing a kickstool with his toe.

'What's the fucking noise for?'

'We got to talk to you, now,' said Harper. 'Your man, the big guy who works here, where is he?'

The short guy stood up and looked them up and down. 'Not again, for fuck's sake.'

'Where is he?'

'He's out. What's it to you?'

'Listen, Mr Marconi, we're investigating a homicide case and we need to speak to the big guy. Where is he?'

Benny laughed out loud. 'Are you kidding me? Fuck you! We don't hear nothing out here. We don't know nothing. All I know is he's not here.'

'I promise we ain't kidding you,' said Eddie, moving up tight to the storekeeper. 'I can have twenty detectives tear the store to pieces, close you down for so long you ain't never gonna open again.'

'You think the fucking shakedown is gonna work on me? Forget it. Show me a warrant. You ain't got a thing. Go find him yourself.'

Harper turned quickly. 'What name does he go by here?'

'He's called Redtop, on account of his preference for wearing the same top every day of his life. I gave him the name.'

'What about his real name for payroll?'

'I pay him cash. He's called Mo. I don't know any more.'

'You got an address?'

'No. Don't know where he lives. I pay him peanuts and I pay him daily. He's only just started. He's the cheapest labour I ever had so I ain't asking questions.'

'You want to be an accessory after the fact in a major homicide case, Mr Marconi? Now, give us his address.'

The man went into the back store and came out with a ledger. He put it on the desk and turned it to them.

'This is his employment record. It's all I got.' On the page was the name Mo and a straight line under the address. 'I don't know where this man lives or even if he has a place to live. He carries a laundry bag everywhere, maybe he lives out of that.'

Harper handed him a card. 'The moment you hear from this guy, you call me. He could be a killer.'

Benny laughed. 'He's not a killer. He can't even swat a fly.'

'Call us,' said Tom.

They didn't know if this had anything to do with the American Devil but Harper felt this was the nearest they'd been since the beginning. They just had to find this guy now. How hard could it be to find a man like that in Harlem?

They walked out of the store. 'I've got a team coming up to watch the 7-Eleven. What do you say we do, Tom?' asked Eddie.

Tom wasn't sure. He stopped for a moment. 'The thing that's bothering me is this. If he's got Lucy James hidden somewhere in the city and we spook him, she could starve to death. We got to tread carefully. Can you get any more bodies up here to walk the streets?'

'I'll call in some favours,' said Eddie.

Chapter Sixty-Five

East Harlem
November 28, 3.00 p.m.

'Here's your guy,' Eddie said as he tossed a folder into Harper's lap. 'This drawing is based on the description given by Lucy James's boyfriend.' The police drawing was a close enough fit to the man they'd seen at the store. The big guy with the red turtleneck. They had an ID but no name.

The next part was harder – finding someone in a city of eight million. Mo was likely to be on foot. As far as they knew he didn't have a vehicle so he was likely to be only a short distance from the 7-Eleven and Washington House. All they had to do was get a team together and start asking the streetwalkers and searching the areas in the radius.

Eddie had done a job on this one too. He hadn't told Tom a thing. They pulled into the car park of North General Hospital in East Harlem and there in front of them were six detectives from the NYPD. Cops who had not taken to the mayor's bureaucratic reforms. They wanted to help out a cop with good instincts. They also wanted to shake the hand of the man who'd floored Lieutenant Jarvis, twice.

A detective called MacGyver spoke for the group.

'We understand you need help on this. Help of the unofficial kind. We're happy to do charity work, we're that kind of people.'

Harper smiled. He outlined the case against Redtop. He was the last person to see Lottie Bixley alive and he was spotted moments before Lucy James's disappearance. And the bonus was that this kidnapper might have some connection to the serial killer called the American Devil. All the team had to do was to spread out and get the low-down from every wino, lowlife and prostitute in the area and then see if they couldn't track Redtop down.

They worked in pairs. Harper teamed up with a rookie cop by the name of Shane Dell. He was a clean-cut redhead with a clear sense of justice.

They walked the area non-stop for a couple of hours. They must've stopped and talked to over a hundred people. Some just ignored them, others tried to help but had nothing. There were a couple of near misses – people thought they recognized the picture but then changed their minds. They had one thing that was helping them, though: solidarity. This was a man who might have murdered a prostitute, so they found the hookers happy to talk for once.

At the western side of Marcus Garvey Memorial Park, they got their first positive identification. Shane Dell approached a group of prostitutes sitting on a low wall next to a basketball court. He talked to them for five minutes and then called Harper across.

'This is Tom Harper. He believes someone took the woman we were talking about.' They looked up and nodded. 'Tell him what you told me.'

A black woman in her late twenties moved her head back and forth and looked around her suspiciously.

'I'm only saying we've seen that guy. Don't know who he is. He's one of the roaming-lonely you see around. Always carrying a heavy bag. Lost his mind.'

'Where have you seen him?'

'Around. Nowhere in particular. He sits in the parks. I seen him sitting in the parks.'

They couldn't help any more so the two policemen thanked them and moved on. At six, the unofficial search team all met up at a restaurant.

Bridges and Swanson had the same experience. Plenty of interest, not a lot of positives, but two who'd definitely seen him around. MacGyver and Lacey had nothing. Eddie and his partner had had better luck.

'We got a positive who identified him as "Redtop",' he said.

'Anything we can go on?' asked Harper.

'They've seen him twice around East 126th Street. We could put a couple of guys on the street corner and see what comes up. How about it?'

Harper agreed and they sent Bridges and Swanson to watch East 126th Street. The rest of them drank their coffee and went back to the search.

Chapter Sixty-Six

East Harlem
November 28, 8.12 p.m.

Mo was standing in a shop front with his suitcase by his side. His coat was buttoned up high to hide his red rollneck. The cops were after him again. He'd seen them around the store and called Benny from a callbox. Benny told him that they wanted to speak to him. They thought he'd murdered someone. Mo hadn't murdered anyone. He'd only ever loved Lottie. He was terrified. He didn't dare go home or back to the store. So he had to hide out in an abandoned building for most of the day, but he couldn't stop himself worrying.

The thought of having no more nights with Lucy was hard. He loved Lucy now. She was warm like a big hound and her skin was soft. She was just about perfect. And now she was up in his dirty little apartment with no one to care for her. It was breaking his heart.

At one time during the evening, Mo walked by the end of his street and saw a cop standing right there, only a few hundred yards from his building and from Lucy James. The fact of the matter was Redtop wasn't going to be able to visit the girl from the park again for a while – not while the cops had his apartment covered. Lucy would just have to wait until this whole thing had blown over. Then he could go back to see her and give her some yoghurt and fresh fruit. In a couple of weeks or so, he could fetch her.

In the doorway, Mo entertained himself by capturing moths that flew towards the bright shop light. He had caught three already. He liked the sensation of their flapping wings in his hand. It tickled him. Then when he opened his hand and they flew out, it was like he was a magician or something.

He wanted to see Lucy so damn much, though. It meant that he'd have to sleep alone for a few days on a hard stone floor. Mo sat down in the doorway and cried.

Less than half a mile away, Lucy James was tethered to the bed in the disused school building where Mo lived. The effect of the chloroform had worn off and no one was there to give her a fresh lungful. Lucy opened her eyes. The room was not hers. She could smell that straight away. It smelled bad. Very bad. She looked up at the cracked, dirty ceiling. Her limbs felt leaden. They ached. In fact, she ached all over. As consciousness began to piece together her situation, she felt her head throbbing. She looked around, left to right, unable yet to lift herself.

The room was dark and cold. She was lying in a bed. The memory was quick. It came in a flurry, like a door opening on to a wall of water – suddenly everything flooded in. The night in the snow, Seth, the fear, the blow to her head.

She tried to sit upright but her arms and legs were tethered to the bed with restraints like they had in mental hospitals. Someone could be in there with her. She looked about. The room seemed clear. There were two doors, one either side of her. She wasn't one of life's copers. She had been spoilt from birth with all kinds of stuff. Daddy and Mummy had spoilt her with toys and gifts when she was little because they never saw her. They both worked so hard. But she had a nice nanny. Then when Daddy and Mummy got their divorce, they both spent all their time spoiling her. So she had never thought about anybody but herself. And she always got what she wanted. And now

Lucy was in real trouble and she had no idea what to do.

She prayed first. Tried to think about God and asked him to protect her. Then she began to assess her position. She tried to look under the bedclothes. She could see by her arms and shoulders that she was wearing a nightdress. Across the room, her clothes were lined up all neatly folded. This was so weird, it felt dream-like.

She'd also soiled herself. The smell was coming from her. Jesus, what the hell was going on! Lucy looked about her for something to help her, but there was nothing. Her incapacity was terrifying. She couldn't even raise her hand to her face. What had her captor done to her? He might have done anything. The white flashes of fear kept washing away her thoughts. It was all too frightening. Even worse, what might he do next?

The man who'd been holding her in this room was clearly deranged, but she didn't know yet what he wanted from her. She shuddered with the thought and pushed it from her mind. She couldn't allow herself the luxury of dwelling. She had to do something. She needed a plan. If he came back, should she be nice, or resistant? Which way would save her? She had no idea.

Mummy and Daddy would be going crazy. She had no idea how long she'd been gone for, but even a few hours would freak them out. They'd be in pieces and then they'd start arguing over whose fault it was. She could hear them in her head.

As she lay there, another thought occurred. This was worse. What if he wasn't going to come back at all? It made her cry as she lay there, the tears welling in her eye sockets and streaming down her face. She couldn't just lie here and die. She knew nothing about living, let alone dying. But if no one came back . . . what would happen?

She was already thirsty. How long could a body survive without water? She'd done it in biology. Was it a few days? Something like that. Yeah. There was time. About three days. She could survive. But Christ, what she'd give for a glass of Evian.

Chapter Sixty-Seven

Senator Stanhope's Home
November 28, 8.30 p.m.

The limousine cruised powerfully over the Hell Gate Bridge. At night, New York had to be one of the most beautiful sights in the world, sparkling with lights over the stretch of water known as Hell Gate. There was nothing like coming home to Manhattan. Nothing in the world, according to Senator John Stanhope. He loved New York. He'd given his life to New York. He'd worked his ass off to represent the 34th Senate District at the New York State Senate and now he was a state senator and everything was groovy. His daughters made him promise not to use that word, but in secret he still did. It made him laugh. Why not laugh? You had to, right?

At fifty-five years old John Stanhope was a family man, a Protestant who worked hard and believed in America. He was brought up very modestly in West Virginia, on a farm in the north-east of the state, and had worked himself into the privileged position of senator after becoming CEO of a pharmaceutical company. It didn't concern his morality that this company was making millions selling drugs to African nations, that was just business. John knew how to separate business from private morality and the lessons of the Bible.

His second wife, Caroline, was a political lobbyist and she

got on with his two daughters, Mary and Rose, who were twenty-one and nineteen. And all four of them got on real well. He was delighted with that. A real happy family.

It had been a busy day for him. It started with a run round the park at 6 a.m. and then breakfast with several newspapers before his briefing at 8.30 a.m. and his first committee meeting at 9.30. He was a member of quite a few committees so he was always back and forth from the State Senate to deal with aspects of Security, Education, Armed Services, Housing, Health and Urban Affairs.

It was amazing what you ended up dealing with, but you just had to listen closely, remember what you were there for and vote or decide accordingly.

Now he was whacked and ready for a whisky by the fire with Caroline and a cuddle from the girls.

His security men got out of his car and stood still, their eyes scanning around. Senator Stanhope climbed out and walked across the drive behind the tall electronic gates.

'We're okay, Bill, don't fret,' he said and saw Rose, his little girl, standing in her socks on the porch. 'Bless her, still like when she was four years old running out to greet me.'

'We'll be here tonight, Senator.'

'There's no need, boys. Go home, see your wives.'

'Even if we wanted to, Senator, we couldn't. We've got orders. So don't you worry. Go and see your family.'

'I insist. I'll see you at six a.m.' Senator Stanhope shook Bill's hand and thanked his driver, then strolled up to the house.

'How you doing, honeybunch?'

'Good, Daddy. How was your day?'

'It was okay but I'm glad to be home with you. Is Mary here?'

'Yeah, you know she is. It's your birthday, you big fool.'

'Oh, that. I forgot all about that.'

He went into the house and his small family was gathered by the open fire in the living room. His heart melted when he saw them. There had been years when he'd worried about the effect on Mary and Rose of giving so much time to politics, but they both seemed stable and settled.

There was a simple banner saying *Happy Birthday Dad* above the fire and a pile of presents on the table. Mary and Rose hugged and kissed him and Caroline brought him his favourite tipple, a twenty-year-old malt from Islay far away in Scotland.

He smiled. Life had been good to him.

Outside in the car, Bill and Adam flipped a coin to see who was going to do the perimeter one last time before they called it a night. Bill lost and he got out of the car. The thing was, the fence was high and electronically monitored so there wasn't a lot of point in walking the perimeter.

Sebastian would have agreed: there wasn't much point at all. He was already in the house.

Chapter Sixty-Eight

Getting into a senator's house, Sebastian had discovered, was a lot easier when no one but the maid and gardener were at home. Then it was fucking easy. You ring the bell, you deliver some flowers, you flatter the stupid bitch and tape the lock. She goes in, you wait. Count to five, go in after her and wham-bam, you're in the house that John Stanhope built.

Of course, then you had to make sure you were able to wait it out, so you hid in the roof space and read books or just sat thinking.

You couldn't turn the security system off either, even if you'd watched her punch in the eight-digit code, because it was a manual system linked to a company who had a pre-agreed list of times for locking or unlocking the system. If it varied by any time without a call, then they'd be there.

So it was best to hide and wait it out. He'd been there all day, as soon as he'd made sure Marty was too scared to tell the cops anything that Nick might have told him. Dee had taken the kids to visit her mother on that tedious retirement estate, but it was good because it freed up his time to hang around inside the senator's house.

And there's nothing more difficult than to kill a senator's daughter and her family in their own home. It would strike fear

359

in the heart of America. Rose was girl number seven. And that was all he needed for his sculpture; one more part and *The Progression of Love* would be complete. He had an idea about where he'd show it, too. The people who were going to look at it wouldn't know what it was. The public were that stupid. They'd always underestimated him and now he was going to make fools of them all. Sebastian listened to the sound of family life emanating from below. Happy families made him want to exert his God-like power of life and death. He wanted to kill happiness and leave fear and pain in its wake.

And why shouldn't he do it? Who said good is good and bad is bad? Who said anything? No one. The universe, as far as he was concerned, was silent, so you just did your own thing. Some worked at being senators' daughters and some worked at killing senators' daughters. That was the happy balance of the universe.

He'd been in the house half the day when Mrs Stanhope came home. She was pretty and organized with a hurried look in her eyes and a hatred of anything out of its place. The first hours after she arrived, he climbed out of the roof space when he heard her shower. He stood and watched her. She had a nice peaceful face. Nice long legs.

It had been hard to resist taking her there and then. It'd been too long since he'd had someone. The delicious Kitty in her own bed. He thought the desires had gone. He actually wondered whether the heat cycle had come to an end, but staring at Caroline through glass as it misted up he felt the surge of desire again – the powerful internal command to control her destiny.

But he resisted. It would be better with the whole family, with an audience to watch his depravity. It would make more of a splash. He had no idea what he was going to do with them all. It was going to be an impromptu party of his own.

That afternoon, he'd watched from a round window in the attic as Mary and Rose returned. Rose was all excited and full of life. She had a beautiful lithe figure that looked about as graceful as a flower. Mary looked a sullen academic type, staring with some deep disapproval at everything she saw. He would enjoy humiliating her. Rose reminded him of his sister, Bethany. Long time before. Sad times, too. He tried not to think of it again.

His golden princess with sunlight in her hair.

When Senator Stanhope returned, the killer was back in the roof. He needed to wait until they were all together; then he would make some theatrical entrance. He wanted to kill them in front of each other. He thought that would give him the sensation he craved. It was getting so difficult to feel anything at all. Each time, he felt the need to go one step further, cross one more taboo just to feel the same deep buzz of sensation.

He listened to the popping of champagne from below and heard the warm conversation of their party.

Enjoy the moment, he thought to himself. *It will not last.*

Sebastian's plan for the Stanhopes was growing by the hour as he lay in that hot close loft. He was getting all horny too, reading about the thoughts and deeds of the psychopaths in a book called *The Mask of Sanity*. He liked to read about sexual murder and mutilation. He had never known why it made him excited. He'd never chosen it. He was just getting his inspiration.

He lay on his back as he read again about his hero Neville Heath. Heath was a good-looking all-star with a strikingly intense appearance who carried out a series of sexually perverse murders. They were remembered for one reason – they were horrifyingly brutal.

Sebastian repeated a phrase from the book. *Acts of memorable brutality and horror.* Such reverence the writer had for the killer. The world was terrified of but half in love with killers. Heath had tortured, killed and butchered two young women, gaining obvious sexually sadistic pleasure from his acts. Sebastian read on, getting more and more excited.

*

Sebastian was about to try it out himself. He had used Heath's methods before. Heath had used a poker, but Sebastian had not found a poker to hand in his own murders. Open fires were not as prevalent as once upon a time. He had used a knife instead. He intended to re-enact the Heath murder with Rose and Mary. Except he was going to go one better: he was going to let Mummy and Daddy watch.

It was five to eleven. Eleven o'clock was party time. Sebastian took up his book again. He had to go through Heath's murder one more time. Just to make sure he'd got it all right.

After all, he wouldn't have time to consult the cookbook when he was baking the cake.

Chapter Sixty-Nine

Marty Fox's Home
November 28, 11.00 p.m.

Marty Fox was sitting at home waiting for his wife. The decanter of brandy was three-quarters empty. He stared from his window and looked at his watch. 11.00 p.m. His wife usually returned by 10.30 p.m. and Marty had been at the window for an hour.

He shouldn't have let her go. He should have taken her and got in the car and headed to the hills. God, this was killing him. And what about Rose Stanhope? Marty felt the horrible sickness of guilt and inaction.

If Nick was right and Sebastian was more than a fantasy, then this girl was in danger, but so was he, so was his wife. Sebastian had shown that vividly enough. Those pictures constituted a threat, not to him, but to his wife.

Marty could still feel the vomit in the back of his throat. He loved his wife, didn't he? He wanted to protect her, but protecting her meant that someone else was in danger. 'I'm not an ethical man,' he said to himself. 'I'm a self-serving rat, a coward, a fucking liar and a cheat.'

He wanted to believe it. He wanted to stop the thoughts, the guilt, the terrible gnawing. He wasn't a hero. No. And if he wasn't a hero, then he had to stay quiet. Whatever happened to Rose Stanhope, happened. Right?

Right?

Come on, Marty! Am I right?

He drowned another quick brandy and walked to the front door. He opened it. The night was quiet, so quiet he could hear the wind in the high treetops. He stepped out in his socks and looked out into the darkness. 'Come on, baby, please make it home.'

He walked further, out to the end of the pathway, and looked up and down the street.

Nothing – not a car anywhere. The world seemed deserted. He looked again. 11.06 p.m. Time was moving so slowly. He turned back to the house and walked towards it. He felt unusually tired. It was a mixture of drink and exhaustion. He felt his body slump as he walked two steps on to the veranda.

Something to his left moved. A sound. He looked across into the darkness.

On the porch, sitting there in the blackness, something.

Marty shook and looked for a weapon. He picked up a broom. Maybe it was just an animal of some kind. A squirrel or a cat. Marty reached his hand inside the porch and felt for the light switch. He clicked it on. The lights on the veranda blazed and blinded him for a moment.

He looked across. A squirrel darted along the handrail and into the darkness. Marty sighed. He was shaking, though. Behind him he heard a car, and holding the broom he ran to the end of his drive. He picked out a set of headlights coming down the street. He stood and waited. As he waited he prayed. 'If it's Christine, I promise, I'll call the cops. Just let me have her back. Please.'

The car approached. It slowed as it neared the drive. Marty smiled as he made out the face of his wife in the dark of the car. It was her. He felt a shudder of joy. He opened the passenger door.

'What is it?'

'We're leaving. We're leaving right now. I've got a lot to tell you, but we've got to go. Drive. I've got to call the cops.'

Marty dialled 911.

Chapter Seventy

Tom Harper was cold and wet through. He had been on constant vigil on East 126th Street since the rest of the team had headed off at dusk, but no one fitting Redtop's description had been by. It was their best chance of getting some leverage on the case, but Tom was beginning to think that this guy Redtop might have flown.

At quarter past eleven, Eddie arrived with a burger and fries. He handed the food to Harper. 'Still here? You're committed, we can say that at least.'

'I've spent longer looking for a lifer.'

'A what?'

'A lifer – a bird I haven't ever seen before.'

Eddie nodded, but he didn't get it. 'What's the attraction of looking at birds, Harps? I never did get that.'

'What's the attraction of anything?'

'Well, the attraction of a beautiful woman is that she makes me tingle with pleasure and if I'm lucky . . .'

'Well, seeing a new bird makes me tingle just the same.'

'That sounds like a medical condition, Harps. You told Denise you got a feather fetish?'

'It's not that kind of pleasure, Eddie, not that I'm expecting you to understand that.'

'Damn right I don't understand,' said Eddie.

Harper ate hungrily. He chewed through the processed meat, which offered no resistance and dissolved in his mouth. His eyes continued to look up and down the street.

'Any movement?' said Eddie.

'Nothing at all. I got a feeling Benny Marconi gave the game away.'

'You want us to get a warrant and blow the place apart?'

'Yeah, I think we should.'

'I think so too. That's why I brought you this.' To Harper's amazement, he saw that Eddie was holding out an NYPD-issue Glock 19. Bemused, he took it.

'How the hell—'

Eddie looked solemn. 'Don't ask, my friend. Just don't let me down.'

They watched the street together in the damp air. Eddie's cell went off. He pulled it out and listened for a full minute before he put it back in his pocket.

'What you got?' asked Harper.

'We got a call. Someone telling us the name of the next victim.'

'Who is it?'

'Rose Stanhope.'

'Was it the American Devil?'

'No, an anonymous call from a psychologist. It's a long story. Seems he was treating a guy who had pictures of Kitty on his phone the day before she died and today he showed up with pictures of Rose Stanhope.'

'What are they doing about it?'

'Getting the Feds involved, checking out the story. They'll send someone over but they've had quite a few calls telling us who's the next blonde to get it, so they're sceptical. The guy wouldn't give his name.'

'Is she blonde?'

'Yeah, she's blonde, twentyish and get this – she's the daughter of a senator.'

Harper felt the tension kick in. 'That's his kind of girl, Eddie. He's been going higher and higher up the food chain since the beginning, hasn't he?'

'Yeah, I guess.'

'Come on, this would be his best yet.'

'No one kills a senator's daughter.'

'Exactly. Let's check it out. If it's nothing, we lose nothing.'

'You're off the case. What do you want me to do?'

'Fuck that. Give me the senator's address, call his home, get a patrol on to it. If Sebastian's there, we've got no time at all. You and me need to go now.'

'You're off the case, buddy,' said Eddie again. Harper stared at him hard and held it. 'Okay, Harps, I'll go with it, but if you're wrong, they'll haul your ass out of the city. Listen, I'll call Blue Team on the way. I hope to God you're wrong, Harps.'

'Yeah, but I know what it feels like when you're close to a killer and it feels just like this.'

Chapter Seventy-One

Senator Stanhope's House
November 28, 11.20 p.m.

It had all gone to plan. Like clockwork, maybe even a little bit better. Downstairs, Sebastian could hear the tinkle of laughter and glass. He loved that sound. He emerged from his hiding place in the roof, took off his shoes and padded through the house. The very idea that he was there in their house excited the hell out of him. He stood at the top of the stairs. How strange for the intruder to come downstairs to greet the family.

By his side he had a simple cane and he used it carefully. With his suit on, he felt quite the man of the house. That was what he wanted. He was about to end Senator Stanhope's ridiculous reign and take his last girl.

He arrived at the bottom of the curved staircase and could hear the senator telling his family a story. They listened to him. They laughed. It struck Sebastian as fake. He hated fakes. This whole house was fake. Senator Stanhope's whole life was a fake. He was going to prove it to them all.

Sebastian stood outside the door of the living room. Conversation crystal-clear now. Smell of burning logs mixed with the scent of cigar smoke. Sebastian felt deeply alone. He let the strange feeling wash over him. He had never understood what he felt or why, but outside this room he knew that somehow that was what it was about. Feeling apart from it all.

An outcast.

Just beyond the door, the senator put his arm round his wife. 'You know what you are, Caroline? You're a saint. No one else would let me get away with it.'

Caroline arched her eyebrows. 'I do it because I get to go to a fancy dinner and see all the handsome men in their military attire. No other reason, darling.'

'Well, I'm glad someone is admiring those guys. They take a lot of time to look that good.'

His two daughters were both in party dresses in honour of his birthday. They sat together on the sofa and watched their parents, sipping wine. 'You tell him, Caroline.'

'I'm not afraid to admit that he's a trophy husband.'

'And a trophy father.'

'Yeah,' said the more cynical one. 'Just right for a glass cabinet.'

They laughed. The sound of four different tones of laughter met in a single chime.

I'm an outcast, thought Sebastian.

'Here's to you and a happy birthday!'

'You gonna croon for me?'

'We're going to do better than that.'

'What?'

'We're going to dance too.'

Cast out.

The door opened slowly. The four faces turned. The white gloss door swung all the way in. In the doorway, a stranger, his face still and intense. Terrifying. Unknown. At that moment, all five people were silent. Sebastian waited. *Who would break?* His big smile moved from face to face.

The senator took a step forward to defend his family.

'Who the hell are you and what are you doing in my house?'

Sebastian let the uncertainty hang in the air for a moment longer. He stared at each of them again, weighing them up like a predator. He looked particularly hard at the two daughters. He liked to feel their eyes try to hold his and then fall to the pale carpet.

'You heard me – I'm asking you politely to leave my house.' Senator Stanhope moved to the phone and picked it up. Sebastian just stood. 'The goddamn phone's dead.' The senator stared at Sebastian. Could he take him? Did he want to with his two daughters in the room?

He turned to his wife. 'Caroline, would you take Mary and Rose through to the drawing room and let me talk to this gentleman?'

'Okay, John,' she said slowly, 'so long as you're sure.'

'I'm sure. Thank you.'

Sebastian moved to an armchair covered in beige silk. He sat and crossed his legs. 'Nobody leaves.'

'What do you want?' said Caroline. 'Do you need money?'

Sebastian gazed at her. He recalled her lithe naked figure in the shower. 'I've been watching you. I liked how you looked in your little shower unit. Real pretty.' Caroline took an involuntary step backwards.

'Please take anything you want,' she said. 'Just leave us alone.'

'Anything?' said Sebastian, staring at Rose. He shook his head and tutted. 'You sure you're offering anything?' He smiled and stood, walked to the fireplace and picked up a poker. 'Are you familiar with the works of Neville Heath?' They all shook their heads. 'You will be soon,' he said, and smiled.

'What the hell do you want?' shouted Senator Stanhope, moving forward.

Sebastian stood and swished his cane. 'Fra Angelico is my favourite artist. Do you like him?'

The Stanhopes looked at each other. Caroline put an arm round each of the two girls.

'He's a Renaissance artist,' said Sebastian.

'Yes, I know Fra Angelico,' said Stanhope.

'Beautiful angels he painted. I like to paint too. I like to paint wings in bright colours just like he did. He's quite an inspiration to me. But I like to use real people, not paint.'

The two girls held on to Caroline.

'I want Rose to come over here to me, Senator.'

'No. You leave Rose alone.'

'I never ask more than once.' Sebastian drew a long sword from the cane. 'Is it dawning on you yet, Senator?'

'What?'

'That I'm here to kill you.'

Caroline screamed. She hadn't even dared to imagine anything like that. This guy was strange but she imagined he was something to do with politics. Not now. Now she saw what he was and she was scared and both the girls were sobbing against her.

'Now, Rose. Please come to me. Your father's a very famous man, but I'm famous too. You might have heard of me. They call me the American Devil.'

They all felt the fear grab hard. Caroline tried to hold on to Rose but she moved forward and stood in front of Sebastian. He smiled. She was trying to be fearless, displaying the pride that had attracted him to her so many months earlier. He couldn't wait to bite into her. He felt the desire welling up in him like a force. 'Thank you, Rose. Now take off that pretty dress.'

Chapter Seventy-Two

Senator Stanhope's House
November 28, 11.28 p.m.

This was their man, thought Harper. On the drive to the
senator's home, Eddie went through everything the psychologist
had said on the phone. It seemed to fit, and what was more it
fitted Denise Levene's profile better than Redtop did. This
wasn't some loner simpleton; this was a white-collar Jekyll and
Hyde with an inability to stop himself.

Eddie and Tom drove in silence for the next ten minutes as
the car neared the home of Senator Stanhope. Harper took out
his Glock and checked the magazine. Sebastian would not give
himself up without a fight. He was dangerous and would be
desperate.

They got to the entrance of the secure residential area and
could see a line of street lights all the way up to Senator
Stanhope's house.

Tom was worried that if it was the American Devil, he might
have killed already. Or would he? They'd never worked out
how long he kept Jessica Pascal or Elizabeth Seale alive. But
they knew he liked to torture his victims for a long time. He
liked to see them weakening. They didn't know how he got
away, either. This guy was a chameleon, or a magician. Or
perhaps he had a trick they hadn't heard of yet.

They turned right and stopped at the huge steel-gated

residence of Senator Stanhope. There were no security guys on duty and they didn't want to alert anyone inside. Eddie parked the car up close to the high wall and they both jumped on top. Eddie threw his leather jacket over the razor wire and they hopped over the wall.

They dropped on to the ground on the other side and listened out for dogs. Nothing. The house ahead was bright with lights in all the windows. They could smell a log fire and see smoke twirling from a high chimney. Without a sound, Harper motioned to Eddie to flank left while he flanked right. Crouching low, they both sprinted towards the house, moving silently on the thick lawn.

At the front door, there was no sign of forced entry, but that wasn't Sebastian's style. He was too clever for that. He saved all his violence for those who could fear him. Harper pulled Eddie close.

'We'll stick together and do a circuit. When we get a picture of what's inside, we can split.'

'Okay,' said Eddie. 'Let's do this.'

They crouched and circled the house, moving quickly under each window and checking for signs of people inside. They came to the windows of the largest reception room. Eddie looked, and pulled back sharply.

'We got a single male suspect standing. There's a girl in front of him in her underwear. The suspect has a sword of some kind.'

Harper leaned down into the grass, out of the pool of light, and looked up into the room. 'There's one woman and another girl on the far sofa. They look tied up somehow. Clasped together.' He moved back close to Eddie. 'Okay, this is it. We can't wait for back-up. I'm going to move back into the darkness of the garden and line up a shot, you want to take the front door. You hear my shot, you bust the front door and go in quick.'

'Make sure you get a good shot.'

'I want him alive, remember. He might be the only key to Lucy James.'

'Well, make sure he can't get up.'

'I will.'

Eddie and Tom clasped their hands together. 'Get going,' said Tom.

Inside the living room, the mother and father were in tears. The killer had brought the second daughter to stand before him. She was now taking her dress off. Then Harper noticed that the mother was holding her side and blood was pouring through her hands. She must've tried to stop him. The senator's face was grey and he looked like the life had been drained out of him. He had cut marks across his face and blood down his shirt.

Tom knelt in the near darkness as the living room gleamed ahead. Inside, the tall black-suited figure stood before the senator. John Stanhope looked terrified. The other man was talking. He was still, but talking. Then he raised a long thin blade. Harper pulled his gun up to eye level. He lengthened his left arm and placed his grip in the palm of his right hand. He took aim and let his breathing still.

He could see the faces of the women. The two younger ones were staring in fear, their faces torn with pain. The other, the wife, did not flinch. Something had been said. Sebastian was raising his sword above the girls.

The killer was shouting now. It was the moment. Something was imminent. Tom moved his sight upwards. He couldn't risk a shot that would just disarm him; he needed to drop this killer with one shot. His sight rose up the killer's chest, up his neck, and stopped on his head. Single headshot. No other options.

The Glock 19 was rock-steady. There was an unearthly stillness. Even the wind seemed to drop for a brief second. Harper was praying. He squeezed the trigger. The silence of the garden was broken. The shot boomed and smashed its target instantaneously. Harper looked, the fear wide in his eyes. 'No,' he shouted. The glass had not shattered. It turned milky white in front of his eyes. Something he had not anticipated. Bulletproof glass.

'Fuck!' he shouted. He started to run towards the window. He heard Eddie's shots take out the front door locks. He kept shooting the bulletproof glass as he approached, peppering it with holes, and then, with a yard to go, he launched himself through it. His body broke the glass and plastic mesh. He flew through the window, hit the floor, rolled and looked up to see Sebastian's sword swirling above one of the girls. The other was already on the carpet, a stream of blood flowing from her neck. Harper let off a shot. It gave the girl a chance, and she threw herself to the sofa as the bullet hit the wall. The killer turned and kicked Harper hard in the face. Harper's head jerked backwards, his Glock flew from his hand and his nose split open. Sebastian ran towards the broken window, running his sword right through Senator Stanhope. Harper scrambled for his Glock. Eddie arrived a moment later and ran to the Senator, throwing his cell phone at the girl on the sofa and yelling at her to call 911. As Eddie tried to staunch the bleeding, Harper was up and at the window. 'I'm going after him.'

He ran out into the darkness, the sound of women screaming behind him.

Chapter Seventy-Three

Senator Stanhope's Home
November 29, 1.00 a.m.

The Senator's estate was bright with flashing lights and the noise of radios. Helicopters were hunting the grounds with powerful spotlights and there were already two teams of dogs, barking and straining to get out on the hunt.

Special Agent Baines from the FBI got out of a car and approached the house. He'd already been briefed by the deputy director himself. How the hell did two NYPD cops, one on suspension, outpace the fucking FBI? Baines took the shots. The truth was, he had no idea. Two NYPD officers stood securing the door. Eddie and Tom moved out of the house to meet Baines.

They shook hands and Baines looked to the floor. 'Sounds like you two saved his wife and one of his daughters. How are they?'

'Devastated,' said Harper. He paused. 'We weren't quick enough. Senator Stanhope and his daughter Rose are both dead. We missed the killer. We saw the bastard with our own eyes. And we let him take out the senator, so it doesn't feel like a success story.'

'You saved him from being tortured throughout the night. You guys acted fast. Good going. Pat yourselves on the back.'

'Not yet,' said Harper.

'Tell me what happened when you burst in,' said Baines, walking through the house.

'The killer ran out, skewering Senator Stanhope. Rose must have been stabbed just as my shot hit the bulletproof glass. He went out through the window I'd bust. I must've been thirty seconds behind him and he was nowhere. We've been looking ever since. Don't know how he does it.'

'Well, he's getting careless, that's one good sign. Leaving the psychologist alive and scared was a stupid move.'

'Yeah. Dr Levene thinks he needs someone to talk to, so he couldn't kill him.'

Baines and Harper looked into the living room. The Feds and the NYPD were working harmoniously and their speed and efficiency was impressive. A meticulous operation was already under way with forensics and weapons experts combing every inch of the place for any signs or clues. Baines stopped at the FBI investigation leader, Special Agent David Mace. 'Tell me, what goes?'

'Two saved, two dead, sir.'

Baines had the look of a dead man. 'Signs of a break-in?'

'No. We found evidence that he waited in the roof space.'

'Fuck,' said Baines. This was way beyond belief. This was the worst he'd seen. They stepped into the living room and Baines stood still and let his eyes move the full length of the sight before their eyes. A beautiful home. A dead man in a chair. A half-dressed girl dead on the floor. Spots of blood on the carpet and sofa. 'Who else was injured?' asked Baines.

'Caroline Stanhope, sir. He stabbed her left side.'

'What's he up to, Harper? I need an answer. I need one right now. What does this mean? Why the fuck does he want to kill a senator's family?'

Tom looked at the senator. 'He's going for the best he can get. He wants to shock the world. But it's also personal. He even took the time to take another trophy.'

'What? How?'

'He took Rose Stanhope's right ear. He must have cut her before killing her.'

Baines looked at Harper. 'I hope to God we can find something here. We are going to be destroyed on this one.'

Harper was keen to look at how Sebastian had passed the time in the roof and one of the CSU detectives took him up there. It was a comfortable little spot. He'd made a seat out of blankets and had left a little torch in the corner. There were remnants of fruit and water bottles. There was also a book.

Harper crawled over and tried to read the title. It was a book Tom knew well, *The Mask of Sanity* by Professor Hervey Cleckley. It was a classic study of psychopathic behaviour, running through various case studies. It read at times like a novel with cause for depraved curiosity on every page.

Was Sebastian studying himself? Was he interested in himself as a subject? Tom Harper had been trying to work something out since he'd seen Sebastian through the window of the living room. He looked similar to Redtop, was about the same height, but it wasn't him. And if the killer was not Redtop, then who the hell was Redtop?

Was Redtop another red herring that Sebastian had thrown their way? Another half-mad patient that he'd met, along with Winston Carlisle? They'd thought that Redtop was the link, but he was maybe just another poor duped guy brought in on this mess.

Was Sebastian trying to outdo all the other killers he'd read about? Was he learning how to be a psychopath? Teaching himself, testing himself? Turning killing into art? Tom didn't know. But the notion was interesting to him. No doubt, if he had a work like *The Mask of Sanity*, he'd have read many books on the subject.

Harper bristled. Next time, he needed to be certain his shot was fatal. He needed to get him. No more red herrings. He had seen the real thing. Now he just had to catch him.

Chapter Seventy-Four

Senator Stanhope's Home
November 29, 5.20 p.m.

It took a whole day before the Feds and NYPD had finished with the senator's house. Special Agent Baines and Tom Harper kept it going for as long as they could, but pressure from above forced them to withdraw. Continuing the search for Sebastian was pointless.

Harper and Baines were the last to leave. The Feds' four black cars were parked in the gravel yard between the main house and its small annexe. Baines took one more look around the empty grounds and then pulled the front door shut.

The team of twelve agents and Harper walked across to the black sedans. There was no talking between them as they walked. They got into the cars and quietly closed the doors. Last was Baines. He shut the door with a heavy clunk and the Federal cars drove off towards the gates in a trailing cloud of fine dust.

Baines was reflecting on the fact that they had been chasing shadows, being made to look fools. He hadn't experienced this before. It was a new feeling. It was called failure and it didn't feel good at all.

Back in the drive by the house, the dust settled on the faint tracks left in the gravel. In the late-afternoon sun, the motes of dust took several minutes to disperse and settle, long enough for the sound of the high-powered diesel engines to have disappeared into the distance.

The house had been left alone again, left to return to normal. All was still, very still. The birds had not yet returned, there was no wind and nothing was moving.

Then, after another hour had passed, a line of small stones moved ever so slightly under one of the tyre tracks. The surface of a dust ridge started to collapse as the top layer of stones fell away. Then a larger movement in the stillness: a large rectangular area of gravel moved and shook. The straight sides of what looked like a trapdoor became visible underneath.

It shook as if it were being banged from below. Then a small crease of darkness appeared at the corner and a large wedge of shade opened up. The trapdoor suddenly creaked wide open and hit the ground.

Sebastian emerged into the evening gloom, his eyes squinting in pain. The stink from the cesspool burst into the fresh air, but Sebastian was free.

The small brick-built cesspool was just over six metres from the annexe and fed by a single six-inch pipe. It was nothing more than a semi-permeable pit where the sewage and waste from the guest house slowly degraded before gradually seeping into the surrounding soil. Senator Stanhope hadn't wanted to pay for connections to the main sewers for a house his in-laws would use for a couple of weeks a year. So he built a cesspool. All night and day it had been Sebastian's hideout. He pulled Rose's ear out of his pocket and ran it between his thumb and forefinger. His sculpture could be completed.

His main issue had been how to breathe, but he fixed a tube to run from the cesspool up the side of the inlet pipe and out through the soil. It was a tube the size of his thumb. If any one of the black sedans had landed on it, Sebastian would have suffocated in shit.

That would've been what he deserved, no doubt. The irony

pleased Sebastian. He liked irony. That such quality agents didn't even investigate the sewage system of the scene of a gruesome murder also amused him.

He had out-thought them all. His feet, however, were a concern. A day in putrid water had left them a real mess. He couldn't walk very well, and that would require some explaining at home. But then again, maybe he wouldn't have to go home if he went to the one person who never asked awkward questions.

Chapter Seventy-Five

East 126th Street
November 29, 6.20 p.m.

Mo had stayed away from his building all night. All through the long night. It had been one of the hardest nights of his life. He imagined that he could hear Lucy James crying and calling for him. He decided that he had to take her away. Take her from the cops and find a new home where they could be together. He didn't return to East 126th Street until darkness had fallen again, when at last he felt safe enough to approach the corner. He stared down the street. There was no cop. Not a single person who looked like a cop. Mo gulped with unexpected excitement. Maybe the cops had gone home. He couldn't hide his delight.

He had a chance now. A chance to take Lucy somewhere safe, but first he wanted to surprise her. Lucy had suffered too and she needed a present. Mo had got her one, too. Something nice from the store.

He was carrying two shopping bags, one from the food store and a special one from the department store. He was feeling all excited. The best thing about having your own girl at home was coming home to her. Especially if you'd been kept apart. He knew that if you could get them to feel at home and safe, then it would all be all right and they would cooperate. He entered the living room and called out, 'Hello, Lucy!'

There was no reply, but he heard a muffled grunt. She was such an optimistic girl. Maurice put his food bag in the kitchen and then went through to the bedroom. There she was, but she didn't look good. She was still real pretty, though. Her eyes were nice. He went across to her and sat on the bed. His big hand reached out and stroked her hair gently.

'I got some things for you, Lucy. Nice things. Would you like to see them?'

'Water,' she mouthed.

Mo fetched a cup of water and held it to her lips. She drank it down in one and asked for more. He liked that she needed him. It felt like heaven that she needed him and drank from his cup. He was smiling broadly. She was lovely. The best he'd ever had.

'No screaming, Lucy.'

'No,' she croaked.

She had to be obedient. It paid to be obedient. If she was good, he would be kind to her.

Maurice stroked her face. 'How you feeling?'

'Hungry. Dirty.'

'I got you things.' Maurice opened his bag and took out a sequined red top. Lucy winced as Maurice showed it to her. He then picked out a long red satin skirt. 'I want you to look nice again. I'm sorry I couldn't come home. I'll run you a nice bath and get these dirty sheets all cleaned up. Would you like that?'

Lucy nodded. Maurice took out red pantyhose and red panties. 'You'll feel nice in these.' Maurice stood up and went to run the bath. 'We're gonna do something special – just the two of us. So I want you to feel real nice.'

Lucy was waiting for whatever it was this maniac wanted to do to her. Perhaps it would come. Perhaps he would grow in confidence. Perhaps he would kill her tonight.

Chapter Seventy-Six

The Station House
November 29, 6.22 p.m.

The lights in the investigation room in Manhattan North didn't go out all night following the killing of Senator Stanhope. The FBI needed to see everything they had on the case and that meant no sleep for Blue Team.

Harper was interviewed over and over again throughout the day, but was left out in the cold as far as the investigation was going. His part in the assault on Senator Stanhope's home had to be covered up. He was off active duty. He shouldn't have had a gun. Late afternoon, a tired and unwashed Tom Harper appeared around the door of Denise Levene's downtown office. He watched her a moment with a feeling close to melancholy. Then he pushed the door further. 'Hi there, Doctor, you got a moment?'

Denise looked up, saw Tom and smiled. 'Hey, the elusive Mr Harper. Come in. It's good to see you. I called you six times. What's been happening?'

'Sorry, we've been strung out, looking for something.'

'I guess you've been through the mill. You look like shit.'

'I feel like shit. We've been tied up like we're under some fucking investigation. It's off the scale, this one. Off the fucking scale.' Tom wandered into the office. He smelled like something

385

that hadn't seen a shower in days. 'It's nice to see you, Denise. You know, I never thought I'd say that.'

Denise smiled and laughed a little. 'How are you coping with the case?'

'Not quite come down, yet.'

Denise sat down on the couch. 'I've seen what the news stories are saying about the senator and his family and I guess it was a lot worse than that.'

Tom nodded and sat opposite. 'Doesn't go away. That's the hard thing. Pictures just floating around your head. Awful pictures of what he might've done to them. It's hard to disengage. It's so fucked up, Denise.'

'You seen all of these?' Denise picked up the day's papers and put them on the glass table. 'You seen what they're saying? "Cops Save Senator's Family". You did good, Tom.'

'I guess I tried, but the senator and Rose died.' Harper flicked through the papers, glancing at the headlines. 'Our killer just went platinum by the look of this. I tell you, Denise, every fucking deadweight from administration wants a piece of the investigation. They can't take a piss without writing a report and sending it to the deputy commissioner. And guess what? It's not going to make a blind bit of difference.'

'Why not?'

'Because it's not that kind of case. You can put pressure on investigations when there's loose ends and shoddy work, but this one is tight. They've just got nothing to go on. They're all out of leads.'

'Except Redtop,' she said.

'No one believes Redtop has anything to do with Sebastian. Not since I saw Sebastian and it wasn't the same guy.'

'But you still think they are linked?'

'I do, but what do I know?'

Denise went over to the door and opened it. Tom was still sitting on the seat, looking unwilling to move. 'I think you underestimate yourself. Come on, let's go out,' she suggested.

Harper stood and followed Denise out of the door. At noon, the President would mention Senator Stanhope at a press conference. He would offer his sincere condolences and fiercely condemn the killings. He would promise every resource available for the brave professionals searching for this killer. Then he would stamp his fist on the lectern and look hard and serious into the camera.

Out on the street, Harper was expecting a cup of coffee and a doughnut, but Denise Levene had other plans. She took him to her car and stood with the door open. 'I know that everyone thinks you're off-beam about the kidnappings and Redtop but I believe you, Tom. And it's the only possible link that hasn't been exhausted, so we've got to find out as much as we can about Redtop.'

'Can't I sleep first?' said Harper. 'Deal with this tomorrow?'

'You could try,' said Denise. 'But you'd just lie there and see dead bodies running around your head. What's the attraction? Come on. We've got to get you back to the only link you've got with the killer and that's East 126th Street.'

Chapter Seventy-Seven

East 126th Street
November 29, 7.15 p.m.

Mo patted Lucy's hand. 'The bath is ready. You take a bath and put on your dress, and I'll cook us something nice.'

Lucy nodded. The hallucinations had faded and she felt almost normal after the water and the prospect of a bath, but she was trying hard to still appear weak. She had learned quickly that you had to humour Mo. It was the only way with him – he was like a great big kid. But she was excited about the bathroom, about being able to wash at leisure. Mo looked at her as she sat on the side of the bed. 'You gotta be a good girl, okay?'

'I'll be good for you, Mo. I will be ever so good.' It was no good just enjoying the freedom, she'd also been thinking through her escape plan. This was a real chance. She would be much quicker than Mo, she would have the element of surprise and her returning strength and balance would give her the advantage. He wouldn't be expecting it.

She had seen that Mo kept his keys round his neck but she would need him to be out cold or disorientated for a moment. She stood up unsteadily, took her armful of shiny red gifts and took them into the bathroom, locking the door behind her. The room had no window so Mo knew it was safe. He retreated to the kitchen. He was going to make pasta for her – something more than tinned mince for his special princess.

Lucy searched the bathroom. She needed a knife or a club of some sort. She found a pair of nail scissors, but they were tiny. The blades were only an inch and a half. She found Maurice's razor next. She unscrewed the cap and pulled out a razor blade. Her armory was placed on the white toilet lid. Then she found a can of deodorant. She wasn't sure if that would do anything or not, but she put it with the scissors and blade. Then she got in the bath.

Lying in the deep bath, even in these circumstances, was a real pleasure. She felt as if she'd been lying in her own filth for a week, sweating unconscious all night and day. She lay in the bath thinking about what she needed to do. How to incapacitate him, take his keys and flee. She'd have to be braver than she'd ever been before.

She heard music coming from the kitchen. He would be off guard. Perhaps he would give her a knife to eat with, but it would be a blunt old thing. She picked up the scissors, turning them in her hand. Looking at them, considering what damage they could do.

When Lucy emerged from the bathroom, Mo let out a squeal of excitement. 'Wow!' he exclaimed. She looked fantastic. All in red with her hair done up and lipstick on. Like a real girlfriend.

'Does it all fit?'

'Just perfect, Mo. How do I look?'

'Lovely, lovely, lovely,' he said. He led her through to the kitchen/living room. There was a small Formica table set for two, two chairs and music playing in the background. Mo pulled her seat back and Lucy sat.

All through dinner as they talked, Lucy was calculating, trying to identify the right time for her escape. When they'd eaten, Mo stood up and gestured to her with his hands.

'What do you want, Maurice?'

'Will you dance with me?' he asked.

Lucy stood up and joined him in the middle of the stark room in the dilapidated building, swaying to the music. It was beyond strange.

Maurice leaned his head on Lucy's shoulder and said, 'You smell pretty.'

Lucy took his head in her hands. 'You look real nice too, Maurice. Close your eyes.' Maurice closed his eyes and turned his face to hers. She stroked his cheek. 'You've been real good to me, Mo. I want to reward you. Would you like that?'

Mo nodded as her finger moved across his lip. Her right hand moved inside her top and found the nail scissors. She withdrew them. Her plan was to plant them firmly in one eye. The shock might be enough to topple him. She was holding them in her fist when a violent knocking broke into the room. Someone was hammering on the door. Lucy quickly hid the scissors. Mo stopped, paralysed. He knew who it was. It was the police, come to get him and take him away. He quickly took Lucy and pushed her into the bedroom. 'It's the police, Lucy. They've been following me and now they've come to get me.' He was shaking all over as the knocking continued. 'I won't ever answer.'

'You've got to answer,' Lucy pleaded from the bedroom door. 'I'll tell them that you were looking after me. They just want to help.'

Mo looked at Lucy. 'Would you?'

She nodded and stepped back into the bedroom. The knocking continued. Mo moved to the door. His hands were shaking as he opened each lock.

The door opened. Lucy was confused. It wasn't a cop.

A tall, wild-eyed figure stood in the doorway covered in dirt and shit. Mo stared at him, his hands shaking.

'What the fuck kept you?' Sebastian shouted, staring at Mo in disgust.

'Sorry, Nick,' said Mo and lowered his eyes to the floor.

Chapter Seventy-Eight

East 126th Street
November 29, 8.15 p.m.

Sebastian looked at the girl in the red dress standing in the doorway to the bedroom, staring out with hope in her eyes. 'I see you took another girl, Mo. What did I tell you? What the hell did I tell you?'

'Don't take no more girls,' said Mo.

'That's right, and what the hell did you do?'

'I couldn't help it.'

'I should kick your ass for this, Mo. You're a fucking liability.'

'I kept her all nice,' said Maurice. 'Better than Lottie. I gave this one water too. Kept her alive.'

'Good, Mo, real good.'

Sebastian walked in, walked over to Lucy and hit her hard across the jaw. She fell backwards and Sebastian shut the bedroom door. 'Speak to me, Maurice. What the fuck is going on?' Sebastian looked around the dilapidated apartment. 'What are you doing in here? What's with the music?'

'Nothing, Nick. Ain't nothing.'

Sebastian shoved past Maurice and took a drink of water from the tap. 'What's been going on?'

'The police have been following me, Nick. I had to stay away for two days.'

Sebastian stopped dead. 'Cops have been here?'

'They were waiting up and down the street, but then today they left and I got in again. Lucy's medicine had worn off and she was okay. She looks better now, Nick.'

'How did the police find you?'

'I don't know.'

Sebastian sat at the kitchen table. He thought for a moment. 'Listen, Mo, this is what you need to do. We got to get the girl out of here right now. I want you to go back to Benny and borrow his van again. We've got to take her upstate. You remember the farm. We can use the farm, can't we? Bring the van back here soon as you can. You understand?'

'You not going to hurt her, are you, Nicky?'

'Course I'm not, Mo.'

Mo nodded gratefully and headed for the door. 'Soon as I can, Nick, I promise.' Then he was gone.

Chapter Seventy-Nine

7-Eleven
November 29, 8.45 p.m.

Harper arrived back at Benny Marconi's store with Denise Levene, having stopped only to take a quick shower at the station. They made quite the investigating couple – a demoted ex-Homicide cop with a suspension hanging over his record and a psychotherapist with a family background in crime and a yearning to be a profiler.

'I'm going in,' said Harper. 'I want to see if I can get anything from Mr Marconi. We can hang around East 126th Street all night, but this guy knows something.'

'He didn't give you much before, did he?' said Denise.

'I brought a couple of crime scene pictures to see if I can't jog his memory.' Harper got out of the car, walked across the street and pulled open the door. Benny Marconi appeared immediately from an aisle, holding a price gun. 'What a great surprise. I kinda knew you wouldn't leave this fucking guy alone.'

'Has he been back?' said Harper.

'I don't keep a close enough eye on his movements.'

'He hasn't shown up for work, has he?'

'No. Not with you clowns on his tail.'

'Just let me know – does he ever alter his routine? That's all I want. You'd notice, right, if he did something different?'

'I ain't got nothing to say.'

'I know that, but just nod or something. Does he ever change the routine?'

Benny stood dead still. 'You going to get that warrant you promised or just waste your time? I'm not in this conversation. You're ruining my fucking reputation sitting on the door like that.'

'Hey, I'm just hoping you care about people getting killed. They're getting fucking cut to pieces.' Harper threw three photographs across the counter. 'Look at what he's done!'

'I keep myself to myself.'

'Damn you! Look at these women. Look at the pain they went through. You not interested even if this guy is murdering local girls? What if he goes for one of your family, someone you know?'

'Hey, this killer takes rich girls, no skin off me. And Redtop, well, he's no murderer, trust me, he's gentle as a puppy.'

'Tell me about his movements. Where is he now? I know that you know.'

'Get out of here. I'm not no piece-of-shit informant.'

'He rapes them, you know that?' Harper watched Benny's expression change. 'He tortures them real slowly – you want that on your conscience?'

'Not Redtop. You're chasing the wrong guy. You need an arrest, he'll do. Just cos he's slow. It ain't justice.'

'Mr Marconi, the killer pushed a knife into a young girl sixty-four times. Small, slow, shallow cuts so she wouldn't die. Sixty-four times, Mr Marconi. Is that not worth your attention?' Harper looked, but Benny Marconi wasn't going to talk. Harper turned to leave. As he stood in the open doorway, he noticed the van was missing from the kerb. A thought ticked like a second hand in his mind.

'Your van got towed?'

'No, it got fixed.'

'Where is it?'

Benny Marconi turned away from Harper. 'I don't know.'

Harper moved across the store quick and grabbed Benny before he had a chance to pull the Beretta from his waistband. He threw him hard against the wall and jammed his forearm into his neck. 'I'm gonna kill you, that's all I'm gonna say,' whispered Harper.

'Redtop takes it, sometimes,' gasped Benny. 'He goes to the Bronx. Yeah, he drives it to get stuff from the food market.'

'How long is he gone?'

'I'm not saying anything. You understand? This is not happening.'

'I understand.'

'I let him take the van. Kind of a favour. He works for peanuts. Least I can do.'

Harper froze like someone had hit him. 'You gave him the van? He's got it now?'

'Yeah. Took it twenty minutes ago.'

'Thank you, Mr Marconi, you've been a great help. Shit.' Harper ran out of the door and straight across the street at speed. He reached Denise Levene's small car and yanked open the door. 'Drive. Get going. We need to get to East 126th Street.'

She looked across at him.

'No questions, just drive! I've got to get on to Eddie and the department. We should've checked this out. We missed it. We fucking missed the van. He's going to try to take Lucy somewhere tonight.'

395

Chapter Eighty

East 126th Street
November 29, 8.50 p.m.

After Maurice left, Sebastian went through to the bathroom and ran the water in the bath. He started taking off his clothes. Lucy was still out cold from the blow he'd given her. He was furious with Mo.

'You're going to get yourself fucking caught, Sebastian. The cops are going to find you easy, if Mo keeps taking girls. Why can't he get himself a fucking dog? What's wrong with a dog? He should get a dog if he wants something to stroke. For fuck's sake. Get a dog and leave these girls alone.'

His hands took the bar of soap and tried to get a lather under the running tap. 'What a fucking place this is! It's a shithole. It's a shithole and it stinks.'

Mud and shit ran brown and black around the porcelain and into the drain. Sebastian looked at himself in the mirror. He looked pale. He hadn't eaten much in days.

He came back into the bedroom, rubbing his wet hair with a towel. He looked again at the girl. She was a problem.

He wandered over to where she lay on the floor, pulled her up and threw her body on to the bed. Lucy's eyes were open now. He sat on the edge and stared into her terrified eyes. The small, innocent face of Lucy James looked back at him.

'You're not a hooker, are you, sweetheart?' Sebastian said. 'I made him promise only hookers, cos that way the cops couldn't care less, but you're worth more than that, aren't you?' Lucy stared in fear. 'Only hookers. Only hookers. What a fucking mess!'

Mo reappeared at the door holding a set of keys. 'I got the van for you, Nick.'

'That's a good boy, Mo. Well done.'

The two men looked at each other. Sebastian saw Mo looking down at Lucy. 'You like this one, don't you?'

Mo nodded, his eyes heavy with pain.

'She's not a hooker, Mo. That's why the cops are chasing you.'

Tears welled in Redtop's eyes, and he started to cry like a baby, big fat tears rolling down his face. 'Please can I keep her, Nicky? Just for one more night?' Behind Sebastian, Lucy looked on in horror.

Sebastian moved across to Mo. 'Hey, big feller, maybe we'll get you another soon. This one's had her stroking. They go bad if you keep them long. She'll be mean to you just like Lottie, and the cops will be hunting this one. You got to let me take her away, just like I did with Lottie.' He led Mo to the door. 'Now quit crying, go and get me an outfit and I'll take care of this. We're going to have to move her right now. Get some clothes for me and I'll tell you what we're going to do.'

Mo opened the door and left. As the door shut, Sebastian shivered. Alone with a girl. He walked across to her and pulled up her dress. Lucy didn't move. She was just like a princess. It was uncanny how they all looked like one of his princesses. Uncanny. He touched the girl's face, softly. Stroked her long hair.

'You're pretty,' he said and her eyes, dark and intense, stared at him. Sebastian found his trousers on the floor and pulled out a plastic bag from his pocket. His appetite seemed to be growing. He moved on top of her.

Lucy stared up at the man moving above her. He had a

handsome face, but his eyes were dead. She was dreaming, perhaps. She tried to move, but like in a dream found she couldn't move her limbs. He had her pinned down. She was utterly helpless.

The man calmly lifted her head and pulled the bag down over her face. Breathing became more difficult as the bag kept being drawn into her mouth, but if she breathed slowly she could still get some air.

She was keen to wake up from her nightmare now. Very keen. This was wrong. This was all wrong. Wake up, she was shouting, wake up. But she didn't. She didn't wake up at all. She tried to remember how she woke herself up in her dreams, but none of it worked.

Through the crumpled bag she watched him looking down at her body, then at her eyes. He was looking deep into her eyes and seemed to be transfixed.

His hand came forward and closed the bag around her neck. She gulped for air. Her body was young and not ready to die. It didn't want to. Every fibre kicked out against it. Every atom and every molecule wanted to carry on. To live. She bolted and tugged and kicked, but she was held tight and the man rested his body on top of hers, pushing the last breath from her lungs.

Chapter Eighty-One

East 126th Street
November 29, 9.40 p.m.

Harper and Denise arrived at East 126th Street and parked up. They saw Marconi's truck sitting on the side of the street. High up in the building, one of the boarded windows glimmered with light.

'He's in. We'll wait for the other guys.'

On the way over, Harper had called up Eddie. Kasper had, in turn, called in the Feds working the task force. They might need to have people with Federal jurisdiction. They were all heading over. This had to end tonight. There was no time for convincing Lafayette, no time for the deputy DA and no time for any warrant. They had to take Redtop out and try to save Lucy James.

In the apartment building, Sebastian was dressed in one of Mo's shirts. He'd rolled the dead girl in a sheet and already put her in the back of Marconi's truck along with two canisters of gasoline. Mo knew what to do. Mo should've left already but he couldn't stop crying. He'd loved Lucy and now Nick had taken her away. He was crying so much that Sebastian was afraid he'd draw attention to himself. It took him nearly half an hour to calm Mo down. In the end, Sebastian promised him another girl. Promised him a keeper if he did a good job getting rid of

Lucy. Mo packed a small bag and left the apartment, for the farm he knew from a long time ago.

Across the street, three unmarked cars sat waiting for Redtop to make a move. Eddie Kasper had turned up with another couple of detectives, Garcia and Mason. Harper got in with Eddie and Denise left for home. The third car contained Special Agents Asa Shelton and Isaac Spencer.

The pack didn't have to wait long before Redtop appeared at the fence to the disused schoolhouse. He pushed the fence aside and got into the van.

Harper looked up at the building. 'You think someone else is in there?'

'I think the body's in the van,' said Eddie. 'If he's going out of the city, then he's already killed her.'

Harper looked again at the light. Something wasn't right.

'Let's go, man,' Eddie urged. 'We've got to find his dumping ground.'

Maurice didn't give Harper any more time to think. He pulled away from the kerb and drove off. After a few seconds, the three cars followed.

The journey upstate was slow. Maurice was driving carefully. Kasper hadn't told Lafayette until they were on their way. He would've stopped them, no doubt, but now it was too late.

Lafayette was covering his back lately and always went straight up the chain of command. The top brass wanted to know every development in this case. He had to tell them that Tom Harper was with Kasper in the chase. He had to reinstate Tom Harper in his absence. Then he had to run for cover – if this fucked up, Lafayette was staring down a serious barrel of shit. They'd got the wrong man once; it didn't bear thinking about what would happen if they got the wrong man twice.

They followed Maurice upstate, the three cars taking turns to lead and fall back. They were heading north on Interstate 87, travelling up past the Catskill State Park. After forty minutes they turned off and within an hour were driving through the dark in some slow, narrow rural roads.

The woods and trees of New York state loomed in the shadows and darkness at the side of the road. They might be driving half the night. Eddie focused on the road ahead. On the winding rural roads, keeping a distance was hard and keeping hidden was harder. If Maurice had a body in the car and he got a sense that he was being followed, then he could easily disappear into the hillside, switch off his lights and they'd be none the wiser.

'You regret not checking the apartment?' said Eddie.

'I will if Lucy James isn't in that truck, but I think she is,' Tom replied.

'You're sure?'

'No.'

'We've got a lot riding on this one. I can call Lafayette and get them to take a look, what do you say?'

'Yeah, you do that.'

'Shit, we think this guy's carrying a carcass, but if he's not?'

'Then I've just signed myself off the NYPD for life.'

As they got further and further from civilization, it became clear that Redtop knew exactly where he was going. It was hard going, all right. And then it got harder. Maurice's truck disappeared.

The three following cars stopped. Mo's van had just vanished. The drive back to the Interstate would take an hour, then it would take another hour to find a motel. It wasn't on the agenda. Kasper led the cars about three miles up the road and the three dark saloons pulled into a yard on the edge of a pine wood. It was a working yard with a yellow digger and a hut of some kind.

The six men got out. It was cold. It was coming on for midnight and the chill was creeping deep beneath their clothes. They hadn't dressed for a night on the mountains.

'What are you two guys thinking?' Kasper shouted across to Asa Shelton. They shook their heads and looked around.

'Either he pulled off the road or he cut his lights and kept on going.'

'You think someone could drive on these roads without lights?' Kasper asked.

'Maybe, if he knows the roads.'

Harper walked over to the wooden shack and took out a screwdriver. With a small torch, he unscrewed the padlock plate and opened the door. Outside, the other five men looked on as a light went on inside.

A minute later, all six men were in the wooden shack. It was a sizeable working hut, with a small stove, a table and some hard hats and logging gear. Kasper was going through the cupboards looking for food and the two Federal agents had set up their laptops. 'I can't believe we came out here with nothing to eat. It's fucking unbelievable.'

Harper was standing by the large old map of the region on the board. 'This is useful. Come take a look.' The guys crowded around the map. 'Here we are in this cut just under the mountainside. There's one road going through the hill, so he's got to be up here for only one reason. There's a pig farm up the road. Looks a small operation. I say that's where he's heading. There's nowhere else this road leads to. What do you say?'

They all nodded quietly. Harper was still one of the most respected detectives on the force.

'Okay, then,' said Harper. 'If he saw our headlights in his mirror then he might have taken one of these old tracks. It takes him way off track but if he follows it round, it'll come back to the farm. I think he's got scared and taken the long road. So what I suggest we do is get ourselves up to the farm and dig in. If he's coming, he'll take a couple of hours to get around the mountain.'

'Okay,' said Eddie. 'Let's go watch some hogs!'

Chapter Eighty-Two

The Pig Farm, Upstate
November 30, 1.12 a.m.

When they arrived at the pig farm, the teams hid their cars up in the trees behind the farm and scoped out their positions. Harper and Kasper set up about two hundred metres above the hog field, looking down a gentle slope. The hog field was an enormous brown enclosure where the pigs churned up the earth as they ran around freely and lolled about in patches of mud.

There could have been a hundred bodies in that muddy mess and you'd never find them. At night, it appeared the hogs all went into the great barn at the end of the field. Eddie and Tom stared out into the darkness. It was a quiet, starlit night. The big old moon was full.

'You think he'll come?' Tom asked.

'He's maybe sitting and watching. He's a nervous cat,' said Eddie.

'Or he's spending one more night with her,' said Tom.

'Jesus, is this not bad enough without imagining him fucking a corpse?'

'The guy likes these bodies,' said Tom.

'I guess he does, but we don't need to hear about it.'

Harper nodded. They both looked down over the darkened hillside.

Beside the barns were the two holding ponds. These great round vats of slurry and blood were as much as thirty feet deep and contained excrement, blood, old carcasses, afterbirth, urine, chemicals and drugs. They were a horrible cocktail of thick, viscous shit. And sitting above them in the hills, Harper knew that they stank to high heaven.

A couple of hours later Harper was standing on the edge of a clump of trees, staring up at the fading stars. Eddie was sitting on the ground with his eyes closed and a blanket around his shoulders. Every few minutes Harper took a look round with the binoculars.

A faint purple glow on the hillside opposite suggested dawn was not far away. The silence was more or less complete, with hardly a breeze. Then, in the distance, headlights appeared on the road.

Heart in his mouth, Harper raised the binoculars to his eyes and looked. He couldn't make anything out except the lights and the fact that the vehicle was moving slowly. He radioed the other team members.

'You seeing this?'

'We're seeing it.'

'What you thinking?'

'Could be our man.'

Tom looked again. Up ahead of the vehicle, the road split, with the dirt track leading to the hog field and the road heading on to the farmhouse.

'How much you want to put on the high road?'

Garcia came back, 'I'll put a fifty on the high road.'

Shelton chipped in, 'I'll take some of that, Harper. A hundred on the high road.'

Harper smiled to himself. They all wanted this to work. 'I'll take your bets, gentlemen. This one's coming our way.'

Three sets of binoculars were trained on the vehicle as it approached the fork in the road. If it did go low, they only had a few minutes to prepare. If high, they could all relax and Harper could go back to watching as a poor man.

The fork approached. The car ground to a halt. They stared in absolute silence. Was the driver looking for the right road or was it something else?

A minute passed.

'Perhaps they've seen something,' said Garcia.

They looked around. Harper spotted it first. There was a torch lying on the ground near to the two detectives. It glowed faintly in the grass.

He radioed quickly. 'Garcia, for fuck's sake, you've got a flashlight on over there. He's looking at the light.'

The torch went out and they all waited with bated breath as the car sat five hundred metres away at the fork in the road. Would it put him off? Did he see it? It was only a faint glow. But he hadn't driven on. He was cautious.

Harper knew in his gut it was him. Redtop. And Redtop didn't know what to do. He was an indecisive soul and now he had seen something that raised enough of a question to throw him. He was probably waiting now. Seeing if the light went on again.

Tom kicked Eddie, who crawled to his feet and took the binoculars. 'It's a Mark 2 Ford pickup. It's his truck.'

'How do you know?'

'Shape of the headlights.'

Tom radioed through, 'Eddie reckons it's a Mark 2 Ford pickup from the shape of the headlights.'

'Okay,' said Shelton, 'if he gets scared we've got to go after him. If it's him, he'll have a body in the pickup and that's got to be enough to nail him.'

They waited. The tension was unbearable. The car sat there, engine running, for fifteen minutes.

'Christ, this guy's cautious.'

They watched, desperate for a sign. The truck just sat and idled. Another fifteen minutes passed by.

'Do we take him out?' Garcia asked.

'Sit still,' said Harper. 'Sit still.'

Another five minutes passed. He'd been sitting there for over half an hour. Tom took the binoculars and put them up to his eye. The light was better now. The sun was still below the horizon but rising. Through the glasses he could make out very little at that distance, just a vague shape and no movement.

Forty minutes after the truck had stopped, it suddenly roared into life and sped down the dirt track.

'All hands, get ready!' called Harper.

The truck jumped and bumped down the path, hurtling at speed. When it got to the edge of the field, it slammed to a stop. The engine was left running.

They watched from the hill. Eddie had a rifle trained on the truck and Harper watched through binoculars.

'No shooting, I want this guy alive,' said Harper. 'He's useless to us dead. We need to catch him.'

They were all suited and booted and ready to roll, they just had to see him do something.

A large figure opened the driver's door. He went round to the back of the truck. He was wearing a coat and hat.

'Is it Redtop?' asked Shelton.

Harper looked, but wasn't a hundred per cent certain. 'Can't be sure.'

'No one move until he's away from the truck. We don't want any car chases.'

The figure stood by the back tyre and leaned into the truck. He pulled out two canisters and took them into the field. Then he returned to the truck. He manhandled a heavy rolled-up sheet with what could be a body inside. He slung the roll over his shoulder and made towards the field.

At the fence he threw the roll over and then climbed across himself. He picked it up again with some difficulty and walked toward the barn.

'Okay, guys, you know the routine. Let's take this guy out. Go, go, go!'

They danced out of the hides and down the hillside, running at full speed, flashlights flickering across the ground. All three pairs descended from different directions towards the single figure in the field.

The figure stopped and turned. He saw the dancing lights coming at him from all directions. He dropped the roll, picked up the canisters and ran as fast as he could towards the barn. He was big, but quick when it mattered.

Mo entered the barn and shut and locked the door. Inside, his heavy frame gulped for air. He felt the terror gripping him. He was being chased down. Like an animal. The men chasing him had just entered the field. Mo looked around. What should he do? What could he do? There were hundreds of hogs in the barn, enormous animals, sitting lazily and snorting. Maurice ran to the feed store and office at the back. He smashed open the lock and looked inside. Nothing, nothing. He looked around at the two cans of gasoline. Nick wanted him to burn the body, but he couldn't do that now. He had to escape. But how? Mo looked at the back wall of the barn. If he could burn his way out he might be able to run and hide in the woods. Mo took a can of gasoline and started to splash it all over the back wall. Then he took the matches Nick had given him and struck one. He heard the men shouting in the fields and he dropped the match. The vapours of the gasoline ignited with a loud whoosh. And Mo was surrounded by flames.

At the edge of the field the Feds were heading for the barn. One of them stopped at the roll and had a look at what was inside it. It was the body of a woman. This was their man and they had him cornered.

This was as near as they had ever been to catching someone who might be connected to the American Devil. The Feds went on. Eddie and Harper headed round the side of the barn. Eddie pulled his handgun out as he rounded the corner, fumbled and dropped it in the mud. 'Goddamn shit!' he said.

As the FBI special agents arrived at the barn door, they could see the glow inside. They couldn't quite make it out, but it was flickering like a fire.

'He's going to burn the barn down,' one agent called. 'What's he up to?'

Then they began to hear a noise. It was a terrifying sound, rising in a crescendo of high-pitched squeals. Something was happening inside. Hundreds of pigs began to panic and move around. Inside Mo was beating at the flames but he was just throwing up sparks, and lighting the straw all over the barn.

The Feds tried smashing the lock on the barn door but it was useless, and they finally opened the lock with two rounds. The shots just frightened the pigs even more. The Feds dragged the door wide open and smelled the stink of burning gasoline and straw. As the door pulled along its steel runners, the volume of the squealing rose and hit them – a terrible, high-pitched cry of pain and fear. They looked up and saw hundred of hogs, covered in flaming gasoline, stampeding towards them.

The hogs bolted, their wide white backs alight and glowing in red and blue and amber. The smell was rich with burning flesh and the stampede was brutal as the pigs trampled and herded their way out, running directly at the two Federal agents, who had skittered backwards and somehow tripped, and were now cowering in the mud at the side of the barn. Hundreds of flaming, panicking pigs brushed past them, virtually trampling their bodies into the mud.

The blazing hogs stampeded from the barn. They sparkled across the field like a howling, terrifying light show. Within seconds they were beyond the barn and bucking and kicking in every direction, screaming out their pain and horror in high mournful squeals as their flesh melted. The special agents, miraculously alive, began crawling away from the barn.

Garcia and Mason further back, tantalizingly near the fence, were not as lucky. Mason was hit from the side full-on by a huge sow travelling at speed and then several fiery pigs ran across him, jumping and cracking his ribs and then his head. He was dragged across the field, his clothes burning against his skin.

Eddie Kasper launched himself across the ground and sprinted towards Mason's flaming body. It was hard keeping up his speed in the mud but he was just about quick enough and rolled Mason over and over in the mud, his face badly burnt.

Garcia was tossed by a headlong charge and his clothes caught the flaming gasoline as he passed over the pigs' backs. He landed not too badly and stood in the darkness, flapping wildly at his clothes with his hands. Harper got to him in time and managed to get his coat off and wrap it around Garcia's body. It saved his life.

Harper looked back at the barn, swiftly realizing that the stampede meant one thing. Maurice was still in there.

'Eddie, look after these guys, call back-up. I've got to get this guy.'

Eddie nodded. Harper raced around the back of the barn and spotted Maurice running away towards the edge of the field. He was slow, though, and Harper knew he was faster.

He gave chase. He knew from the map that after the field were woods, which went on for miles all the way to the river. He didn't want Mo to reach them, but he couldn't take a shot at him either. They needed this guy alive.

In the forest it was hard. Harper couldn't see and had to keep stopping to listen. There was no way to track Mo otherwise. He ran, stopped and listened, blindly following Mo's lead.

Redtop was getting ahead now. Harper kept on. It was so dark in those deep pine woods, he couldn't see more than five feet ahead.

He followed Mo for half an hour, getting no nearer but feeling his strength drain away. Then, through the trees, he saw the flames of the pig field again. They must have come full circle, either by accident or design. Maybe Mo had no idea where to go either, so was heading back to his van. Harper found the last of his strength and began closing in again as they re-entered the field.

In the gathering light of dawn Mo knew he couldn't make it to the truck. He didn't dare get caught, so he ran to one of the holding ponds and climbed up the side. He stopped at the top. The venomous vapours of the shit-pit were caustic in his nose and throat. He felt immediately dizzy. Harper approached slowly, his pistol by his side.

'Maurice, give yourself up,' he panted. 'There's nowhere to go.' Mo turned, breathing heavily. He stared at Harper, who took another few steps forward. 'Come on, we can help you. We can look after you. Don't kill yourself. Come down.'

'I didn't do nothing. I didn't hurt them. I promise. I just looked after them. I didn't ever hurt them.'

'I'm sure you didn't, Maurice, but what happened to Lottie?'

Mo looked round. He didn't know what to say. 'Tell him I'm sorry.'

'Who? Tell who, Mo?'

'I was supposed to give her water. I liked her a lot. I get to like them a lot.'

'Who, Mo? I can't tell him if I don't know who he is.'

'I only wanted to stroke them. I like how they feel. I like them all warm. I didn't hurt them. I didn't do it. I only wanted to pet them.'

For a moment Mo looked as though he might turn himself in. Harper climbed towards him with slow steps, reaching out with his arm. 'Come down now, Maurice.' He could see the fear and tears in Maurice's eyes. He looked like a child. 'Come on, you're not in trouble. We'll help you to make it all better.' Harper was at the edge of the pool. Maurice was within reach. He put out his hand towards Maurice and Maurice's big paw moved to meet it. Just before they touched, Maurice smiled. Then he threw himself backwards into the vast pit of venomous slurry. The pig shit closed over the dark figure in an instant. He was gone.

Chapter Eighty-Three

Downtown New York
December 1, 3.10 p.m.

The streets of the Financial District in New York are much like many other streets across America. The sidewalks are flanked by towers in light shades of concrete grey. Originality can be seen in the little early twentieth-century architectural flourishes around the entrances and windows, but these minor stylistic touches are secondary to the great power of economics and the need to maximize floor space.

Sebastian walked past the buildings, enjoying the sight of their stately confidence. He was carrying a suit bag and feeling good about things. He liked to walk and watch. The traffic streamed down the street and he looked at the rows of expensive cars parked up and down. He came to the entrance to Le Monte, a luxury hotel with a gold and green sign. It lacked any of the pomp of the old buildings and asserted its status with curly gold lettering and plush colours.

Sebastian entered. He had an appointment with an English tailor. He had a weakness for clothes, in particular for bespoke Savile Row suits. He only had one, but loved it each time he wore it. He always thought that it gave him a kind of religious feeling of forgiveness, just like Dee said Christ could. But the suit was more convenient than Christ. He could put it on whenever he wanted the clear lines and balance of superbly tailored fine wool to wash him clean of sin and make him a perfect citizen again.

Sebastian took the elevator to the conference suite for his appointment with the visiting tailors from William and Roger Burke & Co. of Savile Row, London. Many English tailors had taken to these visits to the bigger American cities and the local businessmen and dignitaries loved the old-fashioned glamour and deep subservience involved in being measured and made for.

Sebastian was met at the temporary reception area by a delightfully fresh-faced English girl, who introduced herself as Melissa. She was so finely dressed, so elegant in every way that Sebastian thought she might have been turned on a lathe and made in some gorgeous London babe factory. A twinge in his stomach made him want to reach out and grab her.

The thick red carpet, gold and red colour scheme and low lighting of the suite managed to give this hotel an old English feel. He was met by the tailor and the cutter, Messrs Henry Oldfield and Graham Winder. Henry was in his fifties, white-haired and tanned, wearing a blue pinstriped three-piece suit with a plain blue tie. Graham was in his early forties and wore a rather striking electric blue suit with a red tie.

The new and the old, thought Sebastian. Catering to all tastes, no doubt. He glanced again at Melissa as she placed a champagne bucket and glasses on the coffee table. His mind wandered momentarily into a fantasy and then snapped back to the gentlemen offering their cream-softened hands.

The three men sat in a circle of red velvet chairs for their 'consultation'.

'Firstly,' said Henry, 'we need to understand the nature of your need.'

'That is very hard to explain,' said Sebastian.

'We shall do our utmost to make these decisions simple, sir.'

Sebastian liked being called sir. He turned to Melissa and

met her gaze. He smiled. He could do anything. That's what his gaze said and Melissa lowered her eyes. So like animals, aren't we? Just a pecking order based on power and the capacity for violence and love.

'Is it for a special occasion, day wear, evening wear or business wear?' Henry was leaning in, his kind, understanding head tilted and his warm grey eyes searching to please.

Sebastian didn't know what was next. *The Progession of Love* was finished, but already Sebastian felt that it was not going to be enough to make him stop. Maybe he would appear to his next victim as the perfect, well-dressed gentleman and become in an instant the ogre of unimaginable debauchery. If he was not feeling so cautious, he would have loved to have chosen Melissa as a delicate taster. He'd never killed an English victim. He was interested to see how the different culture might express itself at the moment of death. Would the English reserve remain, or give way to uncontrollable cries?

'I have brought a specimen suit,' said Sebastian. He indicated the suit bag, and the fleet-footed and slender-ankled Melissa held it aloft.

'Unzip, please,' said Sebastian to Melissa. His thumb rubbed against his forefinger as he watched her reveal his suit and hold it up. The two tailors looked at it.

'Richard Anderson, is it?' said Graham with the faintest nuance of disdain.

'It is,' said Sebastian.

Henry went across and looked at the suit carefully. Every so often he murmured to himself. Finally he returned to his client.

'I would like to show you something a little different. I can see the elegance of the long lapel and the single button, it is flattering and undeniably sharp. What would suit, sir, might be something with a little more hint of the dandy. I'm suggesting perhaps a double-breasted classic two-button double-vented jacket with jetted side pockets in a fine nine-ounce worsted flannel. Very elegant. Cut double-pleated trousers with a two-inch turn-up. Very unusual in these parts but just the mix of tradition and modern style.'

Graham went to the long bench behind them to find a nine-ounce Super 100 worsted flannel. He brought a roll of material to Sebastian and offered the edge to his fingers.

Sebastian rolled the material between his forefinger and thumb. 'Superb.'

'Would Sir like to study some of the colours and patterns?'

Sebastian said he would, and stood, turning slightly so that his eye fell on a folded newspaper that was sitting on the table.

Sebastian's attention was drawn by the first word of the bold headline. He tilted his head to one side to see the picture. It was a face. A girl's face in a grainy unflattering photograph. 'A second,' he said to the tailors, and moved to the table.

His heart was beating now.

He took up the afternoon edition and opened it. There in the centre was a large photograph of his Mo, flanked by photographs of two women, Lottie and Lucy.

Sebastian was aware of the people behind him watching him, but the emotion building in his chest was taking all his energy and strength to suppress. He read the opening.

HARLEM KILLER DEAD
KILLER OF TWO YOUNG WOMEN DROWNS AFTER POLICE CHASE

After an intense and dramatic chase, the serial kidnapper and murderer known as 'Redtop' was hunted down to a pig farm in upstate New York in the early hours of this morning.

Detective Tom Harper of the NYPD, working with the FBI, located the killer as he attempted to dispose of the body of recent victim Lucy James.

As the killer fled, Detective Harper chased him through dense woodland before cornering him and watching him jump to his death in a holding pond of slurry.

Sebastian's heart was beating ten times per second. Sweat formed on his brow. He wanted to scream, to run, to kill. His body was caught in a crossfire of emotion – pain and anger in a cauldron of fire.

He wanted to cry. He never cried. He hadn't known what grief felt like and now the unfamiliar feeling was drowning him. He reached out for the table to steady himself.

'Is Sir all right?' asked Henry.

'Would Sir like a glass of water?' asked Graham.

No. He didn't want water. He wanted one thing only – to kill. Tom Harper had taken the only thing he loved in the world. Harper had killed his brother. His little brother Mo. His simple little brother who'd done nobody any real harm.

All Sebastian wanted was to kill. To kill Tom Harper.

No. Better than that. To give Tom Harper more pain than he had ever imagined.

PART FOUR
December 2–4

'How much more grievous are the consequences of
anger than the causes of it.'
Marcus Aurelius, *Meditations*

Chapter Eighty-Four

Downtown Bar
December 2, 7.40 p.m.

Denise Levene was still unable to speak to anyone about her father's death. Whenever she got to that point in a relationship when two people open each other up and peer inside, Denise Levene would freeze. Speaking about him made it seem too casual, too everyday – it put him in the same category as gossip. She wanted to feel it close and hard inside her, like pain. She'd dated in earnest throughout college, swinging from one guy to another like a girl on the monkey bars, always clever enough to leave before anyone was able to claim that she hurt them. She had hated emotional ties as much as she hated white shoes, fast food and television advertising. She liked things sincere. Then came Daniel. She could see why he was in politics. Gift of the gab. He'd convinced her to try something more substantial. She'd found that she liked it.

The tall guy with the salesman smile was already approaching her with a little swagger in his hips. Denise tried to avoid eye contact, but it wasn't going to work with this guy. He thought she was cute, liked her business-like hairdo, her long legs – and the sniffy attitude just turned him on even more. He liked a challenge – chased skirt tasted so much better than skirt on a plate.

'Hey, there, sweetheart, you look a little lost.'

'Not at all. I'm waiting for someone.'

'Well, I've got some directions here you might find helpful.' His large hand pressed flat on the bar and he leaned in close, his cologne suffocating her. 'If you want to know where to go, just follow the arrow,' he said and rolled his forefinger down his tie to the arrowhead at the end. Denise felt his arm curl around her shoulders. 'I'm always happy to take you there, sweetheart.'

Denise pushed his arm away from her. 'If I want to visit a sewer, I'll call Environmental Protection.'

The man smiled, showing his bright white teeth. 'Come on, baby, we can go the scenic route if you want, but I always like to go as the crow flies, if you know what I mean.' His hand slipped round her waist.

'Get your hands off me or you'll regret it,' said Denise, low and calm.

'I can feel you're warming towards me,' he said, still holding her waist.

Tom Harper was at the door of the bar, looking for Denise. His eyes narrowed. The guy quickly let go of Denise's waist. 'Maybe later,' he said, and walked away.

'Was that guy giving you trouble, Denise?' said Harper, approaching.

'Nothing I can't handle,' she said.

'I bet that's true.'

'Yeah, well, thanks anyway. I don't have any scruples about a guy helping me out.'

'Pleased to hear it. Now let's get us both a beer.'

They sat close to each other at the bar, huddled over their drinks.

'Any news yet?'

'Not a thing. I've been working flat out, but we've found nothing to go on. It's been a bad couple of days. Chasing shadows and dead ends. And he's still out there somewhere.

Don't understand it, either. He's gone quiet. No new kills, no communications. I don't like it.'

'You got your badge back,' said Denise with a smile. 'That's good news, at least.'

'Yeah,' said Tom. 'They had no choice. Either admit that some suspended cop had caught Redtop or put me back on the team. But it's good to be officially back on Homicide. We got a lot of working out to do. A lot of good men got hurt.'

'It sounded like a hell of a mess out there,' Denise said.

'Two FBI special agents were seriously injured. Asa Shelton and Isaac Spencer were burned pretty badly. Two guys from our team were hit bad. Garcia was dragged across the field after a pig caught on his webbing. Half his clothes burned into his skin. Mason's face is a mess. Plenty of broken bones too.'

'It's lucky they're alive,' said Denise, her eyes caught on Harper's all the way.

'Yeah,' said Tom. 'They've all got families, you know. Me and Eddie don't and we missed the stampede. Is that called irony?'

'No,' said Denise. 'It's called luck.'

Eddie Kasper had some minor burns from trying to help the others, but Mason was still in intensive care after the showdown at the hog farm. He wouldn't ever be known for his looks again; the skin grafts wouldn't disguise the fact that half his face had been burned away.

'Do you know anything more yet?' asked Denise. 'Anything on who this guy Redtop is? Who was he?'

'His name's Maurice Macy. He jumped in the holding pond and it's pretty difficult to drain. They only just got his body out, but they got his prints from Benny Marconi's truck and he's on file. He has history. And we found a link with Lottie. He was carrying Lucy James in a sheet. They found a match between fibres in Lottie's hair and the sheet. Looks like Mo killed them both. Maybe he took more.'

'Is there any link to Sebastian?'

'This is where it gets interesting. Until two weeks ago, Mo Macy was being held in Manhattan Psychiatric Center. He'd taken girls before. Years ago. He never killed them, just kidnapped them and kept them captive, but he wasn't sophisticated. They both escaped and went to the cops.'

'He was on Ward's Island? The same place Winston Carlisle was being treated?'

'Exactly. It doesn't make sense at all, but it's a link.'

'You think the American Devil was setting this guy up too, like he did with Winston?'

'That was my first thought, but he's not going to tell us now. We checked with Winston, and he doesn't remember him either.'

'So, what happened to Lucy?'

'Yeah, poor kid. She'd been raped and suffocated. Maurice's prints were all over her.'

'Suffocated?'

'There's too many links to the American Devil to dismiss it entirely, but nothing concrete.'

'Except a cherry blossom petal.'

'Yeah, exactly. Mo was living in an apartment in a disused building. That's where he kept the girls. He had hospital restraints on the bed. The forensic team are going over it, but it'll take time before they assess everything they find.'

'Jesus Christ,' said Denise. She shook her head and took a sip of beer. 'Anything new on the American Devil?'

'Nothing. They've got his DNA from the Stanhope house, but the leads are all dead. I don't understand why he's stopped killing. Maybe he's finished what he set out to do.'

'It's still puzzling' said Denise. Then she sat up. 'If Mo Macy kidnapped Lottie, it means that our American Devil profile wasn't right. I should've spotted that sooner. The American Devil didn't need those four days.'

'I'll get it altered.'

'How are you, tough guy?'

'Well, they've reinstated me; that's enough.'

'They've given you the lead back on the American Devil case?'

'Lafayette offered. I declined. I want to work free, you know. Follow my instincts. I'm better working with one or two people. I've even tracked down the five locations in the city where you get winter-flowering cherry blossom and have got some ideas to work on.'

Denise smiled. He was a good guy, for all his faults. He wasn't just honest with others, he was honest with himself.

Alone in a booth opposite, the man who'd hit on Denise sat and watched, sipping his bourbon quietly. He twirled Denise's keys in his hand. It was so easy to slip a hand into someone's bag while they were trying to avoid your cologne. He had what he wanted now: a way to give Tom Harper more pain than he could imagine. He was just waiting for the right opportunity. Sebastian leaned back. He felt sure the right opportunity was just on its way.

Chapter Eighty-Five

Sebastian sat in a hired green Ford. The window was down, the night air cold on his face as he watched the world go by. There was a creased photograph of Mo stuck to the centre of the dash, and every few seconds Sebastian looked at his little brother and his feelings of injustice swarmed over him. He'd never felt so alone. He needed Little Mo. Without Mo, what was it all for? He wanted to hurt now. Just lash out and hurt. He needed to kill. He looked up at Denise Levene's apartment. It was time to get inside and give Tom Harper's little city girlfriend a shock.

Sebastian knew he wasn't wrong, just different – what did Freud say about it? 'A man should not strive to eliminate his complexes but to get into accord with them: they are legitimately what directs his conduct in the world.'

That's all he was, a man in tune with his complexes. A legitimate search for happiness, no different from all such searches. No different at all. Pain would make him happy.

He looked out again. Denise would be saying goodnight to the good Tom Harper across at the bar. Denise would be thinking of getting home. The concierge would soon go to the bathroom again to snort some more low-quality cocaine and Sebastian would slip inside and find a nice warm corner to sit and wait.

424

He wanted to disembowel her and tie her intestines round Harper's neck.

He opened the car door and stepped on to the sidewalk. He watched the concierge take a furtive look round and then head off down the hall. It was simple. Sebastian opened the lobby door with the key pass and walked to the stairs. Denise lived on the fourth floor. Within three minutes, he was standing outside her apartment. He felt the tingle that he always felt, just like the first time when he had stood in Chloe's house. He put on a pair of latex gloves and slipped the key into the lock. He turned it and felt the mechanism click.

Sebastian knew he could've made a great detective. He would be able to catch anyone and destroy them too. But the NYPD had turned him down. He'd failed the psychological assessment. Not good enough for them. His character was deemed unfit. He was not worth an NYPD ID card. Well, he was now, right? He was beating the whole of the NYPD and now he was going to take their best detective's profiler. How ironic.

Denise's apartment was not what he'd expected. She came across as a controlled and ordered thinker. Her apartment was a mess. Sebastian didn't like mess at all. It was a turn-off. He liked his women to be princesses. He didn't like to see discarded clothes and pantyhose all across the floor, empty coffee cups and books scattered on every seat.

He walked through each room in turn. 'You're a slut, Denise Levene. I had no idea.' He opened the bathroom door. Hundreds of products cluttered every shelf, all of them without their lids. On the floor, a bath towel was lying damp and discarded. Sebastian shook his head. He would have to teach her how to behave properly, like a real princess. Then he would kill her.

Chapter Eighty-Six

Denise Levene was about a hundred metres up the road, walking towards the apartment. Tom Harper was at her side. She felt they'd made a connection at the bar. Harper was lightening up. She'd enjoyed herself, too.

'It's nice to walk where there are no TV stations and microphones being thrust in my face,' said Tom, looking around.

'Well, you're always welcome: my street's nice and friendly.' They reached the steps to her building. 'This is me,' she said and looked up at him. 'I'd like to do that again sometime.'

Tom nodded. 'Me too. I enjoyed it. Good to talk.'

'Yeah, good to talk.'

Tom waved at her and wandered away down the road. Denise watched him for a second or two and then went up to the door. The concierge buzzed the door and waved, and Denise walked through to the lift. She stood there thinking about Tom. About how far he had come in such a short amount of time, and how far he had to go. Lisa or not, she knew that he was still a long way from being ready to move forward with his life.

Out of the lift Denise wandered down the hallway to her apartment. She stood outside the door and opened her bag. She searched for her keys for a moment, but she couldn't find them. 'Shit,' she muttered. She was just about to walk right back down

426

to the lift to fetch the concierge when she reached out for the door handle. It wouldn't be the first time that Daniel had shut their apartment door without locking it. She turned the handle and it opened. She shook her head.

Inside her apartment, she switched on the light and winced at the mess. Daniel needed more housetraining. Another job for her list. There was an unusual smell in the air, faint but strange. Denise hung up her bag, took off her coat and placed it on a hanger. She pulled off her shoes and pressed the door shut with her backside. It clicked shut and she turned and bolted it. Daniel had taken Fahrenheit to keep him company up at the senator's cabin in the hills. No doubt he'd ring later and say he'd lost his keys somewhere. She'd have to find them, but looking at the apartment she realized that would not be easy. Maybe tomorrow she'd find the time to clear up the mess.

Denise walked through to the bathroom and turned on the shower. She undressed where she stood, folding her suit on the chair and putting her blouse and underwear into the linen basket.

She stepped into the shower and closed the glass door of the cubicle. The water was as hot as she could stand it and cascaded in heavy, thick streams down her body. Her eyes closed as she flushed the city grime from her pores. It was the only way to end a long day.

Sebastian listened to the falling water. It made a lovely sound. Water was special to Sebastian. He'd grown up by the river. Water was his friend. He opened the bathroom cupboard and emerged from his hiding place beside a stack of towels and un-ironed clothes. He saw Denise through the glass, the water running down her body, her skin shining and clear. He felt a surge of heat and moved into the room. He took the wooden seat from beside the door and pushed her suit to the floor. Then he sat down to watch.

Maybe it was a noise, or maybe she saw shadows flicker across the ceiling. For some reason Denise opened her eyes and

427

turned. The shock was like a well-placed thump to her solar plexus and she gulped, physically doubling up against the shower wall. Her whole body danced with the flood of adrenalin. The stranger from the bar sat just outside the shower cubicle on a wooden chair, his legs wide apart, leaning back as if relaxed and staring with wide eyes. He was staring directly at her. And he was smiling broadly. She cowered and tried to scream, but the sound was a trembling wheeze rather than a loud alarm. Her legs weakened and buckled and her arms covered herself as if it was her modesty that she needed to protect. It wasn't. The man had one of her bath towels in his hand and was shredding it into long strips with a knife.

'Ever been hogtied, Denise?' said Sebastian. 'I'm the American Devil, by the way. I think you already know me well.'

Chapter Eighty-Seven

East Harlem
December 2, 11.20 p.m.

Tom Harper had wandered slowly back to his apartment. He was full of thoughts and ideas, some of which were about the case, some not. The thing that really kept him thinking was the idea that Mo and Sebastian were somehow linked.

Tom walked up the steps to his building. He wanted to forget all about the case for a few hours. There was an envelope taped to his front door, with his name written across the front of it. His heart started beating. He pulled a pair of gloves from his pocket and put them on. Then he opened the letter.

Dear Detective Harper,

Are you afraid of dying, Detective? I've seen the look on their faces when they are about to die. If you kill them slowly enough, they reveal their secrets. Did you know that? They are at their most beautiful just as they die. What will your face look like, I wonder? Shit-scared like Williamson? Proud like Elizabeth Seale?

I'm after you, now, Detective Harper. Just you. Williamson never was good enough, but I'm going to make an example out of you.

All my girls died in their own particular way. I guess,

Detective Harper, that I'm more afraid of dying than any of them. More afraid of loving too.

Artists are like that, unable to love, afraid to die, outcasts from life's feast. We live for our work, nothing else. My sculpture is complete but for one thing and that's you, Detective. I want your blood to mingle with theirs. We'll meet soon, I'm sure of that.

I know you like Denise, Detective, I know you're going to miss her and you are going to try to find her. I know what it's like to miss them. It's like nothing else in the world. I want you to feel pain, Tom Harper.

Think of my taking Denise as a necessary preparation for your ending. First, I will tenderize you with pain and guilt, then I will cut you up and serve you on a plate.

Yours,
Sebastian

Harper swallowed hard. He felt the crawl of fear over his skin. He had not felt this terror before. Not personally. Now he knew what it felt like. Sebastian was after Denise.

Chapter Eighty-Eight

Harper's Apartment
December 2, 11.25 p.m.

The back stairway was painted dark green and echoed to the smallest sound. Harper sprinted down the stairs, jumping the flights of steps in one leap, his footfalls rebounding off the walls and climbing high into the building. He already had his cell phone in his hand and at the bottom of the steps he called Denise. He stood there, breathing heavily, listening to the phone ringing and ringing. 'Please pick up, damn you. Pick up!'

No one did. Harper looked up the street. How was he going to get to Denise's in time? He could get a cab, take a car, but the subway would be the quickest of all. It was a few stops. He tried to calculate quickly and was caught in a moment of indecision. Then he darted towards the subway, a look of panic etched across his face.

All the time he intoned her name like a prayer. *Denise. Denise. Denise.* Perhaps Denise didn't know yet. Perhaps Sebastian hadn't managed to get to her. God help her! As he ran towards the subway, he called Eddie.

'No time for talking, Eddie. Sebastian's gone for Denise. Get a patrol to her apartment fast.' He knew Eddie would be on to the duty supervisor immediately.

He headed down into the subway and stood on the train, staring straight ahead and shaking in the bold yellow lights.

There was nothing worse than fearing for someone you cared for, when your mind could hardly dare to admit that they were only in danger because of you. His shirt was drenched in sweat.

He was trying to think. Maybe it was not too late. Maybe Sebastian had made a mistake. Maybe, he should've seen this coming. Maybe, maybe, maybe, ran through his head with the rhythm of the train.

He couldn't believe how slow the journey was. He couldn't believe he was so impotent. He just tensed and tried to remain focused. She needed him focused. She needed him, period. A busker got on at the next station, carrying a guitar. He stood in the middle of the train and strummed and sang. Some John Lennon number about peace.

The doors seemed to remain open an interminable length of time and then drew together like drapes drawn by a geriatric. Thinking of the killer alone with Denise Levene, her pale skin, her gentle blue eyes, Harper strained to keep the anger and fear from boiling over.

The train finally drew into Denise's station. Tom called out: 'Police! Move!' and started to shove people out of the way as he pushed his way up towards the street.

It wasn't so busy that he couldn't get anywhere, but he came up against more and more crowds. He was drowning in a sea of people. It felt like a lifetime before he made it above ground again and ran towards Denise's apartment. As he turned into her street, he saw the blue and red lights flashing.

He raced to the building, through the doors, and up the stairs. In her corridor, there were cops all over. The rumble of distant voices on the shortwave, the hush of whispered conversations.

Harper burst into the apartment. 'Where is she? Where is she?' No one answered. Their eyes twitched and lowered. He'd seen that look so many times before. It was only ever used on the bereaved. *God, please don't let her be dead!* Tom walked through the door into the bathroom, where he could see the backs of a group of broad-shouldered officers and detectives.

A uniformed officer turned, looked at him dead on and shook his head.

'We got here too late,' he said.

Tom felt as though he was falling down a black hole. His head was clouding over. He stumbled a few steps and looked at what the team was examining.

There was no body. No Denise. The shower cubicle was splattered and splashed with blood and Denise was gone. The monster had her.

Chapter Eighty-Nine

Mace Crindle Plant
December 3, 12.25 a.m.

In 1995, Elliot Crindle of Mace Crindle Corporation, a petrochemical giant, agreed to a settlement with the United States Department of Justice and the United States Environmental Protection Agency. In addition to a very lenient $2 million civil penalty for industrial pollution from leaking sewers and over 65 separate environmental violations, Elliot agreed to upgrade or replace over 18 miles of ageing sewers across the plant.

The ancient pumping centre occupied a large underground site with cavernous rooms formed by elaborate brick arches. The company had closed this unit and sealed it. It lay ten metres below ground, accessible, still, through an industrial elevator in land once belonging to the company and now derelict.

Into this abandoned underground room Sebastian walked, the still body of Denise Levene over his shoulder.

At the centre of the vast and labyrinthine old sewer complex was a large circular space. In it was a set of shelves upon which sat Sebastian's curiosities and artefacts, his own small contribution to the grotesque. His women. He had the clothes belonging to all of them hanging on the walls. There were rows of photographs of each woman taken as they were stalked, then the grotesque shots of their murders and the still, posed bodies hit by the glare of the camera flash.

In the centre, a glass vitrine containing his sculpture of body parts in formaldehyde, *The Progression of Love*.

Behind his display was a dry shrivelled object in the centre of a small shrine. It was Chloe Mestella's heart. Sebastian felt excited being there in the sewers with his girls, seeing evidence that it was real, that it had all happened. He often watched his objects by candlelight so they flickered as if alive. There were body parts from seven women in the sculpture he called *The Progression of Love*: Mary-Jane, Grace, Amy, Jessica, Elizabeth, Kitty and Rose. It was finished. Now he just had to deal with Harper, and Denise.

Across the room was a single bed. Sometimes he slept there, deep in the caverns below the city streets. He had food and drink in there that would last a good while. He could hide out for weeks, if need be, hidden away, sealed in his dark chamber.

He put Denise on the bed. He had time now. As much as he wanted. All the time in the world.

It had been a couple of days since he had seen his *objets d'art* and he crossed to them. He took Jessica's sweat-drenched blouse out of its plastic bag, put it to his nose, savoured the memory, felt it snake through his mind. He could feel his excitement grow. He had planned to bring a body down here many times to play with over and over again, if he ever dared. Now he had dared.

He replaced Jessica's blouse. He wanted the aroma to last. He sealed the bag and turned to Denise. Unlike the rest, she was not there as an object of his fantasy. He had never imagined her ripe in his hands, his fingernails bright with her juice.

She was there for a different purpose altogether. He looked down at her. Such a small, frail bird. He wondered what it would be like – not only to be loved, but to feel love. He knew from long experience that it was not 'being loved' that saved people, but loving.

Sebastian was not yet finished. He pulled Denise's body over his shoulder and went further into the labyrinth, down the dark, lost passages of the chemical sewers, his feet wet with the rainwater that seeped in through the old brick walls. Her cuts had been superficial. Deliberately so. Not dangerous, just across the odd vein or two to create a lot of blood. Blood incited fear so well. He would've liked to have seen Tom Harper's face when he arrived at Denise's bathroom.

He came to the steel bars of the caged prison in the depths of the plant. In there, he would keep Denise. He barged the door open with his shoulder. It took him three attempts and then he took her into her new home, laid her down on her bed and looked down on her face. Like a sleeping princess.

He left her and closed the steel door. The heavy metal clunked in the darkness and Sebastian trudged back up the tunnels like the Minotaur of old myth.

But those old myths weren't true, were they? Minotaurs taking young maidens into the labyrinth to devour them. They were just stories, right? Just old stories.

Chapter Ninety

Mace Crindle Plant
December 3, 4.00 a.m.

Every few seconds a drop of water hit the ground. In the brick cell, the hollow drip of the water on the wet floor echoed, and then silence returned. Silence and absolute darkness.

Denise woke. It was pitch black. She was lying on her back. Where was she? She lay still for a moment. The events returned to her mind. Her heart thumped and thumped. The evening with Tom. The shower. The American Devil. Fear. Horrible fear. A knife slashing at her. She sat upright. Was he watching her? She couldn't hear a thing, just the dripping water. No, wait. There was something. There. What was it?

A mechanical sound.

Yes. A faint mechanical sound in the distance. She couldn't make it out, though. It was so dark. So very, very dark. It was hard to focus, to get your bearings. There was no point of reference. She closed her eyes. That was better.

Her hands reached down. She was naked. She had bandages on her arms. She felt bruising on her lower back as if she had been dragged over something. Perhaps down stairs. And she was stiff all over. Arms and shoulders and legs. Very stiff.

She opened her eyes again. Still darkness. So much darker when you open your eyes. So dark it swallows you. It seemed to swarm about her. A darkness within the darkness. She listened. The mechanical noise had stopped. She was lying on a bed of some sort with a coarse blanket. A blanket like they used to give you at camp. She turned her head and smelled it. The dusty mouldy smell overwhelmed her. *I may not be able to see but I have a sense of smell. I have memory. Yes, Denise, think about camp. Tell me what you can remember.*

Past images swarmed through her mind. The drips fell again and again and echoed against the hard cold walls.

Her hand reached out to her right, but there was only space. She reached out to her left and felt a wall. Her fingers touched it gently. Cold. She felt the groove of mortar. A brick wall. Smooth. The water dripped again. The smell of damp rising from the stone floor filled her nostrils.

Slowly, she was piecing things together. She was in a building. A cold, wet basement. There was something mechanical in the building. A dripping tap somewhere close. The brick wall suggested something industrial. But it might be somewhere that people were near. That comforted her.

She remembered all the tricks her father had told her. She had never imagined that his years in prison would be of use to her. All those hours and days spent chatting away across a scarred blue table.

'Daddy,' she said aloud into the darkness, 'I will be all right, won't I?'

She heard his voice in her head as clear as if he was right next to her.

'Course you will, my little sparkler. I carry you in my cell and whenever I'm scared I light you up and you burn so brightly and so fiercely that I can see for miles and miles and miles. My fantastic sparkler.'

She could light a fantastic sparkler any time she wanted to. She would, too. When she needed to. And she would see everything and see for miles and miles and miles.

'What's the worst that can happen?' he'd asked her.

'I don't know.'

'The worst is they could hurt you, but the most hurt they can do to you is make you afraid. There's no worse hurt than afraid. Hurt doesn't last, but fear has you to himself all night long.'

Yes, she remembered it now. *There's no worse hurt than afraid.*

Denise clenched her fists. She shouted at the top of her voice: 'I'm not scared of you!'

Out of the near darkness, close enough to terrify, came a low, long whistle. The sound echoed around the room and into some spaces beyond.

The fear came rushing back.

Someone was with her down there in the dark.

Chapter Ninety-One

Blue Team
December 3, 9.40 a.m.

Newsflashes and breaking news bulletins over the networks and the internet talked in serious tones about the psychologist and profiler kidnapped by the serial killer. Tom Harper and the rest of the world watched the rolling tickertape at the bottom of the screen. *American Devil returns . . . Serial killer kidnaps police psychologist . . . Victim feared dead . . .*

The horrible carnival of the media rolled on to the screens. The pictures of the seven dead girls. The endless theories. The old experts rolled out to give their thoughts. The recriminations. The hypnotic pace and endless repetition. Then the pictures of Denise Levene smiling at graduation with a voice-over about a bloody shower scene, 'like something outta *Psycho*'.

Denise Levene had entered the public arena. She belonged to them now. Inside the electronic world. Nothing was personal; everything was in the public interest and appetites were vast. You just couldn't satisfy the machine. They wanted more and more. It didn't matter if it was useful or trivial. Even now, there was a high school friend of Denise's from Chicago saying how sad she was and how Denise was such a great student.

There would be more. Many more.

Harper turned round to Blue Team. The faces were all tight-jawed and determined. Harper felt the weight of their indignation and anger. She might not walk the front line as a psychologist, but Denise was one of them and the American Devil had made it very personal. He wanted to hurt Harper. The question was – why?

Harper breathed deeply and kept his hands flat on the desk in front of him. 'I know how you're all feeling, guys, so I'll keep this brief. We need to put a lid on our emotions here. Denise deserves our best efforts.' He looked from man to woman across the team. They all nodded.

'Okay. Here's where we are: Maurice Macy is not, and never was, the American Devil. We just have to accept that we don't know if and how Macy and Sebastian might be linked, but the links keep coming. The man who has kidnapped Denise Levene has killed seven women and he has also killed Detective Williamson and Senator John Stanhope. He will not baulk at killing Denise or any one of you. He is ruthless and determined. He's spreading his wings, too: his targets are getting more and more risky. Just before Denise was taken, I received a threat. The letter's on Denise's board. For some reason he's taken Denise to punish me. We need to figure out the reason for this. We've got nothing from the concierge at Denise's building, but one sighting from the street. A man was dragging a suitcase on wheels along the sidewalk outside her apartment. It was late, so it was a strange sight.'

'Just like with Lucy James,' said Eddie.

'Yeah, that's right. Another of the links between these two men. Also, about the profile – Denise told me to take off the four-day period related to Lottie and ask the papers to re-release the profile. Can you get that done, Eddie?'

'Sure thing,' said Eddie.

'Then we've got to clean up this photofit. We've got plenty of sightings. The guy was spotted during the stalking and just prior to the murders of Amy, Elizabeth, Jessica and Rose. We've got the FBI working on these images, taking off the disguises, trying to work the best fit between the various sketches. They're going to give us a picture that they think is a good fit to the killer. We'll put this out with the profile while the story is still hot. The networks will flash the killer's image all over the world.'

'Is she likely dead already?' asked someone from the back.

Harper paused as if the thought hadn't even occurred to him. 'No. We're working on the assumption that she's alive, but that gives us forty-eight hours maximum. He didn't kill her and leave her body at the apartment, like the others. There's a reason why he didn't do that. He wants to try to get to me. Let's not think the worst, let's think about how to catch him. He must have taken Denise somewhere, so he maybe has a lair of some kind.'

'So what do we do?'

'We go back through every case and see if we're missing something. We've got the guy from the botanical department at Columbia looking at our flowers. He thinks the cherry blossom came from a winter-flowering cherry and there ain't that many in New York. We're getting notices out to all the gardening organizations. It might be one small detail that nails this guy. And we'll need detectives manning the phones. The profile is good, people. It's Denise's work, so let's listen carefully out there. And think lucky. We need a break and we need one soon.'

The investigation team scattered. Detective Lassiter patted Harper on the back. 'You sure you don't want the lead? I'm happy to stand aside.'

'No, but thanks. I'm better on my own. I need to be out there, not in here organizing the interior. I need to get across to the FBI. They think that they've traced the psychologist who called in the Rose Stanhope lead. We're going upstate to find him. It was a helluva task finding this one analyst. You have no idea how much therapy this city needs.'

'Hope it falls for you.'

Harper thanked him and walked up to Denise's board. A

photograph of a bloody shower cubicle. Denise's police photograph. The letter. 'Why are you after me and Denise, you bastard? What is it that we've done? What the fuck flicked your switch?'

443

Chapter Ninety-Two

Mace Crindle Plant
December 3, 9.50 a.m.

Denise tried very hard not to think about Daniel. It was just pointless. Thinking of him just made her feel sad that she couldn't control her thoughts. It made her despair, and despair would not help her win this fight for her life. It would not help her survive and that was all she wanted. To survive this. To do all that she could to help Tom find her before Sebastian killed her.

Silence again.

Perhaps this was it, though. This was goodbye. Dying in the darkness for no purpose, without anyone seeing or knowing. Yes, Sebastian was capable of that. Absolutely. She wasn't sure why he hadn't killed her already. That's what really frightened her. She lay back against the hard mattress.

Then out of the darkness, the whistle again. The low, long whistle. Near and now further away . . . moving away. Her flesh bristled with fear.

She had been gnawing at her thumb, nibbling it with her teeth and rocking, like one of those little Rhesus monkeys the psychologists had deprived.

At university, she'd learned about a lot of cruel psychological experiments. Two sets of Rhesus monkeys were put in very similar cages after birth. In one cage was a plastic milk bottle and access to food. In the other was one simple but significant difference – the plastic milk bottle was covered in fur, to simulate the warmth of the mother's body.

That was the only difference – the presence of monkey fur. Given time, the welfare of each set of monkeys was entirely different.

The baby monkeys with the fur bottle were happy, healthy and playful. Then you looked into the cage without the fur. The Rhesus monkeys were all rocking like psychiatric patients, some on their own like lost shadows, others clasped together in lines and rocking as one. And like her, they gnawed their little monkey arms right down to the bone.

Poor monkeys. For want of a scrap of comfort, a pretend mother, they'd started to destroy themselves with the anxiety. Like her, gnawing her thumb. She could taste blood. It was comforting to taste blood. Why was that? Was it food? Or was it company?

Then there was a noise. It was a different noise. Suddenly, she was alert. It was a clanking sound. Like metal on metal. Then a creak. Then a bang.

A door! *There's a door out of the Kingdom of Darkness.* Hope swelled in her chest. Then fear pushed it back down to her stomach.

Footsteps now. They were definitely footsteps. It didn't seem to matter to her then whether it was the killer or not. At that point, the killer was her saviour.

Someone was at the door of her dark cell. She scrambled her way to a corner. There was the sound of a key in a lock. Then the sound stopped.

Suddenly, a loud click and the room burst into light. Bright, bright light – as fierce as the midday sun. Her eyes burned and her hands rose to cover her eyes. Then he was there. In the same instant.

Something was put over her head. It felt like a tight fitted hood. She could smell it. It was made of new leather. Was he just going to kill her like that? Not a word. The hood was pulled tight and fastened below her chin. Then his hands moved away. She was so weak and disorientated that there was no fight in her.

He was behind her, lifting her to her feet. His hands found her bare neck. She was thinking about dying. She didn't mind now. Best to go quickly and quietly.

How long can a body go without air? It's a matter of minutes and seconds. There's such a fine line between life and death, between the infinite variety of being and the singleness of non-being. Why was she thinking these poetic things? The stranger was lifting her off her feet. His forefinger and thumb pressed against her arteries. Her body fought for blood and air, desperate sudden lunges rising up through her muscles, the terrible clawing agony in her lungs, in her veins. Then she relaxed into his body. A scrap of fur, any fur, even pretend fur. Even killer fur.

Chapter Ninety-Three

The Catskills
December 3, 1.14 p.m.

Two black and chrome Federal vehicles sped up the last stretch of the hillside track towards the small fishing cabin. The wildlife hadn't heard noise like that for a long time. The big tyres and wide vehicles ripped the path apart in their wake.

They found the cabin quiet and still. The two cars screeched to a halt and six black-suited FBI special agents got out in unison. The sight was strangely out of keeping with the romance of the small rural retreat. Tom Harper emerged from one of the cars in his long black overcoat. He instinctively looked into the woods and listened out for birdsong.

Special Agent Baines stared at the cabin. He hoped to God he was right. The heart of every investigation was detailed groundwork, nothing else, and they'd done the work on this one. After the kidnap of Denise Levene, they'd gone back to the phone call that tipped them off about the threat to Rose Stanhope.

The recording was clear enough. Baines could tell it was a male and not much else, but the techies at voice analysis could tell a whole lot more. 'What you got, guys?' Baines had asked. 'This is our one and only lead, so it better be good.'

The two guys staring hard at the green EQ on the screen hadn't even looked up. 'Okay, it's a male, in his late thirties to early fifties, probably mid-forties, but this isn't exact. He's a smoker, there's a definite nodule or two in his vocal cords. You can hear it, right? The gruff throaty tone? Well, he's a New Yorker through and through. Probably from Brooklyn. His parents, at least, are from Brooklyn and he's educated. His vocabulary scores high. Degree and postgrad level study. He works with his voice too, by the sound of it. He's got a high score on evaluative language. He's probably science trained, so as he says he's treating a patient, I'd tend to think of him as a psychiatrist or therapist.'

This agreed with what the guy had said on the phone. Baines had been pleased, but it was still a whole lot of nothing. A native New York therapist in his forties who smoked. They still had to find the guy.

Baines decided on a search on foot. Get into every practice, speak to the receptionist, play the tape. Meanwhile, if the guys looking through the professional databases scored a hit, they'd lost nothing.

Earlier that morning, two special agents entered Marty Fox's practice and were told he was still on extended vacation. They played the tape and the receptionist smiled. That was Marty. In a few minutes they had the records of his meetings with a guy called Nick Smith. Dates, times and psychological analysis. He was treating this killer for Dissociative Identity Disorder. It didn't take them long to find out that Nick Smith was another false name, just like John Sebastian.

They still had to find Marty and see if he had more information. That took only forty minutes. He had a cabin registered in his tax records. At that point, the hawks flew from the field office out to the cabin in the hills.

Tom Harper smelled the wood smoke rising from the stack. It was a beautiful place to hide out. They stood for a moment until the door opened and Marty Fox and his wife stood there, like the happy couple.

'Martin Fox?' called out Baines.

'Yes, sir,' said Marty.

'Special Agent Baines of the FBI. We're investigating the homicide of Senator John Stanhope and Rose Stanhope. We'd like to talk to you.'

Marty's face crumpled. 'Christ, no, really? They're dead?'

'Yes, sir.'

'He said it wasn't real!' said Mrs Fox. 'He said he was just being cautious.'

'You didn't leave your name, sir. You could've helped us on this.'

'I thought I had. I thought you'd be able to protect them. I didn't know he was a killer.'

'Sir, we're taking you back to your offices,' said Baines. 'We need to know everything you got on this guy. This is Detective Harper, part of the task force. He'll be in the car with you. You happy to talk to us, sir?'

'I'm sorry,' said Marty. 'I gotta say, I'm sorry. Jesus. I didn't know. I didn't know he'd hurt anyone else. He threatened us, my wife, that's why I left a message and came up here. I've got nothing here. No phone, no TV. Good God. Dead?'

'Dead.'

Chapter Ninety-Four

Mace Crindle Plant
December 3, 1.30 p.m.

She woke up. She was sore but she was alive. How many hours had passed? She didn't know if he had gone or was sitting with her. She couldn't keep silent any more. She was close to breaking point. She didn't want to speak to him, but she couldn't bear it any longer. 'Why are you doing this to me?' she said.

There was silence for a moment, then the low whistle again. It started coming closer. Closer and closer.

Then she heard the sound of his shoes on the grainy concrete floor and the shuffling of a chair, the slight rustle of his clothes. Why was he staying so quiet?

'Why are you doing this to me?'

Was this some kind of game he was playing?

She'd woken up on a chair. She wasn't dead. That was her first thought. Why wasn't she dead? She remembered dying, but now . . . she was here again. She wasn't dead: there was too much sensation, too much pain, too much fear.

Her arms and legs were tied to the chair. There was a tight hood over her head and eyes, but she didn't seem to have anything more than bruises.

'I want to know why!'

The figure behind her stirred. It whistled. The same low

whistle. Her body shivered. She couldn't help it. It was recognition. The whistle was her scrap of sanity in the dark and now it was up close and dangerous. She heard him rise to his feet. Her body tensed in fear. His footsteps were coming round in front of her. What was he going to do?

He touched her. A horrified pulse ran through her spine. A finger on her lips. She went still like an animal playing dead. Dead, dead still. The finger was cold. It was pushing her bottom lip down. She was resisting opening her mouth. She didn't want him to open her mouth. She didn't know what he was going to do, but his finger pressed more forcefully.

He whistled low and long and continued to press.

Finally, her mouth opened obediently. Was he looking at her mouth? Was he thinking? An object moved against her lip, then her teeth. It was hard. No, not very hard. He pushed it in her mouth and closed her lips.

It was a half-moon shape and soon the taste registered on her tongue.

Apple!

She nearly whimpered. The simple pleasure of a slice of apple. She was being fed. Food was sustenance, sustenance was life – he was sustaining her. She sucked on the piece of apple, then crunched into it. The juices on her tongue felt so concentrated, it was almost painful. She chewed and swallowed.

What next? He didn't do anything else. A minute passed. She wanted more. She wanted more apple.

Slowly she opened her mouth before him. As a bird would to its mother.

He pushed another piece of apple into her mouth. So this was what he wanted? He wanted her to need him?

She chewed the crisp, juicy flesh. It was heavenly. She missed the earth and its gifts. Air, sky, fruit, grass and fields. The simple horizons.

451

She felt him close. He was behind her. He was uncuffing her hands. Then he knelt and untied her legs. What was he going to do?

Suddenly, he turned on a water tap. She could hear it, but with her leather hood could still see nothing. The water ran to the top of a bucket. Then she heard it overflowing. They were both concentrating on the bucket. He with his eyes, she with her ears.

He whistled. She felt her body wake up, the saliva form in her mouth.

'Come to me,' said his voice.

'Why?' she said.

'Come to me,' said the voice. Again the whistle, low and long.

She remained in her seat. She could hear the trickle of water as a small stream slowly reached out from the bucket.

'Come to me,' said the voice. He whistled again.

Denise put her foot forward.

The water touched her toe. She recoiled quickly and then regained her confidence. The foot moved back to the edge of the stream. Denise felt the water reaching under the soles of her feet, tickling her.

'On your knees.' His voice was terse and severe.

Denise didn't move. Then the whistle came and she couldn't stop herself. She needed food. She had nothing but obedience to occupy her mind and body. Her legs bent and she lowered herself to her knees.

The water was ice cold about her shins. She shivered and goose bumps appeared all over her.

Her flesh was alive and awake. He wanted to touch her. Feather-light touches in his dungeon. He wanted to touch this one so lightly, his spirit would soar. He wanted to see the reaction of her flesh to his touch.

'Crawl to me,' said the voice. He whistled. She crawled across the ice-cold stream of water. Hooded, bent, cold and vulnerable.

'Lay your head on my lap,' he said. He whistled. She obeyed.

'Good, good girl,' he said. A small piece of bread was pushed into her mouth.

Chapter Ninety-Five

Interstate 87
December 3, 2.20 p.m.

In the ride down from the Catskills, Detective Harper sat one side of Marty Fox with Special Agent Baines on the other. They had to be careful with Marty. He was a definite flake and they needed him to talk.

Harper shuffled in his seat and looked across. 'I need to know all about the killer, Marty. Tell me what he's like.'

'I don't know,' said Marty, scared and confused.

'Just try, goddammit. We know he was being treated by you, so everything's gotta come from you, Marty. You're the only guy we've got who knows him well.'

'Okay.' Marty took a deep breath, tried to compose himself. 'He's got two personalities, as far as I can see. A guy called Nick who's married and frightened, and the devil, who he calls Sebastian. He never seems to know when the devil's coming. Most of my meetings were with Nick.'

'Did you meet Sebastian?' asked Harper.

'Yeah, momentarily. He's the face of terror. Quite rational, quite determined. Demented. Evil. Slow and fierce. I don't know if it's a game or real.'

'What else did you find out?' said Harper.

'He told a story about a girl from way back.'

'So what happened?' said Harper, eager to get some hold on Sebastian's motive.

'It was a girl called Chloe Mestella,' Marty said. 'She was murdered in '82. Horrific murder. She was fifteen. The killer found his way into her bedroom at night on Valentine's Day and cut her to pieces. I looked it up. It's a real case. There was a murdered girl.'

'Chloe Mestella?' said Harper. He looked at Baines. 'You know anything?'

'Not a thing,' said Baines. 'We got to find out a little more detail. Talk more, Marty. We need everything.'

Harper looked across expectantly. He had thought a lot about Denise since she'd been taken. He kept thinking of her face. The thought of her pain burrowed inside him. It felt like he was guilty of her murder or something worse. And sometimes it broke through and he imagined her pain. But now they had something to follow. 'Speak, Marty,' he urged.

'Chloe Mestella. This guy, Nick, loved her. I don't know what the hell happened.'

'Is that it?'

'She got killed somehow. I don't know who did it.'

'That's good, Marty, just keep it coming.'

Harper stared across at Baines. They were both thinking the same thing. If this was true, then Sebastian might have killed Chloe Mestella. Someone needed to get out to West Virginia fast and see if they might just have found Sebastian's first kill.

Chapter Ninety-Six

Dresden Home
December 3, 5.00 p.m.

The garden was stark and empty in the winter. Nick loved spring most of all. Nick was, by his own admission, heavy on the planting. He loved tulips. Strange plants. Upright and singular. In his back yard, he was digging holes about six to eight inches deep and putting a bulb in each. He had bought over a hundred bulbs. They would look great in the spring. He wanted to see the whole lot thick with the red and white throats of scores of tulips turned upward to the sky.

His son William was behind him, halfway up a cherry tree. It was great sometimes, thought Nick. It was great to get out of yourself and relax. He felt like he was doing some good.

He went inside to get himself a soda. William walked in behind him.

'What you up to, little feller?'

'Need a soda like you.'

'You know how to ask for a soda?'

'I say please and thank you.'

'That's right, but you're getting water. Water is good for you, right? We remember that, don't we?'

William took hold of a glass from the draining board. He turned the tap. Nick watched the water stream into the glass. Then he watched William tilt his head back and drink.

'What are you looking at, Daddy?'

William's blond hair was fine and long, his white throat upturned as he drained the glass. Sebastian was crawling somewhere inside, scratching in the distance like a wolf through the undergrowth. Nick felt the tingling rise up his spine and up his neck.

'You need to go away now, William. Go outside and play.'

'I want to be with you.'

'Go now!' Nick shouted. The tingling was getting worse. He felt the spasm starting.

'I don't want to.'

'Go! Run!'

William stared, unable to move or understand.

Nick put his hand in his pocket and grabbed at the nails. He squeezed hard, but it was no good. It wasn't working. The pain streaked across his frontal lobe. Nick felt Sebastian rise in his throat. All at once, Nick was gone and Sebastian's arm lurched forward and grabbed William's hand. He stared hard at the boy. William stared back. It looked like his father but it was not his father staring at him. It was someone else. His wrist was hurting. He began to cry, but his father didn't stop. Soon, William was howling.

Dee suddenly appeared from another room and asked what was wrong. She saw her husband gripping her son and then she began to scream. Inside Sebastian's head it was quiet. The world had stopped. Nick loved these people. He wanted to hurt Nick now. That was all. Hurt the things Nick loved. That was all he ever wanted. To hurt what Nick loved. He hated Nick. Nick was weak. Nick was an embarrassment.

His cold silent gaze moved to the right. A shining spoon caught his eye. He picked it up.

The faces in front of him were red-eyed and twisted in pain. Dee was screaming violently. He could see her mouth open and close. The inside of her mouth was red like a fresh cut. He could see the dangling flesh at the back of her throat. Her teeth, her fillings, her saliva.

At times like these, he felt so cold, yet so full of emotion. He wanted to clean the world up. All the flesh and movement. He wanted everything dead. The whole world. Nick's wife, his children, everything.

Sebastian saw his princess – little Bethany – bright sunlight in her blond hair. Was it real? It was the secret of himself. He held the image for as long as he could. He saw her sweet, open face. Blond hair. Bright, white, sun-starved skin. Naked, she was lily white. Whiter than he thought possible. White, naked, dead.

The secret of him.

The spoon was in his right hand now. William's hand was red. The bones were bending in his little arm and the pain was increasing. His face was intense and strange.

Dee was close now. She was pulling at him.

He moved the spoon across to William's face, until the boy could see his comical reflection in the convex bow of the spoon.

She was his princess. Why did he keep her in his glass cage? He wanted more than anything to let her free, but he couldn't. The glass cage had no doors, no windows. He had only to watch her suffer and suffer and suffer in silence.

He pushed William's face against the table. He was looking out at the lawn. A thrush was fiercely pecking the grass. The thin bare branches of the goat willow moved in the soft breeze.

The spoon touched the edge of William's eye. It was cold. The boy had stopped screaming. His father's hand was tight against his small jawbone.

Sebastian looked down at William. Dee was hitting him now. A heavy-based pan came down on his arm with all her weight behind it. Nothing entered his world when Sebastian was reigning. Nothing. The edge of the spoon moved under the boy's lower eyelid. What was the child saying? Sebastian stopped momentarily. Something deep within him recognized a guttural sound. William was saying something. Sebastian remembered it now. It was something the princesses had said. They had said it over and over again. He wanted to hear it. He needed to hear it.

But to hear it, he had to come out of his own cage. He had to break free.

Nick. He needed Nick now. He let him back. Suddenly, Nick was there. The scream of his wife in his ear, his arm throbbing in pain, his son held under his own hand.

He moved his hand from William's mouth. The spoon fell to the floor and bounced to a stop.

Nick looked down at his son, now able to hear the words he was repeating over and over again.

'Sorry, Daddy,' William was saying. 'Sorry, Daddy. Sorry, Daddy.'

Over and over again.

Chapter Ninety-Seven

East River
December 3, 6.04 p.m.

Nick fled the house and ran and ran until he was at the very edge of Queens overlooking the East River.

This was it. Sebastian had gone too far. He had threatened Nick's own child. His own boy. Nick loved his boy. He loved him so much. Didn't he? He was going mad.

Alone by the water, surrounded by silence, Nick shut his eyes, in tears. Sebastian's girls were banging and thumping the glass. Nick could see them too. He could see them crying in pain. All Sebastian's women crying out in agony in his glass cage.

Nick moved up close to the cage. He had to see what they were saying. He was so close his mouth was against the glass.

He needed to shatter their prison, set them free. He had to hear them, to know if they forgave him. He had to free them because it was they who brought Sebastian to him. If he let them go, Sebastian would disappear too.

At the water's edge, he drew the pistol up to his head. He pushed the barrel tight into his ear.

He promised them freedom. He said he would free them. He only had to shatter the glass cage.

It had been a long journey. Sebastian had killed people to get back to them. Back to his girls. Now Nick was going to end it.

His forefinger applied three pounds of pressure to the toe of the trigger. Another three pounds and the spring would be released. The firing pin would move to the primer. The small explosion would ignite the main charge, the bullet would drive from its case.

Another three pounds of pressure was all he needed to be free.

The water glistened with diamond tips, the seagulls swooped with arrogant ease, their dark voices carrying over the river.

Another three pounds of pressure.

Then the girls stopped screaming. Nick saw them turn and look in the other direction. He saw them close their mouths in fear. He saw why. Sebastian was right there. He had returned.

Nick knew he had missed his chance – and he could not be sure he would get another.

Chapter Ninety-Eight

Harper arrived back in Manhattan and returned to Blue Team. He pushed the door of the investigation room and stood panting. 'Anybody got anything?'

Blank faces turned. Nobody had an idea. It was killing him, knowing that there was almost nothing he could do. He called Eddie Kasper and relayed the story of Chloe Mestella.

'It needs looking into,' said Eddie.

'Feds are on their way to West Virginia.'

'Fuck the Feds, Tom, this is our girl. We got blood ties – we can't leave it to them. You want me to get over there?'

Harper put his hand on Eddie's shoulder. 'You're a waste of space, but I can always count on you. Thanks, buddy.'

Eddie smiled. 'You had to do the insult or the nice part wouldn't come, would it?'

Tom shook his head. 'Not easy for me to say. Now get going.'

Eddie pulled on his jacket and left the precinct. Tom went to Denise's board. He looked at her face. He wanted to know why Sebastian had taken her. He wanted to know why Sebastian had killed Williamson and now was after him. It would take time to get to West Virginia. Too much time.

Harper took a cup of coffee and sat down at his computer.

He had to find something soon. He called up Chloe Mestella on the internet and read about the murder. If it was still an open case, then the records would be there in the local sheriff's office. Harper looked up the number and picked up the phone.

'Sheriff's office. How can I help you?'

'This is Detective Harper of the NYPD. I know you've got some Feds rushing down your way to look into the Chloe Mestella murder, but I'm looking for some help.'

'What can I do for you, Detective?' said the woman on the phone.

'Have you been following the American Devil case?'

'Sure have. Isn't everybody?'

'I'm Tom, by the way. What's your name?'

'Carla.'

'You could make a big difference up here, Carla.'

'How so?'

'Can I speak confidentially?'

'Sure, go ahead, I've got a missing set of tyres that I've got to investigate but other than that I'm free the rest of December.'

Harper laughed. 'Thanks. I appreciate your time.'

'No problem. I read about you, Detective Harper.'

'Call me Tom.'

'Bet you think we're all a bunch of hillbillies out here, don't you?'

'Hey, I'd prefer to be out in the mountains with some spare time to watch the eagles than here in Homicide.'

'You like raptors?'

'Have to say yeah. Must have a thing about killers.'

'So how can I help you, Tom?'

'Thing is,' said Tom, 'Chloe's murder happened way before they started keeping central records. Long before ViCAP and all these clever little tools that help us see the big picture. Do you remember the murder yourself, Carla?'

'Yeah, but I was only six years old. Still, it was a big thing here. Felt like we were important for fifteen minutes.'

'What about the family?'

'Don Mestella still lives at the old house. Mrs Mestella died a few years back. They still keep Chloe's room just like it was. Most of the time, they just used to sit together in silence. It killed them.'

'Could you read me some details of the report?'

'Sure thing,' said Carla. 'I got the big brown boxes out ready for the Feds. What do you want?'

'Give me the basics. I just want to know if it's our guy.'

Carla opened the old box and pulled out the police report. She opened the beige folder. The horror of Chloe Mestella's murder was hardwired into her psyche. As a child, she'd watched the vast opera of a murder hunt unfold in her back yard. Seeing the original report made her shiver.

'I never looked at this,' she said. 'It's spooky.'

'What's the MO?'

Carla flicked through a couple of pages. Memories that were years old came immediately to the surface. Her voice was edgy. 'Chloe was found naked on her bed by her mother. She was posed like a beauty queen or something with her hair all lying out on her pillow, but she had a big cut all the way up her chest. He cut out her heart. It was a botched job. Very messy.'

'It's the same MO,' said Harper faintly.

'She was covered in flower petals. It happened on Valentine's Day. Nice touch.'

It was the American Devil all right. The thought was terrifying. A man had started killing some twenty-five years earlier and he was still evading the police.

Harper and Carla talked through the rest of the details for the next half-hour, but the original investigation had got nowhere. In the end they put it down as a passing vagrant. It was anything but a vagrant.

'What are you looking for, Tom?' said Carla after they'd exhausted the reports.

'I don't know. Anything that might open up an angle here.'

'Well, I'll be here if you need me,' said Carla.

Harper put the phone down. Sebastian had killed before. What did that mean? If Denise's profile was right and the killer was in his thirties, then even if he was approaching forty that put him around mid-teens in 1982. Was that possible? Could this whole horror story have started as someone's adolescent fantasy?

Chapter Ninety-Nine

Mace Crindle Plant
December 3, 8.30 p.m.

'Dr Levene,' said the strange, contorted voice. Denise jerked her head. He was back, but his voice was different. It wasn't so deep and full. It was kinder.

'Are you listening, Dr Levene?'

The way he crept silently into the antechamber worried her. Was he studying her? He might've been sitting there for hours watching her. A patch of light hit the floor of her prison.

'Please, Dr Levene.'

Denise didn't reply. Not yet. Make him work for it.

'I want to talk to you.'

Stay composed, Denise.

'My name's Nick.' Nick felt sick in his stomach. He knew how dangerous this was. Sebastian wouldn't forgive him for intruding. 'I didn't know who you were when I found you down here, then I put two and two together. You're the woman they're all looking for, aren't you? You're in every newspaper. Every one.'

Denise listened. What game was he playing? 'Where's Sebastian?'

'Sebastian hurt my son today.' Nick hung his head low.

466

'Sebastian took a spoon to his eye. He was going to gouge out my son's eye. I've got to stop him.'

'I don't understand,' said Denise.

Nick moved erratically around the room.

'Please don't ask any more. I'm not in control of what he does. I can't stop him. He's going to kill them all, Dr Levene. He wanted to kill you, but I forced him out. I needed to see you. You can help me. He's going to starve you in this dungeon and then . . .'

'What?'

'He wants to use you to get to Tom Harper. I've got pictures of him on my phone. That's how I know. He leaves his victim's pictures on my phone.'

'Why does he want Tom Harper?'

'I don't know. I just know I can't stop him.'

'I don't understand,' said Denise. 'Who are you?'

'I don't know,' said Nick. His voice was low and fearful, with a hint of West Virginia in there somewhere. 'It's in the Bible. It's called demonic possession. He's evil, Dr Levene, and he's taking over.'

'He's inside your head?'

'He's in my head. He's in my hands. I don't want him to kill. He'll kill my family. He knows I tried to stop him. That's why he went for William, see. If I go home again, he'll kill the boy. I love my boy, Doctor. I love my boy.'

Nick paused. She couldn't believe what she was hearing. She couldn't believe that this was the vicious, sadistic killer responsible for nine deaths. And that he was asking for her help. His voice was so soft and considered that it was difficult to imagine that it could belong to a killer.

'If you've got some kind of multiple personality disorder,' she said, 'I can try to help you,'

'How can you help me, Dr Levene? I've tried with psychologists. I've tried, but no one can stop him.'

'We can try, Nick,' she said. She had no idea what she was

intending to do. She was just looking for something that gave her some control. 'I can try some things with you, if you want me to . . .'

'If you can stop him, Dr Levene. If you can stop him killing my children.'

'Yes,' said Denise. 'But you have to understand, you want to think he controls you, but he doesn't. You control Sebastian, Nick, you just don't realize it. Please, sit down, let me talk to you.'

Nick sat without another word and listened to the doctor.

Chapter One Hundred

Mace Crindle Plant
December 3, 9.00 p.m.

In a dungeon forty feet below Manhattan, an old pump room with brick walls was about to witness a bizarre experiment. Nick was going to undergo CBT. Denise was going to alter his behaviour – at least for long enough to allow her to escape. It had to work. But first they had to trust each other, form an alliance. An alliance against Sebastian. And Denise knew that she needed to convince Nick that it was not about Sebastian, it was about himself. It was Nick who let this fiend take over and control things. In that respect he was no different from a drunk or a violent husband or a depressive.

Denise found her mind twisting between the horror of her situation and the practical truth that the anti-social part of his behaviour needed to be removed from his coping strategies. She was even surprised herself that she could switch so easily from a horrified victim to a doctor.

Nick stayed in his seat. Denise was hooded but free to move around. She needed to move to think.

Nick sat patiently and expectantly. In his eyes, she – like Marty before her – was his only hope of escaping this vicious cycle of murder and guilt. He was nervous, though. Anxious about the treatment and afraid because Sebastian would punish him for letting her do this.

She started by trying to find the words, trying to formulate a way forward. It was hard. The circumstances were so strange that she was close to shrieking, but she didn't. She opened her mouth and let the routine come out all of its own accord.

'What this is called, Nick, is cognitive behavioural therapy. What we've got to do is identify the problem we have. I don't want to know about your childhood or any internal feelings, I just need to know which actions and behaviour you find unacceptable.'

'He murders people, Dr Levene! I want to stop him hurting people!' Nick shouted and then hid his face in his hands, ashamed of his weakness.

'What we have to do is to discover the nature of the problem in terms of the pattern inside your head. The relationships between how you feel, what you think and what you do. Do you understand that? Feel-think-do. We've got to look closely at these things.'

Nick stayed silent. He was thinking. Feel-think-do – that was Sebastian all over. He felt the urge, he thought about it and then he killed. Feel-think-do.

'We will agree goals for you and a method of identifying trigger feelings and trigger words, then we will find a simple physical way to re-programme your behaviour. That sound okay?'

'Yes.'

She breathed deeply. This was a journey into the unknown. She knew that CBT had been successful even in cases of extreme schizophrenia, so why not with this guy?

Denise's hunch was that Nick had called on Sebastian early in his life when he needed help to cope with some painful trauma that had made him feel so weak and useless that he basically collapsed inside. Sebastian had been a saviour at some point – a friend, someone who supported Nick and gave him strength. But when strange demonic urges started entering Nick's head, Sebastian was there to take the blame. Then, at some point, Sebastian had started living an independent existence.

'Do you think what you do is wrong?' she asked.

'I know it is. I can see that what Sebastian does is evil.'

She felt that if she could connect to him, she might prevent him from hurting someone else. She continued: 'Let's try some basics. Let's see if we can stop the urges becoming so bad that Sebastian shows up. Shall we? Shall we try to see if we can keep things so quiet, he doesn't even know you're there?'

Nick smiled. 'Yeah, that sounds good.'

She took him through the events leading up to the point where Sebastian took over. She was trying to identify the trigger. The emotion. The thought.

'What sets him going? What brings him out?'

'Fear, I think. Water, too. When he sees the kind of girl he likes, he comes into my throat.'

'That's a compulsion, isn't it? You feel a compulsion, but it's mutated into him. So you feel weak and you feel this strong desire and then he comes, doesn't he?'

'Yeah. I guess.'

'There's something that releases him. What is it?'

'I don't know.'

'Think!'

'This is hard for me!' Nick shouted. He felt the power rise and his spine erupt with sudden anger. He put the tap on hard. Water rushed across the floor. Nick felt the light flash across his mind.

'He's coming,' he said.

'What can we do?'

'Nothing. He's here.'

Denise ran to Nick and put her hands on his arms. 'Please help me.'

Nick stood up. He looked around. He could feel the demonic power coming up through his body. He had about thirty seconds before Sebastian would be there. As quickly as he could, he untied Denise's headgear. Then he ran to the internal door, a single barred exit. He rushed outside, threw the door shut and pulled a key out of his pocket. He was concentrating hard. His hand was shaking as he locked the door. Sebastian was in his head, right there: any second he'd be out. Nick tossed the key through the bars.

'I've locked you in to protect you, Dr Levene. Throw the key down the sluice grate. If you've got it, he'll kill everyone you know until you give it him back or just shoot at you until you come to him.' Nick suddenly went into spasms against the bars of the door.

Denise pulled off her headgear and searched around. She saw the small key, and against all her instincts she lurched to the sluice grate and threw it down into the sewer.

Behind her the bars of the door rattled and thumped. Sebastian was the other side and he wanted her badly. He was snorting with rage.

He stared at her through the bars. She stared back. There was no way out any more. She felt the horror in every muscle of her body.

'The water brings me out,' said Sebastian. 'I always did like the sound of water.' He had arrived.

'Is that you, Sebastian?' said Denise, keeping the tremor hidden in her voice.

'Yes, it's me. Seeing you there, Dr Levene, seeing you there, it makes me . . . it makes me so full of anger. I want to kill you now. Cut you open, put my hands inside that warm skin of yours.'

Once upon a time Denise had watched a man in a cage with a tiger. The tiger had become aggressive. The man didn't back down. He hit the tiger and pushed her away. Even when the tiger broke his arm, he remained in the superior position. It had saved his life.

'I want to feel your neck, Denise. That's a feeling you don't forget. Now I'm thinking about it. I just might do it.'

Sebastian's clear eyes bulged. He reached his arms through the bars. 'Come to me, Denise. Come to me now and I'll make it nice and quick. It'll be over in a minute and you'll be free.' The veins in Sebastian's neck were throbbing. 'Or else I'll keep you alive a long time as I hurt you.'

She saw that he didn't know what to do. He wanted her, but she was out of reach. He wanted her right there. He wanted fresh meat. They were several metres below the earth, hidden and alone, and a single locked door was keeping her alive. It was driving him crazy. 'Come to me, Denise,' he called.

'Sit down and shut up!' Denise shouted. Inside her head, she was imagining a huge tiger. She heard him pace outside her cell.

'Are you trying to provoke a response, Denise?'

'Go away. I'm talking to Nick. This is his session. He doesn't want you here. Nick! Nick! I know you're there.'

'I am the keeper here,' said Sebastian. 'It is you who are in the cage. You are the animal.' He whistled.

'Nick!' she cried again. She needed Nick. 'This is my session, Nick, and my rules. No Sebastian. He's a fake. He's not you. Do you understand? I don't want to talk to Sebastian. He doesn't exist. I want to talk to Nick. To you.'

She felt the risk. She felt the air in the room. She knew that he was staring intensely. She knew he could do anything he wanted – he could cut through the bars of the door given time or just get a gun and shoot her right away. Time was short. She needed Nick.

Sebastian hit the bars over and over again. She heard him scream, then he slumped down against the wall and out of the darkness it was Nick's voice that replied, 'Sorry. I'm not capable of stopping him.'

'You just did, Nick. You just did.'

Denise reached out her hand through the bars. It was risky, but she had nothing. Her fingertips touched his arm. 'Please,' she said. 'I can help you to control him. If you don't he will kill your son. Stick with me here. Help me, Nick.'

Nick stood and looked at her hand. 'What can you do?'

'I don't know. I don't know.' She thought for a moment. No, it was a stupid idea. But she had nothing else. 'Listen, Nick. Find an elastic band. Wear it round your wrist. You twang it whenever you feel him coming. There must be a series of feelings and thoughts that trigger Sebastian. If you stop the train of thoughts, he won't come. He's not strong. You're strong. He's not real. You're real.'

She knew it was a ridiculous idea. Absurd in every way. A serial killer monitoring his own feelings and thoughts with an attitude band. But it might just give her more time.

'Wear a band?' said Nick.

'It seems a stupid thing to do, but it can help you to make you notice your feelings. Noticing them and questioning them helps to neutralize their force. At the moment, your response to the trigger feelings leads you to kill. So when you have the feelings, you must distract the mind from its pathway and give it a new one.' She waited a moment. 'Snap the wristband every time you have a thought that is inappropriate.'

There was a long silence. Nick was thinking. Finally, from behind the door, he said: 'Yes. Okay.'

'Use the band to bring these thoughts to your conscious mind. You must have an alternative course of action when you feel Sebastian coming. Write down a list of what to do. Three firm direct orders that you cannot forget. Then just follow those orders. By the time you have carried them out, the moment will be gone.'

It sounded plausible. Nick looked at her and felt love for her. It was a simple feeling: he loved her because she showed she cared. And then it happened. The headache was so sudden and so intense, it caused Nick to black out for half a second. He fell and hit his head on the wall. When he opened his eyes, Sebastian stood up again. 'Dr Levene, I think I'm ready to go now.'

474

'For what?'

'I have a date with a blonde called Kimberly.'

'It's too early! Don't put yourself in this position yet. Nick! Stop!'

But he was gone.

Chapter One Hundred and One

Denise Levene's Apartment
December 3, 10.20 p.m.

Harper was standing outside Denise Levene's apartment. He was waiting, his head bowed to the ground. A few seconds later, the door opened. Daniel's tired and ashen face looked out.

'They told me you'd come over to get some of your clothes,' said Harper. 'I wanted to catch you.'

'She wouldn't be gone if it wasn't for you, Detective, so I can do without the house call.'

'I can understand what you're feeling, I'm just here to try to help.'

'How can you understand what I'm feeling? You killed her.'

Harper stood and met Daniel's gaze. 'I'm sorry, but I didn't do this. Denise walked into this all on her own. She wanted to help.'

'She's not a cop. She's not trained. She can't even fire a gun. How is she qualified to hunt serial killers, Detective?'

'She's a damn fine profiler.'

'She was a damn fine research scientist.'

'She wanted more.'

'What the fuck do you know about her?' Daniel's voice was harsh.

Harper took a step back. 'I don't want to make this worse for you. I'm sorry. That's all I wanted to say. I'm sorry. Denise is a great lady. I'm doing everything I can. I'm sorry.'

Daniel didn't reply and Harper turned and walked out of the apartment building. He called Kasper from the street. 'Did you get my message?'

'Yeah, sure did. You think Sebastian was a teenager when he killed Chloe.'

'Yeah, and that means I think that if he was in love with Chloe he was at her school.'

'I'm on the same train track, Harps.'

'Where are you?'

'Meadow Trail High School. There's no one here. I'm waiting for the caretaker to come and let me in. I want to check back through the yearbooks. If we can get an ID on this guy, maybe we can trace him back to New York.'

'That's the plan,' said Harper. 'Keep me up to date.'

'Will do,' said Kasper and signed off.

Harper went across town to Maurice Macy's schoolhouse. The forensics guys had finished their search and the lab guys would be busy. He looked into the rooms, walked through. On the floor there was an old photograph, creased and torn. Harper picked it up. Two boys. One big and tall and one small and slight, standing in front of a sign of some kind. Maurice Macy before he turned into a killer. Harper looked close at the picture of the boys. He looked at the sign, but it was obscured. Just the letter A was visible. Harper put the photograph down and turned round. He saw the empty wardrobe: hardly any clothes at all. Then something clicked in his head. There was no suitcase in the apartment. There had been no suitcase in Marconi's van. Harper pulled out his cell and called Blue Team.

'Garcia, get me the evidence list from Maurice Macy's apartment. I need to know something.'

Garcia came back a moment later. 'Got it. What do you want?'

'Did they take a suitcase?'

Garcia looked down the items slowly, his finger on each line. He stopped at the end. 'No suitcase on the list.'

Harper left the schoolhouse apartment. Someone had seen Sebastian wheeling a suitcase away from Denise's building. There were suitcase tracks at Lottie Bixley's dump site and Lucy James had seen a guy with a suitcase. Harper knew that Macy had used the suitcase, but now he was thinking something else. It wasn't just a copycat. Sebastian was using the same suitcase. There *was* a link between these guys. Somehow they knew each other.

Harper got back on the phone to Garcia. 'Mark, that report we got into Macy's background. We got nothing on the guy, right? Get it out for me, will you?'

'Sure. But we got nothing beyond the hospital records.'

'Then we're going to have to look again. I need to know if he's got relatives. Anyone at all. Can you go back to the beginning with him? You know, starting with where the bastard was conceived?'

'It'll take me a little time, but head back over here and I'll try to have it ready for you.'

'I'll see you in twenty,' said Harper.

Chapter One Hundred and Two

Upper East Side
December 3, 10.34 p.m.

Nick was upset. He wanted to escape the nightmare. He wanted to forget the fishing cabin, the fear. He wanted most of all to forget Mr Hummel. Yes, Mr Hummel. He wanted to forget him. He hated him. He wanted to break him. Sebastian was there with him now. Inside him. Co-existing, but not yet in control. Nick had to keep him back.

Twang!

He snapped his elastic bracelet. What had brought Sebastian out? Yeah, it was thinking of Daddy and the girls. He didn't really mean to hurt them. He didn't know what he was doing. It was Sebastian, not him. Sebastian clawed at Nick's thoughts.

Twang!

He told himself to keep going. Keep watching. What's the baserock of it all? Did anything have a baserock? He wanted to know. Sebastian was telling him he would be famous now. Everyone would know how clever he was, how powerful . . . but most of all wasn't this the thing, his mojo, his heart of hearts? Wasn't it that Nick wanted people to see how diseased he was, how bad? That's why he let Sebastian do those things – to shock, to show the very worst of himself that he felt. Was it that?

Sebastian continued to whisper. He was an evil, evil boy. A disease.

Twang!

Kimberly was sitting about four feet from him. She was on a bar stool, as was he. He could feel her there. He had this sense about people, too. He could tell that she was on edge. Maybe something had happened to her. She wasn't her usual cheery self.

Sebastian had followed the same pattern. Spot a mark. Trail her for a month. See if she was good enough for his sculpture. Kimberly had been in the running for a while. Sebastian had trailed hundreds of women to find the special seven that he finally decided upon. Now the sculpture was complete, he was tying up loose ends. Other people's pain was what he was after now and Kimberly could show him a lot of that.

He'd spotted Kimberly at the airport on the way back from a trip to Texas. He was tired from the flight and feeling horny. There was something about travelling that got him excited. It was suspended animation. He had time to think bad thoughts.

It was her shoes he noticed first: green, elegant and expensive. Her face was pretty too – long and narrow with clear bones. He was expected at home but the thought of a new mark excited him, so he walked up close to her as she was waiting for a cab. As she was distracted on her cell phone, he swiped her case.

People wrote their names and addresses on their cases. He took her case and fell in love with Kimberly mostly through her delicate clothes. They were like stolen treasure to him. The secret life of things he was never allowed access to.

He was so aroused that he was shaking. First, the aroma of her. It was the faint smell of perfume mixed with the smell of the various fabrics. Beautiful. So very beautiful. He had picked up each item in turn and touched it lovingly. Laid it all out on his bed. Each thing was impossibly fragile and delicate, like webs of gossamer, but so silky to the touch.

But it was the knowing that this was wrong that really

rocked his boat. This was a perverted pleasure and he liked the powerful secrecy of the taboo.

For days, the clothes had been enough. Just like with Elizabeth. He'd been satisfied with the weeks of trailing, buying the clothes she wore and the photographs. But these surrogates no longer sustained his deeper urges.

He wanted to take her. He had an inalienable right to her.

Kimberly sipped on a margarita. Why was she alone? Her fiancé was fucking around, that's why. She was hurt. He liked that. The beautiful clothes and the pain. The motto of St Sebastian – *Beauty constant under torture*. He licked his lips. He turned to her and raised his glass. She smiled.

Nick was losing it. Here he was in a bar he didn't recognize and Sebastian was hunting. It was too powerful.

Twang! Twang! Twang!

Sebastian laughed and moved into the limelight. Nick was too weak. Sebastian felt the power of Nick's body, flexed his muscles and smiled back at Kimberly.

A couple of drinks later, Sebastian and Kimberly were deep in conversation. It's so easy to seduce when you've been stalking someone. You know what they like, what they feel. People are simple – you reflect back what they want to know about themselves and bingo!

'You know what it is, Kimberly? Good people attract bad people. That's because bad people want to be good but they don't know how, so they use you as a model. But then they find they can't be as good as you and they resent it. Then they punish you.'

She nodded. 'Are you bad, then?'

The alcohol had changed her approach. He'd been working her throughout the conversation, dropping little trigger words like 'punish', 'rights', 'revenge' and 'self-esteem'.

She was taking his lead so easily he was inwardly proud of himself.

'I'm good at being bad, if that's what you mean.'

In Sebastian's blue Mercedes, they drove in the dark. He was talking like a man on uppers. Kimberly had sobered up a little on the journey out to her home. What was she doing? Her head was slightly fuzzy and she was in the car of a man she didn't know, letting him drive her home. He was nice. Sweet. A little overbearing, but he seemed okay. Or was he? Who knew these days?

In the bar, to be honest, she wanted to forget all about it – all about Ray and his mistress; she wanted a bit of company. He was there. What was wrong with that? As she reclined in the leather seat of his car, she knew exactly what was wrong with that – he was after only one thing and she was about to be used like a piece of trash.

She was disappointed in herself. There was one rule in life, and that was don't leave with less than you came with. It was her motto in business and in her personal life. She knew if she let this guy into her house she would come out with less rather than more. Less self-respect, less moral righteousness, less power, less integrity. She now had to think about how to extricate herself from what he might have interpreted as a dead cert.

Sebastian was thinking of getting her inside her room. He patted his side pocket. The plastic bag. He could see her face contort with surprise, shock and pain. He could take what he wanted, how he wanted. Kill. Hold. Rip.

Twang! Twang! Twang! Nick was there in the darkness of his mind, twanging at every violent thought.

The car stopped outside her apartment.

'Hey, look, I might just turn in,' she said. 'I've had a great night, though. You've been really kind.'

Bitch, thought Sebastian. Trying to turn this around. He wasn't going to let that happen. Kill her now. In the car. Her body hot against the seat. Kill. Hold. Rip.

Twang!

Twang!

Twang!

Suddenly it was Nick holding on to the steering wheel with all his might. He was breathing erratically.

'Get out, just get out!'

'What's wrong? I'm sorry if I upset you.'

Nick felt Sebastian pulling back. 'Just fucking leave or you'll die!'

Kimberly stared at Nick and saw the anger smoking in his eyes. She got out and ran up her drive. Alone, Nick slammed the car into gear and put his foot on the gas.

He smiled. It had worked. He had made himself heard. He had regained control. He had won. Kimberly was alive. He couldn't wait to get back to Denise to tell her. He drove off with a schoolboy smile, ready to show his teacher.

Chapter One Hundred and Three

Harper was unshaven, sitting in front of a wall of sketches. He found it reassuring to sketch Denise's face from memory and photographs. It kept her alive. There were sixteen of them now. He'd been sitting and waiting too long. Sixteen pencil sketches of a woman who was probably dead or a day away from dying. Finally, Mark Garcia brought his information across.

'I've assembled everything I could get on Macy. It was a difficult history to plot. He's got so many holes. After his arrest in 1998, he was in a variety of psychiatric units, mainly in New York.'

'What about before 1998?'

'His parents must've died or abandoned him when he was a kid. He was fostered all over. Twelve different homes is what it says on his record from the MPC and that's not the lot.'

'Where?' said Harper.

'It doesn't say. It says he was born in West Virginia, so you got to presume he was all over the state,' said Garcia.

Harper felt himself getting nearer. 'If he was born in West Virginia, he would've been there in 1982?'

'So?'

'I've just been on the phone about a 1982 murder in West Virginia. Looks like Sebastian's work.'

'Shit. You think they knew each other back then?'

'It's possible. There's a lot of similarities stacking up. What else have you got?'

'There's nothing. We haven't even got addresses in West Virginia. If they've got records from the '70s they'll be on paper. We'd have to knock on doors to get them.'

'Look into it, Garcia. We might need those addresses.'

'All right. I'll call around.'

Harper went back to his desk and took a call he'd been waiting for from the guys at the FBI New York field office. Harper wanted to know how long Denise could count on. The Feds had the file on screen. Tom could hear them tapping out details, cross-referencing cases. There were two of them at the other end of the line. He could discern their low, barely verbal communications – a sigh, a grunt, an uh-huh.

They came back on the phone. 'Look, Detective, we've got bits and pieces to go on – nothing but surmise, you know.'

'Just give me the time frame.'

Harper had asked them one question. What was the average length of time a kidnap victim stayed alive when the kidnapper was a known and lethal serial killer?

'Okay,' said one of the agents, 'we've got three point four days. But listen, that isn't an entirely accurate figure. I mean, eighty-four per cent of victims are dead within twenty-four hours, ninety-five per cent dead within forty-eight hours. If they survive forty-eight hours, then the story is a little different. It can go to weeks. You know. Some of these guys keep them for months.'

Denise had been missing for just over twenty-four hours. That gave him another day, tops. Tom felt hope try to scramble and leave, but he wouldn't let it. He knew that Sebastian wanted games. Denise was his kind of girl, but was the game more important? He wanted someone to suffer. He wanted to punish Harper. He wouldn't kill her until he had seen Harper suffer. Harper felt that strongly. He would have a game plan in mind. He'd keep her alive, but what for?

The Feds had taken the lead on the task force since the kidnapping, but the NYPD were still heavily involved in the case. Tom thanked them and put the phone down. He picked up the silver shield and looked at it. It was what he stood for – once. He put it in his jacket pocket and then picked up the Glock.

It felt good in his hand. He held it up, looked down the barrel out of his window to the windows opposite. He felt no twinge, only the need to find and face Sebastian. He lowered his gun and took the clip from his desk and pushed it in. It clicked. He holstered his pistol. He wanted to fight. More than anything else, he wanted a fair shot at this guy.

At 11.40 p.m. he took a call from a very disappointed Eddie, who had been looking through the old yearbooks of Meadow Trail High School, from Chloe's year and upwards. He had found nothing at all. Not a single photograph that looked like Sebastian. Not a single name that triggered off his thinking. It drained him and he was on his way back to New York empty-handed.

In the investigation room, Tom and the team were going through the calls. The search for Denise Levene was in danger of getting lost under a sea of good intentions. Her kidnap had captured everyone's attention nationwide, but in New York the feeling was tangible. They knew an innocent, beautiful woman was somewhere on the small outcrop of rock called Manhattan and they knew that a deranged sexual predator was with her. They were getting hundreds of tip-offs each hour.

Elaine Fittas crossed to Harper in the investigation room and put her hand on his shoulder.

'She'll be all right, Harper. She's tough.'

'She doesn't look that tough,' Harper replied, staring at her photograph.

'She's a woman. She's made of strong stuff. You'll get him. Keep the faith.'

Harper looked up at her. 'Thanks, Elaine. You know what? Maurice Macy still doesn't make sense to me. Why would he kill these girls if he just liked to pet them? And you know what else doesn't make sense? Lucy James didn't just die, she was killed – asphyxiated with a plastic bag. It's Sebastian's style. You think they could've been working together? If so, why would Sebastian kill Mo's girls?'

Elaine looked up. 'Maybe he loved him.'

'What do you mean?' asked Tom.

'I mean, maybe Sebastian killed the girls because he wanted to protect Maurice.'

Harper nodded. Just then, Sergeant Dan Webster appeared at the door. 'Harper,' he called. His voice couldn't disguise his anxiety.

'What is it?' said Harper. He stared at Dan Webster's face and felt the fear arrive in thick noxious waves. There was a silence around the room. Then the voice came back. 'There's a body in the basement of your building, Tom. Female. Blond hair. Wearing Denise's suit.'

Chapter One Hundred and Four

East Harlem
December 3, 11.55 p.m.

The rush through the traffic with fear gripping his throat was something Tom would always remember. The happy energetic college students, out late and drunk, and the romantic couples in units, all living in their little bubbles away from the horror that everyone fears, seemed a world away from what he was experiencing.

Harper arrived at his apartment block out of breath. He had jumped the car two blocks away because of some red lights and just run. His limbs needed to do something. His mind had reached its own red line.

Then the building came in sight and it terrified him. He had been so quick to try to get there and now he wanted to hold back. An ambulance, two squad cars. Yellow crime scene tape across the entrance to his building.

Two cops stood at the entrance to the basement, lips compressed as they tried to brush off the awkwardness. Harper was lost inside his own head, preparing himself internally for what he might have to face. He walked past them and went down the steps into the basement and on into the laundry room.

Another cop was standing at the door, waiting for Crime Scene to seal the scene. Just three uniformed cops and a waiting ambulance.

Tom nodded at the cop and looked down to the floor. Dan Webster had told him all they knew. The body of a blonde woman had been found in Harper's basement.

The upper body was wrapped in a white, heavily blood-stained sheet. Only the hair, the legs and Denise's skirt were visible.

Harper shuddered. 'Anyone taken a look?' he asked.

The cop shook his head. 'Just waiting for the Medical Examiner and Crime Scene. We can't touch it.'

Tom needed to see beneath the white bloody shroud. He looked round the room. There was no blood anywhere else. So the killer had killed her somewhere else and then transported her to his basement. No easy thing to do – carry a bleeding corpse through the streets of New York. Harper looked down and saw the tracks of two wheels in the blood. Suitcase wheels. Sebastian.

'I need to take a look,' said Tom.

'No can do,' said the officer. 'Got to keep it as we found it.'

'I need to take a look,' Harper repeated.

'I'm sorry, man, I'm sorry, but you got to hold off,' said the officer.

Harper moved towards the corpse. The officer was a big guy and he wasn't smart either. He took a step forward.

'No can do, Detective,' he said and put his big arm out. Harper stood and looked at him. He could take him down and risk being thrown out of the NYPD, or he could wait.

Lafayette walked in and saw the two men squaring up to each other.

'Tom. ME's arrived, CSU are here. It won't be long'

Harper moved away from the officer, crossed to the side of the room and waited, his eyes firmly fixed on the white sheet, his heart beating so fast that he was feeling high. He looked at the whitewashed wall, where something was written. A single word.

Abaddon.

'What the hell does that mean?' he said.

He watched for forty-five minutes as the Crime Scene detectives tagged and photographed and swept the scene, not knowing whether Denise was alive or dead. Not knowing what to feel. Limbo. His life was just in limbo all over again.

He watched as the Medical Examiner slowly moved in on the body and it was time.

Tom's throat closed tightly as two assistants in white overalls each took an edge of the sheet and pulled it to one side.

The sheet was so wet with blood it stuck to the corpse's face and chest. It made a low ripping sound as the material was lifted from the sticky wet flesh.

They all looked down. Lafayette stood behind Harper, his arm on his shoulder, squeezing hard.

'Is it her?' he asked.

'Sick fucking bastard,' Harper whispered.

Lafayette looked down at the body. The beautiful blond hair formed a halo around her head. Her body was dressed and covered in blood.

But the face had been completely removed.

Chapter One Hundred and Five

Mace Crindle Plant
December 4, 1.12 a.m.

The silence was more horrifying than anything else in the dungeon. Denise knew he was coming back and the hardness of the thick brick walls was hurting her fists as she beat against them, trying to find an escape.

Poor, poor girl. She thought it over and over again. *Poor, poor girl. Please protect her from Sebastian.*

She hadn't prayed since she was fourteen years old but for hours Denise continued to pray and hope. She then lay on her side and wept for the girl whose life was in danger. And wept, a little, for herself.

It had gotten very cold all of a sudden. She had no food and her stomach and bones ached. She was in a state of half-sleep when she heard the noise of the metal bolt.

She sat upright. 'Tell me she's all right! Please.'

She heard footsteps coming towards the door of her prison. She saw him at the bars. The light above him clicked on and bathed him in shadow. He sat down on a small stool he had carried with him.

The silence was so tense she was sweating even in the cold of the cell.

'Is she all right?' Denise asked. 'Is the girl all right?'

'I think you'll be pleased with Nick. I think he managed to save one of them.' It was Sebastian's voice. 'I should think you will be famous for your techniques, Dr Levene.'

'Well done, Nick! Well done! I'm amazed. Delighted. She's okay? Well done.'

'It was your doing.'

'The band?'

'My wrist hurts there was so much twanging. Nick must've been twanging like a lunatic. There's a red mark all the way round.'

'Tell me, please. Tell me.'

'I wanted to possess her. Of course I did. She was perfect. Unique. Quite self-assured. I wanted just to grab her and take her, but Nick didn't let me. He kept me inside. I couldn't gain control.'

'Jesus! She's alive . . . Thank you.'

'You know, Doctor, I am quite easy to upset. I seem to have a high degree of vulnerability, which is bizarre when you think I could kill these people without a second thought.'

'That's what the killing is for – to hide the vulnerability, to lock it away . . . to disguise it with the most potent thing there is, the power of life and death.'

'I like killing. Like it like nothing else. It's better than cocaine. It's like cocaine but with all your faculties absolutely intact. It's not false. It's a perfect expression of human emotion. Killing, raping, ripping.'

She heard the band twang three times behind the door. Why was he twanging? She didn't understand.

'It feels good to twang. It keeps Nick away, too. Did it not occur to you that it might? Ha! I drove her home, Dr Levene. In my car. I was alone with her in my car. The opportunity was there, but I let her go. I felt so good, letting her go. I felt what virtue must feel like. It was quite a new sensation.'

'Keep going. Keep working on the strategies. You can heal yourself. You must. You *can*.'

'You have amazing faith, Doctor. I wonder what that feels like too. Denise, I have felt lost my entire life. Will it ever end?' He slapped the elastic against his wrist again.

'Why are you twanging? Is Nick there?'

'He wants to be here. Oh, one more thing,' he said as he stood up. 'You will be pleased to know, Denise, that when I dropped her at her home and drove away, I felt proud of myself on your behalf, as if you were my mother or my father. It was a nice feeling.'

'I'm pleased. You did well.'

'Yes,' he said. There was something in his voice.

'What? What is it?' she said sharply.

'Oh, you know, Denise. You deny yourself something. You walk away. You feel satisfied, but then the urge just comes back stronger. Much, much stronger. You know.'

'What do you mean?'

He took something out of his pocket and held it a moment. 'I have something for you.'

He threw something through the bars. It splattered on the floor. She shivered at the cold red slime.

'It's Kimberly's heart, Denise. She was a lovely, gentle girl. I have no complaints.'

Denise threw herself back against the wall and let out an agonized scream.

'We worked on the first phase, Doctor, and that worked very well, but we did nothing on the second phase. I drove off, but I still wanted her. I needed to see her suffer. I had no strategies. None whatsoever. You left me quite unprepared.'

Denise was lying on her side, in pain. She started to cry as the monster stared at her through the bars.

'When you do that, Dr Levene, that crying thing . . . what is it like? What does it feel like?'

Chapter One Hundred and Six

East Harlem
December 4, 1.30 a.m.

Harper didn't wait around to watch the body being bagged, humped on to a gurney and rolled over bumpy ground to the waiting ambulance. He didn't have the heart for anything. He wanted the world to swallow him up and make it all disappear. But he couldn't say any of it. He snarled at Lafayette, walked away from his building and felt the nausea rising in his belly. He'd never be able to go in there again.

The killer had destroyed his home. Had Sebastian meant to do that? Why did Sebastian want to hurt him so badly?

The face of the corpse had been completely removed. How, they could only half imagine. All that was left was a thin layer of bloody flesh over the bone, and the dark holes of the eye sockets, nose and mouth.

Nothing from which they could identify her until they ran all the necessary tests. The agony was far from over. In fact, it was just beginning. *I want you to feel pain, Tom Harper.*

Harper took himself away to the East River and sat down to think. There was a riot of painful emotion going on in his head and he could hardly cut out the noise. He was at breaking point but he knew better than to give in to the chaos. He had to do the one thing he knew would keep him together. He had to go to work.

The East River was like black ink, tilting with bright streaks of moonlight. The odd picturesque boat chugged by and anyone might presume that the man sitting at the edge was just enjoying the scene.

In his head, the discipline was at work. Harper had a ferocious capacity for work and now was the time to draw upon it. Ignore the thump and throb of emotion, ignore his self-pity. Ignore everything except the forces of reason.

Only reason would catch the killer. Harper took a piece of chalk from his pocket and on the paving stones in front of him he started from day one. He wrote the names of the killer's victims:

Chloe Mestella
Mary-Jane Samuelson
Grace Frazer
Amy Lloyd-Gardner
Jessica Pascal
Elizabeth Seale
Nate Williamson
Lottie Bixley
Kitty Hunyardi
Rose Stanhope
Senator Stanhope
Lucy James
Denise?

He took out his notebook and went through the notes he took of each scene. The poetry sprang from the page: *Every angel is terrifying; Subtle he needs must be, who could seduce Angels.*

Then he wrote: *Abaddon.* He looked at his list. What was this telling him? Sebastian had killed the Upper East Side girls. Had he also killed Lucy James and Lottie Bixley? Why did Sebastian want Tom to feel pain now? Why? What was the connection? The marks on the pavement were barely visible in the dark but

Harper just kept staring. He wanted to know what connected these victims and he wanted to know why the killer was punishing him. A half-thought appeared in his mind. It caught his attention and then waited for him to consider the implications.

His mind had starting going there already, but with it all down in front of him it became crystal clear. It was about Mo, wasn't it? It had to be. He had gone for Denise because Tom had gone for Mo. Sebastian had loved Mo. He was seeking revenge. What for and why didn't matter, it just meant that the link was real.

But if he was punishing Harper, he was also playing games. He played a game with Elizabeth Seale. He'd said it was 'sealed with a kiss'. Maybe Abaddon meant something? Maybe Abaddon meant something about Mo.

Detective Harper spoke the word slowly. 'Abaddon.' Abaddon. He recalled something from earlier in the investigation. What was it? The phone call after they released the fake profile. Sebastian had said something about Abaddon, but then he'd said something else. What was it?

Harper flicked through his notebook. He found the transcript of the phone call. There it was. That's what he said. 'I'm the American Devil. I'm Abaddon – that's where I am. I'm a pure breed devil and I was raised in hell.'

Harper had looked up the word Abaddon – it was a name for the angel of destruction and he'd thought no more about it. Now he looked down more intently at the word.

I'm Abaddon, that's where I am . . .

It was a curious phrase. Tom had taken Abaddon to be a person, an incarnation of the devil.

The cogs in Harper's mind turned and clicked. A gear shifted.

He'd gone to Maurice's room. Harper recalled it in slow motion, trying to picture it in his mind. Yes, he was sure. There was a photograph. Two boys. Obviously connected, maybe

496

even family. The sign was obscured. Just the letter A was visible.

Abaddon, that's where I am . . .

What did it mean? And now, again, he'd written it near the corpse of a woman whose identity he dared not think about. As a reminder, maybe? As a clue?

Abaddon, the name of the angel of destruction. Was that all it meant? What was Sebastian trying to tell him? Then it came all at once. Elaine's voice. Elaine Fittas. Just before he heard the news about the body in his basement. What did she say?

'Maybe he loved him.'

Abaddon wasn't a name, was it? It was a place. It was the place where he and Mo started all this. They knew each other all right. They knew each other damn well!

Suddenly, the only sound on the vast dock was the heavy slap of Harper's running footfalls.

Chapter One Hundred and Seven

Blue Team
December 4, 2.28 a.m.

Harper arrived back at Blue Team and ran up to Mark Garcia. 'Garcia, how far have you got on Macy's background?'

'Nowhere beyond a few names,' said Garcia. 'No address as yet.'

'Come on, I need to know where he lived in West Virginia.'

'Why does it matter right now?'

'Maybe Mo had a partner in crime back then, someone who also fucked up.'

'What are you saying?'

'I'm saying that I think Sebastian and Mo knew each other back then. If I can get Mo's details, then I can get closer to Sebastian's, you understand?'

Garcia was nodding. He got it all right. 'I'll make the calls.'

'What about these names? Is Macy his name? Is it his original name?'

'No. He took the name of whatever family he was with, as far as I can tell. I've got six names in his file.'

'Let me see them.'

Garcia handed over the file. Harper looked down the list of

Mo's surnames: Foster, Hummel, Dresden, Doberman, Quiller, Ash and Macy. 'You got any details on any of these?'

'Not yet, but I can ask. Thing is, no one's going to be at work now. It's the middle of the night.'

'Call the local police, go county by county, see if you can get to the files that way,' said Harper.

'Okay, I'm on it.'

Harper paused for a half-second. 'Any more on the girl in my building?'

'Sorry, Harper, but they don't know. Her prints are being checked against the database as we speak.'

Harper nodded and headed off back to his computer, trying not to think about the report from Latent Prints that would soon tell him the identity of the latest victim. He started to search again for Abaddon. Every web reference was to some thrash metal band or some images of the dark destroyer. He wanted something else: a meaning beyond the obvious. He knew this was a message from Sebastian. He found an original definition soon enough; Abaddon meant 'a place of destruction' not a person. That made sense. Sebastian was the American Devil and wherever he was was Abaddon. That's what he meant. He was re-creating Abaddon again, collecting parts of his destruction in one place. But where was the original Abaddon?

Harper stared at the screen. Mo and Sebastian. If they had known each other and they were bad news, then there might be a quicker way to find them than calling every local sheriff's office in West Virginia.

Harper called the West Virginia State Police. A gruff trooper answered and Harper explained who he was and what he was doing.

'What's the American Devil case got to do with us?' said the trooper.

'A girl called Chloe Mestella was murdered in West Virginia in 1982. That murder could have been the American Devil's work. It might be his first kill, back when he was a kid. Listen,

I've got a lead on a guy I'm trying to trace. He was arrested for attempted rape in New York but he grew up in West Virginia, and I've got no records for him. My guess is that he might have got in trouble a lot back then.'

'Give me his name. I can see if our database can drag anything up for you.'

'Thank you,' said Harper. 'Okay, his DOB is December 8, 1969. He was twelve at the time of the Chloe Mestella murder. His first name is Maurice or Mo, but I've got six possible surnames.'

'We can run them all through,' said the trooper.

'He went under the following: Foster, Hummel, Dresden, Doberman, Quiller, Ash and Macy.'

'I'll try them all, Detective. Give me your number, I'll call you back.'

Harper gave his number and thanked him. Like with everything in life, he'd have to wait. He sank back into his chair and started to trawl again through the details of the Chloe Mestella murder. The online archives gave the story he already knew. Another unsolved murder, a cold case.

Twenty minutes passed before the trooper called back. 'Sorry, no arrest records for any of those names.'

'None of them?'

'Nothing. Sorry.'

Harper was about to hang up but he was desperate for a break and panicking at the thought that Denise might be dead. He looked at his notebook in front of him, the word *Abaddon* scrawled across the page. He threw out the line.

'Does the word "Abaddon" mean anything to you?'

'Can't say it does. You want me to run that through our local database?'

'That would be great.'

'Okay, stay on the line, it'll take a moment.'

Three minutes passed. Five. Then the trooper returned.

'You still there, Detective Harper?'

'I'm still here.'

'We got nothing on record for Abaddon. It's not a name or a place around here.'

'Shit,' said Harper.

'Hold on, feller, listen up. The word threw up a link through to the local Cold Case Unit, but I can't tell from this what it's for. You want me to put you through?'

'Yeah,' said Harper.

The ringing tone went on and on. The trooper came back on the line. 'Sorry, buddy, looks like you chose the wrong time of day, but you can take a look yourself.'

'How?'

'Well, the system's showing a hit, Detective. Take a look on the cold case website and call me back. The details are up there. I'll give you the link.'

Harper quickly typed in the link and the case came up before his eyes:

The Cold Case Unit of the West Virginia State Police is seeking information concerning the murder of Bethany Hummel, aged 14. The murder occurred on February 6, 1982. The victim was murdered in an abandoned fishing cabin on Abaddon farmstead in Pendleton County, West Virginia. Bethany was one of three sisters. The other two girls, the girls' father, Mr Ned Hummel, and his two adopted sons were not hurt in the attack.

Mr Hummel became a farmer after retiring from business after the death of his wife. The Cold Case Unit is seeking anyone who may have information concerning Mr Hummel's daughter and this investigation.

If you have information, please contact Sergeant John Eigen or contact your local State Police Detachment. If you wish to remain anonymous, you may submit a tip by clicking on Submit Online Tips on the main page.

Tom Harper's head was spinning with the possibilities. *Abaddon!* Fucking Abaddon. It was the farmstead. It was a message and Harper had found it, right at its source. The American Devil had killed before Chloe Mestella. This was his first kill.

The whole case clicked together in his mind like a jigsaw puzzle that'd been keeping him at work all night. He saw it with crystal clarity. Harper called the state trooper right back. He wanted to know exactly what had happened to the girl. He wanted to know if the images in his head had any substance.

The trooper fetched up the full report. His gravelly voice came back on. 'Bethany was hooded and taken to a fishing cabin by the river. She was kept there for a day and a half, they reckoned. Seemed the killer kept her and petted her. Then the murder was real violent.'

'Thank you,' said Harper. He was also thanking Elaine. Mo and Sebastian had killed together. Maybe Mo had taken this girl and Sebastian had just been unable to resist the temptation of a helpless victim. 'Did they look at the Chloe Mestella case alongside this one?' he asked.

'Sure they did. There were reports of an itinerant farm hand. Both murders were close in date. They figured someone came through town, murdered these girls and moved on.'

'The Hummel girl was held in a fishing hut, right?'

'Yeah. All three girls went to bed and someone must've broke in and taken Bethany from her bed.'

'Without raising the alarm?'

'He probably threatened to kill her.'

Harper doubted it. The truth was harder to imagine than the story the cops had used to paper over the cracks. A crazed out-of-towner who blows in like a bad wind and takes your children. No, the truth was closer to home.

'Do you have the names of the two Hummel boys?'

'I can look them up. Hold for a moment.'

Harper waited on the line, listening to the sound of the

officer clicking away on a keyboard. His heart was racing now. He tapped his fingers impatiently. *Come on! Come on!*

After a minute, the voice returned. 'Here we are, Detective. Mr Hummel had delusions of grandeur, it seems. The two boys were called Maurice and Sebastian.'

Chapter One Hundred and Eight

Dresden Home
December 4, 7.30 a.m.

The family sat round the big kitchen table. Dee, Nick, William and Susan. Breakfast was spread right across the table – cereals, fruits, toast. A ceramic pot sat in the centre full of hot bacon and eggs. A low rise of steam was visible just over the rim. The children were eating in silence, their heads bent down to their food. Nick tried to smile. Such a beautiful family. Perfect. If only it wasn't all a dream.

Endings are always hard, reflected Nick, as he watched his family eat. The end was coming because it had to. He had to end it. He had to get rid of Sebastian.

Dee was picking again. She always picked. What was it with Dee and food? She never enjoyed it. It was a constant struggle. Nick sat without eating. He was listening to the clinking of stainless steel on the china plates and bowls. The clinking always irritated him.

Dee had read the latest profile released by the NYPD. She'd seen the cleaned-up photograph they were publishing of the killer. She noticed that the four days had been taken out. She kind of recognized the man in the picture and she knew that Nick hadn't come back until nearly half past one that morning. But it still seemed to be a story that she could close like a book. She still couldn't believe that the killer might be her husband. The paper was lying face down on the couch.

Nick looked up slowly.

'Can't you two stop scratching your plates,' Dee said quietly.

The two children tried to eat quietly. Nick was not looking good. He was dark and brooding. He'd showered for over an hour when he got home. Dee had been scared all night long. And now they could all feel the atmosphere. They had grown to fear it.

'Why don't you go and relax and watch the TV news or something,' Dee suggested.

'You want rid of me?' asked Nick.

'No, I don't want rid of you. I just thought you might be more comfortable.'

'Stop eating,' Nick said. His voice was too serious to ignore. His children both stopped and looked up. They were waiting now. What would happen? What would he do next?

'I got something to say,' said Nick. He didn't know what it was, he just felt there was something. Something he needed to do. 'I love you all, you know that? But I gotta go somewhere. I gotta do something. I love you.'

The headache came as usual with the suddenness of a shaft of sunlight from behind a cloud. It shot through his mind and his head screamed with pain.

They all looked at him closely.

'I think Sebastian's here. You got to go. You all got to get out of here.'

When they stayed frozen, he struggled to stand, but the pain knocked him sideways. He stumbled, pulling the table and dinner plates to the floor.

Dee's eyes widened. 'Nick, what's wrong?' She rushed over. Nick was prostrate, his hands pressing against his temples. The children came close. Susan was looking terrified, but William hugged his father.

'Speak, Nick. Is it a stroke? Should I call an ambulance?'

Nick's eyes closed and his head shifted suddenly. The pain had gone. Clarity again. Beautiful clarity. Bethany Hummel had been put back in the glass cage. He couldn't hear her screaming any more, or Chloe. There was just beautiful silence.

'Nick? Nick? Should I call an ambulance? What's wrong?'

But it was Sebastian's eyes that turned to hers. 'Frontal lobe atrophy, Dee. That's what the neurologists say. Brain is not quite what it should be. It's kind of broken. Been broken a long time.'

'Nick.'

'Thing is,' his eyes rose to the three of them, 'Daddy's going away now.'

'What?' asked Dee. 'What do you mean?'

'He's got something to finish. He's got to go and sort this thing out.'

Sebastian stood and picked up William, who was still hugging his neck.

'What do you mean, Nick?'

'Come here, darling,' he said to Susan. She approached him and he picked her up, too.

'Nick, I'm not sure what to do . . .'

He held the two children and smiled at Dee. For an instant he looked like her husband again. 'The thing is . . . I'm here to protect you. I want to know you're all looked after, you know. I said I'd look after you all, didn't I? Made you all that promise. He's just got to go away.'

'Who has?'

'Got to just disappear for a while,' said Sebastian. 'You won't even miss him.'

Dee took a step towards him. She didn't like this at all. 'I think the children should go upstairs. Let them go. Daddy and Mummy need to talk.'

Sebastian smiled and hugged the two children closer. 'I'm going to give these two a bath, then we can talk. We need to talk, Dee. A long, long talk. I got a lot to say.'

'They don't need a bath. It's morning, Nick. Listen to me, you're not thinking right.'

'I need to put my hands in some clean water, Dee.'

'Leave the children down here.'

'Do you two want a bath?'

They both nodded furiously. Anything different was fun, right!

'Maybe you should sit down. I can take them up. Please, Nick. I'll look after them. You rest.'

'Hey, you two beauties, should we have a water fight or do you want Mummy to bath you?'

'Daddy, Daddy, Daddy!' the children cawed.

'You have a rest, Dee. We can talk all day. I'm not going in to work.'

She knew from the look in his eyes that there was nothing to be done. She watched them go. Susan and William looked over their father's shoulder and waved, their faces excited.

She listened to him tramp up the stairs. She heard the water rushing into the bath. She stood there panicking. What should she do? The image of William held down by the neck kept recurring. She needed help, advice, support . . . something. She dialed 911 as she listened to the sound of the water running.

'Come on, come on, come on,' she whispered. Her hand went into the drawer for a knife. Her hand trembled, the blade flickering in the light.

'911, what's your emergency?'

'It's my husband . . . He's acting real strange.'

'Are you in danger?'

'I don't know. We might be.'

'Has he attacked you or threatened you?'

'I don't think so. I don't know.'

'What's your name?'

'Dee Dresden.'

Just then, she heard a splash from the bathroom, followed by laughter. She breathed in. Perhaps she was going mad. Perhaps she was the one with frontal lobe atrophy, whatever that was.

'I think . . . maybe . . . maybe I'm just paranoid.'

'Has he hurt you before, miss?'

'No. Yes. He's frightened us before. He gets these moods.' She paused. Did she say or didn't she? What should she do? Suddenly she broke. 'He held William down. Yes! He nearly broke his arm. He's seven years old.'

'Does he have the children with him now, Mrs Dresden?'

'Yes.'

'Where are they?'

'What?'

'Where are your children?'

'In the bath . . .'

'Can you ascertain that your children are safe?'

'I don't know. God! I don't know. I think he's the man you're all looking for. I think he's the killer. The American Devil. Help us!'

Just then, there was another big splash. This time the splashing continued, but without any laughter. More splashing. Then it stopped and there was silence. No screams or shrieks. Nothing. She held her breath. Her hand gripped the carving knife and she dropped the phone.

She darted up the stairs. The bathroom door was ajar. Still no noise. No noise at all. Her lips were trembling with fear. *My children, my little babies. What's happened to my children?*

She pushed open the door and entered the bathroom. She saw him. His sleeves were rolled up and he was leaning over the bath, his hands under the water. The water was quite still. She saw her children's faces under the surface. They were staring out, motionless, their eyes wide open.

All at once, both children burst from the water and gulped air. 'How many seconds, Dad?'

'Nearly forty. A house record!' Nick turned to Dee. 'What's up, Dee? You look scared half to death.' He smiled at her.

'Nothing,' she said, hiding the knife behind her back. 'Just wonder if you want me to take over, is all.'

Chapter One Hundred and Nine

Blue Team
December 4, 8.30 a.m.

It took four hours for Harper to piece the story together. He had been searching for names in directories and databases throughout the night. It was unlikely that Sebastian still called himself Hummel. At some point, the brothers must have decided to change their names again. Mo had changed his to Macy. But what had Sebastian changed his to? Harper's list held over four hundred names already. He was looking for all the Fosters, Hummels, Dresdens, Dobermans, Quillers, Ashes and Macys across New York. All he had to do now was to go through the list one by one and check it out. It would take time. Maybe too much time. There had to be a quicker way. He drummed his thumb on the keyboard. Time was running out.

Harper now understood why the killer was after him, though. He had killed Sebastian's brother.

Now, Harper could see how it had happened those first times. The murders of the Hummel girl and Chloe Mestella were even more horrific than the cops realized; too horrific for anyone to suspect. They were killed by a child. By Sebastian Hummel, a thirteen-year-old boy.

Harper looked again at the cold case details. The brothers were younger than anyone had thought. That's why Eddie hadn't found anyone in the yearbooks. Eddie's maths had been two years out – the killer had been younger than Chloe Mestella, not older. They'd made a poor assumption and it cost them.

He had found the key to Sebastian – his raped and murdered sister. Tom knew what he had to do. He needed to find out what happened to the Hummels. He had called Eddie and asked him to sit on the door of the social security office in Pendleton County. He needed to know who fostered Sebastian after the Hummel family fell to pieces. He picked up his cell and was about to put in another call to Eddie, but Lafayette rang first.

'What's up?' said Harper. 'I hope it's good news.'

'Sure is, Harper. The woman from your basement? It's not Denise. She could still be alive, Tom.'

Silence.

'Tom, you there? It's not her, man, you hear me?'

'Yeah,' Tom said weakly. 'I hear you. Thank you.'

He put the phone down and sat still for about ten seconds, trying to stop the tide of relief from overwhelming him. Sebastian was true to his word. He wanted Tom to feel pain. More pain than he could imagine. He had to find Sebastian. He had to get Denise back. He called Eddie.

'What's up?'

'It's not Denise,' said Harper. 'It's someone else he used to try to make us think she was dead.'

'Sick fuck,' said Eddie. 'How are you feeling?'

'It's good it's not her, Eddie, but we've got to nail this and find her. Are you in yet?'

The line started to crackle. Harper didn't know it, but Eddie was following a young woman through a low door. 'What you say, Harper?'

'I want a name. Where are you?'

'We're in the stacks now. The lovely Julia is giving me a guided tour of their records. Nearly there, Harps.'

'Call me,' said Harper. 'The moment you get a name.'

'Sure thing. Julia and I are on it.'

Harper couldn't count on Eddie's news being good, so continued with his own checking. Twenty minutes in, when he was only a fraction of the way down the list, it occurred to him that he hadn't even run these names through Blue Team's database. Something might click. He took his list over to Garcia. 'Stop the phoning for a moment. I want these entered on the database, see if anything comes up.'

'Sure thing,' said Garcia.

Twenty minutes later, he called over to Harper. 'Listen up, we got a hit.'

Harper rushed across. 'What is it?'

'Nothing definite, but one of the names cross-referenced with a call we got from a lady in Queens.'

'Which name?'

'Dresden. Woman called in a potential domestic situation and blurted out that she thought her husband was the American Devil.'

'When?'

'Call came in under an hour ago. Patrol have been and gone. She was fine. She panicked. Look, Harper, don't get your hopes up. We get fifty of these a day.'

'Sure we do,' said Harper, 'but I got seven names that Mo Macy used when he was being fostered around and I'm thinking Sebastian lived there with him. This woman has one of those names. What's the address?'

'Just off the Triborough road, I think. Hang on while I check.' A couple of minutes later he looked up from the database. 'Got it. And guess what? Your botanical guys came up with five locations for winter-flowering cherry and this address is a couple of minutes from one of them.'

'That's good,' said Harper. He looked at the address. Was this really him? He couldn't believe that he'd just kept his name.

He'd probably just been happy that he wasn't a Hummel any more. He called Eddie.

'What is it, Harps? We're in the files,' said Eddie.

'Look up Dresden.'

Eddie was silent for a moment. Harper heard files moving and papers rustling. Then a woman's voice in the background called out. 'John and Jamie Dresden took two boys in August 1982. Sebastian and Maurice.'

'You hear that, Harper? What you got?'

'I heard it,' said Harper. 'I think we got him.' He paused. 'Remember this, Eddie. I want you to remember what it feels like just before we take down this bastard.'

They had Hostage Rescue Team running the show, led by Special Agent Baines and his fierce-looking colleagues in black uniform with a vast array of weaponry. He took control of the operation, keeping the vehicles quiet at both ends of Nick Dresden's street. Then the teams moved slowly down the suburban road. Four armed men walking in the centre of the road from each direction, flanked by supporting officers running into each house as they passed, keeping the neighbours safe and quiet.

The rest of the team watched from the end of the street. Nick's house was an ordinary working home. A couple of kids' bicycles had been abandoned on the lawn. Nothing but plain everyday signs of normality.

The Hostage Rescue Team fell into position at the front and back of the house and suddenly rushed the doors. The front door splintered in two.

From afar, the detectives of Blue Team could hear almost nothing. The whole operation was over in under two minutes. Then the team appeared on the lawn and radioed to Baines.

'House secured. Suspect is not present. I repeat. The suspect is not present. Wife and kids are unharmed but he's gone.'

Chapter One Hundred and Ten

Time drifted in different ways in the dark. It wasn't linear, it moved in waves and pulses. She was sure it hadn't been long. Certainly not a whole night and day, but the outer door was opening. It wasn't easy. It was stuck, but the killer barged through. Denise was still lying on her side. She sat up. This was the end.

Sebastian was lugging a huge pair of bolt cutters under his arm. He got to the barred door and placed them on the ground. 'How you feeling, Doctor?'

She looked at him and stared. There was nothing for her to say, nothing to do. The killer was going to cut through the door. He was going to be able to put his hands on her. She'd been trying to avoid the thoughts about her future that were chasing her breath away.

Be strong, she kept on saying inside her head. *Be strong*.

'A little preoccupied, Denise?' said Sebastian. He picked up the bolt cutters and started to unwind the wire safety grips. 'It's a beautiful day outside, you know. It's one of those days when you really want to take a long walk across a field or by the ocean. Not so cold. You like to walk?'

514

Denise stared ahead. *Be strong*. She turned away from him. She imagined her father. She closed her eyes. 'What do I do?' she whispered. 'Come on, old man, you always said you'd be there for me. What do I do?'

There was no answer. Her mind was frozen with fear. The sound of Sebastian working away behind her. She saw her father sitting as he always had, his two hands clasped on the prison table, leaning back in his chair, his face pale and still. *Light a fantastic sparkler*. That was what he said. *Light a fantastic sparkler*. She heard it again and again. She didn't know what it meant.

Her eyes darted about the room. Back to Sebastian.

'You're going to taste sweet,' he said. 'I've been thinking about nothing else. Just you and me. I've not slept all night. Nick's gone now, you know that? I think he's gone for good.'

Denise stared past him. She wasn't listening. She was concentrating hard. A fantastic sparkler was what she needed. She looked up at the single light bulb. There was nothing she could do.

Sebastian finally released the cutters, opened the small thick jaws and snapped shut its compound hinges.

'We're ready to roll, Denise. I want to get you ready. I want to get Harper here. I bet you want that too.'

He saw Denise pull the stool to the centre of the room. She stepped on to it. 'What you planning to do, Denise? Jump on me?'

Suddenly, the light went out and the room was pitch dark.

'So that's your plan,' came Sebastian's disembodied voice. 'You think you can stop me by turning out the light. I lived half my life in the dark, Denise. I'm not afraid. The dark is where I'm happiest.'

She heard the bolt cutter chink against the first bar. Sebastian took a moment to check the jaw with his fingers. 'First one, Denise, first cut.'

He squeezed the long metal handles of the bolt cutters and

felt the jaws push through the steel. The resistance increased and Sebastian used all his strength to push until the jaws bit right through. He repeated the operation at the top of the bar and the steel jangled to the floor.

'First one down, Denise. I reckon I could slip through with just two missing, what do you think?'

The metallic chink started up again. Sebastian's breathing emanated from the dark, like the sound of a beast. A low thumping in her ears was the sound of her own pulse. She was focused but terrified. She just kept on hearing her daddy's voice. 'Light a fantastic sparkler, like I always used to do. Then you can see for miles and miles and miles.'

Chapter One Hundred and Eleven

Dresden Home
December 4, 10.20 a.m.

At Nick Dresden's suburban home, Dee was taken into one of the small back bedrooms and interviewed. There was no time for taking people down to the precinct; they needed information now. The two children were taken by social services and the house was pulled to pieces by a team of forty officers from the CSU, Blue Team and the Bureau.

The Feds had their control truck out on the lawn and had everything on Nick Dresden in an instant. He was a nobody from nowhere. His record was clean.

Harper worked on the lair. He knew a thing or two about a man's lair. It had to be close enough to dispose of the trophies and return to the wife. He looked at the blue Merc in the driveway. 'A blue car,' said Harper. Denise's profile had brought them to this address. It was her profile that Dee had read and recognized. Denise's profile had worked.

'If he's been anywhere recently, then this car is going to tell the story,' said Harper. He called in the CSU. 'Give us anything you can on the car.' There would be forensic evidence, but Harper knew it would take time. Too much time.

The Crime Scene detective looked at the car. 'We'll need to

do a chemical spectroscopy analysis on the material. We need the lab.'

'Fuck the lab,' said Harper. 'What can you tell me in the next ten minutes?'

'Okay, but it won't be much.'

'I want a grain of sand. Anything.'

Harper watched as a team got the car lifted and slid underneath it, scraping the tyres and the undercarriage. He looked into each little clear Petri dish. They looked full of plain old dirt.

'Can you tell anything?'

'We've got four minutes left, give us a break.'

A microscope was brought from the van and the samples were quickly put on slides. Each slide was then passed through the microscope.

'Okay,' said Harper. 'Ten minutes is up. This could save someone's life. Where's this car been?'

'Well, it's been somewhere with sand. Probably coastal. There looks like there's faecal bacteria here too. Algae too from the footwell. Possibly somewhere damp, somewhere underground. Sewers?'

'Yeah, well, that narrows it!' said Harper. 'Anything else?'

'Just one more thing. Don't know what it is, but there are chemical traces here too. We'll have to check, but these are refined chemicals. Medical or industrial supplies, possibly.'

Harper chewed over the information. There weren't many places in New York City that stored chemicals. He was near water. Sewers possibly. Industrial zone. It was something. Better than nothing.

Harper crossed to the Feds' operations truck. 'Give me his employment history in New York.'

'Okay. Most recently, he's working in marketing and sales. He supplied beautician salons with nail polish remover.'

'That's how he came across the girls,' said Harper. 'What else?'

'He's got a long history of short-term employment. We've got a two-year stint as a salesman selling art materials to schools; another two years working at MoMA in the acquisitions department. He's worked many places as a salesman – he worked a year at Senderos, Mace Crindle, KCs, Andersons. Take a look.'

'I don't know the names. What are they?'

'Senderos sells paper. Mace Crindle is the old chemical plant. KCs is food, Andersons is art supplies again.'

'Show me more about Mace Crindle. Can you get it on a city map?'

'No problem.'

'Quick as you can. We've got a lot of ground to cover. He can't go home any more, so he knows this is it. And that's going to make him very dangerous.'

Chapter One Hundred and Twelve

The Lair
December 4, 10.40 a.m.

Deep underground, Denise crawled forward towards the bars. She could hear the cutters snip through the bottom of the second bar. There was one more cut to go. Then he would be in.

'It's going to be nice to get some pictures of you,' Sebastian said. 'I've not shown you my exhibition, but you're going be an important part. So is Tom Harper. I'm going to put you out like bait to get him here, then I'm going to kill you. You understand that? I'm going to cut your heart out.'

Denise stayed silent. She was waiting for the moment when the second bar fell.

The final cut, then Sebastian's laugh as the bar hit the concrete floor with a clatter.

'Well now, here we are. Here we are. Now don't try anything stupid, Denise. If you do, I'll make this a whole lot worse.'

Sebastian put his hands on the bars. Denise could hear his clothes brushing against the thin gap.

Then she lit her fantastic sparkler. She flicked the light back on. Except the bulb was missing and the wires had been pulled out of the damp, decaying plaster and wrapped around the steel bars of the door.

The cell lit up like a firework. Sebastian was momentarily bright with sparks, then his body was thrown back against the wall. She heard a thump in the darkness.

Seconds passed. Denise flicked the light switch off. Maybe he was dead. She crossed to the body in the dark. Then a roar of pure rage blasted against her face as two hands grabbed her throat in the darkness.

'I always give my girls a chance, Denise, and that was yours. You failed.' He took out a flashlight and shone it in her face. He pushed her towards the bed.

'I need to lie down, Denise.' He forced her on to the bed. He was unsteady on his feet. 'I feel . . . strange.'

In the dark, damp cellar, Sebastian lay down on the bed beside her and put his arm around her waist. His hands didn't touch her. The electric shock must've drained his strength. She waited, but he didn't move.

Denise Levene lay in terrified silence, feeling Sebastian's heavy body close against hers and his arm resting over her stomach.

She felt his breathing become deep and regular. He was unconscious. There was a sleeping monster beside her. There was nothing to stop her pulling away, smashing his head in with the bolt cutters if she could find them.

For what seemed like a whole hour she considered all her options. She wondered whether she had enough strength to incapacitate him with one blow. She tried to think where she could hit him. Across the bridge of the nose? On his temple? In his groin?

She didn't know, and anyway he was very strong and he was insane. She knew that pain was not the same for psychopaths as for normal people. They could sometimes keep going even if they were shot.

She concluded that she couldn't be sure of hurting him

enough. Her mind suddenly filled with thoughts of escape. She could risk it and try the door. Then what? Trapped underground with a psychopath you'd just betrayed.

She wanted her life. She didn't want to die down here. If he was sleeping heavily, she could creep out, maybe get ahead of him . . . Get out . . . The thought of it already seemed alien to her. The freedom she longed for was so near and yet so distant. It amazed her to see how quickly she'd become accustomed to this hole. And to him. It terrified her.

Now here was a chance. Perhaps the only chance that she would ever have. She lay awake, in the dark, planning her escape over and over in her mind. She would act. And by the time she needed to act, she would be ready. It was then she would make her escape.

Denise lay for another half-hour, rationalizing everything. In the face of all her trauma, she shut her feelings and reactions into a box in her mind. The mind has a capacity for suffering. She imagined a three-inch bubble of gelatinous liquid all around her body. The world was muffled and distant. She promised herself that she would deal with her fears at a later date. She told herself to stop whining on about it. Get over it. People are being slaughtered across the city. You're the one chance they've got.

Stop being so fucking emotional! Stop!

With the thought came the clarity that she needed. Denise looked out into the pitch darkness.

She knew every inch of that cell. She knew how to operate in the dark now. She had that advantage over him. She could find each wall, each corner, the door, almost instinctively. He was not used to it.

Use your natural advantage.

He was also fast asleep, his body in shutdown, while she was wide awake. Her mind was as clear as it ever was. Crystal clear.

Now it was time.

She counted to ten and then began to move her body away from him. The mattress was so hard there was very little give when she moved. Her left leg left the side of the bed and moved, inch by inch, towards the floor. Her pelvis inched sideways too. This was the important moment. Her body would leave his. Contact would be lost.

She slid away. Gone. She was free from his touch. It felt good. She lay still for a moment, giving him a chance to react. He didn't.

It was easier now. Denise's body inched further sideways; her left foot touched the cold stone floor.

It took her ten minutes to move from the bed. She was so careful, aware that this was her one and only chance. If she failed, he would kill her.

Standing upright on the floor, facing the bed, she knew where she was. She had her bearings. Three steps backward and her right hand would touch the cold metal of the door. She listened, but there was nothing.

One step. *Breathe, Denise, breathe.* Two steps. He moved restlessly. She stopped. Fear shot through her like an injection of adrenalin straight to the heart.

Her left foot slid backwards. It stopped. Her body shifted weight. Has your life ever hinged on the sound you make as you try to walk silently across a room after midnight, afraid of waking someone?

The right foot slid back. Three steps. Her right arm came round and touched metal. The door.

Her fingers gripped the bars. One foot went through the space – and her heel hit one of the loose bars. It rolled on the rough ground, making a low gravelly sound as the metal moved against the concrete. Denise's heart jumped as she stood stock still, waiting for the sound of movement from the bed.

There was none. There was no going back now. Nothing but escape. She pulled herself further through the bars.

One inch. Two inches. Three. Six. She was through. She was

523

out of the cell. She kept one hand on the wall and moved up the corridor, her feet making only the smallest sound as they padded on stone.

She could still see nothing. Fourteen steps and then another door. She counted.

Then she was there. The second door, the outer door. There was a sound from the cell, a body moving in sleep. She listened out in frightened silence, but there was nothing more.

The second door now. She pushed it. Nothing. She pushed it again. It didn't yield. Perhaps it was locked. She was trying to avoid panicking but it was hard.

Her fingers followed the door frame round. She was searching for the bolt, but there was nothing at all – the bolt she had heard would be on the other side, of course. Then she feared the worst. Was the door locked with a key that she had not been able to hear from her cell?

She searched for a key hole.

She didn't find one. The door was not locked. If it was not locked, then it was just stiff or stuck and she was not using enough force to move it.

She put her shoulder on the door and tried to push. Nothing. She pushed harder, then leaned her whole weight into it.

If it was going to open, it needed barging. Barging would make a noise. She stood, thinking, but there was no alternative. It would wake him, but she would have to hope she had enough of a start to run and find a way out. It was a slight chance, but it was her only one.

Fear. It can drain your body of all strength. Bite by bite. But it can also surprise you. She set her mind on moving through the door. Like a karate expert thinking his fist through a block of tiles, she had to aim through the object, not at it. If you aim at it, you'll bounce right back.

It was hard to find the power to make a significant barge. She was freezing cold and there was a monster fourteen paces down the corridor. A fierce, maniacal animal who could burst from its cave and devour her any second.

It was true that your imagination could make objects stronger or weaker and she needed this object to be weaker. Her mind concentrated, her body tightened. One shot. One chance. One moment to decide whether she lived or died.

She jumped into the door with great force, but it didn't yield. A loud iron echo erupted and charged down the corridor. She felt as though it was happening in slow motion, the ripples of sound like an unstoppable wave travelling towards the lair. Towards the beast. Towards her destruction.

It was game on now. No surrender. She started to barge the door over and over again with her shoulder, her whole right side, her head and her sheer force of will.

In the darkened cell, the beast woke to an immediate awareness of the noise. He heard the low thud, thud, thud up the corridor. His hand moved around him. Nothing. She was gone. It took him a moment to recover his senses.

'Levene!' he roared at the top of his voice. It was like the cry of a wolf. It meant her death.

At the other end of the short corridor the terrifying voice pinned her to the door. Her hands were shaking so much that she felt she was going into some kind of fit.

Sebastian was disorientated in the blackness. He flailed around, searching for the door.

She had time to try once more, then he would be there. She took three paces back. He screamed her name again. It seemed to propel her against the door.

'Levene! You're dead! Now!'

She hit the iron door with all her strength and power. It pushed forward about an inch and then stopped. It was her last chance. She heard him claw through the bars at the end of the corridor.

Then the beast was in the tunnel and there was no way out. Nowhere to run.

'Levene!'

Her mind seemed to throw her a lifeline. One idea. One advantage. She could move in the dark better than he could. She took a few steps towards him and lay down on the ground. She just had to know which side of the tunnel he was striding up and she could try to avoid him, roll out of the way.

She listened. His hand slapped on the left wall, so she moved to the other side, but then she heard his hand on the right wall. Which side? He was changing sides. Two more paces.

She gambled and threw her body tight to the right wall. He passed her in the dark, not noticing.

'Levene, you bitch!'

If he found her, he would rip her apart.

She lay still. Would her plan work? He reached the end of the tunnel and with a mighty shoulder barge flung the door open. He carried on.

It had worked. He'd broken out for her. She crawled up the tunnel and crouched by the door. There was light here. A low orange light. The corridors ran in three directions. From the noise, she knew that the beast had gone straight ahead.

She looked left and right. She presumed that he was taking the only route out and began to follow him. Along the way, she found a half-brick lying on the floor and picked it up. The corridor came to a T-junction at the end. Then she heard another sound, quite close. A mechanical sound. It was an elevator.

She peered round the corner. He was to the right, at the end of a short corridor, standing by the elevator. There must be stairs if there's an elevator, she thought. Somewhere. But how would she find them?

She peered to the left. The tunnel ran away into darkness. As the elevator arrived, Levene threw the brick as far as she could left into the left-hand tunnel. The monster turned and screamed out her name, then ran back down the corridor.

He went straight past her. The elevator doors opened. She turned the corner. Twelve feet to freedom.

She ran now and burst into the elevator, pressing the single large red button. The beast heard her and turned quickly. She could hear him screaming as he ran up the tunnel back to her. The doors seemed to move so slowly.

He was so near. She crouched in a corner, her heart thudding desperately. Close! Please! Close!

He smashed into the door as it closed. The elevator started rising. Out of hell, out of the grip of this devil. Into the light. She was crying again. She watched the red light roll round. Any moment now and she would be free.

The elevator continued to rise slowly as Denise looked around the cage. Under the metal operation plate there was an old security sticker asking all personnel to display their security passes. At the bottom of the sticker, the name of the company. *Mace Crindle Corporation.*

Suddenly, the elevator shuddered to a halt.

He'd cut the power. She was stuck. Stuck between heaven and hell. She was going to be dragged back into hell. She banged on the elevator door, over and over again, hoping that someone would hear her.

No one did. She sat down and shook with fear as the tears ran down her face.

Sebastian had cut the power and was now in the lift shaft, climbing the internal access ladder up to the motionless elevator car. He shouted out to Denise as he passed and then clambered on to the roof of the car and opened the hatch.

He saw her crouched on the floor. 'Hello, Denise. Seems you're stuck.' He lay there on top of the elevator and looked down at her, excited by the thought of seeing her face. She wouldn't look up at him. She was crouched filthy and naked in the lift, terrified and in some kind of trauma. 'Let's take you back,' he said.

Sebastian felt the much-loved surge of desire as he jumped down into the car. He was so close to her now, he could smell the fear. He wanted to bite her throat open and rip through her sternum. He pushed the feeling back down. He would have her heart, but not now. He wanted Harper to arrive first.

He stooped to pick Denise up. She tried to close her mind as he pushed her through the hatch and dragged himself out after her.

'Down the ladder, Denise, unless you want me to push you down?'

Back down in the dungeon, Sebastian's hand moved over her skull. 'Do you know what a hunger trace is, Denise? No? I can feel one in your skull. A time when food was short perhaps? Your bone stopped growing so rapidly, a slight rise and fall. A hunger trace, Denise. Were you hungry once upon a time?'

In the dark, she nodded. She had often been hungry. Many kids had been hungry. Being hungry was no big deal. You got used to it and ate when you could.

Sebastian laid her back down on the bed. 'I always give them a chance to get away,' he said. 'But they all fail.'

Chapter One Hundred and Thirteen

Mace Crindle Plant
December 4, 12.40 p.m.

A fleet of thirty vehicles streamed across the city, flashing their lights and running their sirens.

The Hostage Rescue Team and Blue Team Task Force raced through the streets. They were prepared for action. They were ready to take out the American Devil.

The old chemical compound to the north of Manhattan was quiet and still. A faint breeze moved across the East River and through the old buildings. A heavy line of metal fencing scarred the landscape in every direction.

Harper sat in the back of the HRT truck. It was too much to bear and too much to hope. And hope was all he had. In the noise of the speeding convoy, he allowed himself a prayer.

The quiet of the compound was suddenly ripped to tiny pieces as the vehicles smashed through the barrier of the Mace Crindle plant and sped across the gravel and sand. Just as quickly the convoy screeched to a halt and the doors flew open.

Detectives and agents spread out all over the compound like little black ants. Baines set up a small operations centre on the hood of his car. Harper watched them all go off in every direction. He didn't know if they had time to check out every single sewer. He wanted to be more definite, but where did they search?

'We've got about eighteen miles of sewer under this ground, Harper, and several thousand square feet of warehouse space. That's gonna take some time.'

Harper barely registered Lafayette's words as he walked out towards the first line of buildings. He looked around him. The American Devil would have arrived at this compound with a body. He would need to get out of sight quickly. Harper scouted the horizons. There were cops all over it, like a war zone.

Harper saw a group enter the nearest elevator house. They were out soon enough. 'Elevator out of action,' said a voice on the radio. Harper stared across. Going down into the ground would probably appeal to the American Devil, appeal to his fantasies. He walked over, gathering pace as he did so. Lafayette watched him from a distance. This was the time to leave Harper alone. Let the thinking man think.

Harper walked round the elevator shaft. There was no evidence of anything untoward. He pulled open the wooden door and put his hand out to touch the button but stopped as he caught a glimpse of something. The silver button had a streak of grease across it, like sweat mixed with grime. Was it fresh from the team or someone else?

Harper pulled out of the room and looked across the plot to the team. 'Did someone try the elevator button?'

'Yeah, it's bust,' shouted one of the guys. Harper went back inside and pressed it himself. Bust. It sure was.

Harper went back outside. He closed his eyes. A shiver ran through his body. He only had his gut and his gut was telling him they were underground.

Harper went back to the elevator shaft. He put his ear to it and thought he heard something. He suddenly felt the scent. He pulled at the doors, but they held fast. He went back outside and ran across to Baines. 'I think I heard something in the elevator shaft. I'm going to see if I can take a look.'

'Keep us updated,' said Baines. Harper ran across to the NYPD truck and took out a shovel. He returned to the elevator shaft, jammed the blade between the doors and pushed. The doors yielded. He held them open a little and peered inside. The elevator was near the bottom of the shaft. Someone had gone down but not come back up.

Harper had to go now if he was going to help her. He yelled across to Baines. 'Get someone over here. I'm going in. She might be down there.'

Baines told him to wait, but even as he said it, he knew that Harper was already moving.

Harper squeezed past the elevator door and clung on to the thick ropes of coiled steel. There were three lines running all the way down. He threw his legs round the ropes and let go of the door. It clanged shut and Harper was suddenly suspended in mid-air in complete darkness.

He pulled a flashlight out of his pocket and put it in his mouth and then edged down slowly towards the elevator. The steel was ice cold in his hands and his progress was slow. A second later, he spotted the access ladder and swung across.

It took a minute to get down the shaft. His foot felt for the top of the car and he dropped on to it. There was a small hatch. He pulled it open. Inside, the elevator was lit. There was no Denise. Harper looked down. There was dried blood on the floor. This was it. He had to be fast.

Harper stared back up the shaft. Another team was just edging the door open. It would take too long to get help. Much too long. And it might even be too noisy.

He had to go it alone.

Chapter One Hundred and Fourteen

The Lair
December 4, 1.20 p.m.

When Denise opened her eyes, she felt a throbbing pain. Her hands rose to her face and felt the bruise. Across the room, Sebastian sat against a wall and watched.

'He's coming now, Denise.'

'Who?'

'Harper.'

'How do you know?'

'I left him a clue. Abaddon. He's good. He's very good.'

Denise stared. Sebastian was holding a piece of rope. He was knotting it carefully.

'Then you should go.'

'I was planning to kill him just like I did Detective Williamson. It has to be here now, Denise. But it doesn't much matter. I have something for you.' He held up the length of rope. It was a noose.

He stood up. 'You're a clever girl. That trick with the light socket. I didn't anticipate it. I didn't know you had it in you.'

'I want to speak to Nick,' said Denise.

'Oh, Nick,' said Sebastian. 'He's dead.'

'Dead?'

'He wasn't strong enough. He's gone now. He can't return. I showed him what I do to the girls and he couldn't take it.'

Denise looked at the ceiling. She saw the exposed metal framework of the concrete. Sebastian moved the stool beneath it and ran the rope through a loophole. He tied it tight. The noose hung in the darkness, swaying slightly.

The next part of his plan needed to be instituted. He didn't need Denise any more. She was no fun at all. She had served her purpose, to get Harper to pay attention. He would end it now. The killer flicked the rope. Then, in the distance, they heard a boom from the elevator shaft.

The killer leaned forward and turned his head. 'He's here, Denise. Time's up.'

'You can stop this!'

'Denise, he's coming to save you. The knight in shining armour might carry you away and you might live happily ever after. Or not!'

He grabbed Denise and held a knife to her throat. 'If I kill you, it will be to hurt him, not you. I like you, Denise. I hope you realize that. Nick especially liked you.'

He was different now. He was in a mode she had not seen before. He was over-excited but under steely self-control, in a world of his own. Was this his kill mode? Was this where he went when he killed? She'd never been this close to a killer. Her mouth was so dry she couldn't speak a word.

He breathed deeply, the excitement coursing through his brain. 'This is the easy way out for you. You will avoid the agony and the pain. You won't have to see me again.' He bundled her on to the stool and put the noose round her neck. 'Jump off if you want.' He bound her hands behind her.

He knew what he wanted to see in this final scene. He wanted to see Harper's eyes burn in pain as he looked at Denise, as his eyes had done when he read that Mo was dead. He had loved Mo.

It was all about love. That's all. Love for Mo and love for his dead girls. They were all he wanted and all he could never ever have, and knowing that they had gone, nothing else in the world mattered.

Once they were dead, he loved them all. He didn't know why, but he had such strong affection for them as their lives dripped away.

'Love and death are so close, don't you think, Denise? Love and death?'

'No,' she coughed. 'I don't think so.' She knew time was running out. She wanted to keep him talking. Talking might help extend her life. 'What happened with Lottie Bixley?'

Sebastian was silent for a moment. 'I don't like them looking at me, Denise. I don't like people judging me. Lottie was a whore. I watched her die through a clear plastic bag. Do you want to know what I did to her?'

Denise couldn't bear any more. 'You're nothing, you know that? You're nothing.'

Sebastian reached up and held her throat. He watched her twist and panic. Outside, a door screeched against concrete. Then footfalls rushed along the corridor.

'Harper's here,' said the killer. 'He's come to save you. Do you know about the judgement of Solomon?'

'Yes,' Denise whispered.

'Which one of us wants you the most, do you think?'

The footsteps stopped outside the door. 'Endgame,' whispered Sebastian.

Chapter One Hundred and Fifteen

The Lair
December 4, 1.25 p.m.

A group of rats scuttled across the path and disappeared through an open drain. Harper's small flashlight bounced from wall to wall. His nerves were wired. He was alone, but somewhere above the ground the task force was going in hard. He felt like every sense was heightened as he darted along the tunnel and reached the heavy door. He held his Glock firmly in his hand. Sebastian would be ready for him, he knew that. He kicked the door open and stood back, his gun raised, his body tense. Down the corridor was a barred door. Two bars had been removed. Harper moved towards it slowly, looking out over the barrel of his gun. The light was dim in the room. It was lit only by candlelight, but Harper could make out a figure standing on a small stool. He reached the bars and staggered back, shocked.

Denise stood in the centre of the cell, naked, bruised and bloody. There was a noose around her neck. Was this Sebastian's final joke? To give him Denise, like this? To take something good and destroy it? Had he just killed her?

'Denise?' he called out, peering through the bars, looking left to right across the cell. No one else appeared to be there.

He heard a response. A muffled, low, cracked voice. He put one foot through the door and glanced left and right. No one. 'Where is he?'

Denise shook her head. She couldn't speak. Tom could see that Sebastian had wrapped something round her mouth. He shoved himself through the bars. The room was silent. He moved cautiously, aiming his gun, but he saw no one. The room was a simple box, and there was nowhere to hide. He moved quickly across to Denise and almost died inside looking at her. Her face was discoloured and swollen, but she was alive. That's what mattered. Alive. He removed her gag. She was trying to speak, but her mouth was so dry couldn't get the words out.

Tom was momentarily confused, then he looked above him. There was someone holding on to the concrete mesh that crossed the ceiling. A set of strange twisted eyes bore down on him. The moment he looked up the body fell on him, taking him to the floor.

Something heavy landed across Harper's right shoulder, cracking bone as he hit the floor, causing the gun to fall and skid across the ground. The metal bar rose again above him. On his knees, Harper cried out. He felt the metal strike his back as the American Devil hit him again and again. His head caught a blow and blood ran down the side of his face.

Sebastian wanted pain, not death. Pain and plenty of it. He could've killed Tom Harper with the first blow but he wanted him to feel the pain. That was his first mistake.

Harper flicked his elbow back hard against the killer's jaw. It was enough of a blow to make Sebastian step back. Tom turned, his fists clenched. He stamped his left foot into the ground and his punch rose from deep below his waist. His fist struck Sebastian's jaw so hard, he felt the bones in his hand shatter. Sebastian flew off the ground and landed a few feet away. Harper moved across and leaned down to pull him to his feet. He found himself facing a long filleting knife. It touched his neck. Sebastian rose, holding the knife tight to Harper's skin.

'I'm not going to kill you, Detective. I'm going to sacrifice you. You ready to be sacrificed?'

He pulled Harper's head up by the hair and exposed his throat.

'This the man you care for, Dr Levene? This pathetic specimen?' He pushed Harper closer to Denise, searching for the artery with the point of the blade. He just wanted a small hole. He wanted this death to be slow. Real slow.

He smiled. He whistled. Denise felt saliva collect in her mouth.

'You ready to taste his blood?'

Chapter One Hundred and Sixteen

The Lair
December 4, 1.35 p.m.

Within the dark cell, Harper's neck strained under Sebastian's heavy arm. He gritted his teeth and his neck muscles started to shake. Sebastian pricked Harper's throat with his knife. A small line of blood ran down Tom's neck.

He stared up into Denise's eyes. They were closed. He saw her eyeballs move under the lids. It was enough. Denise was thinking. What? Harper pulled his head round so he could see Sebastian.

'I'm going to let her watch you die,' Sebastian said as he looked at Denise. She was trying to draw spit into her mouth. She let the saliva gather and roll around her tongue.

'Look at him, Dr Levene.' The knife tensed in Sebastian's fist.

'You're no one!' Denise shouted. She drew a breath and spat hard into Sebastian's face. His eyes shut and his face turned away automatically, covered in her saliva. His arm rose to wipe his eyes. So that's what she was thinking. A distraction. It was enough.

Harper had less than a second to react. He twisted away from the knife, let himself drop away from Sebastian and spread

538

himself flat against the ground. In one fast movement, he looped one foot round Sebastian's heel and rammed his other foot hard into the knee, trying to bust it right open. The killer's body kiltered backwards and fell to the floor.

Harper had no idea what he was doing in the semi-darkness, but hearing Sebastian's body hit the floor had given him the impetus he needed. He pounced across the floor and climbed on top of him and raised his fists. His knuckles felt no pain as they ripped into flesh and bone with pent-up ferocity.

Sebastian felt the blows rain down on his face. He was just letting the pain reach him. Pain was a curious phenomenon. People tended to overreact to it. He smiled. His jaw broke and hung loose. His teeth cracked in his mouth. Then he lifted his shoulder and out of nowhere plunged a short-bladed knife into Harper's arm. The punching ceased. Harper stifled a cry. Sebastian threw him aside and laughed through his bloody teeth.

'Detective Harper!' said the voice of the killer. 'Angry, aren't you, Tom? Were you angry when you killed my little Mo? You fucking asshole.'

Harper stared around the room looking for his options. 'Why don't you run?' he said. 'The cops'll be crawling round here any minute.'

'Oh, I don't think they'll get me.'

'They'll kill you. They want you dead. You understand?'

Sebastian moved to Denise. 'She wants to taste your blood, but if she has to die, so be it.'

Her hands were tied behind her back and she trembled on the old stool. Her head was pulled at an angle, the rope biting into the soft skin of her neck. The stool moved from side to side as she shifted her weight.

Denise was badly damaged, but her spirit had not been broken. She was still ready to fight.

The monster smiled. Harper looked at him, struck by Sebastian's normality. He looked like everyone and no one.

Sebastian's foot was on the stool. He kept pushing it and letting it fall back.

'Tom, my old friend.'

'I don't know you.'

'But I know you, Tom. I know you all too well.'

'No, you don't. You don't know anyone.'

'You took my brother away.'

'Mo?'

'Love of my life, Tom.'

'I didn't take anyone. You killed him.' Harper kept his eyes fixed on Denise. They didn't know the way out of this one.

'You took him and left me with nothing.'

'You killed him, Sebastian.'

'You were investigating his case, Harper. Chasing the poor guy. You knew he was simple. He was the victim, Harper, and you killed him – frightened him to death and let him die. He never killed a soul. That was all me.'

'Leave Denise. Let her go. If it's between us, then let her go . . .'

'Very well,' he said.

The killer kicked the stool away. Denise's body dropped a foot and the noose gripped her neck with a sudden jolt.

Chapter One Hundred and Seventeen

The Lair
December 4, 1.40 p.m.

The light from the candle was filtered through the motes of dust that had risen up from the floor. Harper felt the jolt physically in his own neck and leaped up to grab hold of Denise. His body ached from the beating and the wound in his arm but he managed to lift her to take the weight from her neck.

She choked and spluttered. But she was still in the game. He pulled the gag from her mouth.

'How tight is it?'

'Tight,' she replied with a low groan.

She wasn't dying, but Harper was holding her with both arms. If Harper dropped her, she would swing again and the noose would tighten around her arteries and starve her brain of oxygen. In a few seconds she'd lose consciousness.

Harper was helpless and so was she. Like stuck pigs.

Sebastian turned. 'Do you want to save her, Tom? Do you even know how you feel? I bet you think of what you'd like to do to her, hey?

'I want you to suffer, Harper.' The killer was circling his prey. Harper was feeling the weight of Denise's body. His clavicle felt like it was broken and he was bleeding badly from his wound. Denise was listening. She had to try something. Something different.

'Your blood is making a mess of the floor, Harper. How long can you hold her up and keep her alive, Tom? How strong are you? Big fucking hero!'

Harper didn't know how he was going to get out of this. Denise would die if he let her go and he couldn't catch the killer unless he did so.

Sebastian stood behind him. 'How much pain can you take for her?'

His knife drew across the back of Harper's knee, deep into the flesh. Harper cried out and felt his leg buckle. But he held it.

'Let us go or you'll die here,' he gasped.

'Or you will,' Sebastian countered.

The knife sliced through Harper's right arm. The cut went deep to the bone and Harper grimaced and let the pain be part of someone else. He held tighter to Denise.

'Tom,' she said. 'Let me go or we both die.'

'No,' Harper said. 'No one dies here.'

'If you take him on, you'll win. If you don't – he'll kill you and I'll die anyway.'

'Touching sentiment,' said Sebastian.

Harper was working something out. He could drop her but not for long. If he got into a struggle with the killer, she would die. He had to drop her and incapacitate Sebastian within a few seconds. How?

'Perhaps you will respond to *her* pain,' the killer said with menace.

His knife drew across her thigh. She screamed as her flesh opened. Harper was staring into the killer's eyes. Emotion pulled at him and wanted him, but he had to control it. He remained still.

Sebastian's hands ran between her legs. 'She likes it, Tom.' Sebastian was enjoying himself now, watching his grotesque statue to love bleed and die. He wanted more sensation, though. Harper could see that. Sebastian always wanted more.

The killer held the blade up against Denise's breast. He scored a line and watched the blood begin to run down her white skin. He was almost transfixed.

'You raped and murdered your own sister!' shouted Harper suddenly.

The killer stopped. 'I didn't touch her. I never touched her.'

Go cold, Tom said to himself. His heartbeat dropped, his eyes narrowed. He had one shot.

'You killed Bethany. You raped her and killed her,' he said desperately. 'You held her down and killed her. Didn't you? That's what this is all about.'

The killer's eyes widened. 'You ask Ned Hummel what happened to her.'

It was enough of a distraction. Go cold, Tom. Now.

Harper lowered Denise's body to the full extent of the rope and then he released her and wrapped his arms around Sebastian's knife hand instead, moving through Denise as she hanged. His left arm smashed Sebastian's shoulder as his right arm jerked, and the killer's arm snapped. A sharp crack echoed in the small room and the knife clattered to the ground.

Sebastian bent forward and Harper landed an almighty kick in his jaw. He keeled over with a great cry of pain.

Harper had seconds to act. Denise was choking. He sprang round and grabbed the knife, then jumped and scored the rope. He slashed once, twice, three times until the knife cut through. She dropped and Harper had her in his arms – in his arms, alive.

He kissed her forehead once and then turned to Sebastian.

He stared in disbelief. The killer was gone.

'Where is he?' Harper panted. 'Where the fuck?'

Suddenly, the candle went out and Harper and Denise clung to each other in the darkness.

Chapter One Hundred
and Eighteen

The Lair
December 4, 1.50 p.m.

The FBI arrived at the elevator shaft en masse, geared up and ready. The HRT team was led by Special Agent Baines. The whole team gathered at the elevator and the elite crammed into the lift shaft and made their way underground.

In the vast dark atrium of Sebastian's lair, fifteen gun lights cut lines through the darkness. They saw the sickening contents. Hearts, eyes, costumes.

The team moved through without a word. There were over sixteen tunnels leading from the central atrium at the Mace Crindle plant. The men split up. Two teams, one north, one south.

Baines travelled south, moving quickly through the tunnels. In the distance they heard the shouting of the other team. 'Sewer six clear. Sewer eight clear.' Baines listened. He and his team approached the end of the large drain.

Baines signalled. He was here in this hell. Baines could smell him. The team of seven agents crouched and made their way down the dark corridor towards the cell.

They found the heavy steel door and heaved it open. There

was a narrow corridor leading to another door. They padded through and stopped at the entrance to the cell.

Suddenly, on the signal, the team burst into Sebastian's cell. A rope from the ceiling. In the corner, Baines saw Harper and Levene, lying together. The harsh lights hit their faces.

'Where is he, Detective?'

Harper shook his head. He had no idea. Sebastian had cut the light. Baines handed Harper a shotgun and a flashlight. 'We've gotta keep searching. Hold on.'

Baines pointed to a small sluice grate in the floor. The men went across to it and shone torches through. It was big enough for a man, but not a man in gear or boots.

Baines didn't speak. He took off his gear, helmet, night visor, webbing, boots, body amour. The team followed suit.

Baines dropped to the floor and with difficulty slipped through the gate. He dropped down five feet and then crouched. He signalled for the team. One by one, the hostage rescue team slipped into the sewer in bare feet, vests and combats.

They crouched and shone their powerful torches down into the darkness. Seven separate beams of light flickered around a large arched tunnel. There was a narrow ledge either side of the central stream.

'How deep?' Baines asked.

Agent Santana didn't wait. He jumped in and stood up. The level was at his knees. 'Couple of feet.'

Baines nodded. 'We got to move quick. He's got a lead on us and he knows these sewers. We want him alive.'

They moved out in single file, like a team of marines in a jungle river. Rats scuttled by on each ledge, sniffing the air and moving on quickly. The tunnel ran ahead but they couldn't see how far. Baines set up a fast pace and the cavern echoed to the sound of the team driving through the sludge.

Within five minutes, they spotted something ahead. The shrill call of the leader went up through the tunnel. Something turned and stared, its eyes glinting in the dark. They followed it deeper into the tunnels.

They came to a narrow channel thick with rats, hundreds and hundreds of rats – small mountains of them, crawling across and over each other, writhing and twisting. Their tiny eyes stared, their whiskers twitching in the torch light. The stream was a glossy surface of matt wet fur, rodent snouts held high above.

The team began to follow. Santana, Bodie, Jessel, Warnock. They moved through the pool of rats, slowly now, the rats investigating, swimming all around them.

The whole team were a hundred yards into the rat tunnel when they came to a dead end. Baines stared into the darkness. The men shone their torches ahead. No go. Baines looked back up towards the cell. The tunnel was a mistake. Sebastian wasn't there.

Chapter One Hundred and Nineteen

The Lair
December 4, 2.04 p.m.

Harper clasped Denise in his arms as they walked through the corridor back to the main atrium. They heard the distant calls from the HRT team echoing throughout the sewers but they didn't seem any closer. Sebastian had disappeared. Harper waited for a shot. Nothing but shouting. He held Denise closer. Sebastian had always managed to escape capture. How?

Suddenly, Harper stopped and pointed his torch up the wall. They'd reached the main atrium. Harper's torch picked out the clothes belonging to the dead girls. They both stared. Then the light spun sideways and they saw the glass vitrine. Shrunken green objects floated in the tank. Then the big sodium lights came on. Harper and Levene looked around. 'Who's there?' shouted Harper.

Then he appeared. Sebastian. He was standing behind his sculpture of body parts.

'Welcome to my museum, Detective Harper. Welcome. You like what you see? This is my masterwork – *The Progression of Love*. Seven women. I love them all.'

Harper levelled the shotgun. 'Nicholas Dresden, you're under arrest. Now put your hands where I can see them and come out front. One wrong move and you're dead.'

Sebastian moved out to the side of the tank, pointing a gun. 'Don't shoot. He's gone,' he said.

'What are you talking about?'

'He's gone,' he shouted. Suddenly, he had changed. His whole frame seemed to have shrunk a few inches. His voice wasn't so deep. His tears started. 'I'm Nick. Don't shoot me. Tell him, Denise. I don't know what he's done.' Nick looked down at the gun. 'Don't shoot me.'

'Put the gun on the floor,' Harper shouted.

'What have I done?'

'Put the gun down!'

Nick turned the gun on himself and jammed the muzzle into his ear. 'I gotta stop him, Denise. I really got to stop him.'

He walked towards them, the gun against his head. He looked shocked and confused. Harper released a shot into the ceiling. 'Last chance, whoever you are.'

Nick was shaking now. He knew he had to kill himself. He had to shoot the glass cage in his head.

That was all.

Alone in his own mind, surrounded by darkness, Nick watched the girl banging and hitting the glass. He wanted to let her free. Bethany. His sister. She was screaming something. He was up close to the glass. So close his mouth was against the glass.

Harper watched. Nick was concentrating intensely, alternately pointing the gun at Harper and turning it back to his own head. 'Put the gun down,' Tom shouted.

'Don't come near me. I'm going to kill myself,' Nick shouted back.

Six ounces of pressure was all he needed. The rest was pure physics, like the rest of the universe, a moral vacuum in a world of physical laws. Then the endless darkness.

Harper moved in close. 'Are you going to set yourself free, Nick?'

Nick closed his eyes. Denise watched him. She couldn't tell if he meant it or not.

'The sculpture!' she said suddenly. 'Sebastian loves his sculpture.'

Harper understood. He turned the shotgun on to the large glass vitrine and pulled the trigger. The tank burst and shattered in front of them, the formaldehyde flooding out and spraying body parts across the ground. Then he turned to Nick, who wasn't Nick at all.

'No!' screamed Sebastian. 'My life's work!' He aimed his gun at Harper.

Harper got his shot off first. The shotgun boomed in the high brick room and Sebastian's body was flung into the altar to Chloe Mestella. Harper moved across. Sebastian's stomach was ripped to shreds. Blood was pouring from his mouth.

Harper leaned forward.

'She loved me,' said Sebastian.

Denise moved over and stared into the face of her captor. 'I just want to see his face. The pathetic look they all have.' Sebastian turned his head away. 'Look at me!' she shouted. She had been his victim for too long. She wanted to tear out his eyes, but she stopped herself.

'I was never afraid of you,' she said. 'Not for a moment. You understand? You never had me. Not for one second.' Her father would've done the same thing. It was a little thing, but she knew it would help in the days to come, when the nightmares would drift back to haunt her.

'I was hurt,' she shouted as Sebastian's life ebbed away, 'but I was never afraid.'

Harper followed Denise's stretcher up into the light. The old lift strained under the weight of the paramedics and the gurney. They got out into the cold winter breeze. Denise breathed fresh New York air into her lungs and grabbed hard on to Tom's hand.

The grey sky was lit up with blue, white and red lights, flashing across the whole compound. It was all about clearing up now, and crowds of slow-moving cops sauntered around re-telling the story of the last few weeks. Sebastian was dead in a cavern underground. Denise was alive. Harper was exhausted, but elated at the end result.

Onlookers, unaware of the horror or the danger, stared with grotesque interest from the wire fences surrounding the plant. They knew something big was going down. Harper was feeling the aftershock of receiving a year's load of adrenalin in half an hour. Post-traumatic stress, Denise would call it. He'd go with that. But it was something else entirely he was feeling. What was it? Yeah, there it was, big and central. Faith and hope. Without it, you're just a misguided boy with a devil's mask.

A paramedic was tending to Harper's wounds as they walked across the ground. Harper wouldn't leave Denise's side. She was conscious but drifting off, her eyes picking out clouds above and loving every one of them. She and Harper hadn't even had the chance to speak properly but perhaps they didn't need to say the words. He'd come through. She knew he would.

Harper looked down at Denise. He didn't know what the future held. He'd survived everything that life had thrown at him in the last year but he knew that the events of the last two weeks would strain Denise's belief in the world. Her mind and body had been punished. Harper wondered how she would cope and what deep indelible scars would be left on her heart in the future. Harper insisted on getting in the ambulance with her. He held her hand and watched the paramedics tend to her.

Daniel appeared in his car and pushed his way through the police towards the ambulance. He saw Denise and stopped, unable to take in her survival, his face full of pain. Harper moved himself out of the way. He put his arm out and pulled Daniel into the ambulance.

'She's okay, but she's going to need a lot of time and patience. You okay?'

Daniel nodded. He couldn't get a word out. He climbed into the ambulance. His hand touched Denise's cheek and she smiled.

Harper stared across at Denise. He saw her smile against the flashing lights, her skin darkened with bruises, her eyes unfathomable. He had nothing to add. She was the hero. *Beauty constant under torture.*

Acknowledgements

An enormous debt of gratitude must go to my endlessly encouraging literary agent, Andrew Gordon at David Higham Associates. I could not have had a better guide and advisor in getting my manuscript to the point at which it would be of interest to publishers. I can only apologise to Andrew for the number of times he has had to read the book during its many redrafts. My thanks also go to the whole team at David Higham Associates who have helped to give this book a future.

I also want to thank my fantastic editor at Headline, Vicki Mellor. There can't be many people around with her breadth and depth of knowledge in the genre and her advice, guidance and good humour have been invaluable in shaping this book. Thank you also to everyone at Headline who has helped to make the book as good as possible.

Thanks, finally, to my family for all their encouragement and support. To my mother for keeping the faith. To my wife who has given me the time and determination, evening after evening, weekend after weekend, to get this written. And to my children who played around my feet as I wrote. I'm happy to say I've finished the book, I can play now!

Turn the page for an exclusive extract of
Oliver Stark's thrilling new novel

88 Killer

Coming soon from Headline

Prologue

Love was the heart of everything. Even death. He held the case close to his chest and stared ahead. Sadness overwhelmed him. It was the destruction of happiness he hated most. He saw the victims in his mind's eye as dark red spots with a thousand lines shooting out in every direction. Lines of impact, lines of connections – they represented people, places, ideas. Lines all now dead.

Each death was infinite. He put out his hand against the wall. His mother had chosen the wallpaper in 1985 – a murky brown background with a raised pattern of white leaves. The feel of it was reassuring, not so the images that now lay scattered all across it from the door frame to the window. There were seventeen faces in all; each one was dated – day, month, year and finally, time of death.

Under each photograph was a yellow card lined faintly in blue ink, the kind you'd find in any stationary store. He'd written on each card in thick black pen. The words were precise and accurate, technical even, but they could still catch the breath in his throat, even now. Even after he'd seen them a hundred times.

Each card was titled CAUSE OF DEATH in capital letters and underlined three times, as though the writer had paused to think about the words to come.

The descriptions came next in a fast flowing script. The letters were legible but the writer had not been slow here.

Ts were not crossed, some letters were not completed. They sometimes fell below the line, sometimes rose above it. It created the effect of making the words look like they were floating.

Strangulation with a nylon fishing line
Blunt force trauma to the right temple
Multiple stab wound to the thorax

They went on. Seventeen descriptions. All killed in different ways. Not a single repetition. Below the yellow card was a white sticker with an address on it. The dead came from all over the United States. Seventeen murders scattered across America like confetti. And no one had made the connection. No one except him.

The man in the centre of the room wore shaded prescription glasses that darkened in the sunshine; they made him look older than he actually was. He was also balding fast for a young man, and had fat choppy fingers that seemed to belong to another's hand. The smell of ingrained sweat lingered in his woollen jacket. It had always been hard making friends; he saw the look they had. They didn't want to know.

He stared at the photographs, letting the images come into focus and then fade. There were too many of them now. He opened his brown leather suitcase and took out a photograph of a woman, somewhere between the age of twenty-five and thirty. She was smiling, holding what looked like a red knitted shawl and turning as if she was dancing the tarantella. She had black hair like a raven and looked happy and carefree.

The young balding man was sweating. From somewhere else in the apartment the smell of roast chicken was making his stomach rumble. Food was the start and end of life, if you were lucky.

He took the photograph in his fingers. He looked down at

the woman, his eyebrows raised. He only had a matter of minutes before his mother would call him down the long dark hallway.

Friday. The family gathered as usual.

He pinned up the photograph. She was beautiful. It didn't matter to him that she was or wasn't beautiful. That was just an additional piece of information that caught on his emotions. They all had something that mattered to someone: beautiful children, a sobbing wife, a dedication to their job. None of them deserved to die. They all had so much to live for. It didn't matter at all how attractive or young or rich or full of vitality a victim was. It was the loss of life that was so wrong. The unintended, forced loss of life. He pinned up number 18 and took out a yellow card.

The brown leather pen holder contained twelve of the same thick tipped black pens. He took one, pulled off the top. It clicked in a satisfying way. He wrote the three words that he'd written seventeen times before. Cause of Death. He thought about the details of the crime. He turned it over in his mind as he underscored the words slowly. Once, twice, three times. Then he was ready.

He looked across at the woman caught up in a moment of dance. He put the tip of the pen at the first line and paused momentarily, thinking of how to phrase it. Then he started to write quickly, the words flowing up and down as he tried to keep his hand from shaking.

Point blank gunshot to the forehead.

He pinned up the yellow card. His mother called from the other end of the corridor. 'Hey, we're not going to live for ever, come and carve.'

He took out a roll of white stickers and tore one off. He wrote the location.

Lower East Village, New York City.

He looked at the date. It had been three weeks since her body was discovered on the sidewalk and no one had yet been arrested. It always surprised him that no one had ever been caught. He imagined the police must be stupid. He stuck the location to the wall, clicked off the light and left the room. From outside he locked his childhood bedroom with two separate keys and the mausoleum was closed for another day.

Chapter One

Detective Tom Harper left the precinct at 11 a.m., three hours after the end of his shift. He was already a half hour late for his meet-up and he looked like hell. The night shifts had been his own choice. There were many reasons why a man took the 12 a.m. 8 a.m. shift – some liked the fact that there were no bosses around, others liked the sounds of the city in the quiet hours and some, like Harper, just didn't sleep anymore.

In Homicide, they called them the night walkers. No one needed to ask why; it was just an agreed unknown. Since his last big case, the American Devil case, Harper had tried to get the killer out of his head and while he worked his long hours, he succeeded. But alone, trying to sleep, things started to rumble from somewhere deep inside and he'd feel the sharp pain running down his side.

Being scared of something that was long gone was hard to admit, so Harper never did. He just tried to avoid it.

Harper headed out of the precinct and down towards the subway to catch the cross town train. He looked at his watch. Mary Harper was a lawyer. His sister liked order and she liked punctuality. She was going to have a great excuse to give him a truck load of her big sister wisdom.

The bruises across both eyes were still fresh and swollen. He'd tried to silence the demons by going back to the gym, hoping that he could work it out in the ring. He trained hard and took a bout with a Puerto Rican cop from downtown. He had liked the preparation, the adrenalin, even liked the thought of being a fighter again. But in the ring, it fell apart.

Thirteen hours earlier, he'd sat in the small lonely changing room, with Dillon taping his hands. He couldn't explain what he was feeling, but it wasn't good.

A small group of NYPD officers watched Harper emerge into a cold warehouse that was kitted out with old wooden benches. Harper was six two with the build of a professional fighter. He had a look of cold determination in his eyes. The Puerto Rican looked twice at Harper and both times, he hadn't liked what he'd seen.

In the glare of the lights, against the hard muscles of the smaller, bullish Puerto Rican, amid the shouts from the off-duty, beer drenched cops; Harper let himself be bossed around the ring. The Puerto Rican was small, but strong. He was tough, but no technician. Harper could have taken him down, but you need more than ability to take a man down. You have to want it, and Harper didn't.

Harper danced for a while, but then his feet started to slow. He let his guard fall. He opened up his shoulders. Harper felt the blows landing hard and he let them come.

He moved and ducked but didn't throw a punch. The Puerto Rican gained confidence quickly and started to land some heavy body shots. Harper parried and defended himself, but he couldn't bring himself to hit back.

In the third round, Harper put his chin out, the Puerto Rican took a big swing from the right and Harper went down. His only time on the canvas. He stared up at the rows of lights and wondered what the hell. That was when he decided to make the call. There had to be something more out there.

Harper arrived at his sister's apartment and rang the bell. A young unknown man answered, asked Harper's name and then showed him through to the lounge.

He waited for his sister to emerge. Her apartment was not like his one-bed hole. It was full of abstract art and modern

Italian furniture. He couldn't help himself; he didn't look forward to meeting her. They hadn't ever got on. They were too different.

According to Mary Harper, an over-educated and overly wealthy lawyer, Tom Harper was not a star homicide detective, he was an unrepressed thug.

Mary appeared around a door looking slim, beautiful and glamorous. She was wearing a black pencil skirt and red jacket, her hair worn up on top of her head. She looked at Harper with a gaping mouth. 'Jesus Christ, Tom – what happened to you?'

Harper shrugged. His face was a mess of big purple bruises. 'How you doing, Mary?'

'I thought you gave up that ridiculous macho posturing that you call sport.' She darted a look of horror from his face down to his shoes and back up.

'Thought I'd give it one more shot,' said Harper.

'Bad thought – he looked like he whopped your ass.'

'He did.'

'What am I going to tell Ella and Harry?'

Harper shook his head and sat down on a white leather sofa. 'I don't know – what do you tell kids these days?'

Mary moved across and pulled Harper's arm. 'Don't sit down, Tom, that's $5,000 worth of clean white leather.' Harper got to his feet and watched as Mary inspected the seat. 'Let's tell them you fell over.'

'Lie to them, you mean?' said Harper.

'Oh, I'm sorry, are you against lying? What do you think I tell them every time they ask to see Uncle Tom and he makes some lame excuse?'

'All right, Mary, enough. I don't want to fight. I like your kids, I'm just busy.'

'Well, you go out of your way to make them feel disliked. No birthday cards, no presents and once-a-year visits. You know what, I once considered telling them you lived in Alaska.'

'I keep unsociable hours. I can't help that.'

Mary took out a compact and a lipstick. 'You don't like people, Tom, that's what's wrong. It's not the hours that are unsociable, it's you.' She arched her upper lip and applied bright red lipstick.

'All right, it's me.'

'I don't want them to know their uncle is a boxer. You fell, right?' She paused and cast her eyes down over his clothes.

Harper stared up at Mary. 'I am what I am, Mary.'

'No, Tom – I disagree. You know, I'm not embarrassed about your crudity and I don't mind that you're a throwback to some fifties pulp novel you once admired. I just don't get this look – what is it? Hobo chic? I mean, my kids have been brought up to have sensitivities about these kind of things.'

'Being brought up in a world of rip-offs and designer labels?'

'Hey, there's nothing wrong in realising you can better yourself in this world. You don't have to repeat the violence you were born into, Tom.'

'Cut it out, Mary.'

'God, you really would do Dr Freud proud.'

'You lost me, Mary. I'm just a cop, remember?'

'Tom, let me give you some advice: find a woman, stop boxing, leave the murders to someone I'm not related to and get a desk job.'

'Desk job. Fine. I'll get a desk job. I'll do that Mary, I'll shuffle paper, find a nice girl and we'll buy a place upstate and raise pigs.'

'Oh, I'm sorry, does that not sound exciting enough for you? In which case, you could do what you're doing, closing off from other people, risking your life and destroying relationships.' Mary paused and looked at Tom with pity. 'What was she called, Tom – that Italian girl with the mouth.'

'Lisa.'

'Yeah, Lisa – well, we couldn't see that coming, could we?'

'I didn't see anything coming.'

'That is the remarkable thing about you, Tom – you're just so blind. You think she was just sucking on a lemon for a whole year?'

Harper picked up a glass paper weight from a glass table. He felt the heaviness in his hand. 'How's the husband?'

'The husband is tamed and domesticated as husbands should be.'

'I bet he's pleased to be so tame.'

Mary crossed to the mirror and leaned her head to one side. She pushed a large silver earring through her earlobe. 'Actually, Tom, I know you think I'm some mega-bitch, but people like Steven want someone to define them and tell them what to do.'

'I see.'

'People are happier with boundaries.'

'You speak with mom?'

'Tried to last week. All I got was a dose of self pity with a sprinkle of resentment?'

'She's alone,' said Harper. He had tried too, but their mother was always somewhere between half drunk and completely incoherent. Mary turned and put her hands on her hips.

'How do I look?'

'You're looking good. You're one of those superwomen, right?'

'In my dreams, Tom. I'm a full time lawyer with a neglected husband, a disapproving nanny, and resentful kids I don't spend enough time with. I don't do cookies, I don't do nice birthday parties, I don't even dress them, Tom.'

'Well, it's nice to hear you're human.'

'Believe me, Tom, we're not that different. And I'm not that removed, though I might look it. I see the shit in court that you see on the street. I hear it, I hate it, I hurt.'

'I suppose you do, Mary.'

Mary smiled. 'Now take the kids for once in your life.'

'You're the only person in the world who bosses me about.'

'Someone's got to. I've read the papers, I know you're good at what you do. Very good, they say. But I'm your sister. I don't buy into the myth of Tom Harper.'

Harper and Mary looked at each other, memories flitting across their minds. In truth, he'd spent too much time away from people like Mary who brought him up short and kept him from taking himself too seriously.

'Take them, Tom, I've got an hour to shop, then I'm in court at midday.'

'I'm doing this so you can shop? I thought you said this was urgent.'

'It is urgent. It's my fortieth birthday, Tom. And guess what, my dear husband is taking me to the Caribbean on a surprise holiday I booked for him. I need some things. You know I do not own a bathing suit, Tom.' Mary laughed. It was the careless laughter of a woman in love with her own image. But it was show. Mary had worked like hell to turn her life around. She faced the fears and put a stiletto right through them.

'Where are they?' asked Harper, sensing movement outside the lounge.

Mary called through. 'Eduardo, bring in my babies.'

Harper watched as the door opened slowly and the man who answered the door ushered in two immaculately dressed children. They shuffled across the white wool rug without enthusiasm. Harper tried a casual wave and a smile. There was no response.

'Bustle up, people,' Mary ordered and leant down, straight-backed from the waist, taking one child in each arm and rubbing their cheeks to hers. 'Mommy will see you soon. Be good for Uncle Tom. Don't eat him, we'll meet up for lunch on Fifth Avenue.'

'Okay, kids,' said Tom. 'What do you want to do?'

'Don't ask them, Tom, you never know where you'll end up.

You're taking them to the museum. This is Eduardo, their manny. He's got your schedule. I'll have him stay with you, so if you mess up, he'll be two ticks on your tail. Okay, Tom?'

'You make it sound such fun,' said Tom.

Mary smiled. 'Now, children, in case your memories don't stretch to last fall, this is your Uncle Tom. Do be careful with him. He's not used to children. And he's in fancy dress as a homeless person, so don't be afraid if people try to give him money.'

Two sets of large wary eyes looked up at Tom Harper. He looked straight back at them. Mutual respect or mutual fear, it was hard to tell.